NO WAY OUT

"Open that door, for any reason, and you'll expose this entire biosphere to whatever's killing the whole world!" Quinn Kelsey stood his ground, immovable, but shaking inside.

"Damn you, Quinn!" Jessica shouted. "Brad's my husband. He'll die out there. We don't know that he's been exposed."

"We can't afford to take the chance. If he's carrying the virus . . . if it's even in the air . . ."

"Think about this, Jessica," Quinn continued quietly. "If things are as bad as we think, we may be the last chance the human race has on this earth. We might be it, the only men and women left alive. You can't afford to risk that."

"You be the leader now, Quinn. I don't give a damn what happens to any of this . . . or any of you."

"These people trust you, Jessica. They're yours, all of them. They'll live, or they'll die, by the strength you bleed into them with your spirit."

She was silent for so long, he thought she'd forgotten him. "Oh, God," she whispered finally, "what have we done?"

THE BEST IN CONTEMPORARY SUSPENSE

WHERE'S MOMMY NOW? (366, $4.50)
by Rochelle Majer Krich

Kate Bauers couldn't be a Superwoman any more. Her job, her demanding husband, and her two children were too much to manage on her own. Kate did what she swore she'd never do: let a stranger into her home to care for her children. *Enter Janine.*

Suddenly Kate's world began to fall apart. Her energy and health were slipping away, and the pills her husband gave her and the cocoa Janine gave her made her feel worse. Kate was so sleepy she couldn't concentrate on the little things—like a missing photo, a pair of broken glasses, a nightgown that smelled of a perfume she never wore. Nobody could blame Janine. Everyone loved her. Who could suspect a loving, generous, jewel of a mother's helper?

COME NIGHTFALL (340, $3.95)
by Gary Amo

Kathryn liked her life as a successful prosecuting attorney. She was a perfect professional and never got personally involved with her cases. Until now. As she viewed the bloody devastation at a rape victim's home, Kathryn swore to the victim to put the rapist behind bars. But she faced an agonizing decision: insist her client testify or to allow her to forget the shattering nightmare.

Soon it was too late for decisions: one of the killers was out on bail, and he knew where Kathryn lived. . . .

FAMILY REUNION (375, $3.95)
by Nicholas Sarazen

Investigative reporter Stephanie Kenyon loved her job, her apartment, her career. Then she met a homeless drifter with a story to tell. Suddenly, Stephanie knew more than she should, but she was determined to get this story on the front page. She ignored her editor's misgivings, her lover's concerns, even her own sense of danger, and began to piece together a hideous crime that had been committed twenty years ago.

Then the chilling phone calls began. And the threatening letters were delivered. And the box of red roses . . . dyed black. Stephanie began to fear that she would not live to see her story in print.

DESERT EDEN

J.M. MORGAN

PINNACLE BOOKS
WINDSOR PUBLISHING CORP.

*To Johnny, whose love surrounds
me in the boundaries of my world.*

PINNACLE BOOKS

are published by

Windsor Publishing Corp.
475 Park Avenue South
New York, NY 10016

Copyright © 1991 by J.M. Morgan

First printing: September, 1991

Printed in the United States of America

Author's Acknowledgment

With grateful appreciation, I wish to thank the following for their assistance in the development of this novel: Barbara Jean Boyd of the Glendale Public Library, for her generously offered help in locating resource material needed for the completion of this work; my Monday night writers' group, for their encouragement and valuable critiques; my agent, Lori Perkins, who saw worth in my ability as a writer, and believed in the potential of both me and this book; and Gloria Miklowitz, who made the dream come true.

Chapter One

Christmas Eve, 1997

Alexei Danilov lay dying. Viscous mucus clogged bronchial and tracheal passages, slowly suffocating the man. The wet slurp of his breathing sounded in the heavy silence of the room — air drawn through the sieve of a glutinous mass. Weeping yellow pustules marked his face, neck, chest and arms — all the flesh visible above the bed sheet. Another round of coughing brought a fresh bubble of blood to the Russian's lips, intensifying the putrid smell of his decay.

Mikhail Vasili Kapov, team leader of Biosphere Four, the Siberia-based station, observed the death throes of Danilov with mounting fear. Only three days ago, the young man had worked beside him on the CXT experiment. And now. . . . Worse, another member of their four-man team had taken ill today. It was all too obvious that something had gone very wrong.

Kapov's life was on the line, and he knew it.

A loud groan and the sound of torturous retching came from the room behind him where the second sick man lay. "Mikhail, help me!" Sergei Tarlkin called. "Mikhail!" Tarlkin cried again; then the voice was lost amid the torrent of agonized groans and other loathsome noises.

Kapov made no move to help either man, held from it by his own terror of the contagion. In this isolated satellite there was little he could do for them, save human kindness, and even that impulse was blocked by fear.

A ragged scream spiked the air. Tarlkin moaned, "I'm all blood. Look!"

Kapov did look, then wished he hadn't. A black, grainy smear coated Tarlkin's chin and down the front of his chest. A greasy stain, like oil with sand mixed in. It was the seal of death, Kapov knew . . . and the stench of bile.

"Ohhh!" Tarlkin cried again, gripping his stomach with both hands, fingers digging like piercing claws. "Don't let me die like this!" he pleaded with Kapov.

But Kapov backed away, horrified. Another demented shriek, and Tarlkin was blessedly still . . . and forever silent. Trembling, Kapov fell to his knees and wept, passionately grateful that the terrifying sounds of Tarlkin's agony were over.

He was still trembling, ten minutes later, when he punched in the symbols for Jordan Exeter's private satellite code.

A wide, red light blinked from the shiny black surface of Jordan Talbot Exeter's office desk. The highly advanced computer, built directly into the flat plane of the tabletop, was pressure sensitive to his lightest touch. It compared the print analysis of his index finger to the key-file in its memory bank, releasing the system's lock. The message ACCEPTED flashed on screen. Exeter pressed the key pads for his personal communications satellite, scrambling the coded reception and accepting the call.

"What is it now, Kapov?" The Russian scientist had become an irritant of late. A trail of whining complaints from the Siberian Biosphere station was the only result of these last few days.

"We have a problem," Kapov's strident voice came through the speaker phone.

Exeter smoothed the sleeve of his cashmere suit over the white shirt cuff. Failure annoyed him. He had no patience for it. Even the higher pitch of Kapov's Serbian accent irked him. He was beginning to think this secret project had been a mistake—a very costly one.

"Has the testing continued?" Exeter asked. "I don't want the experiment skewed because of your irrational fears." He was blunt when he had to be. It saved time.

"Yes, yes. The tests have continued, but there is something very wrong," Mikhail Kapov insisted. "A man is dead."

Exeter's interest peaked. Death was harder to cover up than failure. Not impossible, but harder. "Who?"

"Sergei Tarlkin," Kapov answered, "and Alexei Danilov is seriously ill. Blisters, fever, and swollen glands. The experiment has—"

Exeter cut him off. "The experiment has done nothing. The illness of these men bears no relationship to the tests you are completing on altering a virus."

"You don't understand!" Kapov interrupted, his anger giving him the courage to take risks. "Manipulating genetic material can produce unknown possibilities. We have introduced specific virons into the gene pool," he argued. "If it is these virons that have killed Tarlkin, it means the compound has mutated and can be directly transmitted through lung and nasal tissues. Everything is happening so fast. We are in terrible danger and must leave the unit."

Jordan Exeter considered that possibility. A lethal virus that attacked the body through lung and nasal tissues. . . . Not a cure for cancer, as he had hoped, but . . . germ warfare?

"Negative. Your men remain in place. I repeat, do not breach the satellite seal. We have to know what you've created in there before we expose it to the outside."

"We'll not stay here to die like mice in a bottle!" shouted Kapov.

"No, of course not," Exeter calmed him. "I'll send a rescue team. It'll take two days to reach you. No one leaves the compound before that time. Is that clear?"

"No, no! We may not have that long," Kapov's voice grew louder. Insistent. Exeter could hear the man's fear in it.

"It's the only option you have at the moment, unless you'd like to notify Soviet authorities of what you and your friends have been playing at. I'm sure the KGB would be interested." He left that thought for Kapov to chew on. The Russians would look unfavorably on prohibited genetic engineering experiments conducted secretly by one of their own citizens on Soviet soil.

While he waited for Kapov's reply, Jordan Exeter's thoughts were racing ahead. Far better to leave the four men—three now, he reminded himself—in situ for the next few days. If they died, and that seemed likely, any chemist could break down the components of the CXT vials. They had Kapov's notebooks detailing the project. The experiment wouldn't be lost. Only the incriminating evidence.

"Surely, there is a way to reach us before two days," Kapov pleaded. "It will kill us all before then. You must do something! You promised your protection. Bring us out of here!" he demanded. "To America."

"Yes, of course," Exeter agreed. "Far safer for you here, my friend. But such things take time. Be patient. I'll make all the arrangements. You mustn't worry."

"I pray all of us are not dead by the time your *arrangements* have been made."

Exeter detected a tone of defeat in the man's voice. He hit the computer exit key twice, once for switching off the scrambling device, and once for terminating the call. He sat back against the soft cushion of the calf's leather chair, considering, not making the slightest effort to summon anyone. There was no hurry. If the Siberian team died . . . so much the better. Indeed, it had become necessary.

When the bodies were discovered—in a week or two—the assumption would be of a Soviet indiscretion. With his own carefully selected biosphere investigation team to conduct the inquiry, he would have control of the experiment—and the Russians, the blame.

It was a gamble. He'd have to be very careful, he realized, avoiding all connection to himself with any hint of the outlawed genetic engineering.

With this realization, it seemed the deal of the cards had changed from a pair of deuces, to a full house. Overall, his luck looked good. Exeter was a man who believed in taking chances. He hadn't gotten where he was today by playing it safe, or following the rules. If the stakes were high enough . . . he'd never been a man afraid to take a risk.

The cold was getting to Mikhail Vasili Kapov. Much colder here, with the windchill factor, than any of them had planned. Biosphere Four, the experimental space station in the frozen regions of Siberia, had deliberately been located in this remote valley, sheltered from the prying eyes of the public.

The blizzard outside the dome was savage, increasing the load on the system's temperature controls. A heavy layer of ice formed, adding pressure to the stress bars built into the substructure. They bowed with the extra weight. Bowed, and pushed against the crystal walls of the building, pulling at the seal.

It was a tiny sound, like the rip of paper, signaling a thin tear in the seal. The hairline crack did not register on the main computer; the dome's glass casing had not been violated. The structure indicated its usual secure reading.

Mikhail Kapov wasn't thinking about the wind, or a crack in the substructure of the building. He was lost in thoughts of whether Jordan Exeter would really send anyone for them. With this worry on his mind, and wondering if that odd feeling he had begun to notice in the pit of his stomach meant the beginning of the virus, the idea of a break in the seal never occurred to him. Not that it would have made any difference. It was already far too late.

Following its own course, the CXT compound reached maximum concentration—a live viron, new to earth, and to mankind. It was this compound, this viron, that escaped through the infinitesimal tear in the silicon base, emerging into the icy Siberian atmosphere—viable, and able to multiply at the incredible rate of doubling its potency every hour.

The extreme weather, far from killing the viron, triggered the development of a protective enzyme cap around the individual molecules, strengthening them against heat or cold. Siberia, as it turned out, was one of the worst places for an accidental leak of such material into the environment. To survive in that region, everything, all organisms, had to be strong. The extreme temperature made CXT protect itself, building its enzyme shell, creating a hardier strain than any virus ever known to man. And a hundred thousand times more deadly.

Chapter Two

On the high Texas desert, the glass beehive dome glittered in the morning sun. A stark presence against the white sand, the irregular-shaped crystal formation jutted across five hundred acres, rising to a height of three hundred feet at one end. Nicknamed the Crystal Kingdom by the press, the building was in reality a living laboratory, self-contained and completely autonomous from external atmosphere.

Biosphere Seven, most elaborate in a series of six manned, earth-based stations, was the crown jewel of the system. Five years of planning had gone into the design of these intricate prototype units, years of compiling meticulous investigation into the maintenance of diverse ecological environments. The result of this painstaking monitoring was the replication of them within the sealed habitats of the biosphere domes Two through Seven—Biosphere One being earth itself—scattered across the continents of the planet.

In Biosphere Seven, six distinct ecologies were represented: high desert, tropical rain forest, swamp, savannah, two-hundred-foot ocean, agricultural land, and a designated laboratory and housing area for the ten-person research team assigned to sustain life for two years within the closed colony of this module.

A single car approached the structure, driving slowly up the narrow macadam road. At the crest of the hill, the vehicle stopped, and one man got out. He stood for a few minutes, watching the dawn break over the horizon, touching the just completed crystal dome with a faint blush of color. Opening morning. Day One.

It wasn't the first time he had been here. His was one of two cars allowed on the private roadway — the other being an emergency vehicle. He was Texas multi-millionaire, Jordan Talbot Exeter, founder of the Biosphere Project. Biosphere Seven existed largely due to the tenacity of this one man. He had pushed for the showpiece of the series to be built in his home state. It was his money, and he generally got what he wanted.

Biosphere Seven was his baby. Every part of the system was personally known and understood by him. He always worked that way. If you were fool enough to leave the homework to someone else, you deserved to get screwed.

When satellite space stations went into production, his would be the operation that put them there. His company would build the units on the basis of information they'd gathered in the two-year research programs on earth. The Biosphere Development would provide the only experienced teams, the only qualified programs, and would therefore be chosen.

And not just chosen by the United States, but by every nation that participated in space station technology. The profit to be made from such a widespread venture staggered even Exeter's aggressive reasoning. He would wield more power than any premiere, prime minister, or president. With the controls to the satellites of all the great nations in his

14

grasp, he would be, without question, the most powerful man on the face of the earth.

It was a dangerous concept, the kind of game Jordan Exeter liked best. He hadn't gotten where he was by being tame. *The meek shall inherit the earth,* his Bible quoting mother had taught him when he was little. There hadn't been much in the west Texas town he'd grown up in worth inheriting, so he'd never put much faith in that one. The quote seemed all wrong to him. The meek worked the earth; the shrewd inherited it.

His mother's people had been dirt-poor farmers, but Blanche Exeter had named her son Jordan, after the river of redemption, and Talbot—her maiden name—after the father she'd adored. It never occurred to her that a manicured-sounding handle like Jordan Talbot Exeter might be difficult for a redneck Texas farm boy.

Growing up in the bleak setting of a small west Texas town taught the boy, Jordan, all he wanted to know about scratching and scraping for a living. He'd seen what it had done to his mother, and knew how it had made him feel.

It was from Blanche that the boy, Jordan, learned his goals in life. His mother died in that same spirit-crushing poverty. The message was clear. Never be weak like her. Never be like any of them. Power was the game. The young man, Jordan, fed his ravenous hunger on the feast of that power and was never satiated.

And it didn't hurt to have an ace in the hole—that was the one thing he'd learned from his gambler father. Kyle Exeter never risked a game of chance without a back-up plan. If the loan sharks were after his ass, he had a ticket on the nearest Greyhound purchased in advance. He never played that ticket, or left himself without some kind of security net.

No one ever touched Kyle Exeter—until cancer finally killed him. By then, Jordan had long since wished him dead and was glad to hear it had been slow and painful. He wasn't a forgiving boy. He'd grown up since then, but never changed his mind about that. His old man had deserved just what he got.

Texas schools educated Jordan, despite his early lack of enthusiasm for learning. He'd been a hard case, testing the rules in every institution of knowledge along the way. His theory was, the only thing important enough to work for was money.

For money, he worked very hard. It was real. It bought his way out of that town and freed him from the way people looked at him. They no longer saw the farm boy with his blue jeans riding above two inches of socks. Instead, they saw a man whose clothes cost three times their weekly pay, and whose shoes never saw a white tube gym sock. He was no longer the boy whose mama cut his hair with a salad bowl, but a man whose hair was styled at a place where he could feel the beautician's breasts bob against his forehead when she shampooed his scalp.

When they looked at him, they saw cash—cash that he had pulled out of the earth with his own rough hands: first in oil, on a little strip of ground he'd purchased, just big enough to erect three rigs; second in real estate, buying and selling of the land itself; and third, from judicious investments in the sciences—that exotic language of the earth—genetic biology being his odds-on favorite.

Jordan Exeter never forgot the only good thing his gambler father had taught him, to bury an ace in his own business deals. Only this time, the ace had to be a big one, something that would pull him out with cash in his pockets if Biosphere Seven failed. Even with all that had happened, his backup was still Biosphere Four, the Siberia unit. With luck, he'd still turn things his way and come out ahead.

The sun cleared the horizon, and light spread like water across the sand, dissolving the dark. Exeter's car made a wide turn, marking deep ruts into the desert floor, then headed down the small hill, descending back into the shadows—trailed by the golden light of dawn.

A stack of press releases lay on the foyer table as the journalists entered the conference room. They were here from every outpost of national and world news agencies. What was happening today was a media event of unprecedented proportions. One of the journalists picked up the sheet of paper and read it:

Claypool, Texas—December 25, 1997: This Christmas morning, when much of the world is quietly celebrating the birth of Jesus Christ, ten young volunteers representing thirteen scientific backgrounds—five men and five women—entered the enclosed ecosystem that will be their world for the next two years. Smiling and waving goodbye to family and friends, the ten stepped inside the dome and sealed the door, beginning an experiment that may have untold value to manned space stations, genetic engineering, and the increased understanding of the better stewardship for mankind's own closed sphere—the earth.

Slamming it down again, the reporter strode into the conference room.

The news conference held in Biosphere Seven's adjacent press room had been going on for fifteen minutes. Shouted questions were directed to the spokesman, Brad McGhee. This morning the verbal attack from correspondent Lyman Chandler of *World News* was turning into an assault. Tempers flared, not the least McGhee's own. Chandler kept coming at him, tactful as a needle-thorn cactus paddling a bare leg, accusing Brad and the whole Project of being a giant plot to dupe the public.

"Deny if you will, Mr. McGhee, that Biosphere Seven has been funded by businessmen whose interests are in the commercial profit they can make from the by-products of recombinant DNA and other genetic engineering. Those are not scientists doing research for the benefit of mankind, as you'd have us believe, but paid technicians of wealthy corporations experimenting with a Pandora's Box of deadly possibilities. Nuclear age assassins, that's what they are!" Chandler shouted, shaking his fist at McGhee. "And your word can't be trusted. Your own wife's one of them!"

Brad weighed the pleasure of his fist finding secure lodging in Chandler's face, against the bad publicity such an action would make for the Project. Violence breaking out in the press room on opening day wouldn't do Biosphere Seven any good. Or Jessica. Chandler wanted to pick a brawl. It was this fact that kept Brad from giving the jerk exactly what he was looking for. Chandler's motive was too obvious, to smear the Project any way he could.

McGhee ignored the outburst and went on with his briefing. "As of dawn, six-forty-five this morning, the members of the Biosphere Seven team have set out on a great adventure, possibly the greatest ever attempted." He sensed a feeling of genuine awe among this core of hard-shelled reporters. They recognized the importance of this day, in spite of all their arguments to the contrary. Brad only wished he were inside the dome with the research team, instead of serving as the Project's spokesman out here. Inside, with Jessica.

"James Burton of the *Taos Tribune,* Mr. McGhee." A white-haired, rumpled-looking journalist stood in the audience.

Brad knew of Burton. The man had a reputation for being what veteran reporters called a bulldog. When he sank his teeth into a story, he didn't let go until he got the meat of it.

"We've been hearing some impressive things today about Biosphere Seven—that it's the largest development in the area of controlled environment of any publicly or privately held agency. Quite a jump from the glass ecospheres full of tiny shrimp, algae and microorganisms that began all this twenty-three years ago. You could hold them in your hand," Burton did a full turn and spoke more to the audience than to Brad. "Any of those globes still working, Mr. McGhee?"

"In so far as I'm aware, they are."

"Are they? Well now, that was a bargain. Cost about two hundred and fifty apiece, those little globes. I remember. You could buy them through the mail." Burton was speaking for the benefit of the other reporters again, setting his snare.

"If that's all then. . . ." Brad turned to go.

"Just how much does this biosphere cost?" the loud, clear voice of James Burton called out. "I'll tell you what I've heard from a very reliable source. That it's upwards of a three-hundred-and-fifty-million-dollar greenhouse."

The bulldog still had teeth. Brad felt them gnawing halfway up his ass. And the old man wasn't through with him yet.

"I've done a bit of research on the Project in the last few weeks," Burton went on, "talking to a few science-minded types. From what I understand, Biosphere Seven is constructed on a much grander scale than anything either the Soviet Union's Bios or NASA's Ecological Life Support System have yet attempted." The old man's voice dripped with the syrupy elegance of the southern gentleman.

Brad waited, sure that Burton was warming up to a wow finish.

"My friends tell me that the Soviet government's version, Bios, is way out on the ice, where — should they have any serious trouble — " Burton paused for dramatic effect, "they might not endanger the lives of their people."

Here it comes, thought Brad.

"An awful lot of these same people are saying you folks are trying to fly before you can walk. Making this thing so huge, when you could easily — "

"What's your point?" Brad interrupted, tired of this good old boy sashaying around the issue.

"My point," said Burton, gaining a few sympathy points by looking offended at McGhee's tone, but jumping easily back into the fray, "is that with so large and complicated an environment, won't the chances of something going wrong be much greater?"

There it was, the planted seed.

"Mr. Burton." Brad felt confident that he knew the Project well enough to defend it. "Biosphere Seven is much more than a three-hundred-million-dollar greenhouse. It's an entirely self-contained world. Think of it as a separate planet." That got them thinking.

"The only calculated risk we are taking with this prototype space station is in learning how to control our own environment. What the men and women of our team gain in practical knowledge may be of enormous benefit to mankind in controlling such

20

conditions as world hunger, preventing the erosion of good farmland into desert, and management of pollution from both air and sea. Far from risking the earth," he stressed, "we are blazing a trail straight into mankind's future, sure as any pioneer."

A few heads nodded their agreement in the audience, and there was a low murmuring of approval at this remark. Brad knew he had won over some of the less hard-liners.

"One final question, Mr. McGhee." Burton's incisors were still hanging on. "We all heard what my colleague, Lyman Chandler, said earlier. He might have phrased the remarks a little more bluntly than I would have, but the question he raised was fair. Since this is a privately funded corporation, and the public has no knowledge of what it does, the situation seems that much more potentially dangerous. What protection does the average citizen have? What, if any, genetic engineering will be going on inside that glass dome? Will the world be safe when two years from now those ten people walk out and expose us all to whatever it is they've made?" It was a backshot. The entire audience picked up on it.

Brad gave his best return fire. "I think the point is something you and your colleague have chosen to misunderstand. Experiments such as what you're suggesting—with recombinant DNA, for example—are going on in laboratories and agricultural fields all across the country this very minute. All across the Soviet Union, and many other nations, too.

"Genetic engineering, that scientific witch's brew you're so afraid of, is taking place in test tubes today—not two years from now. The future you're worried about is already here. It's fact. What we will be doing inside Biosphere Seven is an effort to understand how to protect our world, not how to destroy it."

Brad McGhee turned from the podium and walked away. The first press conference on the first day of the new world, at an end.

Chapter Three

Quinn Kelsey entered Biosphere's systems control room. He was the master wizard here, magician of the computer maze that diagnosed operations in the Crystal Kingdom. Computers didn't run things, much to Quinn's regret. The design of each habitat had been developed around a concept of natural control of the elements, with minimal human assistance and adjustment. Instead of regulating such functions, computers merely observed all experiments. Kelsey wasn't happy with that. He understood computers. It was people he didn't trust.

In Quinn's opinion, he had been chosen as part of the team for both his ability with computers — which was impressive — and for his work experience with viable land reclamation for the Peace Corps. By working in the fields beside the poor of India and South America, he had contributed the practical skills of both his physical labor — lending the strength of his back and muscles to each assignment — and the systematic clear thinking of his mind.

At thirty-two, black Irish in heritage and disposition, his need to be a part of the Project was a curious one, for unlike many of the others, he had no lurking ambition to become science officer on any future manned space exploration, no desire to leave earth. It was his very real cherishing of the earth that had propelled him into this capsulized world, his love of what was already given unto man. His reason for devoting two years of his life to cohabiting with nine strangers inside this airtight jelly jar was the sincere hope that some contribution he might make would play a hand in saving the natural abundance and beauty of the planet.

He scanned the central block of monitors displaying the current tally of readings—temperatures in each of the regional zones, humidity, saline content of the two-hundred-foot-deep ocean—looking for any abrupt changes. The numbers varied from day to day, still remaining safe within the range of norm. What he was checking for was any radical shift which would tell him something had gone haywire.

Nothing remotely disturbing appeared on his screens. All systems were functioning if not perfectly, at least adequately. He had to be satisfied with that.

Josiah Gray Wolf knocked softly and entered the systems room. He was an American Indian of mixed tribal heritage, tall and powerfully built. Josiah's dark eyes moved quickly over the screens, assessing the same readings Quinn had recorded. Quinn liked the man for his strong jaw, darker-pigmented skin, deep-brown eyes—nothing pretentiously hazel about them—and jet-black hair, which he wore pulled straight back and bound with a band at his nape. Josiah was exotic against Quinn's own Irish coloring of blue eyes, brown hair, and pale flesh wholly unsuited for living in a world of sun.

"What's up?" Quinn asked casually.

"I still can't believe I'm here," Josiah confided. "That I was chosen over some of the other applicants who were much more qualified. Instead of Brad," he specified.

Quinn shook his head at this sanctimonious shit. "Climb down off the cross, would you? I don't deal well with martyrs before dinner. Gives me indigestion. You were picked because you're damn good at what you do," Quinn threw at him. "Don't start getting pathetic on me, Gray Wolf. You're the one person I'm counting on to make these next two years bearable. Everyone else in this place is either a fanatic over the noble Project, or so boring it doesn't matter."

Josiah smiled at that. "You're starting out with a good attitude. Got a great opinion of our fellow team members. You've been here one day and you're already feeling trapped?"

"Trapped? No, not really. I see things as they are, that's all. I can feel the desperation of some of our selectees to see space. They've got science officer written in big letters across their eyes. That's what this whole thing's about—to them,"

"You're a little tough on people, aren't you?" Josiah came back at him. "What's it about to you?"

"To me. . . ?" Quinn laughed. "Ah, Gray Wolf, it's about living. I want to be damn sure this planet keeps going, that we don't destroy it. We will," he added, his expression serious and hard, "if somebody doesn't stop us."

The door opened. Jessica Nathan, wife of Brad McGhee and team leader of the Biosphere Seven Project, stepped one foot into the doorway. "Meeting in five minutes," she announced. "No stragglers tonight, Quinn," she added. "Our first full day here, I want everyone together at the table for discussion."

"Right," he answered, still staring at the space long after she had left.

"Good-looking woman," Josiah reflected. "Nice ass."

"Our Lady of the Sphere?"

"You think I'm crazy?"

"Unless you've been eating funny little mushrooms, I do. That one's not human, Josiah. Don't you know that? No blood in those veins. She thinks, eats, sleeps and dreams the Project. She and her self-sacrificing husband were both hand picked by Exeter, himself. What does that tell you?"

Josiah looked at him through half-lidded eyes. "I don't know, Quinn. What does it tell me?"

"That he owns them, Gray Wolf. Exeter bought those two, and whatever consciences they may have had. McGhee makes a great mouthpiece for Exeter's spiel. Clean-cut spokesman, offering up his wife on the altar of science. It doesn't get any nobler than that, you know."

"I think maybe you just don't like to take orders from a woman, huh?"

Quinn had to admit there was some truth to that. "Josiah, you might be right."

"Come on, we'd better join the others," said Gray Wolf. "They'll be waiting for us."

"Right about that, too. It wouldn't do to go against the powers that be on our very first day of school," agreed Quinn. "Teacher might get mad. Let's go see what Our Lady of the Sphere has to tell us."

The ten members of the biosphere team were gathered around the conference table in the habitat biome. Jessica Nathan waited while the last two, Quinn Kelsey and Josiah Gray Wolf, seated themselves. The other seven had arrived for the meeting pretty much on schedule.

Seated to Jessica's left was Griffin Llewellyn, entomologist. On her right was Mike York, biophysiologist. The others around the table were Diana Hunt, chemist; Daniel Urquidez, horticulturist; Maggie Adair, molecular biologist; Cathe Innis, botanist; and Piper Robinson, ichthyologist.

She studied their faces, having known each of them only as biosphere candidates until today. Today they were a family, inhabitants of an isolated world which would, if successful, fulfill the dreams of space futurists and earth-based ecologists, alike.

"Let me say first," she began, "how proud I am to be here with you today. Each of you, in dedicating your life to this project for the next two years, has contributed an irreplaceable gift to the earth, and to its people. No one can offer more than the talents of his or her mind and body, as have all of you."

She noticed Quinn lean sideways and whisper something in Josiah's ear. Both of them grinned, but Josiah tried to hide it.

She continued. "I know that we have worked together preparing for this day, some of us for months, some of us for only weeks, but each has contributed a good deal to the concept of this biosphere, and to its potential development."

If they were pleased with her remarks, none of them registered the emotion by their expression. Instead, it was more as if they were waiting for her to make a wrong move, say something stupid, or step on somebody's toes. She felt a palpable barrier between them, like a block of ice.

She needed to pull them together, to coordinate their efforts as a working team. Unless they were operating as one unit, their attempt would fail. That was the purpose of this experiment, to pro-

27

duce the prototype for a world that was a blend of mankind and earth, in unison. From the expressions of these individuals, coordinating the human counterpart alone would be difficult.

"What I need from you," she directed her statement to Quinn Kelsey, the toughest challenge to her leadership, "is a unity of purpose."

Quinn leaned back in his chair in an attitude of studied insolence and rested the toe of his shoe on the table. "And what if our goals are at cross purposes?" he asked. "I'm not here to make money for Jordan Exeter, or to feather my nest in some manned space venture. I'm here for my own purpose, lady. Not yours."

"And what is that purpose?" Jessica pressed, ignoring his attitude and hoping for the right answer. She could use him to bring them into a unit. He was a needle, but instead of bursting them apart, he could stitch them together.

The toe of his shoe slid off the table, and he leaned forward. "I'm here to learn what I can about healing the planet," he said, anger percolating in his voice. "That's all. End of speech. We've screwed it up, and I want to do what I can to fix it."

"And so do I," said Jessica, placing her palms on the table and leaning toward him. "So do we all. It's why we're here. Isn't it?" She turned slowly to face all of them.

"If we can do that," said Piper Robinson, "we'll have made a difference."

"That's right." Jessica smiled at her. "And we will make a difference. Each of us has the opportunity to forge a new beginning to our world." She let the tone of her voice carry the excitement she felt, the excitement she wanted them all to feel.

"We *are* one with this biosphere. To be a blended

28

part of it, we must work to be in harmony with each other. Our goals must reflect that unity of spirit. We are one earth, one people, and one purpose—to achieve a lasting relationship with our living planet."

They didn't applaud; it wasn't necessary. She had them; she could see it in their eyes—a kind of fervor. *Now, if I can just keep them on that straight line for the next two years,* she thought wistfully, and went on with the meeting.

Later that night, long after the meeting, the television monitor in Jessica Nathan's bedroom transmitted her husband's image. *Not real,* she thought. *Not like flesh you can touch.* And she missed that—today, of all days. Touch.

"Catch the press conference?" Brad asked.

"No, sorry. I haven't stopped all day. How was it?"

"Okay. Opening day stuff. You can imagine."

The look in his eyes said more. She felt terrible that she'd missed it. "Was it bad?" She wished she could lay her hand on his arm.

"Something of a slaughter, I think. Am I still bleeding?"

"You look all right to me." He looked wonderful to her, but vulnerable and lonely. "What did the bastards say?"

"Hey, I think we're being monitored here," he reminded her. A smile broadened the soft lines of his mouth.

"Do I care?" she shot back. His smile made her feel better. It was the physical trait she loved best about him. Second best. "It was Lyman Chandler, wasn't it? That man's had his head crammed up his

29

ass so long, he has to fart through his nose."

Brad laughed, water shining in his eyes. "Glad you're on my side."

"Always." She felt the gulf between them like a weight on her chest. A single day, and she felt this. How would they last two years?

He was watching, she knew, on the same kind of hook-up monitor. "I didn't interrupt your work to talk about Chandler," he started. "I just wanted —"

"You don't interrupt," she stopped him. "Ever. I needed to see your face."

"Rocky start?"

"A little," she admitted, "but I don't want to waste any more energy on that."

"Kelsey again? He can be handled from the outside, you know. I can get together a committee to speak to him. There's no reason for you to take any shit from the guy."

Jessica could see from Brad's expression he wasn't going to let it drop. It was always that way, him trying to control things she could handle. An issue of power. "No, I'll take care of it," she told him, a hint of finality in her voice. "He's excellent at what he does," she explained, "a good member for the team. It's just that male/female thing. It chafes him to take directives from a woman."

Brad was quiet. Thoughts were tumbling out, but she couldn't get a sense of them. Not from a monitor. The silence was another wall.

"Ask me what I did today," she prompted.

"Okay, what?"

"I hoed weeds between rows of ripening corn, carried the mulch to the compost mound, dug potatoes for our supper, collected goat feces for the manure pile, transferred two hundred tomato seedlings from a starter tray into a prepared bed of soil, and drafted a report of our first day's accomplishments for the Committee Chairs."

"That's why they picked you as head farmer." He looked like he was only half-joking.

Tender feelings bared? Buried inside, there was resentment that he hadn't been chosen team leader, she knew. How to handle that? As a team leader, it was one thing. But as a wife. . . ?

"I miss you," she told him.

"After one day?" He made as if to laugh it off, then didn't. "I miss you, too. Are we going to get through this? I mean—"

"We'll get through," she promised. "And when it's finished, we'll start our family." That was something they'd talked all around but never settled. Their lives were too unpredictable for long-term plans. "All right?"

"Sure," he said, sounding as if he didn't believe it. "Good night, Jess."

"G'night," she whispered. Added, "Love you," and switched off the monitor.

It had been a hard decision, splitting up for two years. They had wrongly assumed that if selected for the Project, it would be both of them, as a married couple. It hadn't worked out that way. When the decision came through, Jessica had offered not to go, but Brad had talked her into it. In his place, she would have done the same. Still, somewhere inside, she knew how much it hurt him that his wife was chosen and he wasn't. A blow to his pride.

She leaned back against her pillow and closed her eyes, more tired than she'd ever felt before. It wasn't the day's work. It was being alone. That was a weight she carried. The only married woman here, and she was alone.

Easily giving in to the pull of sleep, she slipped

into a dream, as if waiting on the edge of her consciousness. She was floating over the horizon. Looking down, she could see the earth below, and clusters of people. Surrounding her was what seemed to be a soap bubble, luminous and clear. It held her up, away from the world, away from the people.

Brad stood among the others, holding out his arms to her. The bubble drifted higher, separating them. She struggled to bring it down, beating at the thin, shining wall and crying, "Brad! Don't go!" But it was she who was lifted higher on the current of air, pulling them apart.

Above, she saw a dark and empty silence. It waited like a great bird with wings outspread to swoop her up. She knew the sight of it and shuddered. It was the Vast Alone.

The strangeness of the dream woke her, images gone, but the hurt and loneliness remained. Was that what she had done? Taken herself to a place far away from Brad? Separating them?

And then she recalled the name she'd overheard Quinn Kelsey label her earlier that evening. "Our Lady of the Sphere," she whispered, remembering the image of herself trapped inside the bubble.

Hard awake now, Jessica turned on the light, forgoing all thought of sleep until both the dream and the troublesome thoughts were far away. The light guarded her, and later, in the protection of its watchful glare, she closed her eyes and slept.

Chapter Four

Because of the extreme secrecy of Jordan Exeter's plans, neither the Directors of Biosphere, nor the other station members, were informed about the Siberia unit's experiments.

Had there been a visual monitoring system to view the dome's interior, the leak might have been noticed sooner. Since the tear did not register on the main computer terminal as a break in the unit's seal, it went undetected. The other stations knew nothing of the problem until inter-satellite communications to the Siberia unit went unanswered for several days.

Without a monitor hookup, there was no way of surveying conditions from the outside. Reluctantly, the board agreed that the seal of the Siberia unit must be violated. A team of six troubleshooters was assigned from Project Headquarters.

Silently, each director held to his or her personal opinion of what had happened.

Well south of Point Barrow, Alaska, the investigating team made its last stop to pick up Chukchi Eskimo, John Katelo, their interpreter. Living close to the Bering Strait, Katelo spoke English, Russian, and the Chukchi dialect, similar to that of the Siberian Eskimo. His face was a chop of dark bangs, polished malachite eyes, cheekbones wide as knee-caps, and the broad crescent of a permanent smile. He wore Levi jeans and good leather boots, a Northface down jacket, and a necklace of carved walrus ivory. Katelo kept the scientists laughing on the flight across the Bering Sea, with stories of the Inuit hunter and the walrus-woman.

Travel to the isolated station of Biosphere Four took two days. Dog sleds were needed for the last few miles of the trip. The unit had been built in the center of the vast Siberian steppes called Yakutia. The nearest village, a Yupik Inuit settlement, had no access to anything modern.

"Ask them if they have snowmobiles," Ariel Jastrow told Katelo.

The Yupik ignored Katelo's request and brought out two mixed teams of Samoyeds and Siberian huskies, which he tethered together and tugged into the semblance of four parallel lines.

"Will he take us to the research station?" Jastrow asked, spreading a fan of rubles between his fingers.

Katelo put forth the question, and the Yupik answered. The words were a rush of unbridgeable sound of which Jastrow could make no sense of.

"There is sickness in his house," Katelo informed the team leader. "He does not say it, but someone has died. See the singed ends of his hair, and the dark smudge of ash rubbed across his forehead and cheeks?"

The Yupik spoke again, and John Katelo nodded, then translated. "This man will stay with his people, but he will lend us the dogs."

The village was strangely quiet. Only the dark moons of one or two faces peeked out of their doorways to watch the strangers. The unnatural silence felt uncomfortable to Jastrow, who had imagined a far different scene of arrival, with children playing and curious Inuit crowding around the outlanders.

"Get someone else, then," Jastrow tried. "Another man?"

The Yupik took the proffered rubles, shoving them deep into the folds of his anorak. He went into his wooden house and brought out a Samoyed pup, speaking again to Katelo. He did not look at any others.

"He says *Kablunait*—white man—must take *kipmik*—the little dog—for its mother is one of the sled team. He asks that we feed the dogs well and do not run them too hard."

"We don't need to drag along a pup," Jastrow argued, shaking his head.

"Still, we must take him. If we do not bring along the little one, this man will not give us the use of the others."

Reluctantly, Jastrow agreed.

Katelo showed Jastrow how to manage the Samoyeds and huskies with the same rough-coaxing tactics the Yupik had used. The dogs stood quarreling in their traces, the lead runner of each sled dominant, snarling at the younger ones to show his place in the hierarchy. Jastrow made ready to drive one sled; Katelo, the other.

"There is something very wrong in this village," John Katelo spoke quietly to Jastrow when the dogs' owner left them alone for a time. "Did you notice the houses?"

"What about them?" Jastrow threw back at him. He was tired, cold, and the prospect of driving a team of snarling canines made him irritable.

"Many have rough planking over one wall."

35

"So?" Jastrow continued loading supplies onto the sled.

"We Inuit are a superstitious people," Katelo explained. "We will not bring dead bodies through the door of a house. Bad luck. If somebody dies, we lift the corpse out a window, under tent flaps, or knock a hole in the wall, but we never carry it through the door."

Jastrow looked at the houses more carefully.

"And something else," Katelo went on. "You saw the ashes on the Yupik's face? He is mourning a death. Inuit rub their faces with ash and stay in their houses for three days after somebody dies. It's our custom."

"You should have asked the man if they'd had trouble here," said Jastrow crossly.

"I did," Katelo answered.

"Well, what did he tell you?"

"He lifted his shoulders and said, 'Ayorama'—It cannot be helped."

The words left Jastrow feeling colder than the snow.

"Look around," Katelo added. "You see any villagers?"

Jastrow didn't.

The sleds loaded, they cracked their whips high in the air over the dogs' heads, feeling the draw as the lead huskies led them out. Ariel Jastrow looked back, as they moved past the Yupik houses, at the broken side walls in many. A sense of dread built in him, dread of this alien landscape, of the dogs, and of what awaited them at the Siberian station.

"See there." John Katelo pointed as they went past a small hill at the outer reaches of the village. On the summit of the hill was a long row, with

36

stack after stack of anoraks, boots, kayaks, umiaks, and sleds.

"Why have they put those caches of goods out on the snow?" asked Jastrow.

"Those piles of goods are not caches," said Katelo, losing his broad smile for the first time since Jastrow had met him, "but spirit homes of the dead."

They moved in stunned silence past the mounds of death, the nagging sense of dread growing heavier in Ariel Jastrow's mind. It pressed on him with the weight of dead bodies stacked and frozen in a row of mounds on the chalky Siberian snow.

The glass dome of Biosphere Four was covered in heavy frost, more like an Inuit igloo than a clear glass structure. The snowfall altered the recognizable shape of the unit, making the simplest exploration difficult. Jastrow had a hard time finding the one door created for such emergencies.

The Samoyeds and huskies were snapping at each other. Jastrow ignored them for the moment, concentrating on finding the door. More than just finding Kapov and the others, he wanted to be away from the barking and out of the freezing wind. The unit offered shelter and the promise of warmth.

It was a system of air locks. He punched in the computerized code, signaling the large, sliding door panel to open. The team quickly entered the small holding space. The panel slid closed.

"Take a deep breath," Jastrow warned his men, just before a powerful vacuum sucked all the outside atmosphere from the room. A rubber sleeve released the inner door with an audible hiss, and a warm rush of oxygenated air flooded the chamber.

It was like opening a tomb, fearful and sacrilegious. Jastrow felt a raw cut of fear at the lack of response to their forced entry. The six men followed his lead into the silent chamber, uneasy and watchful. At least, Jastrow noted with relief, there was no evidence of any other break-ins. That meant the problem was contained within the unit. He felt himself relax a little.

They found the body of Mikhail Kapov—face and hands marked by blisters closely resembling pockmarks—lying in the narrow hallway, just outside his laboratory. His body, swollen grotesquely in death, had the stench of several days' undisturbed corruption.

"Good God!" the man just behind Jastrow exclaimed, bending an arm up to cover his nostrils. "What the hell happened?"

Jastrow turned his face away, but that didn't erase the picture from his mind. Blue and bloated, the body of Mikhail Kapov was scorched into his senses, both in visual image and in the reek of rotted flesh.

They discovered the bodies of the other three team members in swift course, two in their beds and one stretched out on the floor near the computer terminal. Each bore the same curious yellow blisters.

Heat from the station had promoted the corruption of the four bodies. The stink of decay was too strong to be ignored. It permeated the entire unit, making breathing difficult. Whatever had killed Kapov and the others, they couldn't search for it with the reek of death inducing such nausea in the team. The corpses had to be evacuated from the station.

"Carry these bodies to the air-lock chamber," said

38

Jastrow. No one moved. "Consider that an order," he added. "Williams, Chen," he specified, "remove them — now."

Peter Williams pulled a cover from the lab equipment, laid it next to Kapov and, with his foot, shoved the Russian's remains onto the tarp. Then he and Gordon Chen picked up the folded corners of the body bag and hauled the first corpse away, laying it on the floor inside the air-lock chamber, just inside the dome. They followed the same procedure for the other three, then coded the computer to seal off the area without exhausting the holding chamber's air.

By the time Williams and Chen returned, Jastrow had found evidence of the laboratory experiments the Russians had been working on.

"What is it?" Williams asked. He stared at the vials. "Do you think that's what killed them?"

"I don't know," Jastrow answered. "If so, one thing is clear, none of us are safe."

It was the Soviets, he was sure. Somehow, they had convinced Kapov and the others to violate all project directives, specifically those against any and all genetic or biological testing now banned in recognized Biosphere cooperating countries.

Ariel Jastrow took the understanding one step farther than Williams. He knew that all seven of them, exposed as they were to an unknown, potentially lethal substance, would be quarantined in this outpost until answers could be forthcoming about the nature of whatever was in those vials.

He looked around him at the confines of the unit designed for four men. *God help us,* he thought, *we might be here a very long time.* And then another thought followed on the heels of the first: If whatever killed Kapov and his men was still in an active state, they might never leave. When the team realized the level of danger, keeping them here would be difficult.

Forcing open the Siberian satellite had achieved two purposes: It had released viron molecules into the outside atmosphere and directly exposed the seven-man investigation team.

The red communications light flashed. Jastrow pushed the coded response numbers, and Jordan Exeter's voice came over the system hookup, Texas to Siberia. "Your men made it, I see. Fine. Until we know exactly what happened in there," he said to Ariel Jastrow, "you people stay put. Understood?"

The Israeli scientist clenched his jaws as he listened to the arrogance of Exeter's voice. The man didn't ask, he demanded. He spoke to them with the same brusque aloofness he used for his ranch braceros.

"Have you any idea what kind of testing was going on here?" Jastrow wanted answers. It was good to know your enemy. If he was going to die, he damn well wanted to understand why.

"Negative," said Exeter. "We're making efforts to clear channels to the Soviets now. You men just hang tight, you hear?" Exeter's voice boomed over the system hookup.

"If I can make them stay," Jastrow responded with the same curt tone, disconnecting the line.

Chapter Five

Piper Robinson, a tall, lean, black woman, stood at the corner of dawn. This was where her mornings began, watching the sunrise over the biospherean ocean. She knelt on the sand, in an unconscious act of prayer, staring across the sea to where shades of pink and gold filtered through the glass-panel wall.

She had dreamed of being part of this program, a project that would help the earth heal itself and teach man to better control his irreplaceable resources of land, air and water. It was as though she had come to a point of reckoning in her life, an epiphany moment of certainty that this place and this project were where she was meant to be and what she was meant to do.

The long years of schooling needed to prepare her for this day had been a struggle for her family, financially and emotionally. Her mother, a strong-willed black woman, had worked two jobs in order to keep Piper in college, and later in graduate school. It had been this soft-spoken woman's voice, overruling Piper's father, that had kept Piper in the university that last year before completing her degree.

"Your mother's too old to be carrying two jobs," her father had said at the beginning of her senior year attending University of Texas at Austin. "You're a grown woman now. You need to see that you're putting too much on her back. You've had enough schooling. Time to go out and find yourself some work, like the rest of us."

"Let the girl be," her mother had said, quick to defend her. "She's learning for all of us."

That was how she felt now, that this place and this project weren't just for her or for the corporations that financed the biospheres. It was for all of them, for everyone. This was something she had been moving toward all her life. Whatever the outcome, she knew she was on the right track.

A sound behind her made her turn.

"It's beautiful, isn't it?"

Josiah Gray Wolf stood a little distance behind her. She was glad he had kept back, not intruding into this space that was her own. There was very little she could claim in the enclosed world of Biosphere Seven. This place was it.

"Starting to feel isolated from the world yet?" he asked. "I see it out there"—he pointed to the vista beyond the glass—"but it might as well be a backdrop. We're not a part of it anymore. I didn't expect to feel like this so soon."

"I find myself wondering about my brother," she told him, as if continuing a conversation that had been going on a long while.

"Where is he?" Josiah asked, seeming genuinely interested.

"Florida now. Tampa."

She was comfortable with Josiah; he had nice eyes, and he didn't push. Hadn't asked what she was wondering. Anyone else would have. He didn't pry. Leaving her spot on the beach, she walked

42

back toward him. She wouldn't have talked about Matt to anyone else. "I'd just like to know how he is," she said, standing close enough for Josiah to touch her if he wanted to. Did he? She wondered.

"You could call him."

Her lips pulled up into a smile at that, moving on their own in some queer tug of nervous gesture. "It's not that simple. We haven't spoken in years."

She expected him to ask, Why not? It would be natural enough, but he didn't. He was silent, waiting until she was ready to tell it. "Matt and I had an argument about his daughter. I said some things . . . we both did . . . and he hasn't forgiven me. I don't think he ever will."

"Maybe if you made the first move—"

"Oh, I have," she stopped him. "Several times. Matt doesn't respond. I'm dead to him." She felt the sting of tears well in her eyes, but forced herself to think of other things to keep them back.

"Let him go," said Josiah. "The rest of your family must—"

"No. Matt's it," she said. "He's all I have left. My mother died in my final year of graduate school. My father died a year after that."

"Blood relatives can be more trouble than they're worth. I could be your brother," he offered, laying his hand on her arm.

She looked at his hand, touching her. It was wide but thin, an artist's hand, with fine bones etched beneath the surface of the skin. Is that what she wanted him to be? A brother?

A smile stretched lazily across her lips. "Two weeks in this upside-down ashtray, and I'm ready to be analyzed. Imagine what will be left when they pull me out of here." She laughed at the thought.

43

"You'll be fine," he said, the smile only in his eyes.

"Think so?"

"Oh, yeah." He sounded sure.

Josiah started walking away, not saying goodbye, just moving across the wet sand of this man-made, inland sea, then turned and called out, "How'd you get a name like Piper, anyway?"

"My dad fell in love with an airplane!" she shouted back, feeling good.

He laughed.

She watched the way he moved, liking the straight lines of him. There was a grace to the way he walked. A strong man, she'd noticed, he lifted heavy things easily, but his build wasn't that of a weight lifter — more like a skier, or swimmer. After he'd gone, she still felt the warmth of his hand's touch on her arm.

"No, Josiah Gray Wolf," she spoke over the steady wash of the morning sea. "Whatever else I'm unsure of, I know one thing. I don't want you as a brother."

She turned back to face the soft colors of morning. Her mother's memory was with her in this place, and her father's, too. All of them. So many voices. So many lives all moving toward one unforeseen goal: to bring her here.

Her mother's words came back to Piper now. "She's learning for all of us."

"You were right, Mama." Her whisper carried across the sound of this small sea, across the biosphere itself, and to the earth, beyond. It *was* for all of them. She shivered with the thought. *Whatever happened here, it was for the world.*

44

John Katelo remembered the teachings of his grandfather, Akilo. As a boy, John had been sent from the village of his childhood, to the white man's school, in Kodiak. The lessons learned there were enough to make him ashamed of the superstitious ways of his people. Upon returning home, his mind was closed to the mystical beauty of the old beliefs. Only now, in this place that felt of death, did he draw them forth from this long submergence and look again.

He was Eskimo. The Real People were his tribe. The enforced confinement in Biosphere Four chafed at the freedom ingrained into his soul. He had come to this place as the white man's interpreter and guide. Now he must become Inuit—must act the current of his blood—and escape this house of death before his spirit was contained within it.

Ariel Jastrow had shot one man who'd tried to leave.

"I'm getting out of here," Peter Williams had said, breaking suddenly and running for the door. "You can't make us stay, Ariel. I don't give a damn what happens to the rest of the world. I'm not a martyr, like you. We'll all die in this place."

"Don't touch that door!" Jastrow had shouted, holding a gun that appeared out of the inside pocket of his jacket, as if from nowhere. "I won't let you violate the seal, Peter. Believe me."

Peter had kept moving.

"Stop!" Jastrow had shouted once again. He hadn't taken a chance on aiming for the leg or shoulder. A bullet might miss and go through the glass dome, accomplishing Williams' act without ever disturbing the lock. Jastrow had aimed for the largest target, Williams' back, and fired.

The body of Peter Williams remained within the unit, a warning to them all. Jastrow refused to allow anyone near the air-lock chamber, knowing that once inside, they could force an exit and he would be powerless to stop them. Besides that, he worried that additional exposure to the bodies might induce the same illness in the members of this team. Williams was left where he fell. His rotting corpse scented the air with the stench of decaying flesh, creating a more genuine sense of what they had now become, a charnel house.

It was after this, Katelo decided that if he were to live, he must find a way to escape. Ariel Jastrow slept with the gun in his hand, and his back to the only door. No one would leave that way. Digging a trench under the wall was useless; there was a steel-plated floor to the unit.

In the days that followed, one by one, illness touched them. The sickness came in fevers, sharp pain, and in fear. Jastrow had it, Chen, and all the others—all, except John Katelo. He waited for the first signs of the disease, the blisters, the agony in joints and muscles, but no evidence of sickness came to him. Still, he waited. With Jastrow guarding the only door, he did not know how to get away.

It was the memory of his grandfather, Akilo, and the legends of what the Inuit people did when an Eskimo died that gave Katelo the answer. With one updrawn cut of his pocket knife, the wire to the alarm bell was split in two and no longer functioned. There would be no warning signal.

It was through the roof of Biosphere Four—in the secluded room used for storing food and other supplies — chiseling with his pen knife at the sealant between the heavy blocks of glass, loosening and removing them like the dome of an igloo, that John Katelo escaped. It was a space just wide enough for his body to slip through.

His spirit freed, he moved with the silence of the hunter, untying seven of the twelve still-tethered sled dogs. It hurt him to do so, but he left the other dogs tied as they were, in case anyone else escaped the dome and needed the dogs to cross the open range of snow and ice. Marvelling at the survival of the white-faced pup, Katelo scooped it into the folds of his jacket and fled, gliding like an arctic wind across the face of night.

Chapter Six

Ariel Jastrow stood before Biosphere Four's computer terminal, analyzing the system's control readout. The monitor was a warning device built into the unit, designed to detect any change in the level of oxygen, humidity, or other atmospheric conditions potentially dangerous to the team or their environment. The air pressure graph displayed vivid red.

"Almighty God!" Jastrow swore, angry but not surprised. With a gaping hole in the roof, the monitor could scarcely read anything less. Still, on top of everything else they'd discovered in this frozen hellhole. . . . No alarm bell had rung, but the cut wire beside the control panel explained that.

Furious, he punched in the code for Jordan Exeter's private satellite linkup. The steady white light signaled when the line was open.

"Exeter" came the low-pitched voice.

"This is Ariel Jastrow," the Israeli identified himself.

"Jastrow, good. I'm anxious to hear the results of your team's investigation. First, do your men show any signs of illness? Any fever, or—"

"Dammit, Exeter! Shut up and listen for a change. One of my men is dead. I shot him. I had to stop him," Jastrow needed to explain, "to keep the others here. Another man has escaped, the Eskimo interpreter."

"What the hell—"

Jastrow didn't wait for him to say more. There was so little time. "There's fever, yes. All of us have it. Swollen glands, savage joint pain, poxlike blisters covering our bodies, and elevated white counts that just keep climbing."

"A virus of some kind?" Exeter sounded worried.

"Yes," Jastrow gave him, "a virus. But something worse. I'm not sure what the hell it is. We've been going over Kapov's notes, and it's clear they were working on the modification of a viron molecule. There's reference to a 'cancerlike rate of attrition,' and 'forming a bacteria-resistant viron that attacks leukocytes, the body's defense mechanism.' They weren't making a cold tablet in here," he said, his voice caustic and unforgiving.

"Nothing specific?" asked Exeter. "Any mention of the Soviets? Or who else might be connected with this?"

"No. Kapov was a careful man. His notebooks refer only to the experiment." A painful spasm of coughing held and shook Jastrow like a ratter. He wiped the back of his hand across his mouth and saw a streak of blood. *Pneumonia?* The cold was savage. It whistled around the edges of the patch-board hole in the roof.

Ariel Jastrow had no illusions about getting out of Siberia alive. Whatever the nightmare was—created in those vials that killed Mikhail Kapov and his men—its legacy was already destroying this team as well.

"What's your best guess?" Exeter pushed.

"Biological warfare," Jastrow gave him. "I think

49

that's what they were playing at. A modified viron molecule, capable of attacking the protective cells of the body. Designed to kill huge numbers of people, without bullet, bomb, or army."

"You have the components of it in the notes?"

"It's all here, each test result. CXT Compound, Kapov called it. He didn't specify its purpose, but I'm sure he—"

"Where are you keeping the notes?" Exeter interrupted.

"In my quarters. They're safe."

"I hope so. We'll need all the evidence we can get to prove our innocence. When the world gets news of this, there'll be hell to pay. I mean to see that the Biosphere Project doesn't wind up the scapegoat."

"You don't understand," Jastrow contended. "None of that matters now."

"What the hell does that mean?"

"It means that with the massive leak in the unit, air pressure within the dome has dropped—radically."

"All right. What of it?" Exeter replied, clearly not understanding the significance of Ariel Jastrow's words. "I don't give a damn about the integrity of the unit at this point."

"We're talking about an enormous leak," Jastrow blasted him with the searing words, "a hole in the roof for God's sake. It means the viron molecules have already escaped the dome. And if we are dealing with biological warfare . . ." he paused, uncertain how to conclude his worst fears, "then you'll soon see the results of that in the areas nearest this satellite. We were exposed to the first hard evidence of it when we came through the last miles. There

50

were dead Inuit in the village," he said. "A lot of them. The seal must have been broken even before we arrived here."

A long pause followed; then Exeter tried bargaining. "Even if it did get out, a virus can't survive sub-zero temperatures outside the confines of the dome. Can it?"

"If there are dead in the village, apparently so. A virus isn't alive in the sense you mean," Jastrow explained. He was tired; this conversation cost him. "It doesn't die like bacteria. It can lie dormant for hundreds of years, thousands, then when conditions are right, reactivate into bubonic plague, or Asian flu, or . . . God knows what.

"In this case, with the shield of a protein coating which Kapov and his team introduced, I doubt even Siberian temperatures will have any effect on its potency. It was only after his men became sick that Kapov noted a change in the viron molecules, a mutation into an airborne form capable of invading lung and nasal tissues upon inhalation. That's when he knew they were in trouble."

"Are you telling me that this thing is already out in the world? That maybe for thousands of years, all it will take to get it is to be around somebody who's coughing?"

"All it will take is breathing," Jastrow corrected him. "If you're breathing air, you're at risk."

"Jesus!"

"Jesus indeed," echoed Ariel Jastrow, tired and sick. He was exhausted. The virus was weakening him. "The world has need of a savior. Now it seems, more than ever."

"What the hell do we do?" Exeter asked. "Blow the unit up?"

"No! Don't do that. Neither heat nor cold will destroy it," Jastrow emphasized. "It's not a bacteria. You can't take an antibiotic and make it go away. You blow up this lab . . ." he paused, his breathing becoming labored, "and all you'll accomplish is to shoot the virus into the atmosphere that much faster."

"Dammit, Jastrow! Don't make me start chasing my tail. I won't sit here and just wait for it to—"

"That's exactly what you must do," Jastrow stopped him. He was starting to feel awful, his head throbbed with fever and a flare of pain burned in his gut. He was too sick for this, but reminded himself that he'd been willing to kill a man to keep the world from such contamination. This was important; he had to make Exeter understand.

"Viruses need host organism cells to feed upon—animals or people. Without these, they may lie dormant—contained within this area—or mutate into some milder form. It's to the virus's benefit to mutate if the host cells are restricted."

"Hold on," Exeter broke in. "I don't need a seminar in basic biology. You're the scientist, not me. Put it in terms I can understand."

"Okay. Very simply, if everybody's dead, the virus can't feed. It needs live cells. So it changes, mutates, to a form that makes its host only mildly ill, but doesn't kill him—the common cold, chicken pox."

"Measles?"

"Right." Jastrow was rapidly feeling much worse. He needed to lie down, but this information was too important to put off. "With a milder form, the virus has the world as a potential host. It will continue until something is introduced to stop it."

"You mean, like a vaccine?"

"That, or a way to block the host cells' receptiveness to the virus. Keep it confined—"

"A quarantine? You mean a goddamn quarantine?"

"Yes, it might be necessary, restricted to this area. If we're lucky, nature may work with us. What we'll end up with is the Siberian flu, and not a pandemic. If for no other reason, restricting it may buy you time."

"I'll get back to you," Exeter said, dismissing Jastrow's illness and sacrifice—his and the other members' of the team, including Peter Williams—and disconnecting the line.

Time was something Ariel Jastrow and the rest of his team had little of. They were dying. As his last clear act—before he collapsed on the floor of the lab and lost consciousness of the world—he went outside the biosphere dome to shoot the Yupik Inuit's five remaining sled dogs. Katelo had taken the rest.

Jastrow looked at them. All were starving. Some would certainly die from the cold, but if left alone, one or two might chew their way free. It was possible that the dogs had been exposed and were carriers of the disease. If they went into the villages, they might spread the virus beyond this isolated point.

He aimed the barrel of the gun at the first of them.

The dog whimpered and pulled at the chain which held it. It was a male husky, its thick, double coat a salted gray and white blur. Jastrow could barely see; the brightness of the morning sun on the glaring snow blinded him. He held the gun in two hands and tried to pull the trigger.

53

Have to kill the dogs. The husky lunged toward him, tail wagging, yanked back by its chain. He had killed a man to keep the virus within the boundaries of this satellite. He'd demanded the sacrifice of all their lives. *Have to kill the dogs.*

Something unyielding in Ariel Jastrow hesitated. The dome roof had been violated. The surrounding atmosphere had already been exposed to the virus. And he'd had enough of death and killing. With all the strength left in his arm, in the decision of an instant, he threw the gun away from him, sailing it across the field of brilliant snow. He freed the dogs, giving them their chance.

He then gave them the last of the food intended for his men. They ate hungrily, waiting beside him with wagging tails and eager eyes. "Go on!" he shouted, cracking the sled whip to drive them away.

They scattered across the snow, living springs of muscle and fur, and he wished them well. He wished them life. It was more than he could ask for himself.

Chapter Seven

Daniel Urquidez stood in the partitioned ecospace of Biosphere Seven's ag-wing, before the moving track of hydroponic garden. Biogenetics was his field of expertise. The propagation of new plants, and botany in general, was his specialty. It was why he'd been chosen as a team member for the unit.

He didn't like the way things felt. He got a clue sometimes when something was going wrong, not any kind of psychic shit, but a clue. It felt fucked up.

Why hadn't Exeter, or any of the other high brass, told them what was going on in Biosphere Four? What was the big secret? That was how the game was supposed to have been set up, everyone open and sharing technical experiments and knowledge, a pooled resource of collective minds. Except, it seemed, when something failed. Then the system shut down like a slammed door in their faces.

"Something bad's going down," Urquidez predicted. "They'd tell us if there wasn't much wrong. No big deal." He paced back and forth the length of the hydroponic garden, throwing the weight of his wide shoulders and long legs across the terra cotta tiles. He was a big man, broad and tall, with a heavy head and an unruly helmet of thick black hair. "They don't pull this kind of shit for no good reason," he added, staring hard eyes at his companion. "It feels bad, Cathe, for all of us. Real bad."

Catherine Innis, Cathe, closed her eyes and recited the ten generic names of hydroponic solutions.

Cathe had received her bachelor's degree in botany and ecology. Before being selected for Biosphere, she'd conducted summer vegetation surveys in Greenland and acted as consultant for Texas State University's wildflower preservation venture. She was twenty-eight years old, with a body that was short, plain, and verging on dumpy. She wore heavy glasses to combat the Innis family's inherited farsightedness, with lenses so thick, her green eyes looked like bulging cabbages. She was known among her peers—not unaffectionately—as The Brain.

"Are you listening to me?"

"No," she told him flatly, mentally going back to solution one. He was hard to ignore, but she did not want to spend another morning hearing about the plot the higher-ups were keeping from them. Daniel's imagination was as fertile as solution six, and grew faster than these tomatoes.

"So you don't think there's anything wrong?" he pressed, not letting up on the drill of his penetrating eyes.

"Look," she said, "it's clear they've got a problem with the Siberian unit, but they'll handle it just fine without us. It's not a big mystery, Daniel. They don't need your input, that's all."

"Okay," he conceded, "let's assume you're right. You're not," he stressed, "but let's assume you are. That doesn't explain away the virtual shutdown of communications with the Soviet's biosphere."

She opened her mouth to argue this, then decided against it.

Tomato plants, heads of lettuce, cabbage, cauliflower, and melons rotated slowly around the wide feeder belt, passing from one nutrient level to another. At the end of the line, the crop would be ready to harvest. She concentrated on that.

"You don't believe any of this, do you?" he asked, angry.

"I believe one thing, Daniel." She turned to face him. "You got into the wrong field. You should have been a spy." With that, she twisted two fat, red bulbs off a forked branch, set them on the table, and walked away.

"I'm going to find out!" Daniel shouted after her. "Those fuckers are keeping something from us. I know it. I can feel it crawling inside my skin." He stared at the wide belt of starter cabbages revolving around the room. "That's what all of us might as well be if we don't find out what the hell's going on, just a bunch of cabbage heads moving round and round.

"Shit!" he yelled, hitting his fist through one of the fat tomatoes Cathe had picked for supper. It exploded under the weight of his hand, sending seed, red flesh, and sprayed juice flying across the table and all over the front of Daniel's shirt. A few minutes later, when his heart had stopped whoofing in his chest, he cleaned up the mess and left.

In the honeycomblike quarters of room six in Biosphere Seven's personal habitats, molecular biologist Maggie Adair lay beneath the straining body of biophysiologist Mike York.

57

She watched him as he moved above her, the well-spaced set of his eyes, the rough stubble of one day's beard on his cheeks, the clean lines of his jaw and squared chin. Her glance moved over his shoulders, well-muscled and tan, the strength of his arms as he held himself away . . . as he lifted her in those same arms and pulled her to him.

All of the teachings of the Catholic girl's academy of her youth deserted her in that moment. She was no longer Margaret Mary Adair: shy, cautious, responsible. She was Maggie.

Now, with his body still, his head a heavy weight upon her breast, she held him . . . remembering how it started.

Among the ten final selectees for Biosphere Seven, Maggie had been chosen — one of only five women. Her research on the harnessing of photophosphorylation — light causing the phosphates of the biospherean ocean to be combined with larger molecules, creating energy storage for the unit's use — proved of tremendous value to the selection committee.

The product of a strict education, Margaret Mary was plain as a nun in her style of dress and physical appearance. Her flesh thinly covered the sharpness of fine angular bones, her pale skin of that nearly translucent sort so common to redheads. Every vein could be traced beneath it, like roads of life, exposed. To camouflage this, she hid behind bulky layers of brown wool sweaters, long gray skirts, or loose-fitting pants in neutral shades of tan.

Her eyes, clear orbs tinted with the faintest wash of blue, looked out over the two-hundred-foot inland sea. She saw the ocean, but her mind beheld a tempest. Within the vortex of this chaos was Mike York.

Of another race of humankind was he, that secure, witty, handsome one, so distant from her own. Everything about him was confident, from the sun streaks marking his light-brown hair—seeming to go right through him like a blessing on a favored child—to the ready laugh he carried in his eyes. There was about him a brightness she could see and feel. People loved him without any effort on his part—a life of easy wins.

And yet, something about him made her angry. It was an anger that withdrew her from the smooth feel of his glance sliding over her skin, from the look in his eyes, intimate and unnerving. She had pulled back, alarmed by the fire of emotion such thoughts bred in her.

Standing alone, she stared out across the even plain of the glittering blue sea. Morning had tamed the burning of her restless night. Dawn hallowed the cool radiance of the water, and she felt the peace of it enter her, soothing and warm.

"Maggie." The voice coming from behind her was as calm as the morning.

She turned, knowing it was him. The ocean was behind her, and beyond that, the dawn.

"Hi," he offered, holding her with his gaze.

"Morning," she breathed the word, unsure of herself, unsure of him.

"Maggie, I came here to say I'm sorry for coming on too strong last night. I assumed it was what you wanted, too. You just seemed . . . oh, I don't know. I got my signals crossed, that's all."

"Please," she stopped him, nearly paralyzed with

embarrassment. "Don't apologize. I overreacted. You didn't do anything wrong. I'm just not used to men. . . ." The right words wouldn't surface.

"Making a move on you?" he filled in the blanks.

She nodded, miserable with the admission. "It scared me. I haven't had a lot of experience with. . . ." She had to let that sentence go unfinished, as well. "It isn't what you said," she dared, not looking up. "What you said to me last night was probably a very ordinary remark. It simply wasn't ordinary to me."

"Are you really so shy, or is this a great act?" he asked. Then, "You are an innocent, aren't you?" He smiled then, dawn's soft light resting on him. "Beautiful Maggie," he said, his smile melting away to seriousness. "You're not pretty, you know. Not cute, either."

He said this as if she had made him angry, but she didn't know why. She pulled back from his words, hurt and confused.

"But you are beautiful. My God, look at you." He did look, and she felt a warmth as his glance touched her, as though his hands were on her, stroking her skin. It made her breathless, shaky.

"I won't ask you again," Mike promised, "not until you tell me you're ready to be asked—if that day ever comes. Till then, I'll wait."

Stepping nearer, he laid his open hand against the side of her face for one instant, brushing the tips of his fingers down the rounded line of her cheek. His eyes were searching hers for some response, some answer she didn't know how to give. He moved away, and when her trembling stopped, she looked up; but he had gone.

"Beautiful Maggie," he had said, shattering the

60

protective chrysalis she had lived within, his words transforming her from a drab gray moth into a butterfly fired of a thousand brilliant hues.

And now, these weeks later, she lay beside him. A decision changing what she would forever be had been made, and she had never regretted it. Nothing in her life had prepared her for the way she felt with Mike. There had been no other men, no lovers to teach her what this feeling was. This desire. Only Mike. Only his coaxing fingers on her skin, drawing a line of current along her body. Clinging to him, only the warmth of his breath against the cold of her bare flesh — heat rising from a slow, simmering boil.

That he loved her was the wonder. They were absolutely and completely different. Mike's temper could flare up in anger — shouting over the waste of funds for a poorly executed tissue culture, bright arcs of red blistering his light skin — then he could be found calmly recording ocean saline data ten minutes later, calm and undisturbed. For Maggie, such emotional skyrockets left her limp and shaking, useless for hours for any serious work.

In his arms, she learned the voice of her own heart, a quiet voice which spoke to her in a language she had never known existed. It spoke in the calm beat of her pulse when she lay beside him, curled into the warmth of his body . . . in the quickened race of her blood when the sweet ache of passion coursed through her, rising . . . rising . . . leaving her frail and clinging to him — and in the vault of silence, which also spoke to her, when he was gone.

No God of her faith had promised Maggie such a love. No lesson learned had earned it. He was a gift, unexpected and rare, a hope she had never dared to dream.

But one day, she knew, all of this would end. The sealed lock to Biosphere Seven would open, and Mike York would walk out of her life. Would he leave her? Could she bear the hurt when that day came?

Two years from now, she told herself, easing the weight of stone in her chest. A lifetime. She touched his lips with her finger, tracing the soft line of his last kiss. He pulled her back into his arms. Until that day, she was safe.

Communications with biospheres Two (on an island off the coast of north Wales), Three (in a rain forest of the Amazon in Brazil), Five (in the Outback of Australia), and Six (in northeast China), were excellent. The satellite hookup made the connection between the ecospheres sound as close as phoning down the block. Jessica kept in frequent touch with the other team leaders of all the units, comparing experiences shared by the groups as a whole.

"What's been your input from Bio Four?" asked Paul Schefield, leader of Biosphere Two in north Wales. Paul was British, soft-spoken, and unflappable. "We've been making attempts to contact them, but they aren't responding. Have you talked with anyone at Four in the last few days?"

Jessica hesitated before answering. It was true, she had been experiencing a communication breakdown with the Bio Four unit, but she wasn't ready to admit it. She needed to check with Brad first, find out what he knew about the situation. The Siberia station had been ignoring all of her incoming calls for over a week.

"We've had no input from them, either," she arranged her wording carefully. "I'm not sure what's going on. It's possible they're conducting some kind of deprivation testing, or experiencing a planned isolation silence. If the order came down without warning, we wouldn't know about it. And, if there is an enforced silence, they won't respond until the test's over."

"Yes, perhaps." Paul seemed unsatisfied with her conjecture—*as well he should,* thought Jessica. "It wants keeping an eye on," he warned her. You'll let us know if you hear anything?" He knew her husband was Bio Seven's spokesman.

"Yes, of course I will. I'm sure we'll all know what's happening soon. They keep on top of things."

"Absolutely," agreed Paul, letting the matter drop. "Everything going well?"

"So far, so good."

"And you're getting used to the isolation? That was the hardest part for our team, the permanence of the isolation. You'd think none of us were ever leaving the dome." He laughed, and she felt better for the feelings they shared. They all felt this kind of loneliness, and it would pass.

"Thanks, Paul," she said at the end, her spirits lifted by their brief conversation. "It's good to know that after a year in one of these glass cages, it's still possible to have a sense of humor and relate to others." The call to Bio Two had improved her mood, except . . .

The questions concerning Biosphere Four bothered Jessica all that day. It was more than just a little odd, those unanswered calls. Surely, Exeter and the others knew what was happening at each of the bio units. She thought of the silence within the Siberian habitat, and wondered, making a mental note to check up on them. If there was a problem, she meant to find out about it. And if her team was in danger, God help the bastard who hadn't let her know.

Chapter Eight

"Honored Doctor"—the Chinese man from Chu-Nang province lowered his head—"my son is very ill. Will you come with me to see him? I fear for his life. Even now, it may be too late."

Dr. Xian Chan met the worried father's eyes. "I will follow you," he said politely.

As they walked the small distance from his home and office to the man's house, Dr. Chan considered what might await him. He did not ask the father what the boy's symptoms were. It was more interesting for Chan to speculate on the possibilities himself. Probably a childhood croup, he thought. Such wheezing often frightened parents. Or perhaps something more serious, a perforated appendix or internal bleeding. The father turned in at the corner house, and Chan cleared his mind of all such speculation.

The house was well kept. A woman's voice sounded from behind the far recess of a bedroom wall. It rose in a keening wail, standing the hair on Chan's arms on end.

"My wife," the man apologized, hurrying the doctor along through the outer corridors.

Stepping into the close-sided room, Dr. Chan beheld his patient. All thought of croup or internal injury fled before the horrifying apparition of this

65

child. The boy's face was swollen and marked with yellow pustules, as were his neck, arms, and all visible skin. A foul reek of death breathed into Chan's body with each lungful of air.

He moved back. "I have no medicine for this," he said, fearing to advance one step closer.

"No, no!" the father shouted, dragging Chan nearer. "You must examine him. There is something you can do. Please, Doctor, see his pain; it is terrible. Ease his suffering. My wife will go mad if you do not help him."

Chan struggled to wrest his arm free of the man's hard fingers. Forcing open his medical case, he pulled out a bottle and shook four tablets into the palm of his hand. Aspirin. "Here," he offered, "give the child these, dissolved in a cup of warm water. It is all I can do for him. He will surely die."

The father released Chan then, holding the precious white tablets in his own trembling palm.

Taking this opportunity to escape, Dr. Chan fled the house. Hurrying home, he washed himself thoroughly, rinsing his hands in bleach water, again and again. It was a full hour before his heart stopped quaking.

In the next few days, Dr. Chan had no need of a messenger to tell him that the boy had died. Summonses of case after case of sickness identical to the boy's arrived at his office. Mothers pleaded through his locked door. Armed men threatened to murder him, but Chan would not open his gates to anyone. He hid behind the thick walls of his home, waiting for the one patient he could not turn away. Himself.

In Chu-Nang province—a medium-size district with one million Chinese—within the span of one week, all inhabitants died. All mothers died. All fathers died. All old, and all children died. The born and the unborn. All. The breath of death rose across the land, smothering life, and carrying the fetid stench of Hell.

The virus moved on. Where the air current carried it, life ended. It cast a deadly sweep across the Soviet Union and China, then into the body of Europe, traveling among man—its host carrier—going everywhere he went, on cars, trains, ships, and airplanes. Inside one of those planes—a 747 out of Paris—borne in the lungs of a seven-year-old girl, it made its way to America.

"What's happening, Brad?"

Jessica tried to force truth from her husband's eyes. The monitor hookup showed her his image, but it wasn't really him. She needed to feel the rhythm of his breath, see the way he held his hands. Was he telling her everything?

"Our communication link with Biosphere Four has been cut off for over two weeks," she pushed for answers. "Our news coverage is being censored, too. Quinn can tell. What's going on?"

He looked away, refusing to meet her eyes. That scared her worse than anything else. What was he hiding? Something so bad that even Brad wouldn't tell her. . . . Dear God, just how awful was it?

"I'm sure in a few days we'll have—" he began, but she cut him off.

"Brad, I mean this. We're not waiting another hour. You tell me everything right now, or we're walking out."

"You can't do that, Jess." His gaze connected with hers, a final acquiescence to reality.

"Why not?" she demanded. "Don't bet on our loyalty to the Project, Brad. We're not all married to the company spokesman."

"You can't leave . . . because it's not safe." The sound of his words were hard and flat, lifeless. "You're in danger the minute you break the seal of the dome. I won't let you do that, Jess. Not now. Everything's gone to hell out here."

It was worse than she'd feared. Each of the ten men and women on the inside had his or her own idea of what had happened, and a best guess scenario. "Dammit, Brad!" she blew up at him. "How could you keep me in the dark about something so important? God, I can't believe you're doing this."

She was ranting, but he didn't offer any excuse. His manner was more like that of waiting for her to calm down and be ready to hear what he had to say. Which meant it was bad. Which meant it was terrible. If it wasn't, he'd have told her flat out. There'd have been no reason to stall.

"You're scaring me," she admitted.

"We're all scared," he said. "Jess, I don't know how to make this any better than it is."

His eyes were, his eyes. . . . *God, what was wrong?*

"Something awful's happened, hasn't it?" Her stomach muscles tightened, just saying the words. Fear chewed at her gut, gnawing little holes where the acid poured through, burning. "Not a nuclear war?" she said the words, trying not to give credence to the worst possibility her mind could envision.

"No" — he glanced away, and she relaxed a little — "but something just as terrible."

Looking at his face, she didn't want to know. She was scared, bottomless-pit scared. "I'm coming out."

"No!" he shouted, his eyes glaring hard. "I'll bolt the door from the outside if I have to. You're not leaving the dome, Jessie."

"Why?" Her chest hurt with fear. "Why the hell not?" She was angry, wanted to beat his face with her fists. "Tell me! Dammit, Brad. Just tell me!"

"We're experiencing a pandemic."

"What?" She felt her whole body decompress, like pressure from a balloon. "An epidemic?" She was still confused, but now at least could take a breath without the stab of knives in her chest. *A disease? That was all?*

"We have a global disaster," he explained. "It started in Biosphere Four. A genetic experiment that produced a lethal virus."

"That's it?" Her voice was loud, brittle. "That's what this whole cloak and dagger mystery is about? My God! You scared the hell out of me, Brad."

"Listen to me!" he insisted. "You don't understand. It escaped the sealed atmosphere and mutated to an airborne state—a modern-day plague, killing everything it touches."

"But surely—" she tried to understand what he was telling her—"with antibiotics . . . you can isolate—"

"No! It's out of control. We're attacking it every way we know how—and we're losing."

She got it then, the message he was trying to send home. It struck with the force of a ball kicked into her stomach. "Brad?"

He didn't speak.

She asked, because she had to, because she was leader in this biosphere. "How bad?"

"Bad," he said, unable to hold the horror back with his silence.

69

"Give me numbers."

"No."

"Give me the goddamn numbers!" she shouted, furious and afraid, so damned afraid. Then softer, "Please, Brad, we have a right to know."

He stared at the monitor with glazed, unseeing eyes; they were dead eyes, and she felt them look through her. "Everyone," he answered softly.

"What?" She thought she'd heard wrong.

"Everyone!" he shouted. "The world, Jessica. All of it. Everyone is dying." He was crying. Tears were spilling from his eyes in great drops, running down his cheeks. He rubbed at them with the wide backs of his hands.

Watching the man she loved break down and weep with helplessness, Jessica at last believed the horror of what he was saying; he'd given her no choice.

"Brad, listen to me. I'm going to let you in. Do you hear me? Come to the west gate entrance. Right now." She wanted to pull him through the monitor, grab his hands and drag him away from whatever hell was out there. He was her husband; she wanted to save him. "Do what I'm telling you," she insisted, held fixed to the spot by the sight of his tears. "Please, oh, God, please don't cry. You're coming inside, Brad. You're going to be with us. I'm going to let you in."

"Oh, no, you're not."

Her head jerked back at the sound of the unexpected voice. Turning, she saw Quinn Kelsey standing inside the open doorway of her room.

"Goddamn you, Quinn!" she yelled. "Get the hell out of here!"

He stood as unmoving as a solid wall. "It won't

work. I've been here long enough to hear everything. You're not letting him in, Jessica. I won't let you."

Chapter Nine

The monitor was switched off. Quinn had done that.

"Didn't you hear what he was telling you? Dammit, Jessica, you have to listen to him! Open that door, for any reason, and you'll expose this entire biosphere to whatever's killing the whole world." Quinn Kelsey stood his ground, immovable, but shaking inside from the weight of the message he'd just overheard.

"How in hell do you imagine you have the right to tell me anything!" Jessica raged at him.

"Right? You're asking me about rights? Christ, that's rich. From what I just overheard, there's a lot of dead people out there. Anybody asking about their rights?" Quinn threw back at her.

"Don't try to put that on me," she shouted. I'm not responsible!"

"No," he said with slow emphasis, "you're not. You're responsible for the people within this dome."

"Damn you, Quinn!" She came at him as if he were the virus and she were the cure—like a hammer on a bug.

"You took on more than you bargained for," he gave her, "more than any of us intended, but you're a scientist. You take life the way it is, not the way you want it to be. And the way it is right now is deep shit. What you decide to do in the next few minutes will affect every person in this overgrown greenhouse."

"Stop it!" she shouted, hating him, he knew, for what he was making her face. "I'm not God!" She was raw, tormented. His truth too close to the nerve. "Brad's my husband. He'll die out there." The level of her anger dropped. Her voice took on a lower, calmer tone.

"He'll die either way," said Quinn. "He's already been exposed."

"Damn your dark Irish soul to hell, Quinn," she said quietly, like a sentence. "I don't. . . . We don't know if—"

"We can't afford to take the chance," Quinn cut her off, "and you *do* know it. If he's carrying the virus . . . if it's even in the air. . . ." He let the thought finish itself.

"Think about this, Jessica. If things are as bad as Brad made it sound just now, we may be the last chance the human race has on this earth. We might be it, the only men and women left alive. You can't afford to risk that."

What he was demanding of her was more than she had to give, more than her heart was willing to feel, or her mind accept. And yet, it did accept. He saw her slump inwardly, as though the weight of her body caved in upon itself.

"He's going to die, anyway," she repeated his words.

"Probably."

"Nobody knows for sure."

"No," said Quinn, not arguing the point. He'd already won.

Her eyes, when she looked up again, were dulled

with an impenetrable wall of sadness he could not enter, a space where nothing could ever intrude again. In accepting the truth, some part of Jessica Nathan died, never to be reborn. He witnessed the death in that dark wall of her eyes.

A different woman stood before him in Jessica. In the cold flatness of her words, he knew she hated him. "You be the leader now, Quinn. It's what you've always wanted."

Was that true? Was it what he'd needed from the beginning? From the first day he'd met her? "I'm not the leader," he said, refusing to yield. "You are."

"Not anymore. I don't give a damn what happens to any of this"—she held her arms out to encompass the room—"or any of you."

He was glad of her anger, life reasserting itself.

"That isn't true," he argued, refusing to allow her to slide into this well of depression. "You do. You're a damn good leader, and you care about each and every one of them. They trust you. Hell, they've heard my radical opinions often enough. Most of them think I'm crazy. Do you honestly believe I'd be able to hold them here? After this?" He shook his head. "I couldn't. They don't belong to me. They're yours, Jessica, all of them. They'll live, or they'll die, by the strength you bleed into them with your spirit."

She was silent for so long, he thought she'd forgotten him.

"I'll tell the others about the virus tomorrow morning," she said, "when we're all together. You'll help me explain?" she asked, not looking up.

"As much as they'll let me," he promised.

He almost left, believing she had dismissed him, mentally if not physically. Something urged him to remain. He felt it was safe to leave her—that she wouldn't do anything to endanger them—but planned to sleep by the west gate entrance, just in case.

"Oh, God," her voice silked the room in a whisper, the words not meant for Quinn Kelsey to hear. "What have we done?"

In the absolute quiet which followed, came the softly spoken name. "Brad," she said, as if it meant goodbye.

Before her first tear fell, Quinn walked out of the room and closed the door.

In the upstairs gallery of the White House, a cadre of government personnel met in closed-door session. The windows were locked tight against the city air. It was not pollution the members feared, but the scourge.

Vice-President William Allen stood before the seated members of the committee. "It's only a matter of time before we're forced to admit that the President is dead," he said to them. "I see no point in drawing this out."

"The point, Mister Vice-President," said Joe Turner, speaker of the House, "is that we have quite enough panic in this country already. I don't think anyone out there really gives a warm dog shit who's running the country"—Joe Turner was well known for his earthiness in speech—"but nobody still alive needs the disheartening message that the virus has killed the President of the United States. They've got enough to contend with. Hell, I wish I didn't know it, myself."

President Elizabeth Egan had been a leader to

launch a century—that was what Joe believed when he'd voted for her. She was a vibrant, exciting candidate, assertive about issues of concern to the world: stricter environmental protection acts, enforcement of endangered species legislation, establishing low-cost national health centers for the treatment of catastrophic illness, and a fully supported, continued space exploration program, with the childlike enthusiasm of John Kennedy in the early sixties.

"If that little speech was designed to make me feel inadequate, Mr. Turner, it didn't work. I was elected to this position by the people, and I intend to do my job."

Turner ignored Vice-President Allen's further pontifications. The man belonged to an exclusive club of anal apertures. He'd been the selectee of Wall Street, the comfortable second-spot candidate to soothe the fears of monied America in electing a woman president. Nobody had given a damn about what he really thought, or even if he did, until now. The unimaginable had happened, and President Egan was dead.

"The Communicable Disease Control in Atlanta is working around the clock on this," Vice-President Allen pushed his case. He spoke as if he knew the details well, but Turner knew he had simply read the briefs handed to him that morning. Turner had access to the same material.

"There's been some progress made on a vaccine. Just yesterday, one of the technicians stumbled upon a major clue to the virus's cloning pattern. If they can somehow block that circuitry, then we could turn this into a major flu epidemic, instead of the disaster we have now. Given that, I'm certain the people of this nation will want a strong leader to guide them. We can't deceive the American public—to say nothing of what this kind of a lie would do to international policy."

"Mister Vice-President," Allen wasn't yet sworn in as Commander in Chief, and even though the position was technically his upon the instant of Elizabeth Egan's death, Turner stubbornly refused to give him the official title of president until he heard the man's oath of office, "what we're experiencing is a catastrophe of proportions unparalleled in human history."

Allen started to protest. "Don't forget about the—"

"I know—the bubonic plague," Turner cut him off, then shot him down. "Apples and oranges; they don't compare. Huge areas of the world were never touched by the plague. We're talking about a global eradication of human life! Governments around the world are collapsing, their leaders dead or dying. Mass chaos is rampant. We're experiencing the destruction of the known world." He let that one sit.

"And what do you suggest we do about it?" The question came from General Hollister McKeeghan, Chairman of the Joint Chiefs of Staff. The man had eyes like blue-steel traps, waiting to snap down in anger.

Turner was ready. "This is an unprecedented event, and something unconventional is called for. We're not struggling as nations," he reminded them, "but as the human race as a whole."

"The point. . . ?" McKeeghan prodded him.

"The point, General, if we're to salvage anyone, is that it's time for one world government. Only by pooling all our resources, all the knowledge of our collective minds, can we hope to survive this. Anything less, and this planet will be barren of human life within a year. Maybe less."

The steel traps snapped. "Of all the ludicrous, short-sighted, dangerous ideas I've ever heard! You're suggesting giving away the sovereignty of our nation . . . and you call yourself a patriot?"

"The time for national borders is finished," Turner came back at him. "With this as our heritage, we must begin to look at ourselves as a single people— the human race—or we'll lose everything. We are one world, General. It's time we recognized that fact."

He knew he'd lost them. Vice-President Allen was posing with a shocked, indignant mien. General McKeeghan's aged, chalky face wore splotches of ruddy outrage. The others in the room, seven men and two women, shifted uncomfortably under Turner's gaze. He was the outcast among them, the rebel.

"When are you going to wake up!" he shouted, unable to contain his frustration. "Will we all have to die? Is that the lesson it will take? My God, is that what you want?"

Allen and McKeeghan stared at him in open contempt. The others glanced away. Speaker of the House, Joseph Turner, strode out of the room, defeated.

Ten minutes later, William Harrington Allen was sworn in as President of the United States.

78

Chapter Ten

Within the hemispherical world of Biosphere Seven, the ten were haunted. Memories of those they loved, ones left on the outside, rose in phantom images both in daylight and in the blanketing pall of dark. For each, there was someone. Many someones. Alive or dead—none of them knew for sure—the faces and images of those lost to them ghosted the air, seeding clouds of that enclosed atmosphere with a rain of sorrow.

Except for Maggie Adair. She was unforgivably happy. There were no ghosts for Maggie. Life began and ended in the sealed confines of the dome, in this world, with Mike. Each day was a new Genesis, an oasis of love within the former desert of her life.

Far from hating the virus, she was secretly grateful to it. In destroying their access to the outside, the virus had made it impossible for Mike to ever leave her. Like a covenant with her, it promised continued life. Where Jessica Nathan mourned the loss of all that was passion and love in her being, Maggie Adair rejoiced at the unfolding assurance of her new world. Where Cathe Innes, Piper Robinson, and Diana Hunt chafed at their imprisonment, Maggie exalted in hers. In secret, in the dark, unwitnessed center of her being, she wept with joy.

* * *

"I shot two men today."

"What?" Jessica stared intently at her husband's face on the monitor. He looked exhausted, deep lines around his eyes and mouth. And worse, his eyes looked. . . . Did he have the virus? Was he sick? "You shot them? My God, Brad. What's happening out there?"

"They were the first I've had to kill," Brad went on, telling it as if she hadn't interrupted him. "I've shot at the others, intruders, trying to break into the compound. Couldn't let them do that. Usually, they're just desperate to escape the sickness in the cities. They know about this place, know that the virus hasn't touched any of you. Usually, I shoot above their heads, and they go away. Today, they ran straight at me."

"Brad." She tried to hold him with her gaze, but he was seeing something else, a replaying of the scene, the rifle firing and a look of shock and pain on men's faces—their blood at his feet. She could see it through his eyes. All of it.

"Jessie, I don't know how much longer I can keep them out. If I . . . if something keeps me from coming back, they may find a way to break into the dome. You have to prepare for that."

"Brad, forget about that for a minute. Have you slept? You look so tired."

"You can't let them break the seal, Jess. It's death out here. The air is death. You understand?"

He was thin, the muscles of his face slack. He hadn't combed his hair or shaved, and his speech was awkward, as if the effort of concentration was too hard.

80

"We'll be all right." She tried to calm him. Her hand touched the monitor, fingers pressed against the image of his cheek. *Cold glass. Dead.*

"I love you, Jessie. Remember that. I may not be coming back, after today."

His words stunned her. "Not coming—"

"I may not be able to." He placed his hand on the monitor, over the spot where hers rested. The smooth glass stayed between them. He was outside, beyond the protection of the dome, beyond any help she could give.

She knew what he meant. He had the virus; he was dying. The scientist in her understood. The wife in her fought against that understanding. "Don't leave me, Brad. I couldn't stand being in here if you did." She knew what she was asking was impossible, but the words escaped from her, as if they had been trapped and suddenly freed. Tears spilled from her eyes and ran down her cheeks. She ignored them. "Don't leave me in here alone, Brad," she begged him, frantic because the words "not coming back" didn't hold the heart-stopping panic of the feeling—didn't come close to what she knew he meant. "Please."

"I . . . I don't have any choice," he said.

And then she saw them, the tiny blisters along the inside of his wrist—small, yellow blisters. She pulled her hand away, the horror of this virus staring at her from the ulcerated flesh of the man she loved.

He saw her reaction and lowered his arm. "We can't pretend."

"You have the virus." She couldn't breathe. A sound like surging water thundered through her head.

81

"Jessica?" He waited till she could once again meet his eyes. "There's nothing left out here. We're dying. All of us. You must stay in the dome. Keep the others there."

She turned away. The pain of his eyes was too terrible; the suffering he had seen, too great.

"Remember the way I'm telling it to you, Jessie. Later, when you're alone and you believe you can't struggle any longer—think of what I'm saying now. Alive, I can't be with you. This glass separates us. The virus separates us. But after . . . nothing will stand between us then. I'll be there, on the other side with you."

"Brad!" She knew he was going. Before he made a move to leave, she felt it in the draw of her blood toward him.

"I've always loved you, Jessie. No matter what happens, that won't change. I'll be with you. Remember that."

"Brad! Don't! Please, Brad!"

"God, you're beautiful," he said. She saw the tears ready in his eyes. "Love you . . ." he mouthed the words, and the monitor went blank.

"NO!" she screamed, hitting the blank screen with hands doubled into fists. The raw despair of a grieving world sounded in the hollow wake of that plea—and echoed in the hard silence that remained. "No, no, no!"

Griffin Llewellyn's master's degree was in entomology—the study of bugs. In his achievements before Biosphere, he had designed and maintained the insectary at Los Angeles Natural History Museum while working for the L.A. Inner City Housing

Project. He was an accomplished classical guitarist and had the brooding soul of a Welsh poet.

He was the only light Cathe saw inside this sealed tomb.

Inside Cathe Innis was woman, sleek and beautiful, hungry for the yearning fertility of her race. This was how she saw herself, beneath the shabby layers of flesh, behind the goggle eyes. Anyone could look deeper, beyond the surface . . . but no one ever did. It was her destiny, she believed, to be the worker, the drone, but never the queen.

She had long ago buried her need to be beautiful; with the body she'd been given, it was an impossible goal. And long ago, too, she'd pushed down her desire to be fertile, to be Earth Mother, popping out babies like sausages in a row of links. And the rest . . . all the feelings, she'd forced from the burning center of her heart. Her self would be science. Her self would be work. And now, given this catastrophe, her self would be the kind of mind necessary to preserve and protect this small world she and the nine others so desperately needed.

Burning all the sweet-scented roses from the wheatland of her heart, she'd kept herself steady, pure — save for one deep-buried thorn she could not sear away. It pierced her, and she bled from it. The woman within fed on the blood of this, her soul's welling, and was nourished. It would not die, however hard she cursed and flailed at the wound. Nor could she rid herself of the longing; it was primary to her being and would not be given up.

In this one site of seeded hope, Cathe Innis allowed herself to fall in love — with Griffin Llewellyn. She knew the sweep of brown hair across his forehead, the sage scowl in his blue eyes, with their

83

dark lashes too beautiful for any man's. She knew the strength of his back and the width of his hands. When he spoke, she listened, and his words were songs to feed the empty well of her heart.

All this, despite his disregard of her. Despite the fact that he had never seen her eyes — not really seen — or spoken a word to her beyond the fixed limits of their work, or noticed the woman so close beneath the drone impostor's shell. Despite all, she loved him.

Tonight, she had seen him enter the personal quarters of Diana Hunt. And she had been seen watching, by Josiah. He had come into the hall, witnessed what she was doing, and turned away. Embarrassment and anger needled Cathe like a thorn.

A jealousy that was forged into the being of every living creature grew from the site of that small, deeply-bedded thorn. It twisted around the self of her, binding as strands of cutting wire. She struggled against the gasped breath of unyielding pain; but anger rose in place of hurt, and there, in that warm and nurturing site, it flourished. Anger, fused and blazed hot. Anger, whole and strong.

And hate.

God! she cried out in silence. The word never spoken, the word never finding voice. A rage of fury seared a hole through her hardened shell, through womb and belly, into the center of her — a hurt so devastating, she felt this one lifespring of hope begin to die.

As she would die. As she would. . . .

Rocked to the core of her being with the seething pain of this, she quietly closed the door of her room and went back to work.

* * *

"Did you see her?" Griffin asked. He was raised up on his elbow, one hand idly touching Diana's naked breast. She was a beautiful presence after sex, like a baby's blanket, soft and smooth to touch—a comfort. Not as beautiful as before, when he had wanted her so fiercely that the palms of his hands were coiled heat, and she was cool water. Or, when seeing her standing naked through the shimmering haze of that heat. But that had been something else. Now the fever of his passion had cooled, and she was simply a pretty curve his finger traced.

"Did you see her when she closed the door?" he asked again, having had no response to the first question.

"Who?" Diana Hunt rolled onto her side, away from the toying finger, and from the question.

"Cathe. She was watching us. I saw her. She had this look in her eyes, staring as if . . . God, I don't know."

Diana sat up, the concave surface of her bare back like burnished satin in the low light. He drew closer and kissed the spot where the line of indent stopped and the rounded swell of her hips began. She was warm; her skin tasted lightly of salt.

"You're crazy. You know that?" She stood and slipped a robe around her, then turned to face him. She was dressed, and he was naked, their positions something less than equal. "Am I supposed to care what a woman lurking outside my doorway thinks? Does anything she says or does matter while the rest of the world is dying outside this dome?"

"I just meant—"

"I know what you meant. Christ! I don't give

85

a damn about her. She's nothing to me."

Her words, he believed, were intended for him as well.

Diana's reaction didn't surprise him. They were all handling it differently. News from the outside was scarce. What they knew for certain was all bad. President Egan had died. That had been one of the last pieces of information Brad McGhee had given Jessica before he stopped coming to the dome. That had been . . . how long ago? Over a month? No, two months, surely.

It was as though nothing outside this enclosure existed, because for them, it didn't. The six biosphere units had been built as prototype space stations, designed to test mankind's ability to survive extended periods of isolation in self-contained, completely autonomous environments. With the wildfire spread of the CXT virus, the five remaining units of the Project became just that—living laboratories, secluded outposts of human life, struggling for survival in a world grown hostile and alien.

If the way Diana handled it was to sleep with every man in the Project so that she wouldn't feel alone, that was okay with him.

Griff got up and stood close enough to see the simmer of anger in her eyes. They were pretty eyes, wide open, baby-doll round, and blue.

"I'm not the enemy," he said, putting his hands on her shoulders.

"I know."

He didn't look at her eyes now, but stared instead at the full curve of her mouth, at her bottom lip and the way it parted from the top, falling open slightly as his hand slipped inside the robe and his thumb moved across her breast.

"The world you want isn't out there anymore, Diana. We're all there is—these people. That's the whole of it."

He felt her push away. "Damn you," she said, her voice cold and hard. "And damn this place, too." There were glassy tears in her eyes, but she held them back; they never fell.

Griffin pulled her closer, the crush of her robe a barrier between them. "I don't want to be alone tonight," he said.

She held back. Then, like the softness of her skin warming beneath his moving hands, he felt her body yield.

". . . damn you," she said again, but this time they were in a tangle of sheets and he was deep inside her, her words a low moan against his ear.

The beat of his own need drove him, the heat of passion throbbing to the rhythm of their blood. She arched her back, lifting off the bed to meet his touch, and he crushed her hard against his chest, burying his face in the warm hollow of her neck.

Her words were there, cold as ice against the steam of his skin. He heard them. *Damn you.* He heard them. In the swell of that moment, he did the only thing possible for him to do.

He stopped listening.

Behind the closed door of his quarters, Josiah let his thoughts wander . . . back to the quiet hallway where Cathe had stood, watching. What he'd seen was a hard revelation, the pain of another's soul. What he'd seen hurt him, and bought him an unlooked-for closeness with this woman.

In all the weeks inside the dome, he hadn't noticed her, hadn't seen beyond the role she'd played within the structure of their work. Now Josiah was faced with Cathe as a feeling, caring person. That she was suffering was obvious. That he might help her seemed logical. The question was, Did he want to? And if he did, how?

One thing was clear. What he'd seen tonight was the kind of torment that if unleashed, might sear a burning swath across them all. Knowing this, he made up his mind to get to know Cathe Innis better, and to try to help her, if he could.

The thought of her pain haunted his dreams, and that night, a kind of union was forged with this woman — a union of his spirit and hers.

Chapter Eleven

Quinn Kelsey thought Jessica was right, and said so to the others. "We have to protect ourselves from an invasion from outside. We need to think of ourselves as if we were at war with everything beyond these walls. And more importantly, we need to find a way to keep them out."

The conversation was taking place as a direct result of Jessica's last meeting with Brad two months ago. Since that time, she had moved around the compound exhausted: unseeing, unhearing, empty. Quinn had seen what was happening; they all had noticed, but had left her alone, to mourn. In the sheer weight of her grief, they all mourned.

But now she was back among them, steel in her voice and fire in her eyes, pressing the others for ways to safeguard the unit from sabotage from outside. It had been Brad's idea, she told them. They had to protect themselves.

Not for the first time, Quinn sided with her. He lent the weight of his influence to the argument—and there were those who didn't believe any action was necessary—offering suggestions of ways they could lay a track of live electric current along the two sealed entrances.

"Haven't we had enough death?" Diana made her voice heard. "You talk about killing people as if it were nothing more than planning a cook-out. My God, I'm sick of all this. You want to see dead bodies stacked up outside our walls like cord wood?"

Quinn had expected her reaction. He'd known it wouldn't be easy to convince them that their lives had to come first, whatever their sympathy toward those on the outside. Such feelings wouldn't count for much if the virus made its way into the dome and infected them like the others. Sympathy wouldn't count for shit then.

"What I'm suggesting," said Jessica, taking control of the group again, "is a planned response. We can't wait until an attack happens. All it would take is one minute with the seal violated. We can't afford a single incident."

"But to kill them . . ." contested Griff. "Jesus, couldn't we just stun them or something? Diana's right. I don't want to be responsible for any more agony out there. We've done enough to them. Hell, maybe they ought to open the doors. Maybe it's what we deserve."

A heavy silence followed his words. It wasn't the first time any of them had considered this thought. It was, however, the first time anyone had said it.

Jessica walked closer to him and said softly, but loud enough for everyone to hear, "If death is what you really want, Griff, come to my room after this meeting. I'll give you some capsules that will fulfill your wish. That's your right and a choice you have to make. Nobody here will stop you. Only don't assume to speak for all of us. We're not willing to throw open the doors and welcome the grave with widespread arms."

"I only meant—" Griffin began to back up, nervous in his own defense.

Jessica put her hand out, stopping him. "I know.

90

We all understand what you're feeling. Guilt. It's as contagious among us as the virus. But guilt won't bring back the dead—don't any of you think it will!—and our dying with them won't change that, either."

She had their full attention. "We're going to move ahead from this point—God help us—as if the ten of us is all there is. For all any of us know, that may be true."

Quinn waited a long minute, letting her message sink in, then asked them, "Okay, who knows how to short circuit the doors?"

"Me," said Daniel.

"Urquidez?" Cathe questioned.

"Yeah, me." His annoyed expression showed a reaction to her obvious surprise. "I wasn't born punching tomato seedlings into trays. It's simple, just like hotwiring a car." They all stared at him, and he smiled. "So I had a little valuable education. Now it pays off. Who says crime doesn't—"

"Right," said Cathe, cutting him off before he could cliche again.

He looked like a small boy told to shut up, his feelings wounded.

"We're grateful for your expertise, Daniel," Jessica singled him out for attention. "With your help, we can fortify the dome and gain a better measure of security. All of us thank you."

"Hell, Urquidez, I'm damned impressed," said Quinn. He took Daniel's arm and began leading him away. "Let's find ourselves a quiet corner and talk a little treason."

"Hey, are you some kinda Irish?" Urquidez asked, pulling back and giving Quinn a look.

"With a name like Kelsey, wha'dya think? Daniel, my friend, the Provisionals could'ave used a man like you."

Jordan Exeter wasn't about to die. From what he could see, the rest of the world was going to fucking buy it, but not him. It was time to use the ace in reserve.

One override code existed, a complicated computer chip designed to block the locking mechanism of a secret contingency exit. As the architectural plans stood now, the inhabitants of Biosphere Seven could vacate the unit through two exits—designed as a precaution against medical emergencies or fire—but no one could enter without their permission. The override chip would change all that.

Exeter drove to the site a few hours before dawn. This was not something he wanted anyone to witness. If the public thought there was a way of entering Biosphere, the glass dome would be quickly overrun with a mob of the desperate.

He did have some qualms about breaking the atmospheric seal of the unit, not for any concern about the other members of the team, but for the danger to himself. Opening the door, even for the briefest moment, might mean the virus would enter the biosphere dome with him. If that happened, no place on earth would be safe.

Of course, if the virus was already in his body . . . but then, if that was true, nothing else mattered.

His palms were sweating as he drove up the dark, desert road—not from fever, he assured himself, but from simple nerves. The early morning sky was still glossy black, smooth as ink and dotted with a million brilliant jets of light.

And a mutated virus, he reminded himself, *waiting in the air to decimate human life.* His life. He fingered the door-panel switch and rolled up the windows of the car.

"I'm not going to die," Exeter announced to the silence riding beside him. His fingers touched the computer chip in his coat pocket, talisman of the nineties. "Whatever happens to the weak of this world, I'm not going to die."

He started walking up the sloped rise. Biosphere Seven's glass dome blended into the nearby hills, the shape of a natural mound, still a darkness against the sky, one with the sleep of night. High in the black sea above him rose a horned moon, its crescent curving from the base, tips pointing toward the heavens. Like the crown of the ancient goddess overlooking Earth, her child, it hovered over his act, watching. All the eyes of night were upon him as he made his way up the swollen valley toward the only hope of future he knew . . . to the last Eden of his world. To life.

Exeter left the paved highway well before it veered toward the access road and walked toward the small parking lot for the compound. The main entrance held no hope of admission to him. It would be locked and barricaded — probably rigged against forced entry — if those inside knew what they were doing. Other people had probably tried to break in by now. He thought of the crushed dome of the Biosphere Six habitat in China and remembered the terror in the voices coming over the satellite station intercom, screaming in fear as the heavy glass walls caved in upon them from the force of the mob outside. The screams hadn't ended then — death had not come easy — but he had switched off the station. It hadn't been something he'd wanted to hear.

At the parking structure, he used his key to open the locked garage for the all-terrain vehicles. It was a long way across the desert, too far to walk. He backed out the ATV — all-terrain vehicle — and left the garage door standing open and, from a safe distance away, followed the dawn outline of Biosphere Seven along the sand.

He headed south across the desert, toward the wall of solar panels behind Biosphere Seven's ocean. He kept about five miles from the structure, intending to give no warning to those inside. They would have little choice but to accept his presence once he was within the unit.

It was a risk, of course. In similar circumstances, he would have killed anyone attempting to do such a thing—man or woman—but these people were a soft, bookish tribe: sentimentalists and bleeding hearts. Environmentalists. He'd seen their psychological profiles and wasn't worried. Not a murderer among them. No, he'd be all right, once inside. King of the castle.

The stars disappeared, and a corona of sun had risen over the black backs of the nearby hills by the time Exeter reached the southern division of the unit. Night on the desert had been cold, below freezing. The sun's rays felt good to his chilled hands and face. It would be warmer still inside the humid air of the dome. He hugged that thought to him for warmth.

He parked the ATV a mile from the unit and started walking across the desert floor, his hand closed over the computer micro chip in his pocket.

There was still work to be done.

Piper Robinson waited for the sunrise. Every dawn found her in this same spot, as if the world was made new each morning and she was part of that rebirth. She didn't try to explain it to anyone, but felt a kinship with the beginning of day, and a closeness to whatever god ruled the small, contained world of this biosphere. Standing here, without words, she felt the act of prayer.

She prayed for those outside the limits of this dome, those who still survived. What must their world be, outside? What suffering? What chaos? In the great silence of her being, she thought of them and prayed to the god she believed in, to the mother of earth, the giver of all life.

Piper had grown up in the religion of her father — Charles Robinson, Baptist — and had been taught and trained in his beliefs. As a child, she had accepted his word on the nature of God. He was her father; he knew everything. But as she grew older, questions formed in that instinctual part of her mind — questions that neither her father, nor his religion, could answer.

In trying to find the answers to those questions, she had turned instead to that most primal love of all humankind — to the earth, its mother. Like primitive people of the world, she saw her god — her goddess — in all living things: in the ground itself, and every tree which grew from it, in the solid rock of mountains, and the whisper-breath of grass standing in the breeze, in the flow of water. In life itself, Piper saw the deity she worshiped, and paid homage to this creation in long mornings of solitude and meditation beside the Biospherean Sea.

An overwhelming sense of sadness had bound itself to her since knowledge of the catastrophe outside the walls of this dome. She felt the withering away of human life on the planet, as if each man were her son; each woman, her daughter. She mourned the loss of each child, grieved for them in her heart, and carried the presence of their souls within her.

That was crazy, she knew. No one could carry the soul of another. She shared this thought with no one, for no matter how she rationalized, no matter how well she argued against this strange belief, she could not push the *feel* of them—the lost ones—from her consciousness. They had become part of her. Only in this place could she share it, with the giver of all life, with Mother Earth.

Deep in the pursuit of such thoughts, Piper barely heard the slight scraping sound against the outer wall beyond the ocean. It came simply as an irritant, a noise. Her frail link with the souls of earth was broken, and she was flung back into the emptiness of herself, an aloneness which felt like pain.

Hurting and angry at this intrusion, she strode quickly along the footpath surrounding the shore of the ocean. The sun had risen higher, nearly blinding her as she stared at the spot where she'd first heard the sound.

Halfway around the length of the sea, she saw him.

"Jordan Exeter?" At first she was simply stunned that he was alive. That he was here. What was he doing to the wall of the small room behind the—

He saw her, and the look on his face told everything.

"Oh, my God!" She understood; he was breaking in. And the virus would enter with him. "No!" she screamed, believing he heard her, but he didn't stop. *What was he doing? What was that sound?*

It was five feet to the wall with the intercom. To get to it, she couldn't watch him. It was hard to tear herself away, hard, knowing he could kill them all.

"Josiah!" she screamed, running to the intercom. He was her first thought. If Exeter got inside, Josiah would die.

Her hand hit the intercom button hard. "Come on," she urged them. "Come on, dammit. Somebody answer!"

"What the hell—" Quinn's voice roared from the speaker.

"Break-in," Piper said clearly, holding the panic-tremor from her voice. "Break-in at sector seven, utility access room, south wall. God, Quinn, it's Exeter."

"What?"

"It's Jordan Exeter!"

"Christ!" The pause of a single heartbeat, then, "I'm sealing off the access room. Stay clear of—"

His words were cut off by the shriek of the automatic alarm, a security device set to go off if the walls of the unit were disturbed. Originally intended as a safeguard against animals scratching or sharpening their horns on the glass framework, now the alarm sounded the warning for the real threat—man.

Piper ran back to where she could see Exeter. He glanced at her, but kept working, his fingers twisting something on the steel-enforced wall of the access door. "Bastard. God damn you." She said the words softly, like a curse.

A thunder of sound—nine sets of feet running toward her—made her turn away. Only for an instant. Voices shouting. Someone screaming. Was it Maggie?

A mechanical groan reverberated beneath her feet, and the double steel doors began to close, sealing off the utility room. Jessica was waiting before the doors. Piper remained where she stood. If the seal of the outer wall was broken before the interior doors shut. . . .

She heard the solid *CLUNK* as metal slammed against metal, but her eyes remained fixed on Exeter, watching as his hand turned . . . as he slid the panel open . . . as he stepped—

"He's inside!" She no longer tried to mask the terror in her voice.

Quinn was running, tearing at the wall face with his bare hands, ripping the plastic panel box free at the baseboard. She saw him at the peripheral edge of her field of vision. "Help me!" he shouted. Daniel and Josiah rushed toward him. Jessica remained before the door.

In the space of an instant, they had a long snake of twisted wires pulled from the channel along the floor-board. Quinn split through the length of it and stripped the plastic coating off the wires, dividing the snake into two sets of bare, joined whips. He lay one set of wires against the steel doors and threw the other set toward the water—to Piper. She caught the thick bundle to her like a sheaf of metal wheat, cradling it in her arms. "What. . . ?"

"In the water! Throw it in the water!" Quinn shouted.

Then she understood. They would have to kill him. If Exeter pushed open interior doors—and he could from inside the utility room—they would all be exposed to the virus. There was no time to try to talk him out of it. This very minute, his fingers might be forcing the steel plates apart.

"Now!" Quinn shouted.

She threw the wires.

"Okay!" someone yelled. *Was it Josiah?* "Power on!"

They all heard Exeter touch the doors, the slide of his fingers moving over the seam.

"Why isn't it—" started Jessica, running now toward the wires at the door. All of them running. Rushing forward. Voices shouting.

And then Piper saw it, the reason the massive voltage hadn't stopped him. Her bundle of wires hadn't touched the water. She hadn't thrown them far enough. It was too late. He'd be inside in an instant. Her fault.

She ran, scooped the track of wires up in her bare hands and stumbled forward with them . . . into the water.

The steel doors turned blue-white, the sound loud and harsh, the noise of something popping. It lasted perhaps a minute, the hard white light and the crackle of. . . . The smell of burning flesh stung their nostrils.

"Cut the power!" shouted Quinn, coughing. "No need to fry the fish."

Josiah turned off the switch, the one controlling the motor that aerated the ocean. The sound of a power rev whined and sank. On the other side of the door, they heard a heavy slump.

"Phew! What a stink," said Daniel. "Why the hell does it smell like that if. . . . Hey, Quinn, if the seal wasn't broken, why do we—"

"Oh, God!," moaned Cathe. "Look!"

Except for Cathe, who had already seen, they turned as one body. Away from the white-hot doors. Toward the cool of the man-made sea. Toward the charred remains of Piper Robinson.

Chapter Twelve

They buried Piper Robinson at the corner of dawn. Josiah Gray Wolf took it upon himself to tell the others about this place which had been sacred to her, and how she had come here each day to watch the sunrise. He tried to tell them how he had felt, too, seeing her in this spot the first time, how she had seemed so much a part of the land, still as a rock, kneeling before the sea. He tried to tell them; but his voice broke, and the words choked in his throat.

"We are ten in this world," said Jessica Nathan, standing at the head of Piper's grave. "Nine of us are left alive, but we are ten."

Diana began crying. She made no effort to control her sobs.

"Because of Piper's sacrifice, the giving of her life to save ours, we will go on. To do otherwise would be to waste this unselfish act. Sometimes, when we were alone, she spoke of the world as if it were a single being, and all of us a part of it. We were of the earth, and the trees, and the rocks. We were of the water and the sky above. It was her belief that all life was truly one life. And in the turning of the land, in the changing of the seasons, there is no death, only rebirth.

"So I tell you again, although you see nine, we are ten."

Maggie was crying, and Daniel. Not Cathe. Jessica noticed the unnatural look in the other woman's eyes, as if nothing of any significance had happened. It chilled her to see the emptiness in Cathe's glance.

"Are you—?"

"I'm fine," Cathe stopped her, not allowing the words. Not allowing the question.

"I want to talk to you later. Today," Jessica insisted.

Cathe gave her a hard look, but nodded.

Jessica let it go. They were as strung out as addicts without a fix. Grief touched them all. She had been lost for a time after Brad's death in her own private mourning—and now this.

It was time to remember her duty to these people. They had put their faith in her, trusted her, and she had let them wander alone these past weeks, without any guidance from her. For that, she was ashamed. It was as though she had been dead, with Brad.

But she wasn't dead, and neither were they.

The grief would always be with her, but the paralyzing numbness was over. She was back among them, ready to fight to keep them alive. And they wouldn't lose anyone else, not if she could help it.

"I wanted to see you privately," Jessica began, "because I noticed how withdrawn you were at the funeral today. It's the kind of withdrawal I associate with depression, Cathe. God knows we all have a right to be depressed, but I think this may be something more."

Cathe Innis's eyes were simmering vats of hostility. "It's none of your damn business, Jessica. Who the hell do you think you are? Mother Superior?"

"Last time I looked, I was still the leader of this team," Jessica shot back, standing her ground.

"Bullshit! You stopped being that when the whole fucking world caught a bullet train to Hell. I don't give

101

you shit, Jessica. You're no more in charge of anything than I am."

It was so unusual for Cathe to swear that Jessica stared for a full minute, shocked by her choice of words. She wished now she'd been a psych major in school. Something serious was going on here, and she had only the tools of her own instincts to guide her.

"Look, let's put aside labels like leader for the moment. That's not important right now. I'm concerned about your anger, and how it's going to affect all of us. You seem—"

"I don't have a right to be angry? Jesus-God! What kind of nonsense is that? You're crazy if you're not angry. You're all goddamn, fucking crazy! *Shit!*" Her back was rising and falling with shudders, but no tears crossed her cheeks. Her eyes were icy and dry.

"We all have anger. Do you think you're the only one? I know it's hard, but—"

"I don't want to hear this." Cathe stood up and made for the door.

"Wait just a minute! We can carry on this conversation outside my room if you want—and that's exactly what I'll do if you walk out the door. I don't care who hears us. We're in here for your sake, to allow you some privacy. You want to take it out there in front of the others, that's fine by me." She waited. It was Cathe's move.

"I've got nothing to say to you." She didn't leave.

"Sit down, Cathe. Please."

The other woman slumped heavily into the chair. They sat through a long silence, Jessica waiting for Cathe to speak. She didn't know the questions to ask. Only Cathe could move them forward. Jessica counted the minutes of stony silence and waited.

"I come from a struggling kind of family, not like yours. Did you know that?"

Jessica shook her head, but kept quiet.

"We worked for everything we had as kids. Never had anything handed to us. And I worked harder than any of them. I was going to make something of my life. I was going to wriggle out of the trap, poverty — you know?"

Jessica didn't speak.

"This place was how I was going to achieve it. Working here would be like a stepping stone, and I'd be on my way. Stepping stone," she repeated, and laughed, a bitter sound.

"You're alive," Jessica offered. "The rest of the world can't say that."

"For what? What's our future?"

"I don't know."

"Well, I do. I'll tell you what I see as my shining future. I see a life of hard work and loneliness. The rest of you will pair off."

Jessica started to argue this, but Cathe stopped her.

"Don't. Just don't, okay? It's already happening. Haven't you noticed? Maggie and Mike. Diana and Griffin. Even Josiah and Piper were. . . ."

In the words Cathe didn't say, Jessica heard the truth. It wasn't that the world outside the dome had died. It was that her world had no one in it to love her. And according to her fear, never would.

"I'm not pretty. I know that," admitted Cathe. "I never thought it would matter this much, but it does. Things like that do matter, don't they, Jessica? I work as hard . . . harder than anyone . . . and it doesn't matter, does it? Does it?" she asked, her voice loud and breaking with emotion.

"Oh, Cathe."

"I saw Griffin go into Diana's room — oh, a few times. They're lovers." She stared hard at Jessica, defying her to contest this fact.

So, it was Griffin. Jessica waited for the flood of hurt to follow, but Cathe said nothing more.

"Do you love him?" she asked, finally.

Cathe didn't answer . . . not with words, but the tears she had held to her so tightly flowed freely now. Tears of outrage and of wounded pride. Tears that once might have been caresses, and the hungry cry of desperate love.

Oh, God, thought Jessica. *What the hell am I doing here? What the hell do I know about any of this?*

"I don't think he loves her." It was the only truth Jessica knew to offer.

Cathe looked up, her eyes glittering. "Why do you say that? I don't need lies."

"No, I wouldn't suggest any. Too complicated for me. I'm very simple, really. I just meant . . . I think he's with her because she's . . ."

"Beautiful," Cathe filled in the word.

"Right. Well, she is. And I think that's why he's there. But I don't think he loves her."

"Why not?" Cathe wasn't going to let it go.

This was turning out to be harder than Jessica had thought. How to say the truth without offending either woman. Maybe there was no way to do that. And Diana wasn't here. It felt wrong, as if she were cutting down her own people, but she gave it to Cathe, anyway. Something had to stop the flow of blood.

"Because Diana's not a whole woman. She's a toy. I think Griffin knows that, in spite of whatever attraction she may hold for him. She won't be able to keep him. And when he leaves her. . . ." She left the rest open-ended. Let Cathe fill in the blanks any way she wished.

Cathe sat back, stunned. The tears had stopped. "You really think. . . ?"

"It's just my opinion," Jessica stressed, wishing she could back away from the condemnation of one of her own team, but the words stuck.

"My God, Jessica. If I believed that there was any chance of that. . . ." She stood up and paced. "I just

104

couldn't . . . I didn't want to keep trying, not without some hope, but if you're right. . . ."

She moved toward the door. Her hand rested on the knob, and she turned. "Thank you, Jessica. I know I've been acting pretty stupid, and I'm sorry for that. I'm sorry about what I said to you, too. I just. . . ."

"It's okay. Forgotten. We go on from here. That's what all of us have to do, Cathe, go on from here. We're all lonely."

"God, I feel like such an idiot. It was just eating me up inside. I couldn't help the way I felt. You really think. . . ?"

Jessica shrugged. "I don't know."

"Right," said Cathe, smiling for the first time in many days. "I won't say any more about it, only . . . if you ever need anything, Jessie, I'll try to be there for you. I guess we all need each other, huh?"

Jessica nodded.

"Thanks."

Her hands were trembling by the time Cathe left. She had held them behind her, hiding the exposed pain they would reveal. Cathe didn't need to see that. Pain was something they all had to deal with, and alone. Besides, this was a hurt Jessica didn't want to share. Not with anyone. It was her last link to him, the aching she felt. That and memories were all she had left.

"Brad," she said his name aloud, as though he stood beside her. "I love you, Brad. I love you."

"Cathe," Josiah called from the corridor leading to Jessica's quarters, "are you okay?"

Cathe spun around, facing him. "I'm all right. Sure. What are you doing out here?" She stared at him suspiciously.

He walked closer, smiling a little in embarrassment. "I saw how you were at the funeral, and I knew Jessica wanted to see you. It just seemed to me that you might need a friend tonight."

"Yeah, I guess," she admitted.

He moved away from Jessica's door, and she followed. "No one wants to talk about it, you know?"

Cathe nodded.

"What we're going through is. . . ." He struggled to find the right words, and couldn't. "It's never happened in the world before. I think we've got a right to fall apart a little."

Cathe was silent, but kept walking beside him.

"All of us are scared," he said to her. "We need each other."

She stopped walking and looked at him. "Why are you telling me this, Josiah? What are you trying to say?"

"That I understand how you feel," he told her. "That I feel it, too—that kind of loneliness. You aren't alone, Cathe." He touched her cheek with his hand. "I just wanted you to know."

Chapter Thirteen

When the first Europeans came to the New World, they brought with them a language that was unfamiliar to the native people, a religion that was alien to them in concept and in deed, the moving terror of a horse, and weapons forged of steel. They also brought death — in the form of smallpox, measles, and influenza — against which the Indian nations had no immunity.

When the first Spaniards set foot on the new land, twenty-five million American Indians shared the continent. A century later, less than one million Indians remained. Disease and virus brought by these Europeans and other newcomers killed more native Americans than any field of battle.

Yet some survived.

Mankind, as a species, had endured plagues, epidemics, viruses, and the changing whims of nature. And always, some remnant of human life remained. Only this time the virus was not a creation of nature, but of mankind, itself. This time, man's own ingenuity had moved the species one final step closer to its own destruction.

Nature, that most pragmatic deity, stood aside and let the death throes begin.

Outside the safety of the five remaining biosphere

domes, a panic, the likes of which the world had never known, was taking place.

The streets of London were deserted. Its majestic cathedrals, museums, historic buildings, and expensive homes stood empty, their doorways left open — the city abandoned by people in favor of the forests.

As if returning to their beginnings, Londoners fled to the country, to the thickly wooded groves, away from their fellow man. It was man who brought the disease, and man who would spread it. They hid among the game, their own fearful eyes peering out from behind the shelter of a rock cairn, waiting among the beasts — for animals did not die of this virus.

Around the world, in places of concentrated population — hospitals, army barracks, government buildings, churches, and schools — the disease advanced quickly. In places of lesser density, it teased and lingered, taking this one and that one, leisurely, as if toying with the race of man. In the end, it had them all.

Only the most isolated pockets of the world remained free of the virus: parts of the Amazon rain forest, sequestered, inner reaches of the Congo, some desolate stretches of Antarctica, a single monastery on a remote mountain peak of Tibet, a few solitary South Pacific islands such as Easter and Pitcairn, and other far-flung outposts of humanity. But even in these places of sanctuary, the winds carried. In time, the virus would come to them, as well.

The cries of a dying world rose on the swell of a blustering gale, churning across the unprotected surface of the continents. Its lamentation sounded in the ears of those few who remained, an unleashed howling like a vent of steam, screaming from deep within the earth's still, liquid core.

Slowly, slowly, the demented wailing ceased. A low and mournful moan replaced the cry of human life at its end. The warm desert wind, the zephyr, coursed its way along the vacant canyons that were once cities, over empty houses and abandoned farms, through the forests and the jungles, across the open back of lands — above an earthen plain now silent, bereft of human voice.

John Katelo had survived the scourge. Living off the frozen wastelands of Siberia, he had made his way across the ice and snow to the Bering Strait. There, he borrowed a fishing boat and, with only the companionship of the white-faced dog, Kip, as Katelo now called him, crossed the frigid water, home.

The land had not changed. On the outer stretches along the Bering Sea, John Katelo knew a kind of peace. The land there was the same as he remembered. Nothing seemed wrong or out of place. Only in the villages, when he moved through the empty houses like a spirit walker, did he feel the terrifying loss. The people were no more.

He had hoped. . . . But hope was not a thing a hunter counted on. Hope was for children and old women. A hunter must see with truer eyes. He must act upon the wisdom of his knowledge, and with courage.

Nothing in life had cost John Katelo more courage than living through that first winter alone.

He saw the scattered bodies with a kind of shield over his vision. He saw the faces of old men, children, and Inuit hunters like himself. Some, the polar bears and packs of dogs had savaged. The bodies were a food source, and the dogs especially were hungry. They had been tamed by the hand of man. Now they fed their hunger from the bodies scattered on the snow.

For the first of the dead, John Katelo rubbed his face with the ashes from his campfire. He was Inuit, and would honor the spirits of his people. But soon he realized, the dead were everywhere. He alone walked among the empty villages and threw sticks at the snapping dogs. He stopped rubbing his palms in the charred remains of the fire, stopped wearing the sign of mourning, and went on. Grief could not be worn forever.

Alone, he tried to recall the stories of his grandfather, Akilo. They kept him company on the long trek across the white wilderness of snow and ice: stories of the Real People and their journey over the soft-footed land of snow and the hard-footed land of ice; stories of following the tracks of the mammoth, and of the standing bear; stories of Sloki, the Inuit hunter, and of his wife, Walrus-Woman.

With only the dog for company, Katelo crossed the endless sweep of white-shrouded land. He spoke to the young dog, Kip, and called him friend. For answer, there were warm, brown eyes shining back, the animal's eager body twisting and wriggling in happiness when he bent to stroke the dog's coat, and the nearness of another sleeping beside him in the cold. But there were no words. For the sound of a human voice, John Katelo had none but his own.

The first winter was the hardest of any in his memory. Within the borrowed shelters of other Inuit — those hunters who now walked the land as spirit guides — Katelo waited out the storms. The four winds of earth blew with a strength that marked the event of the passing year. To the lone Eskimo huddling for warmth against the blizzard, it was as though within the howling winds were the voices of the tribe of man, hovering over and haunting the lands on which they had lived. Their cries carried over the sound of the screaming blow. Shivering, he held the dog closer to him, and listened.

Each night, before he went to sleep, John Katelo removed every article of clothing he wore and, in the low light of the fire, beside its warmth, carefully searched his body for signs of blisters or of rash. He remembered well the sight and smell of the yellow pustules on the men in Siberia. Each night, it was the last thing he thought of before sleep.

Each morning, the first thought to come to him upon waking, and perhaps the only words he would say all day: "Still, I am alive."

He was not completely silent, as he might have been without the dog. There were the short commands he gave to the animal, words of the Inuit to his hunting companion. "Watch!" he would say to the pup as he moved in slow motion toward a small herd of caribou. The rifle was part of him, moving in the same easy strides. No sudden actions.

The dog quivered, his back rippling in waves of excitement, but stayed silent. He did not whimper, as he would when Katelo had food to offer. Now he learned the lesson of the hunt. Now he learned to kill.

Bang! The herd scattered, leaving only the fallen caribou, thrashing its agony on the cold ground, and the taste of blood on the snow. Then, "Go!" John Katelo would say to the pup, teaching the dog the ways of the wild, the ways of survival for the wolves and dogs that now ran feral. He stood aside and let the dog finish the kill, let him feel the throes of death in the caribou and taste the lure of blood.

The dog was young and ignorant. He played with the dying deer, a torment that was hard for Katelo to watch, but he didn't interfere. The dog must learn to hunt and kill for himself. One day, Katelo might not be there to bring food to him. In everything, there was a cost, and the cost of this lesson was the life of the deer.

Closing his ears to the struggle of the caribou, Katelo thought of dog sleds, of huskies and Samoyeds. He thought of pack ice and the black-faced seals, fishing from a hole cut in the frozen lake, and of the standing bear. In all of this, his thoughts were the same. They were of life.

In the first winter of the world without man—for human life was few enough to not be counted—the nature of those tamed and domesticated animals that had once been dependent upon mankind changed. On the plains where farms once cut into the earth, herds of cattle tramped the ground, feeding upon the growth of vegetation standing ungathered in the fields. Some died, penned in barns from which they could not escape, or of burst udders and infection, but many lived. They grazed the rich grasslands, feasting on the unclaimed harvest.

Pets of all kinds transformed from the hand-gentled creatures of hearth and home, to feral cats and wild dogs, and to horses galloping free on the range, intent upon surviving in a world gone bare of human restraint.

By the middle of the first winter, when the cold was hard and food was scarce, packs of these wild ones, starving and forced back into hunting by their desperate hunger, stalked the land. The weak were their prey; like Kip, they were still learning how to kill. The tall, straight form of the human was not among them. They forgot the voice of man. In its place, they heard again the cry of the wolf, and of the wild.

A low and cry went up from the face of the planet. It was the suffering of animals, those who had once been in the care of man. The hand that had led them home, sheltered them, and given them food was gone. On empty hillsides, the bleating lambs cried witness to their master's end. They, the weakest, became hunger's cease for others. They, the weakest, became the keening voice of lamentation, the bereavement of earth.

The virus moved across the earth in a matter of a few weeks, a global carnage, sweeping the world free of the dominance of man. Yet . . . on every continent, some few survived. Not the strongest, nor the weakest. They were, instead, those whose natural immunities kept them from getting the virus, or if they did get it, they suffered a much milder illness.

It wasn't likely that any human had a true, natural immunity to the specific virus, CXT, since the pandemic was man-made and not an ancient scourge of nature's own. But some people had immunities that were so closely related to the virus — from an inherited genetic pool — they showed little or no reaction to the contagion.

No single race of man was protected, but individuals — few in number, and through no efforts of their own — held a genetic advantage, and survived.

One of these few was John Katelo.

He was one of the *alone*. For him, it was as though he had stepped through a veil, and the world had turned into one of his grandfather's myths. He was the lone hunter, a savior of his race. With him was the young dog, the only companion Man Above had given him.

For the first full winter, they tread the land in a harmony of terrible silence. The cold winds blew the Old Woman's howls at them, and no one was there to band together and mock her phantom wails. Only John Katelo. Only Katelo, alone. Only he, to hear the growl of bears or the scratching of the dead on the tin roof of his shelter. Only he, through the dark days and nights of winter, wondering if the veil would lift, if the spring would ever come.

And through this mystery, he wondered, too: Why had he been spared?

Chapter Fourteen

Our second Christmas Day, 1998, has passed within the boundaries of the dome. We remaining nine are in good health, physically, at least. Some of us show symptoms of stress-related psychosis: Diana, in the way she relates to others; Cathe, in the way she refuses to relate to any of us; and Daniel, in his hard anger.

In some way, we all suffer this disorder. I wonder: Is it a disorder, really? Or, are those of us who react the most to this unnatural life the most sane of all?

To this date, I still maintain a certain leadership over the group. We find that this is useful for decisions that might be harder to make by committee. For everything of any importance, I consult with each member of the team. It seems, more and more, that everything is of great importance. In our world, the smallest change matters.

Jessica saved the latest entry of her ship's log on the computer terminal and waited while the information loaded into the printer. Both ran on solar energy, a renewable source of power, but the paper she used for the printing was a precious commodity, irreplaceable in their present circumstances. And yet, she used it to record the history of their lives within the dome. It mattered. If they were the last humans on earth, perhaps it was all that mattered.

A knock at her door stopped the distant train of her thoughts. She was no longer the observer, but had been pulled back into the whole as one of them.

"Come in."

Quinn stepped inside Jessica's room and closed the door. "Still keeping track of us? We're the experiment in the big terrarium, the sideshow freaks. Come and pay a quarter for a glance at how they lived." He moved across the room, closer to where she stood. "Who's going to read it, Jessica? Who's going to care what we did?"

She rose to his attack. "If you've come in here to bait me, Quinn, I —"

"No, I didn't come in here for that," he cut in quickly.

"What, then? I'm busy, as you can see, and I want to get back to this." She was curt and formal, keeping a barrier between them. She was always curt with Quinn, she realized. He pushed the wrong buttons, or tested her in ways that felt like pressure, always. And she pushed back.

"There's something I wanted to discuss with you, apart from the others."

She stared at him, waiting for an explanation. When he didn't offer one, she did a little pushing of her own. "What is this, an insurrection? Are you planning a mutiny?"

"In a way, that's exactly what I'm planning. A breakout, if you will."

"Break-out?"

He smiled, looking too pleased with himself.

"You *are* crazy. Now, go away and let me —"

"Hang on. You haven't heard the details. I'd sit down if I were you. This may take a while."

She went on standing, but as he spoke, she leaned in closer to the idea and to Quinn. Her legs felt shaky, trembling with the excitement generated by his words. After a few minutes, she pulled her chair near to his, and sat.

"I'm not sure it would work," she said.

"Neither am I. But there's a chance it might. I've lived in this petri dish long enough. I'm ready to take that chance."

"But, to leave the dome. . . ." She hesitated. One of them was already dead. Could they risk another?

"I only want your approval to check it out, to do some initial testing. Later, if it seems feasible, we'll bring the plan before the others. No point in raising their hopes until then."

"No," she had to agree, "there isn't."

"So you approve?"

She didn't answer. It was opening Pandora's Box. They were safe inside the dome. Outside. . . ?

"Jessica" He reached across the gulf between them and took her hand. "It's worth a chance. Don't say no."

The decision was one she couldn't back away from — and didn't want to. "All right, as long as nothing you do endangers the security of the dome." She was uncomfortable with his touch.

"It won't. That's a promise." He gave her hand a squeeze, then turned and took off with a quickness in his step. "Hell, it might just work," he called over his shoulder from the open door.

She sat facing the computer, but never lifted her fingers to the keyboard. Instead, her mind was seeded with possibilities. It was a risk, but if one of them could go outside. . . .

The room felt smaller, and the weight of time more oppressive. A year. They'd been inside the dome a full year. Another question haunted her. If what Quinn suggested was possible, and one of them was willing to take the risk, which one could the team afford to lose? If it came to that, this wasn't a decision to be made on the basis of courage alone. In their world, the smallest change made a difference. As all of them had learned, everything mattered.

It couldn't be Quinn, she decided quickly. He was vital to the team. They needed him for the computers, and for long-term systems planning, and for protection in case of another attempted break-in, and. . . .

She stopped listing, realizing that if she were honest, it was for more than any of those arguments. She couldn't let Quinn leave because — *God, why can't I admit* it? The pain of having feelings for someone again, after losing Brad, was too raw. The truth was, she couldn't risk losing Quinn because she couldn't bear the thought of living the rest of her life in this dome without him.

She remembered the feel of his hand on hers. More than friendship? Something that had remained hard and closed within Jessica, something she had thought died with Brad, opened. She felt the freedom of it, the new hope, the need. And in the dawning of that recognized need, she cried.

Josiah Gray Wolf had no illusions about what the next twenty years would be like. He was a spiritualist, but he was a realist, too. If the entire race of mankind was gone — with the exception of the nine people inside this glass structure — he wanted to be sure of it. Something in him didn't believe. Wouldn't.

His work inside the biosphere was that of a horticulturalist. In reality, he was a glorified gardener. That was the simplest description of his duties: grounds keeper for the Garden of Biosphere.

The lab research he did on plant propagation and possible medicinal properties was separate from his main force of labor. That was Indian lore, herbal concoctions, or as Quinn called it — mystic shit. It was this work that kept him sane. The other kept the biosphere alive.

And it was alive, this sphere of earth and plants and man. *We are of each other,* he thought, *providing for and nurturing one another — an interlinked balance.* In order to main-

117

tain its viability, the ecosphere needed the hand of man to caretake it: man, to manage the animal life, the ocean salinity, to reseed the ground, to control the climate. People, in turn, needed the resources of the earth, water and atmosphere to live. *We are one being*, Josiah thought, as certain of this as he had ever been of anything.

Today, in this place, he recalled something his uncle had told him years ago. He had been a boy of about seven, and his uncle had taken him fishing. A warm day, the sultry heat of summer baked their backs as they sat in the slowly rocking boat. His uncle, father's brother to him, was a quiet man, given to long spells of silence when catching trout. As if from nowhere, the words came to the man's lips, and Josiah, amazed, had listened.

"The sea is the home of man, Josiah. You know this? From rivers like these, we climbed onto the wide back of the turtle, on rocks, and pulled ourselves out of the water, oh, long ago. You believe this, little Gray Wolf?"

Josiah had made no answer, too surprised to speak.

"We are of that water, still. Our skin holds back that long-time-ago ocean in our bodies, the river of life. The salt of that water is in our blood. You taste it when you cut yourself, eh?"

It was a long speech for such a man as Josiah's uncle. A window of imagining had opened for the child with the magical words. Lying still, it seemed to him that he felt the currents of that long-ago ocean in his body, the ancient sea, surging through him.

Later, in school, when he learned about biology, Josiah saw a quick comparison to that earlier lesson of his uncle's. The atmosphere was another kind of skin, a seal to hold against the bowl of life, the earth. And now, the glass plates of Biosphere Seven acted as another, third kind of closure.

They had risen from the sea, from the wet womb of that ocean home itself, and set their feet on other worlds. But always, they took earth with them, its water, its atmosphere, its vegetation. Through man, the land was now duplicating itself, creating itself anew. Through the nurturing environment within this biosphere, the world was creating its own offspring.

This concept was a new one to the scientists Josiah had spoken to in the days before the virus. They had found it hard to accept the idea that the earth itself — rocks, ground, mountains — was alive. And that man, the creation nature had allowed to succeed, would be of ultimate benefit to the planet, by carrying these replications of the original — these biospheres and ecospheres, space stations and oceanic habitats — into space, undersea, and on to other worlds. And perhaps, far beyond the imagination of man.

Will we be needed, he wondered, *when earth sends out its children? Yes. We are the caretakers,* he thought again. *We are the keepers of the ground.*

More and more, Josiah felt an inseparable union with earth. It wasn't enough to save the land alone. It wasn't enough to know there would be plants and animal life. Man's voice was the voice of the land. Man's eyes were the vision of the world. And man's mind would carry the Genesis gardens, those and other Edens, into places as yet undreamed.

He wanted to be part of that. For now, this garden, this earth, was his home. If things didn't change, it would be forever. If the time came, he decided, he would be the catalyst for change.

New Year's Day, they were gathered together. "If you would all listen carefully for just a minute." Jessica stood, gaining their attention. "I want everyone to hear what Quinn has to tell us about — well, I'd better let him explain it. Quinn."

He didn't rise from where he sat, legs stretched out before him and body slumped into the curl of the chair. *He's not a showman,* Jessica thought, *and won't put on a performance for any of them.* His deliberate

119

indolence irritated her, but some part of her responded to that self-confidence of his, the ego that didn't care what any of them thought.

"What's in the works for us now, Quinn?" asked Daniel. "Bomb shelters?"

That brought a half-hearted laugh from some. Quinn had earned a reputation among them for his spark-start temper, his non-existent politics — "Politicians are all mouths with heads up their asses" — his fanaticism on the twin subjects of total Irish sovereignty — "Let the Brits of Northern Ireland pack up and leave, and good riddance to them!" — and his plan for the strictest possible enforcement of environmental protection measures designed to save the planet — with offenses punishable by stiff prison terms.

"Let him talk," said Josiah, and the others soon quieted.

Quinn's voice never rose above a close conversation level. As he spoke, he stared only at Jessica. "This is something I've been thinking about a long time. Working out the details. I wasn't sure at first . . . didn't want to say anything to anybody until I ran some tests . . . but, I'm sure now."

He paused, and they leaned forward to hear his next words.

"The thing is," he said, looking at each of them in turn. "I've found a way for one of us to leave the dome."

Cathe showed no reaction at all. Her face remained set in that non-expression she had mastered of late. "Jesus!" Daniel swore, pacing the room like the oscillating tongue of a grandfather clock. The others moved as a unit toward Quinn, questions rising like yeast in a loaf of dough.

Two didn't come forward. Jessica stood well behind Quinn and watched as the surge of excitement at his news moved through them. All of her thoughts were centered around one question: Would this make it worse? Whatever other considerations entered the picture — and there were plenty of them — as team leader she needed to be sure of the safety of her people, and of the unit.

One of them gasped in a kind of terrible fear at Quinn's suggestion. Maggie hugged her crossed arms to her chest. Afraid. The sanctuary of her world was crumbling. If it became possible to leave the biosphere. . . . What would happen between her and Mike? Would he be the one chosen to go? Would he volunteer? And if he left her, could she go on?

"No," she cried softly, rocking back and forth, then standing and praying almost silently to a deity she had forgotten and cast aside in her happiness. "We can't leave here. Not now. Help me. Please, please God . . . not now."

Both women stood alone: Jessica's mind crowded with thoughts of freedom . . . Maggie's, full of fear.

Chapter Fifteen

Quinn's news affected each of them differently. If they had struggled with any personal demons over what had happened to those in the outside world, that struggle was harder now. Going outside meant facing those demons. It meant seeing a truth they had been sheltered from. Each of them took a risk in allowing the horror of the outside to invade their lives. And for the one who would leave, the prospect was terrifying.

Quinn's plan involved using PAL, the Planetary-All-Land vehicle. Because all six biosphere stations had been designed as prototypes for space exploration, each satellite also included this experimental unit.

PAL was battery operated — in recognition of the fact that on many planets, solar energy would be insufficient to fuel the vehicle's engine. It was a sealed environment, complete with a clear bubble dome in which its own breathable atmosphere circulated, and its own communications system. Best of all, it was housed in an access branch of the Biosphere Seven unit — one that could be sealed off from the rest of the structure.

PAL could be loaded into the release area — a thumblike extension of the biosphere working space — then the area sealed off from the unit by a weighted steel sliding door and by a pressurized air-lock system. When the system was operational, the outer door to the chamber could be opened, and the vehicle released into the outside, without exposing anyone inside the biosphere-contained unit — including the driver — to the external atmosphere.

"And what are we supposed to do when it comes back?" asked Diana. "The staging area will be contaminated as soon as we open the door. Or, are we planning to send someone out permanently?"

"The area has been designed for that contingency," Jessica answered, shifting the weight of her approval to Quinn's proposal for the first time. "Biosphere Seven was planned, remember, as a functional prototype of the first planetary-based habitats in the Colony Program. It was the design engineer's hope that we would not only test the vehicle, but also the vacuum chamber's capability."

"Vacuum chamber?" repeated Mike.

"It's a venting device," Quinn explained, "programmed to evacuate all air from the sealed-off chamber after PAL returns. Then a blast of radiation from the ceiling ducts, and the room is virtually sterile."

"What about the driver?" Daniel spoke up. "Is he sterile, too?" That drew a low, worried laugh.

"You're assuming it will be a he," Cathe remarked pointedly.

"Cathe's right," said Jessica. "The driver selected could be male or female. And the answer to your question, Daniel, is neither he, nor she, would become sterile. The PAL unit protects the driver from intense radiation and provides the needed breathing atmosphere while the staging area is being swept clean of outside air. Half-an-hour after returning to base, or docking, the air level in the isolated chamber will resume normal biosphere proportions, and the steel door separating the docking area from the main unit will be opened."

A profound silence held them in its grip. Taking this step would allow knowledge of the outside. It was leaving the boundaries of Eden for the world beyond the pale.

"It's too dangerous." The others turned to face Maggie. "No one should go out there. What if they get sick? What if they bring the virus back to us? You're risking all of our lives. And for what? What do you expect to find outside? Everyone's dead!" These last words she shouted, then ran from the room.

"Maggie." Mike went after her. He turned back at the door. "This whole thing has her pretty upset. She's afraid."

"Go talk to her, Mike," said Jessica.

That left seven: Jessica, Quinn, Daniel, Griff, Diana, Cathe, and Josiah. It was from among these that one would be chosen to go.

"Are the rest of us in agreement that we should attempt this?" she asked when the door shut.

"I'm ready to cut out of here," said Daniel, still pacing. "And I think it should be a man," he added, glancing at Diana. "We don't know what the situation is outside the dome. There may be gangs of people, survivors, living by their own violence. No sense tempting any problems by sending a woman."

"Now, wait a minute," Diana shot back, angry and her words hard biting. "Who the hell do you think you are? The object is not to leave the transport. Isn't that right?" She turned to Jessica for confirmation of her facts.

"That's right, but I think we ought to consider this carefully. Dan may have a point."

"What? I can't believe you're siding with him," Diana said bitterly. "The only point he has is the one between his legs, and that's—"

"All right, enough! Let's get back to the question at hand and not get sidetracked. And for the record, I'm not with any one person over another. If I didn't think

124

women were just as good at leadership as men, I wouldn't be in this position, would I? I'd be out there with the rest of them. I'd be dead." Her anger had risen to the surface, and Diana backed down.

"Sorry. It isn't you, Jessica, it's . . . I'm going nuts inside this glass marble. I'm not sure I can stick it out." The words were a hard admission, and they cost her in pride and dignity.

"We're all feeling that way," said Quinn. He had stood back and said nothing until now. "Each of us wants to escape—" he met the eyes of everyone in the room—"but that's not the purpose of this expedition."

"Well, what the hell is the purpose?" asked Daniel. He had stopped pacing and stood with both hands on his hips, glaring.

"To find out if anybody's alive—for one thing. To see how bad the damage is to the world . . . if anyone survived the virus. It'll be a trip into Hell," he warned them. "Whoever goes had better be prepared to face that. If we're right about what happened, it's fair to suppose that not everyone died in bed. There'll be bodies in the streets. And if the animals got to them—"

"Stop it, Quinn." It was Josiah who had spoken. "You're not helping anyone in this room by saying such things." He nodded toward Jessica, who was standing with her back to them. "We have all had dreams of what we might find outside."

"Nightmares, you mean," said Daniel.

"Dreams, or nightmares, it's all the same," Josiah told him. "We see what our minds tell us is there. If we face that—" he paused to give them courage, "then we'll find the strength to face what is left of our world."

"I vote that Josiah be the one to go." It was Cathe who spoke up, surprising everyone. "Both Jessica and Quinn are needed here. Diana's on the verge of a break-down. Daniel's afraid. Maggie needs Mike; I think she's pregnant." There was someone's sharp intake of breath at this, but she didn't stop. "That leaves three of us; Griffin, Josiah, and me. Although he could be spared"—she stared at the floor now—"Griff would not make as good a risk as Josiah. He's a brave man, but it will take a kind of strength he has little of, to face what's out there—and Diana needs him."

"Someone stop her!" Diana shouted, angry. "Damn you, I'll shut you up, myself." She lunged toward Cathe, but Griffin caught her arm.

"Go on, Cathe," he said. "Finish."

She looked up at him, hurt in her eyes, and faced them again. "I would gladly be the one to go," she offered, "and if Josiah refuses, I will. Each of us could be spared," she said honestly, "if anything were to happen, and each has no ties to this place."

"Why him over you?" asked Jessica.

"Because, for me it would be running away. For him, it would be running to. Our Josiah is a mystic; he sees things and knows their truths. He has already seen himself out there"—she turned toward him—"and knows he is the one to go. That's true, isn't it, Josiah?"

They all looked, their eyes telling their judgement of him. "Something waits for me," he admitted, as though revealing a layer of his soul. "What it is, I don't know—but, I believe it is out there."

A silence followed; then Jessica took control again. "Would you be willing to leave us, Josiah?"

He didn't answer quickly, but when he did, they all knew he was the one. "I would," he said, the words spoken slowly and with strength, as if sealing his own fate. "For the sake of the earth, I would go back to it."

Jessica felt his words cut through her, a cold, awakening blade. *For the sake of the earth,* she thought . . . *God help us. For the sake of the Earth.*

"What the hell was the matter with you back there?"

Mike caught Maggie's arm, dragging her to him like a reluctant child. "I don't get it. Are you crazy, or what?"

"Leave me alone."

"No dice. I want answers. What the hell—"

"I'm pregnant!" Maggie shouted at him, using the news as a shield against his anger. She couldn't face him because his eyes were glaring. She felt the heat of his hate.

"Pregnant! That's not possible," he countered, lifting her head and forcing her to meet his eyes. "Is it? Is it, Maggie?"

She wouldn't answer.

He held her by the shoulders and shook the words from her. "Did you lie to me? You said. . . . You did this deliberately, didn't you? Didn't you?" He shook her again.

"Yes!" she cried, the sound a long and wounded wail.

"Why? God, Maggie! Why?" He took his hands from her, and that was harder than the shaking. He pulled back, disgust hollowing his eyes.

She grabbed at his shirt. "I was afraid." The words spilled from her now, unchecked. "I needed something for myself, something to keep—even if you. . . ."

"Dammit, Maggie. Can't you think of anyone but yourself? That's a child you're talking about, as if it were a watch. You want to bring a baby into this?" His arm swept back, displaying the biosphere. "The world's dead out there," he shouted. "Dead!"

"Mike, don't," she pleaded.

"I've had enough. I'm through with you." He yanked his shirt free of her desperate grip and walked away.

"Mike!" she cried again, grabbing at his back. "Don't! Please, don't."

"Get away!" he shouted, his face red with fury. He shoved her. "It's over, Maggie. You did this; you live with it."

She didn't try to hold him to her again. Inside, something as thin as air crumpled—something that had been shelled with love and faith and beauty. It wasn't a surprise. It was just an agony she had known would come. She laid her hand over the still unfelt presence in her womb.

"Don't be afraid," she whispered to the child within her. "It's all right." The words came like the litany of her soul. "I love you, baby. I love you."

"You're a strong woman." Josiah said it like a sanctification.

Cathe bowed her head and almost smiled.

"And lonely."

He had waited until after the meeting with the others, then went to Cathe's room to talk with her. Her living space was bleak and bare. She had made no effort to personalize the room or display any telling of her presence in it. As if she'd never been there. Had she? Was she a part of them? Or was she isolated, in some private sphere of her own?

"Everything you said today was right," he began. She hadn't asked him to sit down.

"Yes."

The emptiness of this room filled his soul with tears. Inside, he wept for her. "I've thought of what might await me if I were to leave the dome," he confided, "more times than I can count. It comes in dreams, and in wakeful thoughts which fly from my head like ghosts. I've thought about it, and knew it would happen."

"I felt that," she said, offering nothing more.

"You might have gone." He knew she had wanted to go.

"Yes," she admitted, "but could I have come back?"

She keeps her dignity, he thought. *How cold it must be inside that hard and voiceless shell.* "Neither you, nor I, are

128

of this place," he gave her. "When Piper died"—the words burned in his throat—"this world became a tomb to me."

She looked at him, and there was understanding of his pain in her eyes. "She knew you loved her," Cathe soothed the wound.

He held that feeling to himself and silently blessed her. "For you, it was when Griffin moved in with Diana. From that day, remaining here has been a living hell."

"Was it so obvious?"

He had touched a raw nerve, and she pulled away from the sharpness of this suffering. "I don't think it was to him, but to me, yes," Josiah admitted.

"And to Jessica. She saw it, too."

"Did she? Our Lady of the Sphere is a mystic woman, wise and all providing."

"What?"

"Nothing, just a name Quinn calls her. He loves her, and he doesn't know how to say the words."

She looked amazed. "Quinn loves Jessica? Why do you say that? I don't think—he's always standing up to her, testing her, or something. Quinn doesn't love anyone but Quinn."

"He loves her," Josiah said again. "One day he'll show it."

"Hmm," said Cathe, slipping back into the silence of herself.

"It was decided," he told her simply, "that I should leave tomorrow."

She made no comment, but he could see her eyes were darting from side to side with unasked questions.

"If we wait," he explained, "someone might sabotage the transport."

"Maggie," she agreed. "Or Daniel."

He neither agreed to nor disputed her conclusion. "Do you believe in the power of nature, Cathe? Do you think there's life in this dome? I mean, that it has a life of its own?"

She didn't answer his question, but asked one instead. "You don't think you're coming back, do you?"

"No man can know his own fate," he answered. "I carry the Indian people within me. We are the mystics, the shamans of the world. We are the voice of the rock, and the land. What troubles me is that with my death, that voice too may die."

He said nothing more. They stood quietly in the silent room, each one sensing the other's need.

"What do you want from me, Josiah?" The question was of itself an offering. She was opening her soul to him, allowing this man to take from it.

"I leave tomorrow morning," he told her. "Until that time, I would like to stay here, and be with you. It may be that if what my heart tells me is true, I will never return to this closed world . . . but a child of mine may live on. Through that child, my people will continue."

"You offer me no words of love."

"Would you have false words between us?"

"A woman wants to hear such things."

"No," he said. "Your love is for someone else. What we might share is something greater than the love you hold within the boundaries of your heart for that man. There is another kind of love ahead for you, Cathe. There is a love of people. I recognize a like-being in you. You will gather souls and lead them."

She hesitated no longer. "You asked if I believe in nature, Josiah. I do. If a life of its own exists in this biosphere, I will catch it to me this night and begin your child." She held out her hand to him.

"May you be the mother of nations," he blessed her, and followed the guidance of her hand to the lonely alcove of her bed.

Chapter Sixteen

Quinn had been waiting, sitting up all night. "Josiah," he called out softly to his friend as the man stepped out into the hall and closed Cathe's door behind him.

"Quinn?" he asked, surprised. He didn't ask for explanations—*What are you doing here? How long have you been out here?*—but the questions were in his eyes.

"I've been waiting to talk to you," Quinn told him. "Let's go someplace where we don't have to whisper."

Josiah glanced back at the door, understood, then followed Quinn in a silent walk along the sandy pathway to the waterfall.

"This is as far as it goes," Josiah shouted over the thunderous pounding of the cataract. "So, let's have it. What do you want to tell me?"

Quinn seemed extremely reluctant to reveal what he'd brought Josiah all this way to say to him.

"What is it?" Josiah asked again, laying his hand on Quinn's shoulder.

"This is something the others don't know," Quinn started, then stopped, seemingly unable to put the thought into words.

"You've been keeping a secret?"

Quinn didn't deny it.

"From Jessica, too?"

"She's better off not knowing; they all are."

Josiah pulled Quinn far enough away from the falls that they could speak without shouting. "You've been waiting all night for this. Say it."

"It didn't matter—not to us," Quinn threw at him. "I made a decision—what was best for everyone. It wasn't easy, but I did it. I've lived with that, but now . . . you have to know."

"Know what?" Josiah didn't raise his voice. His eyes were calm, inviting Quinn to tell him the truth, not scaring him off. Opening the door. Easing the way. Ready.

"I have reason to believe there are people still alive out there." He said it simply, stating a fact.

"What?" The question came like an exhale after a long breath had been held. "You know there are people alive?"

Quinn seemed easier, now that the words were said. He nodded. "I heard them speak."

Josiah's voice was held in his throat, restricted by a band of fury so tight, it left him mute. He could only shake his head in disbelief. At last, the band eased, and he asked, "When?"

"A month ago, that was the last time. Before that, five or six contacts in all."

"And you didn't—"

"Tell anyone?"

"Yes, dammit. Why not? We've all believed everyone was dead out there . . . that we were all that was left of human life. You let us think that." His voice grew louder. "We've all been going through our own private hells, thinking—"

"What I found out won't change any of that. If there was any way it might have helped, I would have told everyone."

"You had no right to make that decision on your own."

132

"Didn't I? Maybe you won't be so quick to judge when you hear what I have to say."

The muscles of Josiah's jaws clamped down hard. It took tremendous effort not to close his hands around Quinn's throat and shake him. But there was something to be learned, something he needed to know before he left the dome. He dug his fingernails into the palms of his hands and waited for Quinn to speak.

"I don't know who they were. Just people. I heard them on the computer access, first in Biosphere Five, in Australia, another time at Bio Three—the Amazon basin rain forest—and then at data headquarters here in Texas. Ghostly voices, that's all they were. The monitors had been left on by whoever had been manning the stations. The people I heard weren't the teams living in the bios. They were intruders. Hell, they may have murdered the men and women inside the domes; I don't know."

"Did you speak to any of them?"

"No. They didn't seem to be aware of the fact that the monitor was on. They were looking for something, information I guess, tearing the place apart."

"How many?"

"Hard to guess. Altogether, I'd say no more than three or four, maximum."

"Three or four?" Josiah couldn't catch his breath.

"Only one at the data center. I'm sure of that. Same voice, talking to himself. He sounded . . ."

"Sounded what?"

"Demented." Quinn held the word like a bomb. "He sounded crazy, Josiah. They all sounded crazy."

"What?"

"I think it's affected their minds, being out there alone. Or, maybe it's a result of the virus. There's no way to tell. The man was muttering something, and screaming, too. He was screaming, Josiah. I listened

133

as long as I could stand it. When he started crying, I turned it off."

"He had good reason."

"The two others I heard were the same. It's the loneliness, or, Jesus. . . ."

Josiah felt a tremor in his chest. His heart was moving so fast and so hard, he could feel it kicking against his ribs. There were people alive out there. Some had survived. If these few had, there might be others. And when he left the dome, he'd find them.

"You can't tell the others, Josiah. I'm telling you this so you'll be prepared, but you can't say anything of this to anyone else. Promise me that? I need your word on it."

"They have a right to know." Josiah refused to be bound by Quinn's insistence.

"A right? What good will it do? How will it make them feel? They can't go out there. Will it help them to know that the only people left are—"

"Then, Jessica, at least," argued Josiah. "She's the leader, Quinn. She should be told."

"No, especially not Jessica. God, no." Quinn's face turned hard as stone.

"Why not? Why do you want to keep it from her? Are you still jealous of her, Quinn? Is that it?"

"She can't know."

"Why?" Josiah wouldn't back down. "I'm leaving in a few hours. Tell me why, or I swear I'll—"

"Because the man was Brad! The crazy one, the voice I heard wailing like . . . like . . . oh, Jesus God. Because it was Brad."

Josiah felt the world swimming inside his head. He closed his eyes and tried to make the spinning stop; but it moved on, and he couldn't break away. He stood like that until his heart slowed and the black mist lifted from his eyes. His legs were still trembling.

134

"You won't tell her?" asked Quinn, at last.

Josiah's own voice surprised him. It sounded muffled, as if filtered through a shallow river. "No," he answered. "Don't worry, I'll keep your secret. I promise. I won't say anything."

They stood in unbroken quiet, the thoughts of those whose voices Quinn had heard, their minds' companions. It was morning before either of them spoke again.

"Take care of Jessica, Quinn." Josiah turned to his friend with the dawn. "You love her. I think you know that. Be there for her. She'll need you."

"You'll be back. Quit talking like you'll never—"

"I know," Josiah stopped him, "but promise."

At first, Quinn said nothing. Then he turned his face toward the rising light, and the words came. "I will," he said. "If she'll let me, I will."

"Okay, let's test the radio on this go cart," the loud voice filled the sealed driver's capsule of PAL.

"I can hear you fine, Quinn," said Josiah. "You don't need to shout."

"Good. You look like an Easter chicken in a big plastic egg. Just thought you'd want to know."

"Thanks."

Jessica took over the radio controls. "Are you ready, Joe?"

"Ready, pretty lady."

"You'll lose contact with us during the seal lock. We'll pick you up again when the system doors are shut and you reach outside. Clear?"

"Clear. Let's break out of this shell."

"Okay. Joe. . . ?"

"Yes?"

"Good luck," she said. "And come back."

135

Those were the last words he heard before the heavy doors moved into place behind him. They were slow and ugly slabs of steel, cutting him off from the only world he could count on. He waited, his hands slick and sweaty against PAL's steering wheel. A minute later, he felt the slight jolt of the floor when the doors locked. Next, the outer door would open, and he would be free to drive out of the biosphere and back into life outside the dome — if there was a life for anyone out here.

A hard sunlight penetrated the room as the outer door rose like a squinted eye, opening. It wedged onto the floor before him and, as the door lifted higher, layered both PAL and Josiah with the warming grace of its light. He was blinded at first; but then the glare softened, and he felt a sense of peace hallow him. He shifted the gear stick into drive and moved forward, rolling out onto the golden track of the sun.

The outer door lowered. Behind him, he heard the sound of exhaust fans forcing all intrusive air from the docking room. It would be followed, he knew, with a radiation bath to kill any virus or germ introduced into the chamber's atmosphere. Only then would the steel inner doors be opened and the docking arena flooded with new air.

The land was white desert before him. A blue overlay of sky stretched the limits of his vision, unobstructed by any fixture of man for as far as he could see. Endless sky. Endless land. Wide open to the face of the sun. Within him, Josiah felt a desperate longing for this land, this sky, this sun. It was immediate, coming with the urgency of a heartbeat.

"How's it look out there, buddy?" Quinn's voice broke into Josiah's concentration, but not interfering with the soul-awareness.

"Beautiful. A sky like a robin's egg, and white sand laid down like a nest."

"You're a poet, Josiah. Sure your tribe's not Celtic, way back?"

"Who knows."

"Right, who knows. Maybe it was the other way around and the Irish were really Indians."

"With red hair," said Josiah.

"Why not."

"Nobody out here, Quinn. From what I can see, there's no tracks or evidence that any people have been near the dome. I'll do a circle around the building, and then head up the highway."

"Funny to hear it called that."

"What?"

"A building. It doesn't feel like a building anymore. It's a world to us, isn't it? Maybe the only world we have left."

"I'm not ready to believe that," said Josiah. "Not yet."

He followed the paved road around Biosphere Seven. Turning the curve that marked the ocean access area, he saw a blue all-terrain vehicle in the distance, parked about one mile from the face of the glass wall. At first, it startled him, fear that there might be someone out there—someone waiting, and watching the dome. Then he remembered, and realized what it had to be. He drove a little farther and saw he was right.

"Quinn, I've found Exeter."

"Oh, Jesus."

Jessica's voice came over the speakers. "Leave him where he is, Josiah. Drive away. He can't hurt anyone anymore."

He turned the vehicle toward the main highway, followed the flat ribbon of macadam, and headed into town. On the way, he felt the presence of the sphere lift from him. Past the first rise, he couldn't see it anymore. It was behind him, and that unreal world with it. On the way into town he hummed a little tune.

Chapter Seventeen

The humming stopped as soon as he reached the main crossroads. Abandoned cars littered the highway, with the remains of what had been their owners still in them. That the virus had been through this part of Texas was extremely evident.

The driver's door was open in one car he passed, with a pair of swollen legs stretching from it, oozing something waxy and dried brown. The gorge rose to Josiah's throat, hot and sour. He knew he would be forced to breath his own vomit if he threw up — trapped as he was inside the sealed confines of PAL — so he fought hard against the urge, stroking his hand down his neck and stomach, soothing the spasms that threatened to engulf him. Without looking again at the corpse, he drove on.

"A lot of bodies," he said into the speaker phone.

"Only corpses?" asked Jessica.

"Yes."

In town, the scene was different. The main street was empty, a ghost town of forty thousand — but they were there, he knew: in their beds, within the buildings, in the charnel houses of the damned.

Quinn had said some people may have survived. If anyone still lived in this town, they were well hidden. He drove by the theater. Its lobby doors were open, and a blue neon sign still burned its bright message, AIR CONDITIONED. *Air Poisoned,* he thought; that's what it should have read.

"What do you see?" Quinn asked.

"Dogs everywhere. They're sitting on the steps of the buildings, watching me. Oh!"

"What is it?" Quinn asked, his voice sharp and too loud.

"I found where they threw some of the bodies— piled into a trench at the north side of town—and why the dogs are here. They've been feeding on—"

"Josiah! Keep moving," said Jessica. "Don't stay there. Drive out of town. Do it now!"

Instinct to follow the orders she gave him pushed his foot against the pedal, but his eyes still burned with the image of that mound. The vision was seared into his retina . . . into his brain . . . white thigh bones gnawed by the packs of dogs, worried loose from the ragged flesh. At the base of the mound had been a skull, a small one, like that of a child's.

He wished he could pop open the canopy and fill his lungs with huge draughts of fresh air, to cleanse the sickness of the scene from his soul. But of course he couldn't—not and hope to survive.

Outside the business section of town were long stretches of residential neighborhoods. The houses were mostly white clapboard, with wide porches at the front. From inside one, he heard the sound of music.

"There may be someone in that house," he said into the speaker.

"Can you see into the windows from the street?" asked Jessica.

"No. The drapes are heavy. I'm going to pull into the driveway."

"Be careful," she warned him.

PAL's wheels hugged the concrete arches of the driveway and pulled up the slope to the top of the small rise. From here, Josiah could see that the front door was open. And the bodies. He could see the bodies scattered like discarded clothes on the floor. Nothing alive moved in that house. He shifted PAL into reverse and backed down the driveway.

"Nothing," he reported.

"You sure?" asked Quinn.

"Yeah, very sure."

Animals were everywhere. He saw chickens in the yard of one house and, unbelievably, a cow grazing on the grass of another. A broken tether of rope still hung at its neck.

As he drove out of town and into the farmlands which skirted the area, he saw the dead animals he had expected to find everywhere. They were those penned and otherwise dependent upon man for their survival. The bloated carcasses of horses locked behind wooden rail fences, pigs in sties that had held no water, and masses of black flies settling on one decaying mound after another, moving like living clouds, descending to feast on death.

"Everyone's dead," Josiah told them. "Most animals survived, but the people are gone."

"Keep going. Keep looking." Her voice didn't break, the tone wasn't a decibel higher than it had been seconds before, but he heard the desperation in it. For all of them, the desperation was close at hand.

He was well into the farmlands when PAL stopped.

For a moment, he couldn't think of what to do. Panic flooded through his veins like blood, and his heart pumped it to his brain. A block on the dash panel shone red. Beneath the alerting color was printed the word, BATTERY.

It wasn't possible, and yet . . . the air in the vehicle had stopped circulating, as if a door had been shut and an oven turned on, baking away all the oxygen. He tried the motor again, receiving only the dull sound of a metallic *click*.

Sweat beaded on his forehead and lip. The heat was rising in the driver's capsule. He took a deep breath and felt his lungs struggle to draw oxygen from the leaden air. If he stayed where he was, his own carbon dioxide would poison him. Already, his body was urging him to lift the clear, bullet-shaped dome top and breathe fresh air. He'd do that, he knew, before he'd suffocate in his own waste air.

"I've got a problem," he said into the two-way radio when the crushing panic in his chest finally allowed him to speak.

"What? Say again." Jessica was in charge; Josiah could hear it in the timbre of her voice.

"Battery's dead. The engine won't start, and the air-flow system has shut down. I'm stuck out here in the middle of a Texas hell-hole, with nothing between me and the virus but a thin bubble of plastic."

"Christ!" Josiah could hear Quinn's oath in the background. The sound of his fist hitting the table was clear as well.

"Try the starter again," said Jessica.

"I've already—"

"Do it again!"

He pressed the button, receiving only the same dull click.

"No power. Battery's dead."

"Say again. Reception is breaking up."

"Battery's dead!" he shouted. Sweat rolled into his eyes. His chest was starting to hurt. It would get worse, he knew.

Static crackled on the two-way radio. He caught a tinny fragment of Jessica's message, "Remain where you . . ." but the rest was lost to the scrambled garble of white noise.

It wasn't hard to figure out what she had meant, even without sound wave clarity. He understood, all right. The problem was, the advice was for shit. Remain where you are until you loose consciousness. Remain where you are until the carbon dioxide permeates your brain. Remain where you are until you die. Not for him.

"I'm popping the top," he said into the speaker, not knowing if they could hear him. "I'm going back into the world, as far as I can get before the virus stops me. If I live, I'll try to find any survivors, and I'll come back."

His hand was steady when he pulled the cover release. All fear was gone. What could it do but kill him? He heard the break in the seal, a hiss, and then he shoved the plastic dome up and back.

Fresh air washed over him, a breeze. He hadn't felt a clean-scented wind blow through his hair in months. There were no breezes in Biosphere Seven. There were fans, but that wasn't the same. There were no breezes in air-conditioned offices, or airplanes, or submarines. The open air of earth was the only place where there was such a thing as a breeze. He reveled in the pleasure of it.

He climbed out of the driver's section, his feet on real terra firma for the first time since entering the biosphere on Christmas Day, over a year ago. The feel of the earth beneath him was soft, a cushion. A sadness welled in him at this softness, and the breeze, and the color of the `sky. *For us*, he thought. *All this was for us. What have we done?*

He started walking then, with the sun at his back. As he walked, he thought of all the names he knew of people. He listed them, remembering their faces, ages, and when he'd last seen them. He felt them close around him, a healing layer of friendship, guarding him from the shock and the terror of being absolutely alone.

With these memories, he walked across the land . . . toward hope.

"He's gone. We've lost him." Jessica stepped back from the console speaker.

"My God," said Cathe, "he'll die out there. He's leaving the car."

Jessica hadn't seen Cathe enter the room. "The battery —" she started to explain, words spilling from her brain like sand from a torn bag. Spilling uselessly.

"He never intended to come back," Cathe stopped her. She was calm, as if she'd known it would happen just this way.

"Of course he did. There's nothing but certain death out there. Of course he meant to come back." Jessica was angry, furious that Cathe had even suggested such a thing. "If that's all you've got to say" — she turned away from her — "just get out of here."

"He told me last night," Cathe went on as if she hadn't heard a word Jessica had spoken. "He said it, but I didn't believe him. I thought . . ." her voice fell lower, flatter, "I thought he was just afraid. But, he wasn't. He wasn't afraid of anything."

She turned to Jessica, her eyes bright with belief. "He knew exactly what he was doing, Jessica. He believed this would happen. That's why he slept with me last night, to leave a child in case he never came back."

"You mean he did this on purpose?" Quinn asked the question. Jessica had grown silent.

"No," said Cathe. "I don't think so. He didn't know how, exactly. He didn't plan it. He simply knew it would happen."

The sound of static noise abruptly stopped. All connection with the outside ended. Jessica felt the sudden loss as if it had been a functioning part of her. He was gone. He'd just disappeared, like Brad . . . like Brad.

"Jessica. Jessica." The sound of her name dragged at her. "Listen to me," Quinn said.

He pulled her into his arms. Cathe was gone. *When had she left them? How long ago had Josiah. . . .*

"We're going to be all right," Quinn said. His face was pressed against hers, the breath of his whisper on her cheek. "Do you hear me? I promise. We're going to be all right." His lips touched her skin— rough beard on cool, smooth flesh. Then he kissed her.

They were alone, two of only eight people left in their world. In that vast aloneness, she drew comfort from his touch. Something in her responded to life: to needs that were real, to feelings that had bubbled to the surface of her like heat from a kettle.

And the heat rose. She pushed other thoughts, other memories away and gave herself into the warm surrounding of his love.

Chapter Eighteen

In the six months since Josiah left us, we have maintained our small colony of human life within the glass walls of Biosphere Seven. We are eight in number: Quinn, Cathe, Griff, Diana, Mike, Maggie, Daniel, and I, Jessica.

We call our home, Inside, dispensing with the clinical name and number of our former title, Biosphere Seven. All that lies beyond this dome is referred to as Outside. That is our reality, and our truth.

It is summer Outside. Our season is a pale comparison to the blazing heat of the Texas desert. The louvered panels on the walls and ceilings protect us from the worst of the sun's rays. We are sheltered in more ways than one from the atmosphere of earth.

Today, on 31 May, 1999, the first child of the Survivors' Generation was born into our lives. Maggie Adair gave birth to a son at 5:32 this morning. She named him Trinity, after the Holy Trinity which watches over us. I wonder, is this name a recognition of our loss, or an act of hope?

Jessica completed the entry and closed the computer file. She was the record-keeper, the historian. Funny occupation, she thought, for a woman who had hated history above all other subjects in school. She'd never had the patience for turning back to the past. Her life had always been geared toward the future, toward space, toward . . . God, toward the stars. And now it was she who kept the history of their people.

The birth this morning had been an experience she would never forget. All of them had been afraid that something might go wrong. Quinn had worked with the Peace Corps, and although he had learned basic midwifery as a required course, it had been a long time between the lesson and the real-life test of that knowledge.

Quinn, Jessica, and Mike had been with Maggie for the birth, Mike having decided to lend his support despite his misgivings. Daniel, Cathe, Griff, and Diana had kept to their own routines for the day, but Jessica believed each of them had thought of little else this morning except Maggie and the child. Through her, came their own continuance — and perhaps that of the human race.

The intercom on the wall at Jessica's right buzzed: Section Four. She pressed the keyed finger-pad, opening the connection to the agriculture sector. "Yes, Griff."

"I think you might want to come down to the ag-wing."

"A problem?"

"Yeah, I'd say so. We've got a termite infestation in the orchard and vegetable plots."

148

"How did the termites get from the savannah to the ag-wing? Isn't that what the screen doors between the zones are supposed to prevent?"

"It is, but they got in, anyway. Not only are they here, they're eating everything in sight. The numbers are incredible. We have to do something, and quick. As it is, we stand to lose half our crop."

"Hold on," she said. "I'll be right there."

Griff was the entomologist, an expert in the field, figuratively and literally. If he said there was cause to worry, there was.

Great care had been taken in choosing the type of termites selected for the savannah region. Of particular consideration was that they not eat the sealant along the base of the dome or between the glass blocks. Termites were needed to turn over the dead grass at the end of the growing season, just as much as larger grazing animals would have done, so that the grass would reseed itself. They had been introduced only into that zone and up until now had kept to the area. What an invasion of hungry, winged termites could do to a harvest, or to fruit trees, was a serious matter.

If, because of the termites, the crops were destroyed, there wouldn't be enough surplus grain to feed the livestock: the chickens, goats, pigs, and sheep. Without animal waste, there wouldn't be fertilizer for the fields, so the crop yield would sizably decrease for the next harvest. Without livestock or crops, the humans would starve. And without humans, the biosphere would die.

A few too many termites mattered.

Jessica entered the ag-wing after passing through a series of four screen doors designed for preventing the introduction of insects, which were necessary to

149

the other eco-zones, from entering the agricultural area. Although kept on hand for major emergencies, no pesticides were used throughout the biosphere. Any chemical sprayed on plants today would be in the drinking water tomorrow. The same thing happened in the outside world—here, it was just quicker.

Instead, natural forms of organic gardening were practiced. Ladybugs were used to combat aphids, beetles to aerate the soil and control insect populations, and parasitic wasps to attack white flies. Four hundred kinds of insects were deliberately brought into the ag-wing: some as food for the birds, fish, and beetles; some as predators to maintain a balance; and some as necessary enablers for plant propagation.

Even the trees planted in the ag-wing were selected with insect control in mind. The neem tree, a native plant species from central India, held a prominent spot near the vegetable fields. It exuded a chemical called azaderachtin, a natural insecticide.

Termites were another matter. A swarm of flying termites could decimate a crop, burrow beneath the bark of trees and destroy them—and they multiplied faster than rabbits.

Jessica stepped into the passageway between the screen doors. Thousands of termites were gathered in the enclosure. They crunched like fresh popcorn, slippery beneath her shoes.

"Over here!" Griff shouted. He was standing at the center of the wheat field on a black carpet. As Jessica got closer, the carpet moved, silvered wings glittering in the full morning sun.

"God," she said. "There're millions of them."

"It's some kind of frenzy of reproduction," Griff

explained. "They go along in controlled numbers for generations; and then a chemical change, or something else we don't understand yet, sets them off, and they begin to reproduce in pestilence proportions—like locusts."

Jessica could see them moving around Griff, a few crawling up the cloth of his pant legs. She had dressed that morning only in a blouse, skirt, and sandals—her legs and feet bare—and instinctively took a step back.

"What do you suggest?" She tried to think clearly.

He gave a hard laugh. "I suggest we'd be a helluva lot better off if they weren't here."

"Well, they are," she said too sharply, feeling them move across her feet, "and we damn well better do something about it."

"Fine. What?"

All she could think of was the scene of desolation left after a plague of locusts had swept through a farmland. It was a memory from a movie she'd seen as a child: the farmer and his wife standing like stones in the field, nothing left of the harvest, scrawny-necked chickens pecking among the devastated grain between the rows of broken stalks of corn and wheat.

"I said," his voice interrupted the connection with that memory, "what do you suggest we do about it?"

The answer was there; she just had to draw it forth. That was the hard part. "Chickens."

"What?"

It came to her all in a rush. "Chickens, and ducks, and geese. Birds. If they want a feeding frenzy, we'll give them just that . . . only they'll be dinner." She started running toward the west wing and the animal pens.

"Where are you—"

"Come on!" she shouted. "Get the others over here. We're going to need all the hands we can get."

"For what?"

"For catching the chickens," she yelled, surprised he didn't understand. "For bringing in the birds."

"Birds?"

"Just get them all, Griff. We're going to need everybody but Cathe for this one. She's so pregnant, she'd trip over the waddlers . . . but everyone else."

She was smiling. "Cheer up," she told him happily. "I'm pretty sure this is going to work."

"Birds. . . ?" he muttered, shaking himself loose of the termites crawling up his legs. He walked to the intercom. "I tell her I've got a termite invasion . . . and she offers me birds."

The ag-wing was a riot of feathers, squawks, and flapping wings. The geese were the best feeders, gobbling hundreds of termites each, but the chickens were the greatest at scratching them out of the ground. Their sharp, pointed beaks found the fat grubbers burrowing in low tree bark; blue jays and black birds reached the others.

A significant part of the crop was lost—the ducks ate as much grain as they did termites—but the larger portion was saved. The fruit and nut trees survived the onslaught, with only a few chickens left roosting in their branches to show for the struggle.

"I feel like some biblical champion." Quinn put his arm around Jessica. He had small, white feathers caught in his hair and a look of boyish delight in his eyes. "We beat them back with beaks and claws." He kissed her before everyone, in the middle of the open field.

"And bills," she added. "Don't forget wide, orange bills."

"Never," he agreed, and kissed her again.

"I love you," she said when the kiss ended. "With feathers in your hair and stuck to your eyelashes, I love you."

"Thank God for that," he said, pulling her even closer. "I was beginning to think I'd have to drag you off to my room by the hair."

"You won't have to drag me," she told him.

"No?"

"No."

He grew serious. "You're sure? It's not too soon. . . ?" There were hard questions in his eyes, questions he didn't ask.

"My whole life would be too soon," she answered honestly. "Would you want to wait that long?"

"I don't want to wait five minutes," he said. He took her hand, and they walked away from the chaos of the fields. They left the ag-wing and started in the direction of the rain forest.

"Where are we going?" she asked. "I thought you said you wanted to take me to your room."

"Not tonight."

"Why not tonight?" She was laughing, enjoying the mystery.

"Wedding nights are special."

"Wedding?"

His hands touched her face, smoothing the laughter from her eyes, her cheeks. . . . "That's what it is, Jessie, isn't it?" He kissed her brow, the sides of her eyes, the closed lids, and then her chin. His lips brushed the hollow of her neck. "There's no one to marry us, but us."

"Marry?" She pulled back.

He held her. "That's what I want from you," said Quinn, not letting her go. "I want that, or nothing at all."

"Why? How could that be important now?" She was struggling, emotionally and physically drawing herself away from him.

"Because"—he took his hands from her—"without it, all I'd ever have is a part of what you are. That's not enough. I want it all."

She stood quietly, not looking at him. Giving herself was one thing; giving her soul was something else. Would this be betraying Brad? Could she live with that? Sleeping with Quinn was something she felt comfortable about—Brad would understand; she was so alone—but marrying him?

"Decide, Jessie. I love you, and it's like a fire that's burning a hole in me; but I won't take less than everything. If you can't give that, then don't give anything at all." He held his hand out to her, an invitation, and a promise.

Her eyes were wet when she looked up, wet with the tears of final goodbye to the husband she still loved. Reaching out with unsteady fingers, she took the hand Quinn offered and joined it with her own.

"All right, you crazy Irishman," she said at last. "I'll marry you."

"We're the future, Jessie," he said, "you and I. How we live each day makes a difference. It's starting over, a whole world . . . starting over. I want it to be right."

She smiled, watching him. "You're a sentimentalist. You have the soul of a poet, Quinn."

"Have I? Maybe so." He drew her back into his arms, his breath warm on her face. "Say you love me."

"I did, remember?"

He kissed her ear, her neck, unbuttoning her blouse. "Say it again," he said. "I want to hear it."

Her blouse slipped to the ground. "I love you, I love you, I love you," she told him. "I—"

His kiss sealed her answer to him. Against the welcoming bed of earth, they made love for the first time, and knew each other at last, as man and wife.

Chapter Nineteen

John Katelo knew a kind of lonely peace that second summer. The land gave up its wealth in generous measure. Food was easy and plentiful. Salmon and trout filled the rivers, herds of elk stretched like moving clouds across the valleys, and the summer sun warmed him.

His world was a garden of flowers, mild days, and soft winds. In the evenings, he laid out a campfire and watched the stars appear in their regular places on the canvas of the night sky. They became his companions, these stars, silent as the moon, but a multitude of familiar formations he recognized.

Growing up, he'd never heard the names of Cepheus, Little Dipper, Andromeda, or the Polar Star, never learned the charting of the constellations or astronomy. Now, when they had become his quiet company, he called them simply by the shapes he saw in the sky.

Straight above was the bright star, the guidepost he found first each night. The others fell into place around it. To him, it was the handle of a fishing net. At one end of the handle was the guide star, at the other end were five lesser lights, arranged in the shape of a cup, or net.

To the left of this, was the whale. Much larger

than the net, it swam the heavens as if they were a sea. A long trail of rope hung from the whale, the harpoon of a hunter caught in its underside. Above the whale, was the dagger; and above that, the twin breasts of the Mother. For Katelo, the Big Dipper and Great Bear were the antlers and body of Father Elk.

He tried to remember the Inuit names of the stars, those told to him when he was a little boy by his grandfather, but it was as though a mist hung over that time, separating the world before and the world now. With each day, his recollection of that other time grew more like a dream.

What had Grandfather called the guide star? The name shimmered in the ocean of Katelo's memory, a thin light shining beneath deep water. His mind stared into the pool, but he could not cross the barrier. The past was gone.

The summer days stretched out before him like long fields of grass, seemingly endless. These were the Trickster's days, the spirit who led man into the dark edges of the underworld, or into any kind of trouble. The Trickster would have Katelo believe that summer would go on forever. He would whisper thoughts into Katelo's ear—how it would be good to rest on such a day, or how this warmth and bounty would surely last forever.

The Trickster was a child-spirit. It sometimes came as an old hunter or a beautiful woman. Like a thoughtless child, it played its games on man, luring the simple mind with the brilliance of its purpose. It was not evil, as that power was known to Katelo, but prankish. Still, if a man listened to the Trickster's words, he would soon follow on that path where evil led.

Katelo closed his mind to the sun's warmth and the endless days of green. He saw through the herds of elk and the flocks of snow geese, to the winter's spare and empty land beneath. It would come again, that hollow time, when the ice wind whipped the face of the earth and called its cry of death.

He remembered. He knew the look of the summer lie and saw through it. Truth was winter. While the fish jumped in the streams and the birds grew fat on the rich grass of the land, Katelo turned his thoughts to the emptiness of white starvation and prepared for the cold. It would come, surely as summer's bounty would leave the land. He would be ready.

In the next days, he would travel south, away from the land of the white bear and the seal. He would follow the streams, going always with the water. Where there was water, there was life.

It was life Katelo sought, among the ruins of earth, among the empty houses and abandoned cities. The search would lead him south, where the hope of other people waited. If there was a chance of finding even one, he must take it.

The spirits of earth had chosen him to survive, when all others had died. Why? It was a question he asked himself each day, each night, each hour. Why?

From the east, a sound of thunder rose above the mountains. It rocked the ground and shuddered in the air, pressing the fist of its voice hard against sky, water, and land. The terror of it rolled into Katelo. He sat, hugging his knees, feeling the pounding of his heart beat at his ribs.

Fat drops of rain scoured the land, thick with the storming rage of heaven. Spikes of silver-white lightning cracked the sky, and the waters of the upper world opened to the land below. They poured from the great fissures like rivers and flooded away the stars.

Kip trotted over to Katelo and nudged him with his white muzzle. The Samoyed, too, was alone—separated from the animal-kind that bore him. By living with the man, he had forsaken the world of feral dogs. Packs of wolves and escaped sled dogs ran, but he was an outcast among them. They held him as a rogue animal and watched him with suspicious, careful eyes . . . as they did the man.

Katelo laid his hand on the dog's neck, his fingers sinking into the thick, shaggy coat. "You feel it, too? . . . the cold of their souls walking over the night? . . . the dead, still with us?" He looked into the dark brown eyes of the dog. "You hear them? You feel it when they pass through you?"

Kip whined and moved closer.

Katelo hugged an arm around the animal's back. "We walk in a sea of souls, my friend. They remain, the lost ones. They sit in the deepest holes of the earth, and they climb the sky; but always, they are here beside us."

Another split of thunder racked the night, and the rains fell. Man and dog sat beneath the wide-open heavens, afraid of the houses where the dead lay waiting. They huddled together while around them wailed the torrent of the storm.

Josiah Gray Wolf kept to the back roads; the cities were a vision of Hell. In the cities, the stench of death swelled like furnaces, and the grim reaping of bodies fouled the land. The air throbbed

159

with the power of the destroyer, and of loss.

Today, Josiah drove a red GMC pickup. The frame around the license plate read, BAD BOYS DRIVE BAD TOYS. The size of the truck made Josiah feel safer, not from other cars on the road — he was fairly certain he'd have the right of way — but from anything else he might come into contact with.

Packs of wild dogs roamed the highways as if following hunting tracks. Most were scared if Josiah came too near them; but some others had turned savage, and he was glad to have the barrier of the truck between him and their snarling teeth.

He kept the truck doors locked when driving, for he'd heard what he'd thought were human voices twice since leaving the dome, both times a kind of high-pitched wail. The memory of what Quinn had told him in confidence about the voices heard on the station hookups, "He sounded crazy, Josiah. They all sounded crazy," stayed with him. There were many things worse than death. His doors stayed locked because he feared those things.

In the first weeks, he had feared the virus, too. He'd waited for it, like a timed sentence. Each morning, he had woken up surprised that he was still well. Each night, he had gone to sleep fearing that he was getting sick. And the days passed.

When the truck ran out of gas, he found a new one, and then others. Some had the keys still hanging from the ignition. Some keys were in the purses of dead women. It meant entering their houses, and that was hard; but he'd done it. He'd done a lot of things that were hard since leaving the dome. He'd survived. That was hard. He'd survived, and he wasn't crazy.

But, he hadn't found any people.

160

Stacks of compact discs kept him company. He sang as he drove, country-western classics by Willie, Waylon, and Alabama. He listened to books on tape, *The History of Civilization, The Bible The Goddesses and Gods of Ancient Europe* — these, and other works of philosophy, poetry, and essays on the human spirit he was drawn to. He heard their voices, sounding so near, and thought of that other life, the place the world had been.

In the evenings, he slept locked in the car or, if it was too cold, beside a large campfire on the open range. Sleep was a silence he feared. It was when he slept that the dreams came. His dreams were intruders he couldn't fight against, forcing themselves into his mind . . . eating at his courage.

In the dreams, he had no gun, no knife at his belt, no lock on the truck doors. He was alone and vulnerable. They came at him, fingers like bony claws, raking scar after scar into his flesh, marking him. He was the one; the survivor. He lived, and they had died. They hated him. In his dreams, he paid a heavy price for life.

He thought about God. Josiah had never been caught up in the moral convictions of any religion. He'd left that to others. He didn't disbelieve, but an organized faith had never touched him.

His mother, a Shoshone, had been brought up to think that all of nature was the Mother, and that the Great Father of the heavens had blended with her to create life.

"Earth," she'd told her son, "is a womb. Think of it as that, a place where life begins and grows. The Great Father touches each place in the heavens in a different way, but Earth is the nourisher, the Mother. From Her, life will gain strength to leave

161

the boundaries of this world and, when we are ready, be borne into the skies."

He wasn't so sure.

Heaven wasn't a place he thought about anymore. It was too distant. The earth, that was something else again. He had begun to feel its sacredness, for the first time, in the rich overlay of life spreading across, and within, and from it. He felt a part of that life, nourished in the Mother's womb, and therefore of importance.

He had been spared. The virus hadn't touched him. It wasn't a chance happening, he believed. He had been chosen . . . but for what?

Alone, he turned to the old ways of his people. He saw life as they had seen it, in the air he breathed, in the ground he walked upon, in the water he drank. *We are all of one boundary,* he thought. He rested in a tree-shaded clearing in the hill country near Austin. He stretched out, lying with his bare back against the sun-warmed ground beneath him, feeling the pounding of his heart carry to the land below.

His friends in the dome were in a single biosphere, and he in another. They had known this before they entered the glass-cased dome, known that the earth was Biosphere One, but it hadn't been real until now. That had been a myth, like his mother's religion.

Now he saw this outside world as a nursery, protected within a living sphere. Gravity and atmosphere were its glass dome and sealant. Like the others of his kind—those within Biosphere Seven— he was the guardian. He lay still, listening to the sounds of life surrounding him. He didn't close his eyes, for the visual was a track of harmonic beauty,

162

too. All was here for him to notice. He was the animate soul.

If there is a God. now's the time to speak to me, he thought. He waited, listening for the sound of thunder or a flash of lightning . . . but nothing changed. All was as it had been before.

Still, something in him had changed. Without words, without a covenant sealed in stone tablets, Josiah himself was different. He had seen the circle of Being as if from a faraway distance. He was the observer, and the participant. He had no need of holy script to tell him what he already felt. Words breaking from the skies of heaven were simple tools; the voice he heard was within him. All of life was his god, his goddess. All of life was part of him — the mountains, waters, air, and land — and he, part of it.

So, he was not alone. Nothing nourished in a world so full could be alone. He drew the thought to him like a cover, warming himself within its comfort.

Some who had survived had gone mad; he would not.

The days for Josiah were a kind of harvest, each bringing a rich store of bounty, for his spirit, for his body, for his mind. He was on the pollen path, an Indian expression, meaning on the road to spiritual life.

His eyes were ever watchful for another human. In time, he would go back to Biosphere Seven. They waited, he knew.

Did his survival on the outside mean the virus had weakened? What limited knowledge he had of a virus told him it had not died. It was not like a bacteria, which could be killed. All the viruses ever known to man were still present on earth. Some had mutated. Some had been weakened by a process of natural selection, in order to insure the continuance of a host source (far more practical to cause mild sickness in the host animal, than to kill it), and some lay dormant, waiting until the precise time best suited for their development.

The other possibility was that he was one of a few people who would always survive a virus. In any plague, some were affected less than others. It might be that an enzyme in his body protected him from the contagion—a genetic code inherited from some ancient source. Had an ancestor of his survived a similar pestilence?

Until he was sure, he couldn't go back among the others.

Josiah waited. He kept his mind and soul directed on the pollen path, trusting in his own source of strength to carry him through the days to come.

Chapter Twenty

Cathe's daughter was born that September, on the ninth day of the ninth month, in the year 1999. She was a frail infant at birth, nearly a month premature, weighing just five pounds four ounces. She was long and thin, with downy tufts of straight, dark hair at her nape. Cathe called the child Sidra, a name that meant, inheritor of the stars.

"I'm surprised you didn't give her an Indian name, after Josiah," remarked Maggie. She held her son, Trinity, in her arms. The baby was three-and-a-half months old, swaddled like a solid lump in blankets up to his neck. Blue eyes peeked out from among the folds of cloth, and curls of pale hair escaped the linen cap he wore. Maggie had made both infant gown and cap from a nightdress she had brought into the dome with her.

Cathe rested in her bed with Sidra pressed against her body, cradled in the warm crook of her arm. "I didn't name her after her father because she isn't just Josiah's," she answered Maggie. "She's the first female born into this world—a new woman—and as that, she's like no one but herself."

Trinity twisted fitfully in his mother's arms, hungry to nurse. "Are you sure about that?" asked Maggie, a smile in her eyes. She pulled up one side of her sweater and let the child's searching mouth find its hold.

"Maggie," Cathe said, her voice taking on a serious tone, "I don't think they're for each other, our two. Don't plan it in your mind."

"Who else would they be for?" asked Maggie, annoyed and too sharp.

"They'll be like brother and sister," said Cathe, "growing up together in this place. It isn't likely that they'd see each other as anything else."

"They won't have much choice, will they?" Maggie finished the point. Her face was cold set, hardening the lines of her jaw.

Cathe could see that this wasn't the time. "Just don't plan it for them, that's all." She laid her hand over the crown of her daughter's head, her fingers warming the small head. Something as instinctive as the maternal drive which coursed like living blood through her veins, told her that Sidra and Trinity would follow separate paths. Their lives would cross, and part. She kept the thought to her, holding it as carefully as she cradled her newborn.

Her daughter, Sidra, was not of this enclosed place; she was of the stars, of the sky. . . .

It began with a hard wind. Through the night, desert sand scraped the face of the dome. Chips of flying stone beat at the glass. Weighty brush pulled from the ground, with the ragged breath of storm hurled against them, one after another, like paper bags in the breeze.

And the dome rocked. . . . It shook the solid mold until walls and rounded summit shuddered, threatening to fall in upon them. The strength of it hit, pounding at the outer barrier with near tornado force. Through the dark tide of night, it raged.

Sounds of the wind from above pulled at them. Solar panels ripped free of the roof, slapping and banging in loose connection, until the final grip of fist claimed them as its own. The wind whipped beneath the uplifted glass disks, creating a company of high, eerie whistles, hundreds of thin, unearthly screams. It was as if the avenging Furies hovered over them, gathering with the storm.

Worse, the cable guide lines for the solar tower ripped loose and thrashed in heavy whips against the frame of the tower. The structure bent and hit the roof, its jointed arm flailing against the glass block in loud cracks, beating at the dome of the biosphere — the pounding fist of an angry god.

Quinn lay awake, listening to the furious press of it. If the seals broke. . . . If one block of glass shattered. . . .

"It doesn't help." Jessica snuggled closer.

"What?"

"Worrying."

He ran his hand over her skin, smooth and soft. The touch of her comforted him. "You've become fatalistic. If the roof caves in . . . the roof caves in. Is that how it is?"

"Pretty much." She sat up, pulling the sheet over her breasts to cover them. She always did that. It was fine with her, apparently, if they were in bed together naked, but if she sat up, or walked around the room, she wrapped something around her. It was part of the feminine mystique, he decided, and enjoyed the soft-draped image.

"And I suppose you're not the least bit concerned about the seal breaking and letting the virus inside?" He trailed his fingers down her nape to the small of her back.

167

She arched forward at his touch, her movement liquid. "I stopped worrying a long time ago. Tornadoes are a common event in west Texas. We knew we might experience something of this kind. The unit was designed for stress. We'll weather the storm."

"How'd you get to be so wise?" He slid closer, pressing his lips to the spot where her hip joined her leg, and began slowly kissing his way up her side, tasting her skin, softly nipping with his teeth. . . .

"I discovered worrying didn't do any good." She touched her hand to his head, a weight, guiding him. Always, she responded to his love.

The fullness of her breasts stopped him, and he lingered there.

Beyond the dome, the zephyr raged. Within the living world of Biosphere Seven, the two Insiders held each other through the night, and waited for the calm.

With the dawn, they knew the worst. The solar generator had failed. The force of the wind had damaged the receptor cells on the main unit and torn huge sections of the system loose. From the desert wing, they could see the ragged wires and metal sheeting lying in twisted chunks on the ground. Trapped inside the dome, there was nothing they could do to repair the damage.

Quickly, the biosphere began to grow cold. A fog condensed in the high tower above the waterfall, forming a vaporous cloud. It hung there, a beautiful mist, dulling the glass walls from the heat of their breath.

Nine days of dark rain followed the storm. Sheets of water cascaded over the glass carapace, streaming down its sloping sides and pooling on the ground below. Soon, a shallow moat surrounded them, and they were set apart like an island from the mainland.

"The trees will die," Cathe told them. "Winter freeze will destroy some, killing the roots; lack of a constant mist of water in the rain forest will eliminate others. I don't hold out much hope for the citrus trees in the ag-wing. We can try wrapping them, but it's just too damn cold."

"We'll dig the smaller ones up, pot them, and bring them into the habitat until spring," Jessica suggested.

"And when they get too big for the pots?" Daniel asked.

"Then we'll start new ones," said Quinn, putting an end to it. "We'll do whatever we have to do in order to survive. You're the horticulturist," he hit back at Daniel. "You figure something out."

Their spirits dropped with the temperature. Moodiness was common. Discussions became arguments. The eyes of each man or woman reflected their waning hope and the chill reality of their future. The truth became clear. Technology could not save them against the forces of nature.

Now it was that small difference, that thing that set humans apart from other animals—the creative ingenuity of man—that became their only hope.

For Diana Hunt, the idea of bringing a child into the world under these circumstances was abhorrent. Insanity. That two of the women had chosen to create life in the midst of this pall of death struck her as stupidity of the highest order or, in a worse sense, an act of mockery against the destruction of mankind.

Diana's world was dead. She saw herself and the

others as living ghosts, free to move around the edges of what had been, but never enter there. Glass walls were her cage. The loss of power after the storm, and the ever increasing breath of cold, came as little surprise to her. She expected death. Awaited it.

The act of causing a child to live, of giving it hope, was a sin she had no strength to commit. Death was at hand, holding an icy blade over their heads. Didn't they see it? Didn't the others know?

She wouldn't look at the babies, wouldn't hold them.

Instead, she found what little comfort she could take in any strong arms that would hold her. She never slept alone. It was not sex that drew her to its hot embrace, but the touch of a man's body against her own, to calm the white terror of her fears.

"I can't be here too long," Mike told her, naked, and coldly entering the warm cocoon of her bed. "Maggie will wonder."

Diana pushed the thought of a waiting Maggie from her mind, pushed everything away but the quickening pulse of her own need. She clung to Mike, not caring. It might have been Griff beside her, Quinn, Daniel, or Josiah; she had slept with each of them since entering the dome. None had satisfied the desperate longing in her. All would not have been enough.

Of the five men, only Griff and Mike would touch her now. Quinn had been the first to see the truth of her that first time—just after they came into the dome—that she was searching for something other than sex, or love.

"What's wrong with you, Diana? You keep flying into the flame," he'd said, "but you've got bars around you, lady. You never let anyone come inside."

170

"Maybe you should leave," she'd told him, angry at this unveiling of truth.

He had never come back for the answer.

Mike had never asked.

"I have to leave," he said, after the fevered rush of lovemaking was over.

"Stay with me till morning." She reached for his hand.

"Can't," he refused, pulling away. "It isn't right, being here like this. There's Griff to consider . . . and I have to think of Maggie and the baby."

"Get out," she told him.

He hadn't thought of Maggie when his body was gliding within her own, when his hands were hard clutching her shoulders, and his lips were on her breast. He hadn't thought of Maggie then.

Alone, Diana waited in the growing cold. The only child nurtured within her was one of raging terror, and loneliness. It quaked inside her . . . screaming like Deirdre from the womb.

It was late fall inside the biosphere. The majority of the harvest crops had been gathered, so food was plentiful. The eight adults dressed in layers of heavy clothing, and the two babies were kept well wrapped, like little Eskimos, with only their heads protruding from the blanketed snug-sacs.

In the summer, the problem would become a build-up of heat. Biosphere Seven was in the middle of the Texas desert, beneath a windowless, glass dome. Without the solar generator, there wouldn't be power to run the fans that circulated the air flow and kept the building cool. The louvered panels on the ceiling and walls could be kept closed; but the heat of the sun would bake down on them, and the temperatures would be unbearable.

Worse, it was the solar generator that powered the wave action and aeration of the inland sea. With a cessation of that movement, the ocean would stagnate. What would be left would be a salt water lake. Most of the fish would die.

Sickness took on new meaning within the seclusion of the dome. Fortunately, the babies were not exposed to the normal viruses that often afflict children. There was no direct contact, secluded within the dome, with anyone infectious to expose them to chicken pox, mumps, or measles.

They did, however, suffer other enigmatic maladies: unexplained fevers, diarrhea, vomiting, and rashes. Most were attributed to teething, with the exception of the rashes. Trinity, they discovered, was allergic to eggs.

No one developed acute appendicitis, no one broke a leg, but each of them thought of what the result would be if something really serious did happen. How would they cope if one of them were cut and a terrible infection set in? . . . if one of the childbearing women had needed a cesarean? . . . if a simple cold turned into pneumonia? Would slow, lingering death be the end for them all?

Was it worth it, waiting for that day to happen?

They were living out of each other's pockets. Too close. Daniel threw the first punch, but Griff had asked for it. The two men were well matched; Griff, more physically powerful, but Daniel, more underhanded.

They were fighting over Cathe.

It had been a chance remark. Griff was living with Diana and had said, casually, "Cathe would

172

probably be a great lay, but she's too damn ugly."

And that was what had set it off . . . because Daniel was in love with Cathe—had been since their first days of working together in the hydroponics lab—and had never admitted it to anyone, especially her.

At first, in the early days of living in the biosphere, she'd been distant, cool to his mild advances. Later, she'd been infatuated with Griff. All of them had recognized that situation, with the exception of Griff. If he had realized, he'd shown no indication of any sensitivity about it. He'd just kept doing what he'd been doing, which included living with Diana. Still later, there'd been Josiah, and their child.

Daniel had never spoken up. He'd held his feelings inside him, remaining silent . . . until Griff made his remark.

"What the hell?" Griff had reeled back from the first blow, stunned by both the fist and the intent.

"Shut your damn mouth!" Daniel had shouted at him. "You've got no right to say anything about Cathe. Nothing, do you hear me? You, with that whore you sleep with. Everyone's had Diana—everyone!"

Griff knocked him down, a solid punch on the side of his head. Daniel fell back, but came up swinging. Blood ran from his ear, a thin trail of it, soaking the white collar of his knit shirt. He lowered his head, moved back a few steps, and rammed his skull full bore into the center of Griff's chest. The sound of cracked ribs could be heard, even over the loud grunt of pain.

"If you're going to kill each other, do it where I don't have to look at you." Cathe stood a few feet back from them. She'd heard enough to know what they were fighting over, and she was red with embarrassment, and anger.

173

"I never heard of anything so stupid in all my life, beating the life out of each other. Don't we have enough to contend with, the cold and the damn virus, without you two breaking each other's bones? My God! Who's going to do your work for you when you can't move? Have you thought of that?"

"What am I supposed to do?" Griff shouted. "The crazy bastard punched me."

Cathe looked at Daniel, who didn't say anything in his own defense. "It looks like it's over now. Call it quits and walk away—both of you."

"I don't think I can get up," said Griff, his face gray-white with pain.

She put her shoulder under his good arm and helped him stand. "I'll walk with you to your room," she offered.

He pulled away. "No thanks. I don't need anything from either of you." He moved off slowly, every step causing a sharp intake of breath.

"That was some scene you caused"—she turned back to Daniel—"and completely unnecessary. It wasn't the first time I've been called—"

"You're not ugly," Daniel stopped her before she could taste the bitter word on her tongue.

"I'm not Diana."

"No, you're not—thank God—but you're more beautiful . . . to me." He remained where he stood, making no move toward her.

"I was in love with Griff once," she said, looking into Daniel's eyes.

"I know."

"I'm not anymore."

He said nothing. His dark eyes watched her. Waiting. . . .

"Well, if you're going to get into fights defending

174

my honor," she said simply, "you'd better come home and live with me."

"Not until you want me," he said, then turned and walked away.

He is the strangest man, she thought, watching his back as he left her. *Strange, yet . . . interesting.*

That night, sleep wouldn't come. Cathe lay awake, restless and anxious. Sidra slept in the soft-blanketed bundle beside her. She had the thick, dark hair of her father — an Indian baby — and the green eyes of her mother. Sidra was Cathe's world, and had been so since the moment she was conceived.

Was there room in her world for anyone else? For Daniel?

She had offered to open her world to him, to bring him home, to be a part of her life, and Sidra's. But that hadn't been enough. He'd given her a qualifier. He'd said, "Not until you want me."

Did she want him?

Did she want anyone? Was Sidra enough?

The long night passed, and the next day, and the next. They didn't speak of it. Except for working together in the lab, they didn't speak at all. It was as if there hadn't been an offer, as if he hadn't fought with Griff, hadn't told her she was beautiful, hadn't walked away. Yet, the knowledge of his unspoken words worked on her, and the fact of the love he bore in silence.

Late into the fourth night, she left her room, carrying only Sidra in her arms, and softly knocked upon Daniel's door. He answered readily, as if he'd known she would be there — or hoped for it — and had been waiting.

"I would have come to you," he told her. "Tonight, I

175

would have buried my pride and come to your place. All the things you need are there, for yourself and the baby. . . ."

"Everything I need is here," she said. "I want to be with you, Daniel. If you still want me . . . and Sidra . . . I want to be where you are, and to love you."

With a deep sigh at the realization of his dreams, Daniel stepped back from the doorway and welcomed Cathe and her daughter into his room, and his life.

Chapter Twenty-one

The winter, when it came, was bitter and stayed long. They had no heat in the dome, no electricity, no fires. Open fires would have quickly caused a crisis—nowhere for the smoke to go. It was inconceivable that the world's most self-sufficient biosphere had turned them into primitive people, bundling in thick layers of clothing to keep warm. But it had.

They had no fires to cook their food, no heat to warm their houses, no light to shine through the dark December days. Outside—the name had come to mean much more than simply being beyond the glass shell of Biosphere Seven. It meant a soaring up from the stone age of this dome. It meant something different to each of them.

To Quinn, it meant computers. With the loss of the solar generators, they had also lost all computer functions. He felt short-circuited, as if the power failure had been his failure, too. A sense of impotence plagued him through the frigid days and painfully cold nights. If the others blamed him, no one said it. Still, he felt their unspoken castigation and condemned himself.

As the days of solid cold lingered, Quinn's view of the world became as ashen as the overhead sky. Daily, he thought of simply walking out. Let them kill him, if they would. It didn't matter. Daily too, he thought of finding a way to restart the generators. With an energy source, the others could remain within the shelter of this enclosed world—safe.

"You're not our priest, or a sacrificial lamb," Jessica said, when his mood became so dark even she couldn't reach him.

"I'm not content to sit and wait until we all die of *natural causes* inside this glorified display case, if that's what you mean."

"What makes you think it's your fault? Who the hell said you were responsible for the rest of us? You didn't cause the storm, Quinn. And you didn't create the virus."

"So?" He was angry, and hurt that she didn't understand his pain, his guilt.

"So, give it up! I'm sick of seeing you mope around like some kind of lost soul. We'll make it through this."

"And if we don't? If we start dying from pneumonia? If the babies start choking in their cots with croup? What are you going to say to them, sunshine? Cheer up?" He pushed her away from him, too roughly.

"What do you want me to say? What do you want to hear? That you should have had a back-up system in place? That we're suffering because of you?"

"Yes, damn you!" he shouted at her, fury standing in his eyes.

"It isn't true!" she shouted back. "No matter how much you want to take the blame for it . . . how much your conscience stabs at you, it isn't true. You're not responsible. If it weren't for you, Exeter would have broken into the unit, and the virus would have killed us all, long before now. Remember that?"

"It was Daniel's idea to hot-wire the circuits."

"Daniel froze. We all froze, except Piper . . . and you. Goddammit, Quinn! What do you get from all this self-hatred? We don't need an Irish martyr."

"The fact is, you don't need me for much right now,"

he said in a low, hard voice. "What you need is someone on the outside, fixing the solar panels."

"I need you." She said it with the same rough edge in her voice.

"Really? And why is that, Jessie? We haven't shared more than a few icicles that passed for words in the last month. If it's sex you're after, you'd be better off talking to Griff, or Mike. I hear they're both glad to provide a quicky to any woman who asks."

"I'm pregnant." Her words were like a slap.

At first, he didn't say anything, as if he were too hurt to speak. Then the grin came back to his lips. "I don't know what you want me to do about it. We're fresh out of doctors."

"Stop it." She didn't cry, or yell, or move away. She stayed exactly where she was and waited, just looking at him.

"I mean it," he insisted, the pathetic grin fading. "You've never had a baby, Jessie. Things go wrong. We don't even have any medicines, for chrissake! My mother had . . . too many kids."

"Are you one of the *too many?*"

"There you go again. You can do anything. Right? You're Superwoman. Dammit, Jessie!" He gripped her shoulders hard with fingers that held too tight. "I've got no control over what happens in here . . . for any of us. Don't you get that? I don't want anything to happen to you." There were tears in his eyes, shimmering at the edge of his lashes, threatening to fall. She sensed the trembling in them, and in the way his hands gripped her shoulders, shaking her.

"Nothing's going to happen to me," she said gently.

"You can promise me that, can you?" He was rubbing away the red marks his fingers had left on her arms, touching her face, her hair.

"I can promise you that whatever happens, it won't change the way I feel about you. I love you, Quinn.

179

Hold me in your arms and tell me you love me. Tell me you want our child."

He held her to him and kissed her, his lips tasting with the salt of tears. Tenderly, he kissed the inside of her wrists, her neck, her eyes. "I won't let anything bad happen to you, Jessie. I won't."

There was such fear in his eyes, such terrible fear. "No," she said, sheltered in that all-encompassing love, the circle of his arms. "Nothing bad."

Trinity slept, but Maggie could not rest. The savage cold made her ears ache and her toes feel brittle. Far from improving, the temperature was dropping with every passing day. Dear God, it was impossible! How had they come to this?

The baby stirred, disturbed by his mother's restless movements. *I'll wake him if I don't get out of here,* she thought. The child was safe enough. No one here would harm him. She left him sleeping and tiptoed out of the room.

It was good to walk, good to get the circulation moving in her legs and arms. The cold was painful when she remained still. If they at least had a fire to warm their hands and feet. . . .

She walked toward the desert biome. The sand was a cushion beneath her feet, warming her toes and ankles with each step, and yielding into a softness which surrounded and warmed her. She knelt for a moment, burying her hands in it, too. The joints of her fingers ached. The sand was gritty, going beneath her nails like tiny stones, but the surge of warmth made the small discomfort worth it.

"Mary, help us." She bowed her head and prayed. Trinity wouldn't survive the winter if they didn't find a surcease for this desperate cold. "Look at my child. Look at Cathe's child. Have pity," she begged the Mother of Jesus. "Please . . . help us."

Maggie's faith had stayed with her. Throughout the long years of her girlhood, her belief in God, and the power of His Mother, remained. She was a Catholic; she was Irish, but it was the strength of her faith that had made it something far more than the combination of either canon or dogma. Where others had turned away or tried to pray and hope, Maggie accepted and trusted. It was as natural to her as breathing. God was real. His merciful Mother was real. Her life, and the lives of everyone within this dome, had begun and was sustained by them.

Yet . . . the dome remained silent. Cold ached in Maggie's bones, behind her eyes, and hurt her lungs. The freezing temperature was an answer, too. Had God turned His back on man? Had even His Holy Mother averted her eyes and stopped her ears to the sound of their pain?

"God!" Maggie cried, loud and wailing as a grief-torn mourner.

She stood and ran to the wall, where the computer panels of useless key pads shone in the moonlight like altars of false hope. She beat her fists on them. Dead things, cold and inhuman, with no pity in their plastic beings for the desperate souls of man.

"Damn you!" she screamed at them, hitting again and again at the lifeless white disks, until her fists were sore. She hated the key pads, hated the panel, hated the biosphere. All of it was alien, a futile imitation of the real world.

Her anger rose like the crowning curl of a wave. It held her, and she felt herself smothering within it. "Do something!" she screamed at the panels. "Why don't you do something?!"

She hit at the level keys, open palms hard against the wall, striking . . . striking . . . a rage boiling in the hollow of her fear. Collapsing, her body leaned and slid down the rigid face of the panel, hands pressing the smooth disks in her fall.

"Mary," she whispered, eyes closed, accepting.

The sound of movement beside her . . . a siren's shrill, unending wail . . . and the emergency exit door to the desert biome . . . opened.

At that same instant, the sliding steel walls dividing the biomes automatically closed, sealing off the desert unit from the rest of the biosphere. It shut, as the exit door opened.

The alarm shrieked its wild terror into the night, covering the sound of Maggie's scream.

Chapter Twenty-two

"Jesus!" Quinn shouted, shoving back his chair and standing. "The seal's been broken."

Jessica was already out the door, running. One red light on the control panel was lit, the one for the desert sector. Her mind sorted through a hundred possibilities. How could there be power for the alarm? — for the light? And God . . . how had the seal been broken?

The siren's wail abruptly stopped. With its hard cease, Jessica felt the drop in her own heartbeat. *What now?* it asked, thudding. *What now?* She ran past the citrus orchard, along the wet sands of the beach, past the salt marsh, toward the desert, toward the gray, steel doors . . .

. . . toward the gray, steel doors.

"God," she breathed the word. "Oh, God."

Then the heavy rhythm of pounding, terrible pounding on the doors. Someone had breached the biosphere wall. Someone was inside the dome, beating on the steel doors. Who? Was it Josiah? Someone else? How many?

The air in the entire biosphere had been contaminated when the seal was broken. The virus. . . .

"What's happening? What. . . ?" Daniel stopped dead, mid-run, staring hard at the new barrier.

Cathe was beside him, silent, holding her baby. Sidra's eyes were wide with interest.

All of them were there, Quinn, Daniel, Cathe, Diana, Griff, Mike.

"Where's Maggie?" Jessica asked. Her voice was high, scared. She couldn't help it.

"Let me in!" The hysterical voice shrilled over the intercom, jolting them. "Jessica! Mike! Open the door!"

"Maggie!" Mike was at the doors, trying to pry them apart with his bare fingers. "Help me, all of you. It's Maggie. She's out there." He struggled harder. "We're going to get to you," he shouted through the black ribbon of seam in the gray steel. "It's okay, Maggie. It's okay."

Only, it wasn't.

"How the hell did it happen?" Griff asked. Beside him, Diana had crumpled to her knees and was shaking. "I thought the doors and the intercoms were run on the solar generator," he went on, "like everything else. How did she—"

"There must be a battery backup on those systems," said Quinn. "It was a fail-safe for the exit doors, and for the system operating both the alarm and the doors."

"Help me!!!" Maggie screamed. Her voice grated the very air, a shredding sound that bled terror into the room, into the biosphere. "My baby's in there!" she cried, beating at the doors again. Pounding.

"Oh, Christ!" said Daniel, realizing.

"What's the matter with all of you?" shouted Mike. "Get this door open. We have to bring her back inside. It's not too late." He looked at them and saw the answer to his unspoken fear. "No! She's one of us, dammit! We can't leave her out there. She'll die."

"We can't let her in, Mike." It was Jessica who told

184

him the truth. "We don't know if the biosphere's been exposed, but we can't take the risk of breaching the seal again."

"She's right, Mike," said Quinn. "The break triggered the doors automatically. What we probably had was a positive air flow. We can't be sure of that, but we absolutely can't open the doors again—for anyone."

Jessica pressed the intercom switch for the outside speaker. Amazingly, the in-use light pulsed green, and it worked. "Maggie, it's Jessica. Listen to me."

"Jessica . . . you've got to help me . . . I didn't mean to do it. I was just angry, hitting the control board—it was dead, Jessie, you know it was dead. I didn't mean to open the door. I'm sorry. I'm so sorry." She was crying, her words becoming harder to understand.

"She touched the wrong panel key," said Quinn, understanding what had happened, "and that set everything into action."

"Maggie, listen," Jessica tried again.

"Don't leave me out here alone. Don't do that, Jessica. Please, please don't do that. I want my baby. Mike, make her give me my baby."

"Don't panic," Mike tried to soothe Maggie's fear. "We've just gotta figure this thing out. Everything's gonna be okay, I promise. Tell her, Quinn. That's right, isn't it? What do we do? Tell her what we're gonna do."

Quinn didn't back away from the answer. "There's nothing we can do for her, Mike. I'm sorry. She's on her own now."

Maggie's distraught sobbing was heard through the intercom, an unending anguish to them all.

Diana held her hands to her ears. "No more! Why is this happening to us? We didn't make the virus. We

didn't kill the world. When will it be over? When???"
She was rocking, her arms wrapped in a protective
cocoon around her head, rocking.

"Griff," said Jessica, "take Diana back to her room.
And please, check on Maggie's baby, too."

Diana moved beside Griff as if she could barely
walk. Griff put his arm around her waist and supported most of her weight as they moved away.

"She's cracking," whispered Quinn.

"I know," said Jessica. "She's been on the edge for a
long time."

"She needs watching," said Quinn.

Jessica wasn't thinking about Diana anymore; her
attention was focused on Maggie. She didn't know
what she could do for the woman, but she couldn't
just leave her like this. Their world was crumbling. It
was still within Jessica's power, her responsibility, to
hold it together—to hold them together—but what
could she do for Maggie?

"I'm afraid," the words came softly over the intercom. "It's dark, and I'm alone."

"I'll stay here tonight," Jessica told her, "right beside
you."

"Jessica?"

"Yes, Maggie?"

"What will happen to my baby? Trinity's just six
months old. Who'll take care of him? Who'll love
him?"

"We will, all of us," Jessica answered.

"I'm his father," Mike spoke up. "I'll love him. Don't
worry about the child. I'll take care of him."

"Promise me, Jessie," said Maggie.

"We all promise," said Cathe.

"Maggie, for God's sake. Don't talk about this now.
How can you think I wouldn't care for my own son?
He's my child, too."

186

"Promise," the mother insisted, her voice desperate. "I'm giving him to you, Jessica."

"Don't say such things," Mike argued. "We're going to find a way to get you back. Surely. . . ." He turned to the others.

"I promise." The vow was sworn by the surety of Jessica's soul. Nothing in either world would ever cause her to break that solemn oath. Nothing.

Quinn brought blankets, and they stayed beside the intercom all night. They took shifts, one of them remaining awake at all times to keep Maggie company. She never slept, but talked through the long hours until dawn, her voice tremulous with cold.

"Will I die out here?"

"I don't know," answered Cathe.

"Will I die out here?"

"God, I hope not," said Daniel.

"Mike, will I die out here?"

"No way. I won't let that happen."

"Will I die out here?"

"Maybe," said Quinn, "but there's something you can still do to help your child. There's something you can do to save him."

"Will I die out here?"

"Yes."

"Thank you, Jessica, for telling me the truth I already knew." With the first soft light of dawn, Maggie closed her eyes and slept.

Chapter Twenty-three

Brad McGhee stumbled over the bank of the rocky ledge, and fell. He was blind, partially deaf, and his motor control was poor. His body hit the packed-dirt cliff wall and rolled, arms twisting in the air in panic to break the drop. Riverbed gravel gouged his legs when he hit bottom, eight or nine feet below.

A wet trickle of water touched his hands, pushing over his scraped, bleeding knuckles and surging on. His clothes were filthy, blue plaid shirt and gray Levi's torn like the grated skin on his fingers and face.

Pain registered, the reaction slowed by shock. His face ached from the cuts and swellings. He cupped his hands in the stream and held the cool water to his lips, rinsing dirt and the salty taste of blood from his mouth.

No bones felt broken. *Might have snapped my neck in the fall,* he thought. *Might have ended it here. Survived one more time.* Was that good? Did life mean anything?

At least his mind was sound.

The worst had been those first weeks, when

death kept pace with him: Wherever he walked, ate, slept, it hovered and struck. Children died, their bodies littering yards like forgotten dolls, their toys left where dropped from small hands.

That was at the last, when no one had the strength to care for the young or the helpless. At first, families hid their sick. A child running a fever meant the whole family must leave. Angry crowds surrounded anyone with the virus and drove them out of the city.

There was nowhere to go. Highways were choked with abandoned cars and drifters living in dirt hovels. To travel the roads without a weapon was to invite the certainty of death. Life became the only value, one's own life.

Marriages held together by the thin glue of a legal union twisted apart, their bonds fraying with the first fears of the contagion. Wives were abandoned like cast-off clothes. Then sickness claimed them. Sickness claimed them all. In the end, the children were abandoned, too.

They had been alone at the last, the babies and the littlest ones; that thought haunted Brad.

The virus had found him and burned through his body like heated coals, fever so high his skull felt like an iron cooker, his brain steaming. For days, he was a part of it. The virus ate at him, made his blood sicken, made his head swim with heat-colored images of rivers afloat with corpses, of shadows moving in the shape of giant spiders across the land—their dark legs jeweled with bloody skulls, their eyes gleaming black as polished stone—and of sweeping plains of chalk-white cold.

The fever left him delirious, his mind functioning in a kind of half-life, not reality, not true madness, but something in between. He had no way of knowing how long he'd been like that. Days? Weeks? There was no one to tell him. There was no calendar keeper, no doctor, no priest kneeling beside him with the offering of last rites, or to say he was alive.

And he was blind. The vision of the death of the human race had nearly driven him mad. In his blindness, he found a lonely peace.

There was a price to pay for everything. For his life, there was loss of sight, near deafness, and physical weakness that left him frail as a one-year-old child, sometimes barely able to stand. The tremors would start in his ankles, then move to his legs, until at the hips, his body would cave in and fall. It might have been the high fever of the virus, which perhaps had caused a stroke, leaving him with this unpredictable debility. It was because of this, that he had fallen off the cliff.

But his mind was sound.

When he had realized that he was going to live, that somehow he had survived when everyone else had died, he had taken himself as far away as he could get from Biosphere Seven, and from Jessica.

He had reason to hope his wife was still alive, and even more reason to keep the knowledge of his existence from her. The man she had married was dead. The shell of him had been burned away in the fever-fire. What remained was a new personality, and a new man. His soul had been purged by witnessing the death of humankind, refined by fire, and purified by the inner vision of blindness.

His life had value; he was convinced of that, but not as the husband of Jessica Nathan. If he had been spared for a purpose, it was one he did not know. Each day he grew weaker. Each night brought him closer to death. In the near silence of his world, he felt his spirit rising away from the body that held it. He felt the separation . . . and his own flesh became as nothing to him.

Lying in the rock-strewn riverbed, he had no strength left to lift his body from the pebbled shale. The water flowed across his open palms, blessing his final hours.

"The earth is my inheritance," he said into the void that surrounded him. "Let my body and my bones nourish it."

In the dream that came to him, he saw past his blindness, visions of life in vast abundance — in the sea, from the soil, in the air. Beautifully colored birds winged across the brilliant skies of his world. Animals of all kinds walked the land. The great whales, dolphins, and fish swam in the clean waters of the sea, and clear rivers moved like veins across the fertile valleys.

His final thoughts were of Jessica.

The hands that touched him were soft and gentle. He felt the warmth of reckoning fingers at his brow, at his throat, and he struggled to stir. Lifted from where his body rested on the mud and stone, he was carried as easily as the weight of a small child, in arms that were both gentle and strong.

Bearing the added burden, his rescuer climbed the loose-dirt canyon up to the rise of the grassy vale. Brad felt himself slipping again into the emptiness of total dark — a darkness that was not of sight, but of mind. He tried to speak, but the effort cost him too much. He fell back into the embrace which comforted him, silent and barely conscious.

"The earth is your inheritance. It will nourish you."

The voice was feminine, yet powerful. He heard the words clearly, despite his disability, and felt their impact sound through him.

I'm dreaming, he thought, just before the last quiet door closed on all awareness. He felt his spirit slipping into the peace and, believing he was dying, let his soul go freely into the healing calm.

"I can't believe it. I still can't believe it," said Diana. She was wrapped in a heavy blanket, crouched on the floor. Her hair was uncombed; her face, swollen and blotchy from a night of tears. "Maggie was part of us. Now she's out there, sealed away from everyone. Sealed off from our whole world! What if the virus came in when the door opened?" she asked again.

The question had come up more than once during the night. It wasn't a single question, really. It was a whole string of what-ifs. What if the virus penetrated the atmosphere? What if we get sick? What if some of us die? What if? What if? What if? Griff was ready to kill her himself if she didn't shut up.

"Quinn said it was a positive air flow, pushing the air out the door—not in," Griff assured.

"He said probably," Diana argued. "Probably! God in heaven, I can't stand thinking about this anymore. Look at us. We're prisoners." She had sucked an edge of the blanket into her mouth and was chewing on the corner.

"We're not prisoners. We're survivors. Can't you think of us as that?"

"Survivors for what? What's left for us, Griffin? This glass tomb? Or the freedom of outside, like Maggie? Oh, God, I'm scared. I'm so scared." She began the rhythmic rocking again, blanket pulled close around her shoulders, eyes wide and dark with fear.

Despite his own annoyance with her, something in this posture moved him to pity. He pulled her to her feet, walked to the bed, and sat with her cradled in his arms until she fell asleep.

Her silence brought him little peace or rest, for he was left with the visions of the future she had engendered in his mind.

"How do you feel?" Jessica asked. A weak cast of sun shone through the morning mist.

"Cold." Maggie stretched her aching muscles, standing. She was in the desert bios, the exit door to the outside still open.

"Not sick?"

"No."

"You need to go outside and look around this morning," said Quinn, joining Jessica at the speaker.

"I don't want to go out there. If I'm going to die, I want to do it right here, near the rest of you."

Jessica shut off the intercom. "You're upsetting her."

Quinn wouldn't back down. "We need her to look at the damage to the solar panels and the generator. Of all of us, she has the kind of knowledge to put it back together. Hell, she designed the photophosphorylation process. That's why she was chosen, remember?—extracting a workable energy source from the sea. She could get the solar system working again. We'd have heat in this place, Jessie. There isn't any choice. We need her help." He switched the control button back on.

Jessica didn't stop him.

"Where's Trinity?" Maggie asked.

"Cathe's watching him. He's fine," Jessica replied.

Quinn didn't wait any longer. "Maggie, we may not have much time."

"Quinn!"

"It's the truth." He turned to Jessica. "We've got one shot, and she's it."

"She has feelings. She's not one of your computers."

"I know that," he answered calmly.

"That's a human being out there."

"And there are nine more in here—soon to be ten. I'm trying to save them. I didn't want to scare you, but you've got to think about the truth. When winter really hits, this place will freeze solid as a block of ice. If we live through that—and I don't think the babies will—the summer temperatures reach about one hundred and twenty degrees in this desert. We're sitting inside a glass dome. The heat will build up and have nowhere to go. It'll cook us. Slowly."

Jessica felt the validity of his words in the fluttering movement in her womb. Her child would be born in the summer. She stepped back, giving Quinn clear access to the intercom.

"I'm going to check on Trinity."

"That's good," he said, pain in his eyes for the fear he had caused her. "It's going to be all right," he started, but she was already hurrying away.

194

Jessica had been their strength, and he had broken her courage with this new terror. Now he had to make it right. By whatever means it took, he had to make it right.

Chapter Twenty-four

John Katelo heard the winter winds through the cracks in the wooden house. It was a hunter's cabin, supplied with a glass-fronted gun case stocked with rifles, knives, and ammunition. Katelo had broken the glass door of the cabinet the first night.

He was traveling in unfamiliar land. The rifles and the Browning 9-millimeter gave him a sense of security against whatever danger he might encounter. He kept the loaded pistol beside him when he slept, and the rifle strap over his shoulder whenever he went outside the cabin.

Kip lay on the flagstone hearth beside the fireplace. The white Samoyed's coat was lush and dense for warmth. His tail was curled around him in a snug embrace, and his nose met and nestled under the tip of it. The day was frozen.

Katelo didn't know where he was. He had followed the Alaskan Peninsula hugging the coast. Winter had caught him here. He thought he was still in British Columbia, but he might have made it to Washington before the first true storm of winter struck.

A blizzard had held him in the cabin for the

last three days, and the drifts had not melted. The sky was a sheet of hammered gray, riveted with dark bore holes where storm clouds gathered. They promised another night of snow, and another day of ceaseless winter.

It was as though death had come to the land as well, for nothing moved in the air or on the ground. In three days, John Katelo had seen nothing from the windows of his cabin except falling flakes of ice and the sweep of ashen clouds as they scudded across the shadowed rink of sky.

Kip's ears lifted, and a low growl started deep in his throat. He didn't bark, but stood, staring at the door, waiting.

Katelo had not noticed the first intrusive noise, but—his senses alerted by the dog—he heard the next sound. It was the soft crush of snow. He moved silently and reached for the rifle. The dog's teeth were bared. He did not growl, but his body quivered. Katelo cocked back the hammer.

The thought of a heavy-footed bear came into the Inuit's mind. Would the white brother come this far south? Or, was he in the land of the Kodiak, or grizzly? Would the rifle hold enough shots to bring it down? He put more cartridges on the table and laid the pistol there as well.

In the distance, Katelo heard a cough. It was followed by a series of choking gasps, each heavier and louder than the last. Not a bear—a human. Coming nearer.

The smoke from the fire would give him away.

Did he want to be found? The cough sounded bad. Was it from the virus? Katelo's finger remained on the trigger.

197

"Look, Jack. My God . . . there's a cabin!" the woman said.

"Be quiet!" the man ordered. "See the smoke coming from that chimney? Someone's in there." He was the one coughing.

"Are you crazy? I'm going inside. I'm not going to stay out here and freeze to death. Whoever's in there can't be worse than what's out here." She started walking fast across the snow toward the cabin door. Katelo could hear the *slush-slush* of her shoes sinking into the deep traces of soft powder.

"Salena! Goddammit, woman. Lena!"

She opened the door which was not locked, and stared into the predator eyes of the white Samoyed . . . then into the barrel of Katelo's rifle.

Her scream brought the man running.

"Leave me alone, Quinn. I can't help you."

It was still early morning, well before any of the others were ready to come and check on Maggie. Quinn knew he had to make her see his way before they arrived, especially Mike. It had been hard enough to get Mike to leave her, even to take care of their baby. Maggie had helped persuade him to do that, not realizing what Quinn had in mind. Now she was alone with his steady, unrelenting demand—and she was weakening.

"Think of your child, Maggie, if not of the rest of us. He'll freeze to death this winter. There'll be nothing any of us can do to protect him. Isn't it worth trying to save his life?"

"But, I don't know how!" she cried, breaking into fresh tears of frustration. "I told you. I can't do it."

"That just isn't true. I know you're scared, but you're going to start right now," said Quinn, not accepting her refusal. "I want you to get a ladder from the maintenance shed and climb on the roof."

"I'll fall," she fought him.

"Get the ladder, Maggie! Do it now!"

"I can't go out there," she cried, terror in her voice.

She was still in the desert sector, clinging to the wall of the biosphere, afraid to cross through the open doorway. The world outside the dome had become an alien place, full of death and fear.

He had to be hard. He had to find a way to save them if he could. He hated himself for it, but he had to use her fear.

"We don't have time to wait, Maggie. The virus may already be in your system. If so, you'll begin to feel the first stages of sickness in a few hours."

"Tomorrow . . . I'll do it tomorrow," she bargained.

"You might be dead by tomorrow. We can't prevent your death . . . but you can save your child. Do you want him to suffer? Do you want him to turn blue with cold?—to develop pneumonia and drown in the fluid of his own lungs?"

"Stop it!" Maggie begged him.

"Go find that ladder," insisted Quinn, "and stop wasting precious time."

He heard her footsteps moving away from the wall. The sound grew fainter until he could hear nothing more. When he was sure she was gone, he leaned against the cold, steel doors and wept.

* * *

The structure consisted of a rooftop of solar collector plates, a series of interspersed Trombe walls, and a tower-type solar power station. Through a bank of heliostats, the tower boiler collected heat from the sun, then passed that heat into the thermal storage unit, and from there to the steam generator and aerocondenser. A transformer converted the stored energy into usable electricity and powered the network of electronic systems throughout the unit.

The hurricane had ripped the tower station off the roof.

Maggie stared at the gaps, hundreds of missing solar plates. The spaces seemed to be grinning at her, like a hag's snaggle teeth. What was left of the tower station—lengths of spiky, white pipe—looked like bare bones thrown from a grave.

From here, standing on the roof, she could see for miles in any direction. *I'm on top of the world,* she thought. All that really mattered in her world was within the dome beneath her feet, her child . . . Mike . . . all of them.

Her hands were cold. She rubbed them together and began working on restoring the solar tower.

John Katelo's hands holding the stock of the rifle had been warm from the fire, but the sudden surge of adrenaline when the woman opened the door had turned the blood carried in his veins into rivers of ice.

He wasn't a killer. The rifle barrel remained aimed at the doorway, at the spot just above her

200

breastbone. He made no move to invite this stranger into the house. A woman. He hadn't seen one in over two years—alive.

The dog sensed Katelo's fear. His reaction was instinctive. He lunged at the intruder.

The loud report from the rifle blasted just after the woman's scream, an instant before Kip's jaws would have closed on her neck. The sound shied the dog and sent him snarling to the back of the cabin, haunches bent, neck ruff standing out in fury, ready to attack again.

The coughing man joined the woman at the doorway. His face was ashen, save for two red splotches of fever on his cheeks. Dark circles bruised the pale skin around his eyes, the slate-colored orbs sunken back into his head, giving him a look of walking death.

"Call off the dog!" the man shouted. "We're near froze with cold; can't do you any harm."

Katelo wasn't so sure he could call off Kip; the dog was more savage than tame. He had made sure of that for the animal's survival. And even if he could control the Samoyed, he wasn't sure he wanted to trust these people . . . not yet.

The man was obviously sick, probably with the virus. If that was true, the stranger would die soon anyway. It made no sense to expose himself to the illness. Katelo didn't want the man in his house.

The Eskimo way could be as hard-edged as ice drifts. Katelo's people could be coldly logical when it came to matters of life and death. In a time not so long past, old women—when they had lost their teeth to age, when they had no living sons

201

or husband, or when their usefulness to the tribe was at an end—had been put out on ice floes to await death in the form of starvation or the white bear. Such things had not happened in Katelo's lifetime, but he had heard the stories of his people. Survival in this land often made for hard choices.

The sick man would die anyway.

"Don't be a damn fool. We've come so far. You're the first person we've seen in months," the one called Jack tried to persuade him.

It was the woman who changed Katelo's mind. There was caution in her brown eyes, but courage, too. They did not look as though they held lies. She kept her place at the open door, not turning from her fear of either the man, or the dog.

"Who are you?" Katelo asked her, ignoring the presence of the man.

"Salena Cross. This is my friend, Jack Quaid. If you're not going to let us come inside, you might as well shoot us with that rifle. We'll die out here, left to this weather. My friend is sick from the cold—not the virus, if that's what you're thinking. We're survivors of that plague, just as you are. If it was going to kill us, it would have done so long before now." She took one step forward, moving into the room. "We're coming inside, Mr. . . ?"

"John Katelo." He felt his finger relax on the trigger.

". . . Mr. Katelo. Unless you plan to use that rifle, please put it down and call off your dog."

"Kip! Stay!" he commanded the Samoyed, hoping the Yupik's old training would be remembered. "Down, Kip! Stay!"

With that welcoming gesture, the woman named Salena Cross entered the warmth of Katelo's cabin, and his life.

Chapter Twenty-five

By the third day of Maggie's attempt to repair the solar generator, heat began flowing into the biosphere. The system resumed functioning at dawn, and by evening, the biomes were twenty degrees warmer beneath the insulating dome. There was power to cook, and light for the habitats, and the computers were up. It was as though the world was given back to them and man had once again received the gift of fire.

"You really did it!" Jessica's grin could be heard in the sound of her voice. "I can't believe you found the parts and knew how to connect them."

The intercom switch remained on pulse power now. Neither of them needed to touch the panel switch to be heard. "The parts I couldn't find," Maggie told her, "I rigged out of salvaged windfall from the roof. That tornado did serious damage. We're missing a third of the solar panels, and the communications building was leveled."

Jessica thought about that, the communications building and the man who had once been the spokesman for Biosphere Seven, her husband. Brad was gone, and now the building, too. All of that seemed a part of something that didn't exist anymore. She was alive, so was Quinn, and so was their baby who was to be.

"It's getting warm in here, Maggie. You've done it. You've given us another chance."

"I'm glad," Maggie offered. Her voice held a hesitation that hadn't been there before.

"What is it, Maggie?" Jessica became aware of the skin on the back of her neck. It prickled with a cold foreboding.

"I've got it, Jess. The fever started today."

"Maggie."

"Quinn was right. He said I needed to hurry. He said —"

"Maggie . . . don't." Everything that had been hopeful only moments before began falling into ruin at her feet. The virus was still there. None of them were safe. Poor Maggie was going to die. All of them were going to. . . .

"Jessica, you'll tell Trinity about me, won't you? You'll tell him I fixed the tower and the generator, that it was the last thing I did for him. Tell him for me, Jessica. I want my son to know that I loved him, until the very last minute of my life."

"We'll all tell him, Maggie. You've saved everyone."

"It was for him," Maggie insisted.

"I know," said Jessica, wanting to cry, wishing there were tears left to weep for anyone . . . for anything.

"I may not come back tomorrow." Maggie's voice had become softer — was she crying?

Jessica had to ask. "What do you see outside, Maggie?"

There was a hard hesitation, then, "Enough to not go into the cities. It happened, Jessica. We killed ourselves. It didn't take the hand of God to destroy man. We did it. We stirred up our own de-

205

struction in a cauldron and let it loose on the world."

There was more waiting to be asked. She had to know. "You've looked around the biosphere? You've been through the administration buildings?"

"Yes."

"Did you . . . have you seen—"

"Brad? No, Jessica. I'm sorry. I looked for his body, but it wasn't here. I found Exeter, and some others, but not Brad."

"You're sure?"

"I would have known him." Maggie's voice was flat, tired.

"Of course. I didn't mean—"

"Jessica, it feels so strange out here. Alone. I'm going to die totally alone."

She couldn't think of what to say. A pulse point in her neck was thudding, hard. She wanted to put her arms around Maggie and hold her, but—

"I'm Catholic, you know."

"Yes, Maggie." The hurt was building. It was swelling within her and would burst from her soul in screams and sobs, a rage that would tear at everything it touched. The hurt was more than Jessica could bear.

"There's no one else," Maggie started, hesitant.

"What is it? Tell me what you want. Please." *Why can't I cry for her? Why can't I plead with God and cry?*

"Would you say the Mass with me, Jessica? I want to hear the Mass spoken once more on earth before . . . ."

"I don't know the words, Maggie. How can I—"

"In my room, there's a missal. It's on the table beside my bed. Go and get it, Jessica. You'll read the part of the priest, and I'll answer the responses."

206

The thought shocked Jessica. It wasn't that her own faith was Jewish or that she was a woman. It was that Maggie was asking her to say a Mass for the dead — for Maggie's death. The act was premature and filled Jessica with cold horror.

"I . . . wouldn't you rather wait until—"

"I'm dying now, Jessica. Don't be afraid for me. I know it's happening. Only, you need to help me, just as I helped you. I believe in God, Jessica. I always have. You need to listen while I make an Act of Contrition—"

"A what?"

"When I say I'm sorry for my sins and ask God to forgive me . . . then we'll say the Mass together."

"Maggie. . . ."

"Go and get the missal, Jessica. Hear my confession before I die." Her voice was quavering, trembling with sickness, or desperation.

"All right. I'll do it," said Jessica. She went to find the book, to say the words that would give Maggie peace, to make her own peace with a God she had put up walls against. She hurried, knowing in her heart — for both of them — there was little time.

"Oh, my God, I am heartily sorry for having offended Thee. I detest my sins, because I dread the loss of Heaven, and the pains of Hell, but most of all, because they offend Thee, my God, Who art all good, and deserving of all my love. I firmly resolve, with the help of Thy Grace, to confess my sins, do penance, and amend my life. Amen."

On the other side of the glass wall, the response was spoken. "I absolve you of your sins, in the

Name of the Father, and the Son, and the Holy Spirit. God bless you, Maggie," said Jessica. "And may God forgive us both."

The dog accepted the woman's presence in the cabin. He had never attacked a human before, did not think of her as food, and had only lunged for her throat because he had sensed Katelo's fear. When the fear was gone, so was the Samoyed's aggressive behavior toward her.

The man, he watched. There was the smell of death on him, rank and hot as fetid breath. Kip's brown eyes followed, when the man sat, when he stood, when he walked about the cabin. The woman was safe, but the one whose constant coughing hurt the dog's ears was danger.

The tensed muscles beneath the thick, white coat quivered with barely contained excitement. The man was not the dog's prey, but he was a threat to Katelo. Kip guarded his master, waiting for the moment when the man would attack. A primitive knowledge — that of the feral hunter — sensed it would be soon.

"Tell me what happened," Salena asked Katelo. Her voice was calm water and brushed across his troubled memories of that time with easy words, smooth and soft. She was gentle, this flame-haired woman. Her skin was the pale cream of walrus ivory; her eyes, like sea grass, copper-brown in the light.

"You sayin' you were inside that hell-house?" said Jack. "I saw pictures of the place, bodies bloated up like dead cows—stacked like cord wood, some of 'em. You tellin' us you just walked outta there? Uh-huh, I don't believe it."

Jack Quaid pushed his glasses farther up onto the bridge of his nose. It was a narrow nose, as long and thin as an axe blade along the spiny bridge. His eyes were dark behind the thick lenses, like puckered stones beneath a river course, hard and seeded with grit. His mouth was no more than a reddish line, jagged across the width of his face, slanting down.

Katelo tried to remember what feeling had persuaded him to allow this hawk-beaked man inside his house. If it hadn't been for the watchful eyes of the woman, he would have cast the sack of barking bones out onto the drift of snow from which it had arrived, and left it there to freeze.

"Be quiet, Jack," Salena said to Quaid. "Never mind what he says," she whispered. "I believe you." Her face was angles and soft curves, not moon-shaped like those of Eskimo women. Her cheeks were not circles, but concave valleys, pulled snugly at the jaw, and fitted to a pointed purchase at her chin.

"Hell, maybe he's the one 'at done it." Jack leaned over the table, between them, gripping Salena's arm. He started laughing at the idea, chortling, then was struck with a spasm of wet, sludgy coughs. "That right, Chukchi? You the scientist responsible for all this?" The laughter dribbled down his chin, and spittle flew from his mouth when he choked on the thick phlegm.

Katelo scooted his chair back from the table and stood, moving toward the door. "We need firewood," he said, and closed the cabin door behind him. In the shroud of snow, he felt his heat of anger ease. The icy bite of the air gripped his lungs with pincer talons and raked his throat with ragged claws as he drew breath after cleansing breath of frozen air into the hollow of his chest.

A week ago, he hadn't known there was another human being alive. Now, after only a few hours with Jack Quaid, he was ready to kill one. The idea of spending the rest of the winter with the man — all winter — was more than he could stand. He thought about moving on.

Snow made for rough traveling. If the weather promised to remain clear for a day or two, he might make it to another cabin. But if a blizzard struck again, and the sky had a storm-clouds look to it, then he'd be caught in the open with no shelter. It wasn't worth risking his life for Jack Quaid.

The cabin door opened, and Salena stepped out onto the porch. Katelo busied himself loading wood into the cradle of one arm.

"Jack saved my life," she said, as if someone had asked her. "I know he's not easy to live with, a rough-cut man . . . too hard, sometimes."

Katelo's only response to this would have been insulting. He kept the thought to himself.

"There was an enforced quarantine in Brighan, Montana, nearly a year ago. The town was dying, person by person, and no one was allowed to leave. I knew I'd die there, couldn't get out.

"Jack saved me. He shot a man, killed the guard on duty, and we escaped. We ran north, into Canada. I might be dead now if it weren't for Jack."

"Why do you tell me this?" Katelo looked into the cool rivers of her eyes.

"So you understand why we're together. I'm not

210

his woman," she volunteered. There was, in these last four words, an offering. "Jack is sick. He may be dying."

Katelo broke from the hold of her gaze. He bent, adding more wood to the load in his arms, then started back into the house.

"Don't leave, John. I know you're thinking of going, to get away from Jack. But stay, please. I don't want to be alone."

Her words stopped him as surely as a snare around his ankle. He had been without the company of another human voice for nearly two years. In that time, no one had spoken his name aloud. Now she called him John. Her voice said, ". . . stay. I'm not his woman." She was stronger than he had the power, or the will, to leave.

"I won't leave," he said simply, already feeling the weight of the house press on him as he opened the door.

The search of Jack Quaid's eyes met him from across the room, dull black stones beneath a layer of ice. Katelo felt them bore through him, carrion birds, eating their way into his soul. The image left him cold. He rolled one log into the fire, the others onto the flagstone hearth, and warmed his body near the open flame.

"She's a pretty piece, Salena," Jack said as he crossed the room to the fire.

Katelo's anger rose like the lick of copper from the kindled embers.

"Not for you, Chukchi. Be clear on that. The woman's not for sharin'. You get my meaning?" Jack hawked a shiny lump of phlegm onto the red-hot grate. The spittle sizzled.

Katelo grabbed Jack by the neck, shoving Quaid's

211

razorback face hard against the rock chimney. Just behind them, the dog stood ready, growling low. "You don't speak to me—ever. You clear?" He slammed the man's face again, dredging up a cry of pain. "And never—" he struck Jack's cheekbone against the stone mantle—"never spit into my fireplace again."

A sudden draft of cold air made him turn. Salena stood in the open doorway. She said nothing, staring. Katelo let Quaid go.

One side of the dog's muzzle twitched; a spike of white tooth showed beneath the raised lip. A rippling current moved along the muscles of Kip's legs and back . . . shuddering . . . shuddering.

From the doorway, Salena called softly, "John."

"Kip!" Katelo shouted.

The dog trotted to his master's side.

Margaret Mary Adair felt the hard presence of a Texas winter. The sky was an overturned cauldron, grainy and pebbled with the rough texture of loose coal, and sleeting down in great tears along its welded seams. It was mid-morning, yet the weight of the dark pressed on her, suspending all bright and muted color—covering the land with the muffling quilt of lowering black.

Maggie was dying.

The fever had keened through her in swift, sparking currents, leveling at one hundred and seven degrees. Delirium crowded the saner corridors of her mind, erasing memory, erasing thought. Only images remained.

Summer heat . . . lying on a crowded beach, the sun burning her pale skin, turning it red . . . and the waves

212

crashing along the shore, pounding waves, hitting the rocks with the surging force of the ocean . . . the cry of birds overhead, sandpipers and gulls. The water would be cool against her fevered flesh. Its seaweed-green beckoned her.

She rose with the heat, staggering beneath the blistering sun, toward the liquid light of that leafy green, the tide surging like her blood. The sea's wet foamed and sudded its white collar around an emerald cape, bubbled and frothy, a lacy ribbon to tie up her hair. Like her eyes, that green, That was what Mike had said — sea green. her eyes.

She walked toward the smooth repose of the water, felt its coolness touch her skin, and the white sea foam billow around her ankles. Her feet sank into the chill cloud of it . . . step after step . . . until the sea's pulse pulled her down, stopping her heart with its great weight.

With her final heartbeat, Maggie's body fell into the snow. The storm abided. By evening, the spot where she had fallen was buried beneath a shroud of unblemished white.

Chapter Twenty-six

December 25, 1999: Three weeks have passed, following the death of Maggie Adair. We spend our third Christmas within Biosphere Seven. Those of us still living await whatever crisis might be next, profoundly aware of how fragile is our ecosystem, and our lives.

Due to Maggie's courage, we have heat, energy to cook our food, and power to run the computers once again. With the wave action restored, our ocean has begun regenerating itself. Griff has taken deep-water samples and found varieties of living fish he thought were dead. Somehow, they—like the rest of us—have managed to survive.

We are nine—seven adults, and two children. I carry a third infant within me, and wonder if any of us will live to see it born. How long until the next crisis? . . . until the next storm, or sickness, or accident?

In the two years we have lived within the dome, we have lost three of our number. I think today of Piper Robinson, whose heroic action prevented a break in the seal; of Josiah Gray Wolf, who offered his own life in hopes of finding others; and of Maggie Adair, whose knowledge and action has saved our lives.

Thoughts and memories of Outside come to me today, and in some quiet part of every day. I fight against the sweetness of remembering, forcing the images from my consciousness. But when I sleep, the soul of Earth returns to me, and I cannot wrest myself free of it.

The thought terrifies me. Will I die in this artificial world? Will I end my life as Our Lady of the Sphere?

Quinn's hand touched her shoulder. "Come away from the console, Jessica. That's enough journal keeping for today. You need some rest." He glanced at what she had written.

Not wanting him to read her testimony of fear, she quickly scrolled down the page to the bottom, saved the file, and exited.

"Our Lady of the Sphere. . . ?" He caught a flash of the final words and read them aloud. "Uh oh. How long have you known about that line?"

"Since you first said it to Josiah." She shut the computer down and turned back to face him.

His face was a hodgepodge of emotion, eyebrows and forehead frowning in assumed guilt, lips pressed hard together, trying to contain embarrassed laughter which threatened to escape at any instant, and bright eyes that were already grinning the mischief of a little boy. "Did Josiah tell you?"

"No, I heard it for myself."

"I'm sorry. It was just that I was—"

"Jealous," she filled in the word.

"Oh, I don't know about . . . well, maybe just a little."

"Maybe a lot." She kept him squirming.

"All right." The smile broke across his face, and he laughed. "I admit it. And I'm sorry you heard what I said. Still hate me?"

She came into his arms and kissed him. "Yes."

"Good . . . as long as I know. At least I'll be prepared for the poison in my food."

"That would be too easy," she revised the terms. "I plan to keep you around to torment for the rest of your life." She began to unbutton his shirt.

His hand caught her wrist, stopping the game. She looked up. "You were the right choice for team leader, Jessie." The expression in his eyes was serious. "I didn't want to believe it then, but I know it now. You were there for Josiah, at Piper's death; you knew what to say to Cathe when she needed someone to turn to; and Maggie trusted you with the life of her child. You held them together, through all of this. You were the best. I would have been a miserable—"

"Ssh." She put her two fingers to his lips. Stepping back, Jessica untied the soft yellow robe and let it fall to the floor. Her pregnancy showed in the pronounced curve of her belly, but she let herself stand naked before this man, her arms held out to him.

"Our Lady of the Sphere," he said stepping close, and touched his hand to the curve of her body, where their baby lay.

She reached behind her and switched off the lamp. Night folded in around them, a veiled retreat from the watchful eyes of God, and in all the world—in all their world—they were alone.

Food had become a problem. There would have been enough canned goods in the cabin for John Katelo to have survived the winter, but the few remaining tins of chili, stew, and peaches wouldn't stretch to feed three.

The dog hunted his own food.

It was hungry winter, the time when most of the animals either hibernated through the coldest weeks—living off their stored fat—or moved south, leaving the barren wasteland of the Canadian forest.

In a few days their rations would be gone. Katelo knew he must risk going to hunt, with the possibility of being caught outside in another blizzard, in order to feed them through the hardest weeks before spring. It wasn't the danger to his own life or the cold he dreaded; it was the thought of leaving Salena alone with Quaid.

Since the day Katelo had confronted Jack Quaid, a secrecy of intent grew up like a wall dividing the small cabin. Quaid remained mute whenever Katelo was near, apart from the visible message of his coal-black eyes. The only sound coming from the man was that of incessant coughing.

Not only was Quaid withdrawn from Katelo, he was now unapproachable to Salena as well. The sick man's eyes watched them both, hatred burning in the suppressed anger of his silence. Katelo worried that it was jealousy, that Quaid resented the feelings Salena was beginning to know for another man. Until now, Jack Quaid had been her protector. She had been grateful to him. Now Katelo received her admiration . . . and her love,

It had happened two nights ago.

Each had thought Jack was asleep; that had been a mistake. The cabin was bitterly cold; freezing wind seeped through fine cracks in the grout seams, between the logs. A warming fire blazed on the grate of the hearth, sending spiraled waves of heat into the main room. The storm hoared the windows with frost, coating the glass with gray-white rime.

In the cabin, the lovers met before the fire. Katelo stood at one side of the rock chimney face, and she at the other. The heat of the burning logs brought a hot flush of red to her cheeks. The moving points of flame caught and darted in her eyes, reflecting the light. Beauty. Still, he held himself from her. And the fire moved within them.

It was she who took the step toward him . . . into the welcome of his arms.

Through the long caress of night, passion rose like the blazing of the fire. To be with this woman—to let his hand linger on the full curve of her hip, on the silk of her skin beneath his palm, on the aching beauty of her breast—was a magic in Katelo's life. She was the soul-taker, a woman spoken of in the stories of his people. He felt his spirit rise to her.

A soft step behind him alerted Katelo. Jack Quaid stood in the open bedroom doorway. The eyes of the two men met for an instant, Quaid's boring through Katelo's with the sharpness of a killing knife, Then, before Salena realized he was there, Quaid turned away and vanished, closing the door and smothering the cold trace of light.

Nothing was said of it the next day, but Katelo now felt a thread of fear in leaving Salena with Quaid. He warned her to be careful, giving her the Browning 9-millimeter, ". . . for protection." He thought that he should put Quaid out of the cabin, but she told him again how the man had saved her life, how he would never hurt her.

Ignoring the shouted voices of instinct, Katelo made ready to leave them.

"Take that animal with you!" Quaid said at the last. These were the only words he had spoken to him in days.

"No," Katelo refused, sensing the importance of it even then. "The dog stays."

"You might need him," said Salena. A frown of worry creased her brow. "You could be hurt. A pack of wild dogs might—"

"Kip, stay!" he ordered the Samoyed. The dog whined when Katelo left them, but remained at Salena's side.

Gray clouds like battleships raced across the sky, snow and ice crystals held in each billowing mist. The floor of heaven was wet steel, and the building mass of silver storm lashed and scourged the foundry of it. Blizzard weather.

The land was hushed, awaiting the coming storm. A cushion of white softened Katelo's step, hiding the lay of ground on which he might have found a track of game. His breath fogged the air before his mouth and nose, and the astringent smell of ice was in his nostrils.

He walked the white of winter, standing like the heavy-footed bear, listening. The land reached into the spirit of John Katelo—a hard place, this cold, unforgiving scape. It gathered into him: the stretch

219

of trees; the crush of snow beneath his feet; the whisper of an animal, moving.

He stepped as softly as the sound, not hurrying, not running toward the caribou. Each stride brought him closer. The deer was foraging, raking the bark of a tree with its branching antlers and pulling the strips off with its lips and teeth in wide, flat ribbons. It was a buck, four-and-a-half feet at the shoulder, with a pale cream ruche at its chest.

Katelo crawled the last few feet, lowering his profile so that the caribou wouldn't sight him as it stood, black hooves barking the tree. The animal was intent on its work—a great buck, heavy in body weight, but hungry, for all that.

The Chukchi rose to one knee . . . sighted, and squeezed the trigger. The bullet struck at the crown of the animal's head, just as the buck had raised its muzzle to tug at the new ravel of bark. The carcass went slack, a final grunt of air puffing from the caribou's nostrils, and slid to the base of the tree.

The first snowflakes fell as Katelo made the final cut. He bundled the thick wedges of bloody meat into a crude wrap of caribou skin tied at the center with the animal's own wet sinews. The antlered head, he left behind with the remainder of the carcass. He had no need for trophies. It would not be wasted, but would feed another kind of hunter, some smaller game.

Even without the skeleton, the package was heavy, over a hundred pounds. Katelo secured it to the small dredge sled he carried on his back. The sled was made with the same conformity of a snowshoe, a frame of thin wood fitted with crosspieces and tied

220

with leather strips. He took up the long, joined thongs of the sledge, slipped them around his waist, and began to pull. The weight of it, even across new snow, was a hard burden.

And the snow fell. . . .

He felt the ice of it in the breath he drew into his lungs. He felt the freezing air in the wind against his ears and drew the hood of his anorak close around his face. His eyebrows and lashes frosted, and the cold stood like a solid barrier between the Inuit and the smallest advance forward.

Behind him, the howl of a wolf shot the air like heated lead through tender flesh. The smell of blood had lured the hungry. Another cry. Another. Katelo gripped the rifle stock, his finger curled around the trigger, ready. He pulled ahead, moving into the face of the wind . . . away from the crushing jaws and howl . . . away from the shadow of gray death.

The wind carried the scent of fresh kill; the wolves followed.

As Katelo moved through the shouted voice of the storm, a certainty came to him. The wolves would attack; the smell of new blood was too great; and their hunger, hollow.

Hating to lose the desperately needed food which might sustain them through the winter, Katelo cut the caribou skin bundle open and threw half of the kill far from him, onto the snow. He retied the packet to the sledge and, forcing all his strength to the task of pulling, ran ahead through the fierce muscle of the gale.

Behind him came the sounds of snarls and snapping jaws. Katelo knew he must hurry. When the pack had finished the portion he had given them,

221

they would come after the rest. Their appetites had been whetted, and like a razored knife, they would cut through him to sate their hunger.

In the thick of falling snow, he lost his way. All around him was a well of white, blinding his vision to any memory, any trace of the path to the cabin. Drifts piled onto the flat plane of the sledge, and the weight of it was pulling him down.

He wouldn't die for the caribou flesh.

In the end, it was less than ten pounds of meat that he carried from the kill. He slipped the wedge of venison beneath his anorak, layering the portion between his shirt and skin. His belt held it in place. The sled, and the rest of the meat, he left still wrapped in the half-frozen deer skin.

His eyes were blinded by the storm . . . nothing but snow and wind. Even the wolves had left the terror of the freezing wind for the warmth of their dens. The blizzard consumed everything . . . all heat, all direction, all senses.

He took a step forward—his legs unbending, cold solid as the trunks of trees—into the shallow ravine of a frozen streambed, and fell. Protected from the ice wind by the sloping walls of the crevasse, Katelo huddled his body into a rounded core and waited out the storm.

Chapter Twenty-seven

January 1, 2000: Is anyone out there? Can you hear us? Answer. Repeat. This is Biosphere Seven. Is anyone left? Answer. What's happened? What have we done? Dear God, are we alone? Answer. Answer.

Jessica pressed the send key, transmitting the missive to all computer terminals linked to the biosphere connection: the single remaining biosphere dome, all accessible public relations departments, each affiliated corporation, and every unit coordinator of personnel. A maze of computer terminals from Texas to the Amazon Jungle were designed with the capability to receive her letter in a bottle.

She waited.

It was three in the morning. She was dressed in a robe and barefoot. Only the dim glow of the monitor lit the room. The overhead light might wake the others. She wanted no company for this act. Privacy. It was hard to find such a thing in an hourglass world. The green light showed that the message had been received and displayed.

223

There was no answer.

Are we the only people left in the world? Is everyone dead? Answer. This is Biosphere Seven. We are alive. God help us. We are still alive.

The overhead light clicked on, flooding the room with harsh yellow glare. She shaded her eyes, then looked to see Quinn standing in the doorway. He was holding Trinity.

"We came looking for Mommy."

"I see that."

He crossed the room, taking a chair close to her. "Something about the night, I guess. None of us can sleep."

Jessica took the baby from him. "He's dry."

"I changed him."

She hugged the baby to her, wrapping a fold of her robe around him. "You have a conscientious daddy, Trin—a good man."

"Glad you think so." He moved closer, kissing Jessica's neck.

He dropped a note on the table in front of her.

"What's that?" she asked.

"A letter from Mike."

"What? When did you—"

"Earlier tonight. It's about Trinity," Quinn told her. "He addressed it to both of us. I read it on the way over. He wants the boy back."

"Oh, God." Jessica was tired, too tired for this struggle. Mike was Trinity's father—that was true—but Maggie had given the baby to her, insisted on it, in fact. She didn't want to open the letter, so pushed it away with her fingers.

224

"Quinn, I —"

"Read it, Jess. It's all right."

Reluctantly, she picked the letter up. The handwriting was large and blockish, like a child's. It read:

Dear Jessica and Quinn,

This is a note intended to thank you for caring for my son. Since Maggie's death, I haven't been able to concentrate on much else besides my grief for her. Maybe some of that grief is really for myself, I don't know. Anyway, for now, the boy is better off with you. I know he's loved and cared for, and I know it's what Maggie wanted.

Having said all this, I want you to remember one thing. Trinity is my son. Whatever Maggie may have wanted, the boy is my child, too. I'm his father, and I want him to know that. I'm not giving him up — not to Quinn, or to you, Jessica.

One day, I'll come and ask for my son. I'm still a part of his life. Sometimes, the need to remember that is all that keeps me going. I'm his father, and that's never going to change.

He had signed it, *With my thanks. Mike.*

Jessica put the letter down. "He's hurting, isn't he? I don't know what to do for him."

"We're doing it, I'd say. Taking care of Trinity."

"What's going to happen to us, Quinn? Are we just postponing the end? . . . putting off the inevitable?" She was conscious of the baby in her arms, of

225

the size of the room, and of the space beyond it, too. She was conscious of the child within her.

"That's what life is, Jessie—postponing the end. We're no different than any other animal on this earth, just more aware of it."

"Everything's gone, isn't it?—everything we had."

He wrapped both arms around her and the child, making his body a solid core, surrounding them. "This is the world, Jessie. This is all it's ever been—" he kissed her softly—"and it's still here."

She laid her head against the crook of his neck and, for that moment, believed.

Brad McGhee felt the dream begin again. . . .

It was the image of a wheel, turning and turning, three concentric swirls of phosphorous white, spinning alone in the heavens, far above the planet . . . and he was a spoke of that wheel, connecting them. His body lay in a straight line from the curved, outer circle, through the second and third luminous rings, to its center nucleus, the earth. The spokes—himself, and eight other people he didn't know—lay suspended like laser beams, descending in the shape of a cone to the world below.

He felt the power of healing flow through him: above him, into him, from him. He was the connector. The others were connectors, too. He tried to see their faces, but the wheel was always turning; their images were blurred. Like him, they were people. He saw that much.

Am I alive? he thought. *Am I still Brad McGhee?*

The question fluttered through his mind, but other things surrounded it, making the answer insignificant. He no longer thought of himself as

Brad, but as part of the three circles, and of earth. He was a bridge. The light of each circle pulsed within him, coursing through his body to the blue and green sphere below.

In the turning of the wheel, in the radiance of that shadowless white light, he felt his strength return. Peace claimed him—mind and body and soul. Like a vessel, he was filled with it. Light poured into him and from him. He was the tunnel to the heavens. He was the pipe of peace. The messenger.

An awareness of physical strength came to him, a force of might he had not known before. He felt his body heal from the ravages of fever, through the nurturing of the wheel. Less and less he asked the question—*Am I still Brad McGhee?*—until the answer was finally clear. He was not. He had changed.

That which had been Brad McGhee was nearly burned from him. The virus and fever had claimed the physical body of the man, leaving him weak and blind and deaf. Now the source of the dream had cleansed away the rest.

But he was alive. He knew that at last.

He awoke from the dream, into a morning of soft, amber light. The sky was a liquid flame above him; the earth, a living being. He felt its breath in the cool green of the grass and trees. He felt its blood in the flowing channels of the rivers. He felt its heart, in the surging rhythm of the seas.

He awakened on a hillside, in the warm, first breath of dawn. Standing, he felt the ground beneath him, solid . . . the sounds around him speaking the energy of life . . . and the sky above, wide and beautiful. He was no longer blind. He could see and hear . . . his body strong and whole.

Snow lightly dusted the ground. Winter was fading, the hint of spring already in the air. The world was renewing itself, and he was part of that renewal. Life, in its abundance, was generous. In every direction he looked, there was evidence of that opulence of plenty.

His last clear memory of life—before his vision of the wheel—was of the woman whose arms had lifted his broken body from the riverbed, and who had carried him up the ravine to the plateau above. He had felt the comfort of her presence throughout this time of healing. She had supported him in those same arms, holding him close against her. She had brought him water and food, offering a bowl of milk for him to drink and a blanket to keep him warm. Her voice had soothed him when his fear had surfaced, calming, like the stroke of a smooth hand upon his brow.

The name by which she had called him since the moment she'd carried him from the riverbed was not Brad . . . but Prophet.

Like his name, he had changed. It was as the prophet that he regained life. It was as the prophet that the world was revealed to him. It was as the prophet that he would serve as the voice of the messenger—as the spoke of the wheel—to the people of earth.

He called out to the woman, not knowing her name, but calling, "Are you there? Are you there?" A wick of fear held him in its heat, consuming all that was the courage of his heart.

He couldn't see her, as though he were still blind, and his deafness blocked the sound of her voice; but the answer came to him through the channel of his mind. Her answer shuddered through him, rocking the ground beneath his feet. That which was spirit in Brad, knew the message clearly.

I AM BESIDE YOU. THROUGH ALL THAT YOU MUST DO.

No longer afraid, he knelt on the white-laced ground, waiting for what he was sure was the voice of God, to lead him.

Jack Quaid hurt. All of him ached. His whole body felt like a sore that swelled and throbbed. It had started in his throat the night before, a scraping pain when he swallowed, and hard, enlarged nodes at his glands.

The cough was worse, too. Even the bottle of Jameson Irish whiskey he'd found at the back of the cedar chest hadn't eased the spasms which gripped him in claws of the cough. It felt as if his lungs were being shredded piece by piece and hawked up in bloody phlegm.

He kept the cabin warm, throwing a thick stack of branches on the fire. Salena complained it was too hot, but he paid no attention to her. Why should he? She didn't give a damn about him—didn't care if he was sick.

She wanted that Eskimo. The slut had let the Chukchi put his hands under her clothes in the dark. She'd slept with him. The thought of Katelo's body pumping against Salena's sickened Jack. He had saved her life, killed a man and brought her out of the charnel house of that Montana town. He'd saved her for himself, but she hadn't waited until he was well. She'd turned against him with Katelo.

Jack never forgave anyone who did him wrong.

The whiskey warmed his throat, soothing the

229

scratchiness while going down. He held the bottle like a lover, caressing the narrow neck with his fingers and thumb, resting the sloping curve of the glass bottle against his cheek. There was kindness in the amber liquor, kindness that wasn't in any man . . . or woman.

It made him angry. He hated John Katelo for what the Inuit had stolen from him. Oh, yes, he'd stolen her, surely as if he'd taken a loaded gun and held it to Quaid's back. The Eskimo had robbed him of his property.

Another draw of whiskey fueled the fire that raged in him.

If he killed Katelo . . . if he killed the woman, too. . . . There was enough food in the cabin for him to survive the winter if the others were out of the way. He could hunt, come spring, or walk out of here. The place would be his, with nobody to tell him to shut up. If he killed them. . . .

He didn't want the woman anymore. She was filth. She'd let that Chukchi touch her. Wanted it. His fingers squeezed on the cool, glass neck of the bottle, wishing it were hers.

And then Quaid remembered the gun Katelo had left for them. "For protection," the Inuit had said, handing the Browning 9-millimeter pistol to Salena. If he were clever, Quaid could get it from her, find wherever she had hidden it among her things. It was a small cabin.

With the gun in his hand, there'd be no problems.

"We need more firewood," said Quaid.

"You're burning it too fast," Salena told him. She

230

held a cup of hot tea in her hands, palms hugging the rounded sides of the blue china. "It's too hot in here, anyway. Let it die down a little."

"I need heat!" Quaid argued. The terrible coughing started again, this time convulsing him into a doubled-over, low bend. "The cough, it's killing me," he moaned. "Get the wood!"

Salena rose from her chair and started for the door. The dog followed her. "No. Stay here, Kip." She rubbed the back of the Samoyed's ears. "Good boy," she told him, running her fingers through the lush ruff around his neck. "I'll be right back. Stay."

She opened the door, and the wind forced its hard hand into the room, frosting the planked flooring, and nearly blowing out the fire. Salena went out, pulling the door shut and leaving the dog standing with a whine in his throat, waiting for her return.

Jack ran the length of the room, wedging the beam of a two-by-four in the slotted lock across the wooden frame. He'd keep her outside until he found the gun. Then he'd shoot her and drag her body off a distance from the house. When the Eskimo came back—if he survived the blizzard—he'd shoot him, too.

Quaid took another pull from the bottle, a long one, and carrying the whiskey with him, headed for the room Salena now shared with Katelo.

The sound of a booted foot kicked the door. "Jack! Let me in, the latch beam's fallen. The door's locked. Jack!"

The dog barked.

Quaid ignored them, searching for the gun. He tore the mattress from the bed, looked beneath the

231

springs and frame . . . ripped each drawer from the standing chest, and dumped them out. No gun.

"Jack!" the shout was louder now. "I'm freezing out here. Open the door!" Again, the sound of heavy kicks.

The dog threw himself against the door, barking furiously.

Quaid would kill the dog, too, when he found the gun.

The closet held nothing but extra sets of sheets and blankets, folded and stacked on the top shelf. Quaid started dragging them down, one by one, shaking everything.

A loud thud from the wooden porch said Salena had dropped the armload of wood. In another moment, he heard her at the windows, fists on the thick shutters. "Quaid! Can't you hear me? What's wrong with you? Quaid! Open the door!"

He shook the wide, gray-striped blanket. The gun fell from the woolen folds, landing at his feet. Scooping it up, he tugged the magazine cartridge from the handle. The pistol was loaded. Quaid snapped the magazine in place and pulled back the steel slide grip of the barrel, readying the 9-millimeter for firing. Another frame of cartridges lay on the floor beside it. Enough bullets. He shoved the extra case into his pocket.

The dog was clawing at the windows. He twisted around to face the man, and growled as Quaid crossed the room.

He felt the heaviness of the pistol in his hands, the power. *I could kill the dog right now,* he thought. It was tempting. *How fine it would feel to put a bullet through that skulking animal's brain.* No, he wouldn't do it yet. Shooting the dog would give the woman warning. He wanted her to be surprised.

Quaid lifted the wooden bar from the door and walked out. "Salena!" he shouted, his voice carrying over the mad rush of wind. "Over here!"

She fought the storm for the few steps from the window to the front of the house, gaining the corner of the porch — both hands pulling her along the log wall. Her hair was iced with a coating of white, as were her brows and lashes.

"Thank God!" she gasped through lips that were already blue. "Hurry, help me. I'm freezing. You didn't open the door." She started toward him.

His hand came up, holding the gun.

"What are you —"

He didn't wait for her to finish. "There's just you and me, Salena. We'll go for a walk. Over there, by those trees." He pointed to the stand of fir which marked the boundary of forest nearest the cabin. "Walk!"

"Jack . . . are you crazy? We'll freeze out here. You're not thinking clearly. You're sick, Jack. Give me the gun." She stepped toward him.

The pistol fired. The kick of the recoil knocked Quaid back, throwing off his aim and skewing the shot. The 9-millimeter nearly dropped from his hand. By the time he righted his stance, Salena was gone.

Snow blew into his eyes, blinding him, as he shouldered his way into the gale. She was hiding, but he had the gun.

Paralyzing cold swept through him. He felt the ice of it inundate his ski jacket, cross the thin barrier of his skin and enter muscles and veins, drawing all heat from the warm, center core of him. Shielding his eyes with his right arm, he held the

233

gun outstretched before him in his left hand, searching.

Jack Quaid turned at the corner of the cabin and saw Selena crouching against the wall. She looked too cold to move.

"Jack. Don't."

He gripped the gun in both hands, steadied his stance, took careful aim, and. . . .

The dog's teeth sliced through the ski jacket, to the flesh of Quaid's right arm. There had been no warning growl. Now, in this attack, a hard, rumbling sound came from the Samoyed's throat. His jaws locked on the exposed bone . . . thrashing head side-to-side . . . twisting with the entire weight of his body . . . trying to rip the limb free and bring the kill down.

Quaid screamed at the sickening wrench, his arm tearing from its socket. Abruptly disconnected bone stuck out at a right angle along his forearm as the slack bag of skin was pulled and stretched by the dog. Grated nerves hung like white worms from the exposed flaps of Quaid's slashed muscles, and bright red spurted from the severed artery near his shoulder.

With his left hand, Jack Quaid reached for the Samoyed's neck . . . struggling desperately to maintain his balance . . . trying not to fall . . . trying to tear the razored teeth away from him . . . and dropped the gun.

He heard a long, high shriek—thought it was Salena—but it was himself, opening his mouth wide and screaming. The thin, reedy pitch was far above him, like a forming shell encasing his mind.

Abruptly, the demented wailing stopped . . . only when the arm snapped . . . only when the dog pulled Jack Quaid to the ground . . . the squeezing grip of his bloodied jaws on his neck.

Salena fired the pistol. The shot's report cracked against the hard-bitten air. Startled, the Samoyed shied back, a mask of red staining the white coat of his face and chest.

"Kip, stay!" Salena commanded in a firm voice. She took a tentative step forward, reaching a hand toward Quaid. *Oh, Jesus,* she thought, *is he dead?*

The dog moved closer to the kill, warning her away with a loud, threatening growl. He put his paws on Quaid's legs, claiming him.

Salena stared into animal's dark brown eyes. Kip was ready for any sudden movement on her part. A long line of evolution, she knew, had given the dog the ability for reflexive action, a fine-haired trigger of response to the prey's attempt at unexpected escape. If she broke and ran for the cabin, instinct might cause the dog to catch her—an instinct that could cost her life.

"Jack?" Salena held the gun in steady hands. She could not shoot the dog. . . . It had saved her life; she was sure of that. "Jack?" she tried again.

The Samoyed gripped the thick denim of Quaid's pant leg between his teeth and started dragging the body across the new snow, toward the first break of trees. Kip's eyes were yellow-red, and his lips curled into a snarl around the firmly clenched teeth.

Salena waited, hoping Quaid wouldn't groan, hoping he was already dead . . . and terrified that he wasn't. No sound came from Jack, only a scraping *whhhoosh* as the weight of his body was tugged over the freshfall, toward the secret hide—a stain of

235

ruby blood marking a wide swath along the white ground.

Badly frightened, Salena stepped back, and back again, until her foot touched the porch. Turning, she rushed inside the cabin and barred the door. Only then, did she allow herself the awful trembling. Only then, the mind numbing terror.

If John Katelo didn't come back . . . if something had happened to him . . . she would be completely alone. Except for the dog, she reminded herself, shuddering. The terrible image remained . . . a trail of blood and a mangled body dragged across the open ground, into the break of trees. She leaned heavily against the door, her arms adding weight to the wooden bar and holding it in place.

Chapter Twenty-eight

March 7, 2000: Winter is easing. We are witness to the dramatic changes in the weather, although our temperature inside the dome remains at a steady range of moderate. We have seen the snowfalls, and felt the winds against the glass. Life must be hard Outside, for any who have survived the virus.

To date, I have not received an answer to my message. If anyone is alive beyond the dome, either they have not chosen to reply, or cannot. It is possible that someone without computer skills has noticed my message — a child, perhaps — but doesn't know how to respond.

I choose to believe that there are others alive Outside, although scientific fact may prove me wrong. Surely, some people in the other biosphere dome have survived. And, what other places that we are unaware of might have provided food, shelter, and uncontaminated atmosphere for survivors? Were there underwater research laboratories? We have already proved that man can exist beneath the sea for an extended time? Were such places self-sustaining? My heart tells me this is true, although I have no proof.

Today, the last of the snow has melted. The sun brings an early warmth, and we see an abundance of life, Outside. We have seen animals move past the glass walls of our observation windows — dogs, rabbits, a great cat of some kind — and marvel at their existence. It seems the virus has not stricken the animal world with the same vengeance it has had for man. Only the caretakers have been eliminated, and not the flock of life that herds across the land, and sky, and sea. Was the sea spared? Are there dolphins? Are there whales?

I think about horses, their strong necks and flowing manes. The thought often comes to me as I stare at the land surrounding us, that one day I will be at the window and see a horse approaching the dome. I will go out, climb on that horse's bare back, and ride it away from here, across the desert.

We nine remain, seven adults and two children. My child will be born this summer, when the land on the other side of the dome is hot. We have kept physically well, careful of our lives in this unforgiving environment. We are the Survivors, and so must we remain.

The cursor blinked, waiting for the next entry into the log. Jessica stared at the monitor, realizing how little she sounded like the leader of this team. She had written nothing about the practical running of the biosphere, except for listing their numbers, and had taken no skills-based accounting of the other members of the group within her charge. It would matter to someone, perhaps, noting what each person had done to insure their survival. She ought to be recording this information, she ought to, but it simply didn't matter to her.

What mattered more were the people themselves. None of them were units to be measured, timed, and recorded. They were human beings, perhaps the last humans, and what mattered to Jessica was how they felt, how they coped, that they survived. Once again their luck had prevailed; there was no sign of contamination from Maggies breach of the seal. Her job had become very clear to her: keep these nine people alive, any way she could.

It was the year 2000. All her life, that had seemed such a faraway date. The year 2000, and mankind nearly gone from the face of the earth.

"We're not gone yet." She struggled with the negative, forcing the thought from her and holding it back with her own strength of words.

"We're not what, yet?"

Jessica turned, surprised to see Diana standing behind her. She saved the log entry and quickly exited the file.

"You didn't have to do that," said Diana. "I wasn't going to read it."

"You have a talent for entering a room quietly." Jessica ignored the other remark. Diana would certainly have read the entry, and would not have kept its contents to herself. "Next time, give me a little warning, like a knock on the door."

"You're getting secretive, Jessica. What is it you're hiding?"

"What do you want, Diana?" Jessica was tired of this nip and run game. Diana's moods had always been hard to anticipate. In the past, she had experienced big swings of temperament. Now the mood swings were more intense, and more frequent. At times, especially lately, Jessica wondered if Diana Hunt was insane.

"It's just some notes to myself." Jessica tried to put her off the track. "It makes it easier to remember planting schedules and other details. Nothing all that interesting."

"You're lying." Diana advanced a step closer, her eyes unnaturally bright and wide, her bottom lip slightly bleeding from where she had pressed her own teeth into it. "You were writing about me, weren't you?"

"No."

"Liar! You don't care if I die. You're only interested in those screaming babies . . . and the men. You think I'm afraid of you because you're team leader? Well, I'm not." The final words were accompanied with another step closer. "I'm not afraid of anything, anymore. You'd better remember that. If I wanted to, I could hurt you. I could hurt your precious babies, too."

Jessica felt the naked thrust of fear enter her. It probed her body like a sword, twisting and turning, as Diana spoke again.

"None of you care about me. I'm alone in this place!" she shouted. Diana turned around and started for the door. Almost there, she twisted back, the pupils of her eyes large as marbles. "I'm not staying here to die," she insisted. "You can do that if you want, so can the rest of them, but I'm not. You can't watch me all the time. I'll leave this place," she whispered.

"Diana—"

"I'll leave this place." The sound of her voice was like a hissing snake. "You tell the others. Explain it to them; you're the leader. I won't stay—not for them. If you try to stop me, I'll hurt you, Jessica. I'll hurt all of you. I know how, " Diana warned, and rushed out the door.

The threat left Jessica chilled. Diana Hunt was a brilliant woman, a well-educated biochemist and biolo-

240

gist, capable of analyzing and maintaining each of the living specimens within the carefully selected confines of Biosphere Seven.

It was Diana's research that had shown humming-birds to be a better choice than bees for pollination of plant species within the dome, because of the problem of ultraviolet light beneath the glass canopy. Not just any hummingbirds would do. Those chosen were birds whose nutritional needs were met by the variety of food source available, and whose beaks were the right length for reaching the nectar in the flowers and other plants chosen for the agricultural wing.

Diana had decided upon the nursery plants for the rain forest and the mulch and soil needed for each type of tree, or vegetation. She knew the nutrients required for the survival of each neem tree from central India, each halophyte plant which could be irrigated with salt water, each termite used to break down the grass in the savannah.

Diana Hunt was a bright star of intelligence, able to maintain the rich assortment of life nurtured within the boundaries of the dome. And Jessica was just as certain that a mentally deranged Diana was absolutely capable of carrying out the promise of her threat. If someone didn't stop her, she would destroy them all. . . .

"We need to confine her," said Quinn.

The entire population of Biosphere Seven, with the exception of Diana Hunt, met in the wooded shelter of the rain forest. The lyrical splash of the waterfall nearby underscored the setting, like atmospheric back-ground music for a film. Above them fell a gentle mist, dampening their clothes and hair.

"We can't do that, Quinn," argued Griff. "What

gives you the right to lock any of us into a cage? Diana was just scared. She hasn't hurt anyone."

"Not yet," Quinn reminded him.

"She's not going to, either!" Griff yelled, anger standing in cords on his neck and forehead. "I know her better than any of you," he claimed, furious with the look and smile that Daniel gave him at these words. "I'm going to knock you into a tree, Dan, if you don't wipe that grin off your fat mouth!"

"All right," said Jessica, stepping between them. "We're not here to fight among ourselves. We're here to decide what to do about Diana.

"Griff," she went on, "we all know how much you care for Diana, and we're not here to sit in judgement on any relationships she may have had, with anyone. That doesn't matter. All of us have handled fear in our own way." She glared at Daniel until the smirk disappeared from his face.

"What is important," she said to all of them, "is that we come to an agreement on what steps should be taken to protect ourselves from any action Diana might take to endanger all of us. She's been on the edge of a breakdown for a long time. I think it's finally asserting itself. In short, that means she could be dangerous."

"She hates the children," said Cathe, boldly staring Griff down. "I'm afraid of what she might do to Sidra, or to Trinity. They need to be protected, at least until we're sure we can trust her."

"She does hate them," Daniel agreed. "I've heard her cursing sometimes when Sidra cries, as if the sound drives her crazy."

"We can't take any chances," said Mike York. "We owe it to Maggie not to let anything bad happen to Trinity—or to Sidra," he added quickly, noticing the look Cathe was giving him. "I like Diana too, but if it comes down to a choice between the children and her

. . . I know which way I'll vote. Trinity's my son," he announced to them all. "I haven't been much of a father to him, but I'll protect him with my life if he needs it."

"I'd like a show of hands," said Jessica.

Five arms speared the air.

"I'm sorry, Griff. It might not be for long," said Jessica, "only until she's stable again. Believe me," she added, "none of us want this. As it is, she's just too great a risk."

"Sanctimonious shit! You've got no right to judge her. You're jealous. She's not a team robot like you, Jessica, and she doesn't worship at the little shrine of motherhood, like Cathe. She's a woman, with real fears and desires, as Quinn and Daniel already know. And she's not with either of them. She's with me. Hell, maybe she's the only one here who's really alive. I'm not going along with this, with any of you."

Quinn stepped closer to Griff. Jessica saw, and knew what he was going to do, but she let it happen. It was something Quinn was capable of and she wasn't, and it needed doing. With a hard right jab to the jaw, and a left punch to the midriff, Quinn knocked Griff to the ground.

He stood over the man sprawled like twisted limbs of storm-chaff on the forest floor, ready to knock him down again if he tried to stand up. "Listen, studly, you've impressed the hell out of us with your prowess, Dan and I are just drooling with envy." Griff struggled to sit up, but Quinn pressed a booted foot onto his chest, hard. "Stay down!"

He left the foot in place, pushing his weight on it for emphasis. "We don't give Jack-shit for your reasons, Griff. Like it or not, we're a team. A group vote is just that, a decision for all of us, including you."

"I won't be a part of locking her up," said

Griff, his face flooded red with anger.

"Then, we'll lock you up, too. If that's the way you want it. You can be with her." Quinn pressed the boot harder onto Griff's chest.

"You won't hurt her?" Griff asked, visibly weakening.

"No," Jessica answered for all of them. "She'll be treated well, I promise you."

"All right," he agreed at last. "God help me, all right."

Quinn stepped back and, gripping Griff's hand, pulled the man to his feet. "You go back on us, Griff," Quinn said in a low whisper meant only for the man before him, "and I'll kill you—no committee."

Griff pulled his arm out of Quinn's rough grasp. "Just make sure you keep your word about Diana, that's all. Just make sure."

"I'll arrange a place for her," said Jessica in conclusion, "someplace warm and safe. We'll do it tonight."

The object of the meeting completed, the group dispersed, each taking a different trail back to the habitat. Griff was the last to leave, waiting a long time by the waterfall. At last, even he headed back, leaving only the sound of the cascade hitting the rocks below.

She waited. When she was certain it was clear, Diana left the shelter of the rock cavern, stepped out from behind the veil of falls, and hurried away, sure of what she must do.

Chapter Twenty-nine

The riverbank down which John Katelo fell had saved his life. The eight-foot-deep earthen banks sheltered him from the sub-zero wind factor of the blizzard. Protected by a rock overhang from the worst of the snow, he waited out the storm.

His hands were useless, fingers frozen into hard icicles he could not bend, even to reach the wedge of venison tied beneath his anorak and shirt. Shivering with cold, hunger consumed him. He thought of the caribou meat, rich in fat, and would have eaten it raw could he have reached it, so desperate was his need.

Instead, he pulled the wolverine-furred hood closer around his face, leaving only a small, open circle to breathe, and shoved his wooden hands — they felt like tree stumps — beneath the belly of his anorak. He drew his knees up to his chest and huddled the extremities of his body into a solid block, minimizing heat loss.

The blizzard howled above him all that night. After a time the snow stopped, but the shattering cold held him in its deadly talons, making the climb to the top of the riverbank impossible. Late into the night, the winds dropped, as if a silent emptiness had descended upon the earth.

Looking up at the sky between the lapses in the fog of his breath, Katelo saw a bright harvest of stars in the clear, black heavens. He thought of dying here, in the ravine between the banks of the river, and fought against it. The sky was alive with life, and so was he. He stared at the far-off specks of light, willing himself to live until morning.

A brilliant sunrise cloaked the morning. Katelo felt its warmth through the hollow tunnel of his hood. His face ached as the smooth plane of heat touched it. With fingers that were still too stiff to bend, he shoved back the deep pocket of hide and fur, exposing his head to the awakening day.

Except for the thick wall of snow piled high atop the riverbank, and layered in the deep trench beside him, the view from where Katelo sat showed no sign that a blizzard had ever been. The sky was as clear as summer and golden with sunlight.

Tentatively, the Inuit stretched out one leg and then the other. His muscles burned as blood coursed back into tingling calfs, thighs, and feet. After a few painful moments, he tried to stand. The weight of his body came as a shock to the cramped muscles of his legs, and he did no more than stand still for long minutes, waiting until the spasms eased.

One step, and then another. He swung his arms in small arcs until the tightness in his shoulders loosened, until the heavy weights in his hands fell from him, and he could feel fingers, joints, and nerve endings scream in pain at being awakened.

He sang hard answers to the pain, sang in Chukchi, like his grandfathers, and stomped the earth with his feet, keeping a rhythm to the words. His hands moved too, striking the air like small clubs as he sang. It was a song of power, and of sorrow.

"I am hunter of the white bear. See me.
My clothes are seal and walrus skin.

My house is whale bone.

Winter ice does not stop me. I live.
Wind of knives does not cut my flesh,
or freeze my breath.

My brothers, the wind has taken.
Ice floes of rivers are my veins.
My eyes see death.

I move like the white bear, my brother.
I walk the land of snow and ice, standing.
Another day, I live."

The morning sun stretched across the face of the
ravine, melting the newly fallen snow into a wet, moving slush. Katelo knew that when all the snow had
melted, the slush would become a raging river, over-
flowing its banks and destroying all in its path. Spring
thaw would break the ice floes to the south and carry
the added weight of that melt-water into powerful, fast-
moving floods, churning rivulets and streambeds into
seething rapids across the land.

He had to get out.

Above him, crusts of earthen bank draped with
thick, fast-melting caps of snow broke off from the
sloping ledges and fell into the thousand-eyed monster
below — the moving cauldron of river. Chunks of jagged ice, rock, and broken tree limbs ground these huge
clots of earth into pockets of foaming mud.

Katelo chose his steps carefully. One slip, and he
would be lost beneath the crushing teeth of that river.
His fingers clawed and caved little hollows into the face
of the cliff, working steadily at pulling him above the
fury below. Still partly numb, his fingers slipped and
dug in, grasping the makeshift handholds like talons —
digging pointed claws into the earth.

All around him, breaks of sod and heavy snow cracked free and tumbled down embankments, hitting the water with the force of canon shots. Again and again, handholds crumbled away in his fingers, and he was left scrabbling the clay wall for anything to grasp. Anything to hold him above the white ribbon of death.

He thought of nothing but the climb. *Fingers there,* he thought. *Boot toe there.* And the sounds of avalanche echoed about him as high walls of snow slipped free and slid like moving mountains down the hard-packed banks, carving cliff-length gouges of rock and soil free with them.

He heard, but did not listen.

His right arm stretched overhead, reaching to the crest of the canyon and flailing into the marshy surface for something permanent to cling to, something to help pull himself up and over the muddy shelf. It was soft snow, and the more his hand burrowed and tunneled into the depth of it, the more wide mantles of overhang dropped clean of the snow-mounded cap, plummeting to the roiling torrent below.

Bracing his left foot on what seemed a sturdy outcropping of rock, Katelo shifted his weight to it and stepped up. With a splintering *CRACK,* the wall face gave way. The long sheet of solid ground thundered to the valley floor, and river, sending up a wake of water in its trace, shooting up the embankment slopes like a white foam net.

The taste of loam and ice crystals was in his mouth, along with the metal taste of fear. Katelo clung to the unbroken, vertical slant of earth just below the cliff top by the strength of ten fingers, his legs dangling in mid-air. The roar in his ears was the shuddering sound of his heart's blood, coursing . . . coursing. . . . In a moment, his fingers would slip, or the caving ledge would sheer off from the crumbling shoulder of embankment, and he would fall to his death.

Risking everything, the Inuit released one grip. With five fingers holding his entire weight, he scraped his free fist into the packed snow at the cliff's rise. Incredibly, his hand hit solid rock. In that instant, his palm opened and wrapped around the stone.

Quickly, Katelo transferred the bulk of his weight to the new hold on the steady rock. With his other hand, he found a second grip, and held to both. Using these handholds, he swung his left leg up and over the lip of the ravine and struggled to the top.

Not waiting even a moment to catch his breath, he scrambled back from the edge of the drop. Using knees and hands, he crawled across the surface, knowing his legs would sink into the deep snow. *Keep moving! Before the bank crumbles. Before the river claims it.*

A few feet away, the ground was solid—formed of the stone of mountains, not the soft-pressed soil that had shaped the earthen banks. He kept moving, to put the river behind him . . . to put it far behind him.

His breath came in hard gasps, and his right hand was bleeding from where he'd shoved it against the rock. His body trembled, every muscle rebelling against the strain of the last hour. Still, he kept moving.

The ground shook, even before he heard it—that great roar of an entire cliff face giving way, falling . . . shifting the mass of a million tons of earth . . . and thundering into the churning water below. Clouds of brown dust shot a mile into the sky.

John Katelo looked back at where he had been only moments before, remembering an Inuit saying: All things destined by the Spirit will be. Man dies only on his day of death.

He waited another moment, until his heart resumed a normal pace, untied the venison wedge from beneath his anorak and ate a few bites of the raw meat, then started again for home.

Today was not his time to die.

Salena Cross pressed her back harder into the jagged stone facing of the fireplace. She held the pistol, still loaded and ready to shoot.

The dog wanted in; that much was clear. His claws scraped on the wood, throwing his weight at the barrier. She heard him, standing she guessed, with forelegs high on the worked plank door, then sliding down the rough surface, claws dragging in the grain. But what would he do if she opened the door?

He had come back in the night. In the time she had waited for the dog to return — and she had known he would return — Salena had listened for any sound from the woods, any sign that Jack was still alive. Once, she thought she had heard a man's scream, but that was the keening of the wind in the blizzard. Surely, it had been inhuman, that cry — or so she hoped.

The dog would freeze to death in the savage cold.

If Kip had been a wolf, or a truly wild dog, he might have dug a den to burrow into through the storm. As it was, he had lived with the Inuit too long. The Samoyed knew his place was in the warm cabin, and his thick body hit the solid planks with added weight and insistence, the longer she refused him entry.

The dog had killed Jack.

She wanted to let him inside. Something strong in her hated the idea of allowing the slow death of an animal as beautiful as Kip. He had saved her life — when she'd been cowering against the cabin wall, knowing she would die — and Jack had tried to kill her. She wanted to let him in. . . .

Still, something strong in Salena held her in place with the pistol in her hands, with her back against the stone mantle. It was the image of Jack's body, savaged at the neck and dragged across white snow, leaving a

250

trail of blood. And the scream that had followed.

"I'm afraid," she said to the dog, as the hard scratching came less often and the thumps at the door grew steadily weaker. "I'm sorry. I want to let you in . . . I want to . . . but I'm afraid."

Through the dark hours of night, she watched the door, and waited. By dawn, only the infrequent, faint touch against the wood indicated the dog was still alive.

Twice, she went to the door and lifted the wooden bar, but did not turn the knob. Twice, she put the bar back in place, trembling with the terror of her fears.

It was over, she decided. No sound had come from the animal for hours. No movement. Was he asleep? Was he dead? The blizzard had stopped, and the day was clear and sunny. She knew she should go outside and face it, see the dog, see what he had done to Jack. She knew.

It was when she had turned away, when she wasn't looking, that the pounding started again, hard and demanding. High on the door, pounding. *How could he still stand?* Weight thrown at the plank boards. Again. Again!

"Stop it!" she screamed, pressing her hands to her ears. "Oh, God, make him stop it!"

If anything, the force at the door was more demanding, insistent and strong. The dog wanted to live. He had survived the blizzard, survived the freezing night, and wanted inside.

He wanted to live!

"All right!" she screamed, "all right," lifting the wooden bar. "Even if you kill me, I don't care anymore. I don't care."

Salena pulled back the heavy door. Standing in the open space, cradling a snow-covered Kip in his arms, was the Inuit hunter, John Katelo. A mirror of ice clung to his mustache and slight beard, sealing his mouth and preventing speech. His brows and lashes were frosted white, and his skin looked the color of window rime, a lifeless gray.

"John!" she cried, rushing to him. "Oh, John!"

Then she saw it, the dark shape huddled against the wall. Not the dog . . . not Kip, but the frozen body of Jack Quaid.

"No," she whispered, and stepped back. A burning taste of horror filled her mouth, and she swallowed hard.

Katelo moved past her, inside to the warmth of the fire, but Salena held to the frame of the doorway, staring at the silent mass lying on the hardwood porch.

Shirt cloth covered the terrible wound at his throat, a gaping hole torn from the center of it . . . unable to speak, unable to tell her of his presence. With only one arm, with legs so badly savaged, she couldn't look at them, he had dragged himself across the field of deep snow, back to the house. Desperately clawing, nails splintering the wood . . . heavy thumping . . . beating his fist again, again. All night, it had been Jack!

One arm rose above the slumped corpse, frozen solid, the stiff fingers of its hand still raking, even in death, at the unyielding barrier of the door.

Chapter Thirty

I can't let them lock me away, Diana rationalized, pouring the vial of chloral hydrate into the communal coffeepot. She had waited, crouched down behind the habitat wall, listening, until she'd heard Daniel—who had cooked the noon meal—walk back to the dining room, leaving the kitchen unoccupied.

She'd hidden the jar of clear liquid two days ago, in a cache of rocks at the outer edge of the rain forest, knowing even then that she might need it. Normally, the chemical was kept in her lab as a general purpose pesticide, an insurance against severe insect infestation.

As a chemist, Diana knew that in the right proportions, chloral hydrate also worked as a narcotic. Combined in most liquids, such as coffee, it would be tasteless and, about thirty minutes to an hour after ingestion, would induce a prolonged, dramatic sleep. Too much could cause difficulty in breathing, or in rare cases even death, but in the right proportion—and Diana was careful about the dose—it would put them all to sleep.

After pouring the contents of the vial into the simmering coffee and blending the liquid with a spoon, Diana slipped out of the habitat kitchen as silently as she'd come in, hurrying to a place of hiding to wait for the drug to take effect.

"Daniel, have you finished installing the outside lock on Diana's door?" Jessica put her mug down and reached for the coffeepot to pour herself another cup. Her mug was still half-full, but she only drank the heat off the top. She hated the taste of coffee that had cooled enough to drink without steam rising off it.

"I put a slide bolt into the door face, and an outside steel bar which lifts onto two brackets on either side of the doorway. With both in place, there's no way anyone could escape that room." Daniel took the handle of the pot from Jessica and poured himself and Cathe a second cup of coffee.

"And what are we going to do then . . . just lock the door and forget about her?" Griff pressed. He stood up, pacing the room with nervousness.

"Griff, we're not a mob of—"

"What we're going to do is help her," Jessica cut Quinn off before he got rolling. He had come from a long line of Irish insurrectionists, and being accused of playing the reverse, hard face of judge and jury left him on edge. He'd knocked Griff to the floor once already that day; Jessica didn't want to see it happen again. "We're not here to put Diana in jail," she went on, "just to protect ourselves until she's better."

"And if she doesn't get any better?" Cathe had spoken up. She held her daughter on her lap, feeding her bits of bread and mashed potatoes. "You heard what she said about the children. She hates them. I don't trust her, Jessica. I'm afraid to have her around Sidra, or Trinity. We have to protect them."

"She's not a monster!" shouted Griff. "Do you really think she'd do anything to an infant? Jesus, Cathe. She's part of us. She's just scared, that's all. She said some things she didn't really mean. We've all done that."

"Yes, we have," Jessica agreed with him, touching a gentle hand to his back. "I think you're right, Griff. I don't want to believe she'd hurt anyone, especially the children." He looked at her with grateful eyes. "Still, she's on the verge of some kind of a breakdown. That's clear from her behavior. We can't afford to take chances. It's best if we play it safe, at least for now."

"If and when we find her," added Daniel.

"There're a limited number of places to hide within this dome." Jessica leveled out the thrust of his comment, then sat back in her chair, exhausted.

The concern about Diana was only part of her physical tiredness. She knew the pregnancy was also taking its toll on her strength. Lately, she needed to rest in the afternoons, and that condition had her worried. With so much physical labor to do in the individual biomes—just to keep things running smoothly in the ag-wing, animal compounds, and aquatic tanks—the biosphere needed a full compliment of ten active workers to maintain adequate food production, necessary animal husbandry, air and water control, and all the other mandatory systems checks required for survival in the self-contained world.

If she didn't stay well enough to do her share of the work, how would the rest of them survive? *Self-important thought.* It was wrong to think that she carried them, emotionally or physically. They were a team of intelligent adults, fully capable of making the right decisions about governing their lives without her to guide them.

Still, it *was* her place to lead them. If she gave more importance to the role than that, it was nobody's fault but her own. Survival in the biosphere was more than a job, more than an experiment. It was their lives. It was the lives of the only population of human beings she knew to exist in the entire world. It was Eden, all

255

over again, and she'd be damned if they ate the wrong apple.

"You all right?" Quinn leaned close to ask her.

"Just a little tired. I need to rest for a while. Quinn, be careful that you don't—" She wanted to warn him about Griff.

"I know," he said, understanding the rest without the need of words. "I can ride people pretty hard sometimes. I'll back off with Griff. Dammit, Jess, I understand how he feels. But I won't let him risk all our lives for her."

"I know that," she said, touching her fingers to his cheek. "You have a caring heart inside you, Quinn. Don't be afraid to let it show."

She stood up and headed for their room. The walls shifted, moving in her sight. Undulating. Staring at them nauseated her, scared her, too. *Something wrong.* She felt dizzy, and so weak she wasn't sure she'd make it another step.

"Quinn!" She reached a hand behind her as the room began to swirl . . . as the floor slipped beneath her feet, away . . . away.

Weighted blackness caught her. Hearing the muffled cry of her own voice as she fell, she plunged into the blanketing depth of it.

Diana was ready with plastic cord to tie their ankles and wrists. She took more care with Jessica, because of the pregnancy, lying the woman at a comfortable angle on her side. The men, she tied with an additional length of cord, linking each one's wrists and feet behind his back. Cathe, she sat upright—hands and feet bound—like a bag of potatoes stacked against the wall.

Six bodies would be hard to drag to the locked room

256

by herself. That was where she planned to keep them until she had time to figure something else out. She'd slipped the key from Daniel's pocket after he passed out. *Don't want to hurt anyone.* That wasn't what she wanted at all. But, they shouldn't have tried to do this to her. They caused it themselves. Should have left her alone.

The first of them began coming to by the time she finished tying up the last. She stepped back, instinctively moving well away from danger.

They shouldn't have done it. They shouldn't have. If they had never threatened to keep her like an animal in a cage. . . .

"Wha . . . ohhh," Jessica groaned, bending her body almost double in pain. "What have you done? Ohh, God," she cried out. "Diana, what—"

"You're all right." Diana tried to calm her. "It's harmless. Chloral hydrate. Stop sounding like that! I only put you to sleep for a while. You'll be all right in a minute."

"I'm pregnant, Diana. Help me. Untie these cords. Don't do this. Ohh," she groaned again, her face blanching to the color of bone. "I might be aborting. Please, untie my legs."

Diana was breathing hard and fast. Her head felt dizzy with fear. It wasn't right, what Jessica was saying. She couldn't be miscarrying the baby. That wasn't the way it was planned. No one was supposed to get hurt. It couldn't be happening. Unless . . . unless Jessica was pretending. Diana held her breath, thinking. Jessica was smart. She'd use any means she had to save them.

"You'd better let us go, and now," demanded Quinn. His voice startled her, the sound of it hard and fast awake, not weak or groggy like Jessica's.

"Shut up!" she yelled at him, scared.

257

"Unless you're planning to kill all of us—"

"Shut up!" she shouted again, pulling back as if he might strike her. She was confused. Jessica was twisting on the floor, knees pulled up to her chest and moaning.

"Stop it!" she pleaded with Jessica. "There's nothing wrong with you. I know you're lying. You're lying!" she insisted. "Stop it!"

"Diana, baby, untie my wrists. Let me help you." Griff's voice was gentle, not like the others. Not hard and cold like Quinn's. Not trying to terrify her, like Jessica. He loved her. Griff loved her.

"It was just chloral hydrate." She turned to him. "That's all I put in the coffee. That wouldn't make her sick. That wouldn't make her lose the baby . . . would it, Griff? I didn't want to hurt anyone. I wouldn't do that."

"I know," his voice soothed her. "I know you wouldn't. You just panicked, that's all. I understand. You're scared. We're all scared, baby. Please, Diana. Untie my wrists. You know I love you. I wouldn't hurt you, ever. Let me help."

All of them were alert now, struggling with the cords that bound their wrists and ankles. She stared at their eyes and wondered for the first time how she could control six people by herself. She couldn't keep them tied all the time. Besides, now that they were awake, she was afraid to drag their bodies to the room. She was afraid to touch them.

Jessica cried out—just once—sharp and high.

"Dammit, Diana! Let her go!" shouted Quinn. "If you don't, you'd better be sure you kill me."

"You'd better kill all of us," added Daniel, his voice cold and threatening, stinging the air like the sound of a whip cracking.

"Leave me alone. Leave me alone!" she screamed

back at them. So scared. What could she do now? What could she do by herself?

"Listen to me, Diana. I only want to help you," said Griff.

He loved her; that's what he had said. *Words could lie.* But he had stood up for her to Quinn in front of them all. He had tried to talk them out of hurting her, and Quinn had knocked him down. Could she trust him? Could she risk letting any of them loose?"

"Ohh!" Jessica's knees hit each side of the hardwood floor as she twisted and twisted in a litany of pain.

All right, All Right, ALL RIGHT!

Diana snatched the carving knife from the table, ran with it clutched in her hands . . . her mouth open wide in an unsounded scream . . . the blade outstretched before her . . . straight to Griff, and cut through the knot of cords at his wrists.

The knife dropped from her fingers, hard, clattering to the floor. Terror pulsed with beating wings, its frantic rhythm pounding at her chest. Watching him. Would he help her? Watching his quick struggle with the knot at his ankles, and the cord falling away. Watching.

"Cut the rest of us loose!" shouted Quinn.

Diana stepped back, panic rising in her blood. Still Griff hadn't looked at her, hadn't lifted his head, his eyes, so that she could see what truth lay in them. Still . . . still. . . .

His arm snaked out and struck at her.

Never looking up, giving no warning, he propelled himself forward with the spring action of both feet. Grabbing, his fingers curled like claws to tear her flesh, grasping at the sheet of air where her leg had been. . . .

"Get her!" Daniel yelled. "Dammit, Griff. Get her!"

She ran. Stumble-hearted and pulling thin breath

259

into lungs that felt collapsed with fear, her legs carried her. Bone-jarring thuds as each foot hit the ground. Up her spine, into her brain. Running. Through the door. Outside now. Running.

"No, Griff! Don't go after her. Cut us loose," yelled Quinn. "Hurry up, man. Help me with Jessica."

She heard. Some part of her brain recognized that Griff had fallen behind, that he had stopped chasing her. Still, she ran. Nothing calmed the trapped-animal beating of her heart. Nothing quelled the snake pit of her mind, the words in her brain, hissing, *There she is! She tried to kill Jessica. Tried to kill all of us. Get her! Lock her up. She! . . . she! . . . she!*

Where to run? Where to hide? They'd find her. "You'd better kill me," Quinn had warned. Would he kill her now? If Jessica miscarried? But, that wasn't possible. Jessica couldn't die. She couldn't lose the baby.

Panic led Diana—panic which hadn't believed Griff would ever turn against her—to a place of desperate sanctuary. For her, nowhere within the dome was safe.

She stood by the emergency exit door in the savannah biome, muscles trembling, her chest heaving with shuddering gasps. Palms up, she placed her hands an inch above the pressure panel in the west wall. One touch would sound an alarm, seal off the unit from the rest of the biosphere, and open the sliding glass door to Outside.

Didn't want to press the panel. Outside was death.

An emergency door had been built into each biome in case of fire, earthquake, or other natural disaster. It was just such a panel in the desert biome that Maggie had inadvertently opened. And Maggie was dead.

God, she didn't want to touch it. She didn't want to die.

Voices coming toward her. Running, the floor shak-

260

ing with the weight of their thudding steps. Heartbeat pounding. She held her fingers closer to the wall, a breath above the panel.

"Diana . . . don't!" shouted Quinn. He was at the head, leading them after her like dogs in a pack. She was the fox; and they, the hunters.

"Stay back!" she cried out, her voice high and reedy with fear. "I'll do it. If any of you come near me, I swear I'll do it."

They were Daniel, Mike, Griff, and Quinn. Cathe wasn't with them. Where was Jessica? What had happened to her?

"Jesus, Diana. Please don't open that door. Think what you'd be doing. I'm sorry I tricked you. There wasn't any choice."

"I hate you, Griff!" she screamed at him. "Keep away from me!"

"Nobody's coming near you," Quinn promised. "We're going to stay right where we are," he said calmly, "and you're going to put your hands down, away from that wall."

"No. I don't trust you."

"Shit," swore Daniel. "Should we try to take her?"

"I'll do it," she said again. "Don't make me."

"Everybody stay put!" Quinn called to them all. "Take it easy, Diana. It's okay. Everything's going to be all right. We'll just wait till we all calm down, and then we'll talk."

"Get away! All of you, get away and leave me alone. I'm scared, and if I move too fast, I might push this panel by mistake. You're scaring me. Go away!"

"We can't do that," said Quinn.

"Where's Jessica? Is . . . is she all right?" Her voice was thready, pulled thin and flat.

"She's resting," Quinn explained. "Cathe's with her."

"I didn't mean to hurt anybody. I would never hurt

Jessica . . . but you were going to lock me away. I heard you. All of you. I couldn't let you do that," she cried.

"Come away from the door, Diana. If you open it, all of us will die." Quinn's voice was calm, but terrifying. "Don't touch it." He started forward, moving slowly.

"No, no, no!" she shrieked. "I'll do it. I'll do it, Quinn. I'll do it." Her hands were on the panel, fingers touching the cold metal. On the panel. . . . Ready.

Overhead, the speaker system crackled into a shrill of static sound. Loud sparks of blistered air filled the savannah biome, popping and snapping like crickets on a hot griddle. The moment froze. No one moved. All faces turned up, toward the message, and the messenger.

"Biosphere Seven, this is Josiah Gray Wolf. I don't know if you can hear my voice, the equipment here is faulty, but I hope and believe that you can, and that all of you are alive."

Someone within the gathered clutch of men cried out, softly as a sigh, "Oh, Jesus." Was it Daniel? No one else said anything, and the voice from the speaker went on.

"Jessica, Quinn, I'm on my way back to you. I've found others. Wait for me. Don't leave the dome. To all of you in Biosphere Seven, and to any others within the sound of my voice, this is Josiah Gray Wolf. I am coming home."

Slowly, Diana lowered her hands from the emergency panel. Her arms dropped to her sides, leaden weights, holding her down. The thoughts of her mind were high above her, floating on that same static current as Josiah's, in that same electric air.

Josiah's alive. The unvoiced thought channeled like

cold water to the dried rivers of her brain—awakening life. He had survived outside the glass closure of the biosphere. Outside. He'd lived . . . and found others.

"Diana." It was Jessica's voice, speaking to them from the computer room. "None of us must risk our lives now. We have reason for hope. This changes everything. We need you. We all need each other. I'm asking you to follow Josiah, and come home."

"I can't believe it." The careful face Mike always showed to others was unmasked, revealing a raw wound of shock and fear. "How could he—"

"Good God, Josiah," said Quinn, loud and full of strength. "You did it, Gray Wolf. You did it!"

"Did you hear?" yelled Cathe. She was running toward them, holding Sidra in her arms. "He's alive. Josiah's alive."

Diana felt the pall of death fall away from her. She had carried it like a shield since the day Josiah left them. The weight of that pall had worn so heavily, she couldn't lift her heart. Now, with this new hope, it dropped from her and left her free.

Hurrying, she moved to join the others. Whatever had happened, they were still her people. Nothing else mattered, nothing that had gone before. For the first time in months, her heart knew and recognized the quiet stir of simple joy.

Griff pulled her into his arms, and for that moment, she forgot how he'd betrayed her, forgot everything and let him hold her. "My God," he said, hugging her tight and squeezing the breath from her lungs, ". . . he said he found others."

"It's going to be all right," she said, calming him and brushing away the sudden rush of tears from his cheeks.

For the first time since the virus began, Diana Hunt believed those words. The rage of fear melted from her veins, and from her soul. She felt it drop away, a terrible, dark burden she had carried . . . and in its place, the clear light of hope.

Chapter Thirty-one

The revelation that Josiah was alive and coming back spurred a surge of activity in Biosphere Seven. Every area was looked at with new eyes. How would the others—the survivors he'd found—view the achievements here? What would Josiah think of all they'd accomplished?

Jessica didn't lose the baby, as she had feared. The chloral hydrate had made her sick, but by the following day, she was able to walk around the habitat with little or no side effects from the narcotic.

"I came close to losing you," said Quinn, shaken by the experience.

"We came close to a lot more than that," she reminded him, thinking again of Diana, standing with her hands on the exit panel. "If she'd gone through that door, all of us might have—"

"But she didn't." Quinn was quick to lead their conversation away from that memory. "And besides, with what Josiah's told us, maybe Outside isn't a death sentence, after all."

"Don't start thinking like that, Quinn." This kind of speculation scared her. *Maybe earth was safe again. Maybe the virus had burned itself out, or disappeared like an exotic flu. Maybe the nightmare was over.* The worst part was, she wanted to believe it, too, and had to force those hopes down in order to go on living in this smaller, enclosed world.

"I know what you're going to say." He put a hand to stop any lecture. "It's just that—my God, Jess—he's alive. Josiah survived. That has to give us the possibility of a chance. You can't deny us that."

"I'm not trying to deny us anything." She pulled back from this role of parent, she didn't want to mother anyone, especially Quinn. "I know it's exciting. I feel the same way." She had to make him understand. "But what happens if it doesn't turn out the way we want it to? If we allow ourselves to dream of leaving this place"—she painted the image for him in broad strokes, words that wore the hungry colors of life, of longing—"and then, for whatever reason, we can't leave."

"He's out there," Quinn argued. "Don't tell me no one could survive in that world. He's doing it. And others. He's found others, remember? They're living, too. Don't tell me not to hope, Jess. I can't do that . . . not even for you."

She let it go then. The truth was, she not only understood what Quinn was saying, but felt it in her own heart, too. It was why she still sent out the computer message in secret, week after week.

Are we alone?
This is Biosphere Seven.
Answer. Answer.

And now, finally, someone had.

Still, one part of Josiah's message haunted her. If he was alive, if he'd found survivors and earth was safe, what was the meaning of his warning? A line of worry marked her happiness, a line that began with the words, "Don't leave the dome."

Brad stood on the banks of what had once been known in the state of Texas as the Ware River, a branch of the Colorado. Grassy knolls, punctuated with spring wildflowers—bluebonnet, Indian blanket, white poppy, paintbrush, and wine cup—surrounded the promontory crests which sloped down to a wide expanse flowing with clear, mountain runoff.

It was this same river into which—months before, when dry and empty of life-giving water—the blind and stumbling man had fallen, and been saved. Just as he was certain of what had happened in this place on that day, of the physical presence of a savior carrying him from the dry riverbed, restoring his sight and his life, he was now equally certain of why he had been spared, and what he was meant to do.

Survival was exacting on the Texas high desert. He had lived through the trial of winter, and now the land rewarded him with bright colors, clean water, and abundant life. Just as the flowering plants pushed their way through the hard, dry earth, reaching their display of colors toward the spring rains and the mild, sunny sky, it seemed the animals, too, had found their tracks to the high desert, seeking the rich blue-green grass and the cactus plants bending low with sweet, ripe fruit.

The river was where they headed, hurrying across the red dust of the land. It was where they gathered. From his vantage point in the adobe shelter he'd made at the crest of the bank, Brad saw the impressive variety of life nourished by this hard country.

Herds of cattle came to the river to drink. Some were spotted white and black, with lean, elongated bodies, and carrying the long horns that marked them as less domesticated than their cousins, the Herefords. Some were reddish-brown, square-built and heavy, with the protective horns bred out of them.

After the cattle, came wide trails of bleating goats, then scattered lines of leggy deer, their eyes dark, and their quick shapes kicking up the seared brown dust at the first sign of danger. Coyote and fox crept out of their cooler dens, each leading a kit, or pups. And in the nearby rocks, a mountain lion up from Mexico waited.

Eagles spun a weave across the sky, their graceful spirals descending to the water's edge, and up again into the soaring blue. Black-winged hawks glided on warm thermals, and scavenging vultures, with their telescopic eyes, hunted from above for anything too weak for survival in this unforgiving place.

Brad wasn't plagued by mosquitoes or flies—the desert of Texas didn't have many of those—but learned early to be wary of scorpions living under rocks, and thick tarantulas with black-furred legs, moving across the desert sand alone, or in a glistening wave of thousands.

There were bright-eyed prairie dogs and perky rock squirrels, slow-moving armadillos, and blue-black snakes as thick as his forearm. In the spring, the earth gave up its bounty. All of them, the rugged survivors of this country, met at this source of life—the river.

Brad planted a sapling on the left bank of the river, a cedar. Its roots would grow deep into the reddish clay in search of water. Cedar and oak were the noble trees of Texas. Their boughs had shaded the exalted, and the dead. Now this cedar would shelter the new temple which he would consecrate on this site.

His was a vision of continuance and regeneration, that the world would renew and abide. He held to this faith as a scripture, unwritten except in the context of his mind. The strength of the words were there, moving like swift-flowing channels, waiting to impart knowledge. Waiting. . . .

Each day when he awoke, Brad bathed in the cold water of the river. His world had been begun again in the dry sandbed of this place. To him it was the life-giving womb from which he had been reborn.

The land adjoining the river was sacred, hallowed ground, where the vision he remembered had lifted him from the dust and gravel — from the dark fringe of death — and carried him in the strength of gentle arms, above the shallows, toward the rise of the bank where the cedar was now planted, there nourishing his body and soul.

It was her place, this river. Her earth, too.

He had been alone since those days of healing, alone with thoughts that stemmed like vines thrusting up from a barren soil, spreading a transforming veil of life over the reaches of an isolated ground, this haven, this calm. In his solitude, he had not been lonely. His world was alive with new thought, new passion, new belief.

In his awakened consciousness, a preparation was taking form. His awareness of that consciousness grew with each day, expanding past the center of his own being, to reach beyond himself . . . to others. Whom the others might be, he didn't know, only that they were coming, and that he needed to be ready.

In simple ways, he tried to prepare himself for their arrival — tried to light the candle of his soul, so that they might see its burning flame. He had become the prophet waiting in the desert, the consecrated priest. He had become the messenger, the spoke of the wheel.

In the evenings, he saw light shining from inside Biosphere Seven. Several times—only in the cover of dark—he had gone within a hundred feet of the dome. *Where Jessica was* . . . the thought pained him like an aching nerve. *Where Jessica was.* . . .

He had been severed from her life by the cold glass walls of the satellite hemisphere, by the virus, by the very nature of his survival. He hadn't elected to become what he now was; it had been decided for him. He had been chosen.

That didn't mean he didn't think of her.

Jessica believed him dead. He remembered the terrible sound of her voice, the way she had cried his name . . . that last day. Quinn had kept her from coming out to him.

"Brad, don't go!" The sound of her voice had been a physical pain tearing through his gut and scorching a line of agony across his chest. "Don't leave me! Brad! Brad!!"

He couldn't allow himself to bring that kind of hurt to her again. *If she knew he was alive* . . . *if she saw him outside the biosphere walls* . . . *what would she do? Could she lose him twice?*

And if Brad saw her again, could anyone—including God—keep them apart?

In the daylight, he kept away from the sun-glittering dome. His place was by the river, by the adobe house, and the tree he had planted. But by night, he would often hike to within a thousand feet of the dome—its glass walls shining from within, like a lesser moon in the darkness—sit at the edge of the

270

high, flat mesa, and dream . . . not the fretful images of sleep, but the wide-awake dreams of love.

In isolated, far-flung pockets of the world, other men and women — few in number — gazed at the distant stars in the night sky and wondered. Why had they been chosen? Why had they survived when the rest of their world was gone? Why were they alone?

Without evidence of hope, many of them retreated into shock and silence. It was a state from which they would not recover. There was no one to share their fears, no one to understand the terrifying emptiness of the cities. When they cried out, there was no one to hear the little child in their voices, afraid and alone. And so they were silent.

The lucky ones met another survivor and formed bonds greater than any unions they had ever known. They were bonds of human-to-human, and in the vast, barren reaches of mankind, this union was the solid core upon which they began to rebuild their world.

In the first days of the outbreak, the necessities of life, food and shelter, were still possible to attain. Then the trucks bringing supply shipments to the markets stopped deliveries in the early weeks of panic, for fear of possible contagion. Quickly, stores were emptied of everything edible, and people hoarded whatever goods they had. Basic foodstuffs like bread, fresh meats, vegetables, and fruit disappeared from shelves. Before the first month was out, all groceries and virtually all stores of every kind had locked their doors for business. In most communities, there was no food to be had.

Soon, death winnowed the chaff from the competition. Those who had hoarded supplies of canned goods, in death, became the suppliers to those who had managed to survive. In a few well-stocked kitchen cupboards, were the requisites for life.

Going into those houses was the worst, for as often as not, there were the remains of bodies lying on the floors, sitting in chairs, even floating in bath water. Death came in haunting images to so many that hospitals became simply the walled repositories of the dead, and could not begin to handle the ever increasing numbers. In the final days, people died where they fell, and no one made any attempt to move them.

For some, survival meant that they had not been directly exposed to the virus. They lived in isolated environments—on atolls and largely uninhabited islands, in primitive rain forests and jungles where the native population never came into contact with cultures other than their own, or in sheltered laboratories like the biosphere satellites and undersea habitats—and were unaware, at least for some time, that anything had changed in their smaller world.

For others, survival was a fact of genetic preference. Through chance biological favoritism, their systems blocked receptiveness to the virus. An ancestor, with whose illness they still bore a genetic link, protected them.

For those like John Katelo, the link was strong enough to prevent any invasion of the viron molecules into healthy cells. He, and the exceptional few like him, did not get sick. Even those who stayed in the midst of the cities, in the heart of the disease, never became ill. They were the fortunate. They were the blessed. They were immune.

A sprinkling of others were spared, those like

Brad McGhee. In them, the genetic link was distant enough to allow the virus to infect some host cells, yet block enough to prevent or postpone death. Those who had become ill with the virus and survived were now immune. They were like the first group; safe. Those whose systems had fought the sickness off until now — like Josiah Gray Wolf, and Salena Cross — were still vulnerable. They were question marks.

In all the world, less than seven thousand people survived. Of these, five thousand would live through the next six months. Death would come in many forms. It was not always at the breath of fever and blistered skin. Death came to some, like Jack Quaid, in the fierce splendor of nature: in snow, in a rushing river, in a broken roof beam from an earthquake. Death caught them, as the sacrifice to nature would always choose some. They were the unlucky, the ill-starred. They were the offerings.

From a world of over five billion, an entire human race of five thousand — some within walls that protected and separated them from the deadly atmosphere — was all that remained. From this scattered thread of life, a new humanity was being formed.

In the cries of the newly born, the hope of mankind sounded across the face of earth.

Chapter Thirty-two

In the year 2000, the inhabitants of Biosphere Seven prepared to leave the shelter of the satellite dome. In each, thoughts of freedom unfurled like flags, rippling excitement with the prospect of going home. They had been conceived of the planet earth, not of the artificial world of this glass-walled universe. A yearning arose in all of them, to return to that from which they had come.

On the first day of summer, 21 June, 2000, the morning of the solstice, Jessica Nathan's son was born. He was a round-faced infant, with his mother's dark hair and his father's serious, blue eyes.

The labor had gone on for nearly two days — and after, Jessica lay limp as wet rags beside her newborn son. He was quiet, as if exhausted, too.

"Leave it to you to pick the longest day of the year to have a baby," Cathe joked. "You always work too hard."

Jessica tried to smile, but her energy was gone. Her body felt as worn as a plane of smooth glass, flat and empty. She had lost blood, perhaps a lot of it at the last, but what she felt was more than just exhaustion. What she felt was loss.

Within her was a well of tears that would not come to the surface, a river of pain for all they had been through. *Why now?* she wondered, with the blessing of her child nestled in the bend of her arm. *Why now, this reckoning of sorrow?*

"Jessie? Are you all right?" Cathe's face wore an older look than it had only a moment before, one that recognized this pain, one that remembered loss.

"I don't know what's wrong with me," Jessica tried to explain. "I should be happy. I have a son. He's healthy and I'm alive. Josiah's coming back, and . . ."

"And you're worn out. That's what's wrong," Cathe told her. "You've carried the heaviest weight of this place for too long. It's time to let the rest of us share the load." She adjusted the sheet, covering Jessica's arm.

"It isn't that. It isn't *just* that," Jessica corrected herself. "I feel like something's pressing on me." She struggled to make Cathe understand. "There's something closing in . . . something I can't stop."

"Come on." Cathe put her hands out as if to stop the frightening words. "Most of this is because you've just had a baby. You're tired. Rest. You'll feel better tomorrow, I promise."

Jessica didn't have the energy to argue. She nodded, and let Cathe go away. But the pain didn't go away. It stayed, a coiled, hard ache, pressing on her like a warning. . . . *Something waited. Something soon.*

Josiah Gray Wolf leaned against the cool limestone wall of the cave. The summer heat scorched the earth outside this shelter, but the temperature was only eighty at the mouth of the rock, and cooler the deeper you went back into the caverns.

It was too hot to travel with the old one. She held them back, Mrs. Oliveras, with her arthritis

275

and her heart condition, but they waited with patience. She was one of only ten survivors, and each one—each human life—counted as a victory against the yawning maw of death. They would wait for Mrs. Oliveras as long as necessary. She was one of them, the select.

Josiah had gathered the living to him, like a patriarchal shepherd searching for lost lambs and leading them back into the fold. For all the miles he had crossed, these ten were the total victory, the final yield.

All were Americans. He had not chanced crossing into Canada or Mexico, but kept the van on familiar roads, where he was more confident of finding gas in parked cars, or available from the fuel pumps of some stations—those powered by wind generators or battery—and canned food in homes along the way.

They were eleven, including him, and their numbers were seven women and four men. There were no children. This was not because the women were not mothers—some were, and had given birth to daughters and sons—but there were no survivors among them who were children. The little ones had been among the first to die.

The world was a solemn place without children. The sound of an infant's cry would be a welcome herald. Josiah missed the noises made by a troop of running kids, spontaneous laughter, boisterous shouts, and singing—the voice of a child like wind through a reed, high and fragile.

He wondered, leaning against this sea-etched rock, if Cathe Innis had conceived a child from their single night together. Did he have a son? A daughter? If so, would he live to see it?

Anna Oliveras walked from the darkness at the back of the cave toward the light, where Josiah rested. She was white-haired, croned with age—her back curved into a dowager's hump—and had a body that was rounded and softly padded all over, like a comfortable pillow. Josiah thought her beautiful.

"Feeling better, Anna?" The others called her Mrs. Oliveras, out of respect for her years, but she had asked Josiah to call her by her given name. It was an intimacy between them, marking their relationship as exclusive.

"A little sunshine will help my knees," she answered, moving unsteadily on the uneven rock floor. "A body has want of heat at my age. We are cold, bloodless things, past eighty."

"Sit down," he said to her, and stood to help her lower her weight to the hard floor.

She stretched her legs into the hot tracks of sunlight, just at the rim of the cave. Without hesitation, she hiked up her skirt, halfway to her thighs, and eased back against the porous rock. "Ah, that's better. It's too cool in those deeper chambers. How do all of you stand it?"

The deeper chambers she referred to were the caverns tunneling into the subterranean core of the mountain. The chasms there, smoothed from the stone walls by ancient glaciers and rivers, were twenty degrees cooler than the surface air. All except Mrs. Oliveras found these inner cavities a relief from the desert's blistering heat.

Josiah let the question go with a smile. It wasn't really meant to be answered; at least, he didn't think so. Mrs. Oliveras said a lot of things that sounded like questions but weren't: "I wonder where

277

this road's going, Josiah." Or, "Can I afford a trip like this?" And when he'd first met her, she'd asked, "Is this the end of everything?" That question hadn't wanted an answer. He hadn't offered one.

It wasn't that she was senile. She was sharp and witty. Quick. She asked these questions because the answers were already there. He believed she just wanted him to know. She liked him.

"We're going to be all right," he said to her for no apparent reason. They talked to each other like that sometimes, him saying something, her saying something, each of them believing the other would understand. Usually, they did.

"Tell me about your children, Anna." He wanted to understand her, this woman. He wanted to see her life through her eyes, and hear it through her words.

"My children?" She pulled into herself, eyes moving away from his watching stare. A curtain of sorrow draped lines down her face. She was old. Wrinkles were trenched deep. "My children," she said again, the word like a wound he had opened.

"I'm sorry," he started. "You don't have to—"

"My children were many," she began, looking out at the hard, afternoon light. "They were dark-haired sons with large, wet eyes like oil in a deep well; blond daughters with pale skin and eyes like a summer sea. My children had bright, red hair, eyes the color of grass; brown hair and eyes of damp earth. My children were many," she said again, and sighed.

"We're still alive, Old Mother."

She visibly pulled back from her grief, made a sound like, "Umm," and touched his arm. "We are," she agreed. "Man is the endangered species now, but we are alive. We will struggle, and who knows, some of us may go on."

"We are going on," he insisted.

"Yes"—a wan smile played at her lips—"but we have lost so many."

Josiah said nothing. It was true nothing could heal the ache of that loss. It would be borne as a permanent weight on the shoulders of mankind.

"Tomorrow, we'll travel again," he told her, hoping to lighten her mood.

"Good. The others are ready to go forward. They're anxious to see your friends. I have held us up too long."

"You'll like my friends." He tried to interest her in the journey.

"Tell me again how it will be," she urged him. "Tell me of the new world you and the others will create."

"You'll be there."

She said nothing, but her eyes said she didn't believe it.

"Think of what we've been given," he began, knowing she wanted to hear the story. "We are few, but the earth is large and generous. This time, we will act as one with the water, and air, and land— act as part of the whole. If nothing else, we've learned that the earth is a living mother who nurtures us, and whom we cannot abuse. She is our source of life."

"You knew this long ago, Josiah." Anna Oliveras closed her eyes, as if remembering. "Your people, the Indian nations, knew the land was alive . . . felt it in their blood and in their minds."

"We saw a truth that some wouldn't see," he agreed. "It's taken humanity as a whole a long time to come to it, the belief that this earth is the womb of our life. The world has been given a second chance to learn that lesson."

"Will they learn it now, Josiah? Will they see what has always been before their eyes?"

"It's our last chance, Mother." He reached for her hand. The veins were high ropes beneath tents of sagging skin. Blood coursed a thread of life within those veins, pathways of all that had been part of this woman, and other women before her.

"You must take my children there," she said to him. Her eyes were sharp stones, piercing him. There was an urgency in those eyes, a need which could not be ignored. "Promise," she said, a cold wind following the uneasiness of her words.

He laughed, trying to make light of it. "I want to get home, too."

"Promise," she said again, the stones imbedding deeper into his soul.

"I promise," he swore, feeling that it was more than words he gave this woman. A chill came over him, and he felt the tremble of it quake through his flesh . . . into bones . . . into blood. "I promise to lead them," he said, knowing this was what she wanted.

"Don't be afraid, Josiah." She comforted him with the touch of her vein-gnarled hand. "Where you go, I will be beside you."

"I don't believe in hope anymore," said Elizabeth Cunningham, rising from their lovemaking, standing and brushing her long hair in the cool shelter of the inner cave. "I lost all such faith when the virus came, when I watched my children dying, my husband . . . when the outbreak took everything from me. Hope doesn't bring a new tomorrow. I think only of today."

Josiah watched her moving in the half-light, her arms raised over her head, breasts thrust forward, tying back her light-brown hair with a ribbon and a clip. In that stance, she was like a sculptured statue of Venus rising from the sea, or a huntress naked to the waist and reaching for the arrow quiver at her back. She was beautiful, her body arched like a crescent moon, wisps of hair flowing from her brush.

Watching her, he remembered. . . .

He had found her sitting on a hillside in Austin. It was sunrise. He was driving by, noticing the swirls of color in the morning sky — and she was there. She turned when she heard the sound of the truck's engine, stood and waited for his approach, not rushing down to meet him. At first, he thought her aloof, but it wasn't that. She was detached.

Her world and all the things she knew of it were gone. It was the same for all of them, but Elizabeth carried the hurt differently. She carried it as a shell around her. She insulated herself with this barrier, as though she too were in a sphere, safe and hidden.

"Tell me," he asked, "how did you survive the virus?"

She shrugged. "Don't know."

"Why are you sitting up here? What are you waiting for?"

"Death." It was a simple statement, as if she believed there were no other possibility.

Her attitude annoyed Josiah. She *was* alive, after all. She'd been given a gift and was wasting it. So many others had fought desperately to live, while she. . . .

"Elizabeth, would you come with me?"

He told her about Biosphere Seven, that he was looking for other survivors—if there were any—and that he would keep looking and take anyone he found back with him to that place, to begin a colony living near the dome.

"I'd like you to come with me," he said again, reminding her that she needed to answer—that she needed to break the cold-as-death stare, and respond.

"I don't think so," she said, and turned away. It was casual, as if she'd said, *No thanks, I don't care for any dessert.*

"You don't think so?" He couldn't understand it. For him, finding another person alive outside the dome was the greatest thing that ever happened. How could she be so indifferent? "What do you want?—just to wait here until death catches up to you?"

"Maybe." She'd dismissed him, assuming an avid interest in the changing patterns of the sky.

Frustrated and angry, he almost walked away. Almost.

"Look—" he was irritated by her sovereignty, her independence—"if you're determined to give up, fine. I think there might be other people who lived through this, like the two of us, and I'm going to keep searching for them. When I find them, we're going to start again. If you'd rather stay here and wait to die, then you don't belong with me, anyway. I'm a survivor—not a victim." He walked

282

off, furious, willing and ready to leave her.

Behind him, he heard the sound of her hurrying down the hill. Following. "I'll go," she agreed, without any explanation.

That had been enough. For then.

In the next few days, they found no one. They were alone, and slowly, she revealed herself to him. The name, Elizabeth Cunningham, had seemed slightly familiar to Josiah when he'd first heard it. She'd been an author of children's books. He had read one of her novels, giving it to his nephew for a birthday present.

She told him how afraid she'd been when everyone started dying, how she believed each day that she would die, too. Once started, her words were like a river which would not stop its flow. She told him of her husband, a strong, intelligent man who rode horses and climbed mountains, a man she'd loved . . . and of her two children—a son four, and a daughter two; they had been the last of her family to die.

She told him all that there was of her life, and more.

After a wealth of days alone, after they had learned to know each other as few men and women ever know another human being, she came in the night to his bed.

"I'm cold, Josiah . . . cold inside and out. I was shivering just now—trembling from fear, and grief, and loneliness—and I thought maybe, if you wanted. . . ."

He welcomed her into the loving embrace of his arms. Since the morning they'd met on the hill, they had shared each waking moment of their days. Now they shared their love.

The next day, in Florida, they found two more survivors: Emily Pinola from Tampa, an eighteen-year-old with the permanent stamp of worry in her eyes, and the old woman, Anna Oliveras. These two were companions, heading north.

They became a unity, these three women: young girl, mother, and the old one. Although he led them, Josiah felt peripheral to the cycle of life that bound them together. He was the product of these women—of women like these: the lover, the father, the child. They, in their three stages, were the continuity of life.

Josiah and the women continued together, through many days of empty cities and deserted roads, finally picking up Skeet Hallinger—a former construction worker—on the outskirts of Atlanta, Georgia. Skeet was twenty-nine, well muscled, blond and tan. He had been completely alone for the last six months, and had thought himself the only human alive in the world. Unable at first to put his thoughts into words after so long an isolation, his eyes showed he was glad to see them.

In New York, they found their sixth companion, Stephen Wyse. He had a gun in his back pocket, a knife strapped to his leg, and a cartridge of Mace hanging from a loop at his belt. He was skittish—at sixteen, too young for the world to have played such a game on him—and scared as hell. He joined them because there was nothing else he could do, but he didn't trust them. He didn't trust anyone.

Just outside of Iowa, on the Nebraska border, they met up with T.J. Parker, farmer and father of three sons—all dead. Parker almost didn't come with them; it was too hard leaving the graves of his wife and children. He said that without them, he didn't want or expect anything out of life. He told Josiah to leave him, to take the others and go.

It was Mrs. Oliveras who convinced T.J. to accompany them. She talked to him like a grandmother in words that were gentle and healing. Something she said broke through his hurt and sorrow, to the well of life within him. In the end, he stood at the graves of his family, said goodbye, and followed the others on the road.

They drove through the states of Nebraska, Colorado, and Utah—finding no one. The land was populated with animals, but humans were nonexistent. It was as if an angry hand had swept them off the face of the earth with the flick of its wrist. In Nevada, they found Crystal.

Crystal Rivers was a showgirl (had been one, before the virus) in Reno. When everyone started dying, she stayed on at the casinos, dressed in expensive clothes, lived in the best hotel suites and swam at the beautiful pools—until the water turned green with algae and even the best bourbon couldn't blind her to the horror around her. Beautiful, and too silent, her eyes said something had hurt her, something even before their world had died. She came with Josiah and the others, leaving behind the nightmares of whatever that hurt was.

In a grass-green forest of Central California, climbing the hills from Santa Cruz, they chanced upon two young women: Natalie Peters, Merry Logan. Each young woman had been a student at the University of California at Santa Cruz: Natalie a junior, and Merry a senior that year. They hadn't known each other before the sickness struck their families, their friends. When the death throes were over, only these two were left. United by proximity, by age, and fear, they became friends.

In Arizona, just outside Flagstaff, they found the last of their numbers, Rosalina Santos, a woman in her mid-thirties, with a round, comfortable body, and a style of dress as colorful as a Mexican piñata. Everything about Rosalina was a circle, from the brown moon of her face, to her ample bosom and hips, and the curved hills of her legs.

They first saw Rosalina briskly walking down the dusty road, carrying on an animated conversation with herself. She was laughing, moving one heavy arm in the air to illustrate a point, her eyes dark and excited.

"Is she crazy?" asked Stephen Wyse, drawing the cartridge of Mace into his hands.

"No," Josiah assured him. "I think she's just lonely. We all need to talk to someone, don't we? She seems happy; look at her."

Rosalina joined the small party of survivors, an energetic, joyous woman. Quickly, she became a friend to all, especially young Stephen, with whom she immediately adopted the role of mother. It was Rosalina with her soft smiles and warm eyes who finally convinced the frightened sixteen-year-old to put away his protectors of Mace and knife and gun, not get rid of them — for he was not ready to do that — but put them away. In her moon face, bright eyes and rounded form, he found a world of trust.

They went on together, these eleven, driving through other states, searching. Where they could, they lived off the land. Where they couldn't survive without help, they took sustenance from the storage rooms and kitchen cupboards of those who had died.

In the late summer of the year 2000, they gathered at the caverns of Carlsbad, New Mexico. From this place, they would begin the last portion of their journey, traveling with Josiah Gray Wolf back to Claypool, Texas, and Biosphere Seven—to the colony of hope and life they would start, just outside the dome.

That night, in the cave at the edge of the opaline desert, the old woman, Anna Oliveras, died. The assembly of ten buried her within the shelter of the cave, deep at the back of the caverns, in a space where the well of time would not touch her.

To Josiah, the death of this one woman just before they reached their final destination was hard to accept. In her way, she had been a comfort to him, a softness when all the world was hard and unyielding. He would miss her.

In the morning, Josiah kept his promise to the old one. He had gleaned the scattered harvest of the nation's people, returning with them back to where he had begun . . . leading the survivors home.

Chapter Thirty-three

By summer, John Katelo and Salena Cross had made their way down from Canada to the sloping hills and wide grasslands of Montana. The land was good, cattle plentiful, and there was a harvest of naturally reseeded crops in the nearby fields. They picked a log house they liked, and stayed.

The house was two stories, with a spacious wooden balcony fronting the master bedroom, an extended roof-line on all sides of the structure to shade the outside walls, with summer sleeping rooms below. The balcony, and the back of the house, looked out on a lake of such pristine beauty, Katelo felt in awe of it. The soft incline of trees and captured sky were mirrored in the blue-gray oval. He called the place, Mirror Lake.

The lake was fed by a mountain stream which in its ancient past — as a ice age glacier — had broken through the solid rock pinnacles surrounding the valley, and hollowed out the deep basin which now contained the water of Mirror Lake. Unlike most glacier-based water reservoirs, this one was alive with fish, a bird sanctuary, and a natural game reserve. It was the perfect place to settle and begin their lives on the rich bounty of this land.

In all the time since Katelo left Siberia and Biosphere Four, Salena Cross and Jack Quaid had been the only survivors he'd seen. It was Katelo's suspicion that Quaid was already sick from the outbreak when he died, and that if Kip and the freezing storm had not killed him, the virus would have.

He kept this thought to himself, but the idea worried him. If Quaid could have kept free of the virus for so long, and still become so sick with it — well after he'd believed he was safe — the same could be true for anyone else. Death was still with them: in the air, in the water, in the animals they ate. Which thing was dangerous? Which thing would bring on the sickness?

In this place, Katelo did not hear the call of spirits. He felt at ease here, a resting spot after the long journey. With Salena's help, he rebuilt the corrals and fenced cattle pastures. Slowly, they gathered livestock: three milk cows, a bull, and twenty-five head of mixed cattle, several sheep, two sows, a hen house full of chickens, one remarkable rooster, and four saddle-broken horses. To this, they added Kip, who had learned to accept his food from his master's hand, and guarded the ranch from wolves at night.

When John Katelo stepped onto his balcony at sunset and looked out at the incredible vista before him — white-winged birds lowering to the water's edge, an owl hooting a greeting to the rising moon, and the easy low of cattle in the fields — he knew that he had found a paradise.

Each day, each hour, each moment, he remembered the blessings of his world. He never thought of them as blessings. He was not Christian; the word had little meaning for him. Instead, he thought of them as unions, or blendings with the

Living Spirit of Earth. He thought of them as sacred marriages.

I will give you the lake, the wildlife, and the land; you will care for them.

John Katelo didn't know the stories of Genesis, of Adam and Eve, or the garden. He had never heard of a place called Eden. What he knew was sunrise when it lifted like an orange cloud over the glassy surface of the water; he felt a fullness in his breast at the trees greening a perfect oval around this new homeland, and listened for the voice of the Spirit in each thing . . . in every moment of life.

Salena stood beside him outside the log house one summer night, their dinner of fresh-caught trout cooking in an iron skillet over a small, open fire. Hot oil popped and sizzled in the pan, and the smell of crusty, fried fish seasoned the air, making his mouth water with hunger. It was black night above their heads, and a shimmer of jewels scattered across the heavens like glittering ice.

He knew no words to tell her how grateful he was that she was here, sharing this night with him. Yet, something in him needed her to understand, to know how he felt. How rich. He waited until she took the skillet from the fire and moved the cooked fish to a warm platter. Then he touched her back.

"Are you afraid, Salena?" he asked, other words falling away from his consciousness, in a sweep of tenderness toward this woman.

"Of what?" Her eyes were gentle orbs, liquid with love and beauty.

He didn't know how to explain his concern for her. The land was so big and empty. A woman might feel . . . he didn't know. His thoughts were of his mother, and the aunts and sisters of his family.

They had been happiest in a group, working together, laughing at secrets as women did. One alone, like Salena, without a friend to share the hidden world of sisters . . . would she feel lonely?

"When you are quiet in your heart at night," he asked, "do you think of the spirits of the dead? Do they brush your skin and speak to you?" He was afraid of what her answer might be, afraid she would become like Shadow-Woman of his grandmother's tales, and disappear in the smoke of the fire. "Are you unhappy, Salena, without others?"

"No," she said quickly, her eyes judging him. "Are you?"

"No, no," he said, sure of his answer, still unsure of hers, "but Salena, is it enough?"

"Together," she said, "we are enough."

A heaviness, darker than the blackness above him, lifted from his chest and winged its way clear of his soul. He felt it leave, and the clean, sweet hollow of where it had been fill with a bright pain of simple gladness.

He listened carefully, but nowhere was there a sound of spirits calling from the unyielding dark. Only the woman beside him. Only the whisper of their two breaths in the night. And the soft lapping of water against the damp curve of the shore.

"I've decided. When Josiah brings the others, I'm going to leave the sphere." Diana dropped her creme-and-black-patterned silk robe to the floor and stood naked in the cool shaft of moonlight. She let the soft luminescence wash over her, as if bathing in a stream of white mist.

"Come here," said Griff, ignoring her words and

leaning from the foot of the bed where he lay naked, reaching his hand to her thigh.

She moved to him, let him touch her. Lovers was an easy word for what they were. They shared bodies, shared heightening strokes of fingers on fevered flesh, shared and killed the lust that swelled within them . . . but that was all.

They were not partners in the way Jessica was with Quinn, or Cathe was with Daniel. Their reason for being together was one of fear, not love. Fear of a global death outside their door. Fear of a world peopled with ghosts. Fear of being alone — forever.

She lay beside him and stroked the hair at the back of his head as he kissed her breasts. From the point of each nipple, he drew a slow line with the tip of his tongue to the center of her belly . . . circling . . . circling . . . and from there moved downward to the warm softness of her inner thighs. Her body arched to meet him, and when she felt him swell inside her, she cried out in pleasure. Theirs was passion; theirs was not love.

After, when both had cooled of the heat which claimed them, when the pounding of their hearts had slowed, Griff came back to her earlier words. It had taken him this long to face the thought that he might lose her.

"It's too early to think of going Outside yet," he warned. "Too soon."

"Josiah's alive." Her body was still naked when she rolled away, but she covered it now with a sheet.

"He said to stay within the dome," Griff argued. "There's something we don't know yet. He wouldn't have said that if there wasn't a danger. Think of

Maggie," he added. "Think of what happened to her."

"I'm not Maggie." Her voice, though soft, was angry. "That's not going to happen to me." She stood up, slipped on her robe and paced back and forth across the smallness of the room.

"I just want you to be careful, that's all." He was sitting up, a gingering of blond hair falling over his eyes, looking so young, looking like a high-school jock. She wanted a man.

"I'm always careful," she told him, opening the door to return to her room. "I'm going to leave, Griff. Whatever happens. I won't spend the rest of my life in here. When Josiah comes back, I'm going."

She pulled the door shut behind her before he could argue the point any further. She didn't want to talk about it with him; her mind was made up. To Diana, existing caged inside a glass dome was not a life worth living. She felt suffocated, an animal in a terrarium. If reentering the world meant chancing death, that was a risk she was willing to take.

Thoughts of open plains of unenclosed space filled her mind.

Instead of crossing the hallway to her room, she padded barefoot down the corridor, turned left where the annex leading to the observation deck met the interior passage, and climbed the single flight of stairs. A lightweight, metal platform stood eight feet above the floor of the deck, with a disk-shaped panel in the center of the wall before it. She climbed the twenty-two steps to the top and passed her hand over the motion detector on the wall.

Eight segmented curves of gray steel opened like

293

the petals of a flower, revolving back into the recesses of the inner wall. A five-foot circle of clear glass gleamed like the glazed-black pupil of an eye. Leaning forward, she stared into the Outside, mesmerized by the real-life portrait before her.

It was telescopic, as if she were truly suspended on a space satellite, instead of its prototype built on earth, and looking down from a great distance at this black, star-glittering world outside her grasp.

An aching for the freedom of that familiar, remembered space grew in her, a welling up of longing for what she had lost . . . for what the human race had lost. The gloss of night lay like a wet soul upon the land, shimmering softly with the remembered radiance of creation.

It was her home, this place beyond the walls . . . mankind's home. And she wanted it.

Unable to close the panels and leave this vision of an indescribably beautiful earth, Diana lay down on the floor of the platform, hugged her arms and legs close to her beneath the small warmth of the robe, and went to sleep.

Outside the observation window, tomorrow waited.

Jessica and Quinn named their son Cameron, after Quinn's father. It was a strong name, but no reflection of her own Semitic heritage. Her child was Jewish, because she was, but the rules were different now, created for the world they lived in, and not bound to the canons of the past.

Doing her share of the work in the biosphere, and caring for the two children, Cameron and Trinity, kept Jessica busy enough to push most thoughts

294

of Josiah's arrival with other survivors to the back of her mind. She could go for hours without thinking of it, caught up in the technical jobs of maintaining the sphere, or feeding, bathing, and just living with the babies. It might be hours . . . but then, the worry would come back to her. Where was he? Why was it taking so long?

A sense of personal danger rested with Jessica, one which had never been a part of her before. If Josiah returned—when he returned—would she choose to leave Biosphere Seven? Would she be willing to put aside her fear of death and take her chances with the others who had survived, with those Outside? If Quinn went—and she knew he'd go—would she leave with him? Before her son was born, the answer would have been yes.

Now, with a child whose life she was responsible for, asleep in her arms, she wasn't sure.

The days went on, numbered and confined to that small accounting in her mind. So many days. They were listed in a private reckoning. She was the silent witness to each minute, each hour. Where had Josiah been when he contacted them? Why hadn't he sent another message? Where was he now?

Always, after she had made her head throb with pain at thinking of it, the last question would come, a whisper, a taunt.

What if Josiah never comes back?

The baby cried and nuzzled at her breast. A stream of milk flowed from her into him, and he quieted. His eyes were blue and innocent; the dark crown of his head nestled warm in her arm.

What was it she really wanted? If Josiah returned with others, would that endanger her son? If he

295

never came back, would Cameron be safe?

The questions gathered like wool on a spindle, growing larger and larger . . . until the wheel's spinning made her dizzy, and the thread of it snaked from her mind, catching her in its hold . . . and whirling round and round.

Chapter Thirty-four

At the close of the twentieth century, a calamity unlike any the world had ever known swept the face of the earth. Not the act of an angry god, the tribulation was conceived and born of man. In his mind, it was created; through his body—the body of mankind—it was nurtured; and in the scattering of those who survived its wrath, it remained. Through him, with him, in him—the curse abided.

In the first days of the year 2000, a silence hovered over the land, sky, and sea . . . a silence not known since the mist-shrouded beginnings of the world. Never, since the voice of man was first heard among the animals, had the weight of its silence been so profound. If the beating heart of Earth was Nature, and the all-knowing, cosmic mind was God, then surely, the voice of the planet was man.

The cry of birds cawed and screeched their throaty trills across the heavens; cattle and other grazers of the land lowed a mournful psalm to earth, to grass, to water; in the sea, whales sang a rejoice of freedom, and of life.

But the voice of man was hushed, a quiet whispering. In all the world, only five thousand remained.

In this winnowing of human existence, other species emerged triumphant. Without poachers to decimate the last number of African elephants, without people to destroy their natural habitats with cities and villages, or encroach upon their food supplies, the largest land mammal still surviving on earth reestablished its African domain.

Once again, the trumpeting call of the bull elephant sounded over the rich grasslands of Africa, and was answered by challengers to his strength, young rogue bulls from outside his herd. Once again, the shining-eyed calves and matriarchal clans of elephant cows trod the ancient tracks of Africa like nomads, with nothing to impede their progress but hot desert winds and the hungry lioness stalking from the tall, swaying grass.

Other species, too, increased their numbers in the absence of man. The populations of dolphin, seal, manatee, and whale thrived in undisturbed seas circling the globe. Some endangered animals flourished when the hand of man-the-trophy-hunter was suspended: rhino, mountain gorilla, cheetah, leopard, Canadian goose, American alligator, and scores of others.

For a few, however, those most fragile species at the end of the environmental line — the California condor, peregrine falcon, American bald eagle, and the greater panda of China — the damage was too severe. These animals, permanently harmed by man and the destruction of their natural habitats through pollution of the air and water by pesticides, or other chemicals, or by encroachment on their living space, now needed the interference of man to assure their continuity.

Without human intervention to hatch their eggs, which were too brittle to bear the weight of the mother bird's body, and assure that each egg of every clutch survived, these magnificent birds quickly became extinct. Without man to import and supply the once abundant bamboo shoots—the forests of which had been replaced by villages—the panda, whose only food was the bamboo, starved.

Tame animals like cats and dogs renounced the formerly docile behavior of the household pet and become feral. They joined in packs and dens, remembering a nature they had forgotten while under the authority of man.

Vast numbers of domesticated animals—cows, horses, chickens, goats, sheep, and a score of others—thinned their ranks to select only the fittest. The weak, or those too subdued by man to remember such things as finding their own food and water, breeding, and surviving in the winter, quickly perished. It was the wilder ones, those that had been most resistant to becoming servants to the human race, that succeeded in this new ecological niche.

Once again, there was a need in bulls for strong, sharp horns and the ferocity to protect the cows and calves of their herds from wolves, great cats, and other predators. Once again, stallions needed the fury and instincts of the conqueror to gather their harems of mares and safeguard them from danger. One by one, all the tame, the docile, the subdued, relearned their natural order, as if the time spent as the servants of man had never happened.

Earth swelled with life, replenishing the heterogeneity of the differing species. *In the beginning* had rebegun. This new Genesis was the dawn of a world without man, or at least one in which his presence was too small, too insignificant to be counted.

And yet . . . what man had left of the garden, the evidence of his existence—in structures, in the hole in the ozone, in the polluted waters of lakes and dying oceans — would affect the earth and all its inhabitants for thousands of years to come.

Like the Lord God, in His reckoning with Cain, man too had set his mark — and it was upon the face of earth.

The diamondback rattler lay coiled in a neat loop against the flat desert rocks. Stretched from fang to rattle, it was a six-and-a-half-foot North American pit viper, dusty gray, with brown and white diamond patterns on its back. Its distinctive black, gray, and white banded tail was tipped with a set of eighteen rattles at the end. At each shedding of its skin, a single, hollow rattle had been left attached to the tail, and others had been added periodically since its birth. Although rattles often wore off, or were lost by other means, so that the age could only be approximate, the number marked this specific diamondback as at least an eighteen-year-old adult, and one of the most venomous snakes in the United States.

Its wide, heart-shaped head lifted from the shaded stone. The pits — sensory devices on the sides of its head between the nostrils and the eyes, which gave the pit viper its name — detected the presence of the man. Even in total darkness, these homing devices could discern a rise of three hundredths of one degree centigrade, becoming directional compasses to allow the snake to follow the source of heat and make the strike.

The rattler was hungry. It had been two weeks since it had last eaten, and although the diamondback had gone longer between meals, its hunger made the snake irritable. It had felt the thump of footsteps from the man in the *hearing apparatus* of its lower jaw, a simple motion detector. Now it tasted the air with its black, forked tongue, *smelling* what sort of prey was approaching.

The rattle — five inches long, with white, double rows of eighteen buttons, thick as a man's two fingers — lifted from the rock. *Cch-cch-cch-cch . . . Cch-cch-cch-cch,* the vibrations sounded. It moved out from the shade, onto the hot, desert sand.

The heat swelled in waves lifting from the scorched ground. Even with the protection of its scales and watertight skin, the rattler could not bear the touch of the heated sand for more than a few seconds. Nature had adapted the rattler's mode of travel to moving across the burning desert in such a way as to walk on its sides — sidewinding — contracting its body into a series of S-shaped curves which rippled down the length of the diamondback, pushing it forward. Touching only at two points, it marked diagonal slashes, or bars, in the blistering sand.

The eyes of the rattler were not of much use, the desert heat, and its own evolutionary history of having once been a burrowing animal, made both eyes and ears ineffective. Still, the eyes — yellow orbs with black, vertical pupil slits — scanned the space before them, searching.

At the man's approach, the rattler gathered itself flatter against the sand, looping its body into a coiled stance, head raised and sensing the air for danger with its tongue. The man was danger, too large for a meal, yet possibly a threat to the viper's life. Man was a hunter, a predator who killed snakes. The diamondback warned with the

301

deathhead rattle of its tail, its head lifted in attack stance. It warned the man . . . but he crossed the rattler's path, anyway.

A booted foot stepped hard on the spiraled body of the diamondback, crushing soft tissues with its weight. The foot jerked back, stumbling in the shifting sand . . . the man's body falling, landing twisted on the ground . . . directly before the coiled body of the snake.

The head of the viper flared, hinging open to expose the red and white lining of its mouth . . . ruby cords of venom pulsing . . . and the needle-sharp fangs bared for the strike.

Its slit eyes sheathed closed, blind, guided only by the heat sensors on the sides of its head, the force of the rattler's powerful body whipped forward . . . hitting its mark . . . fangs stabbing . . . piercing the man's leg and pumping the twin tracks of poison into the thrashing flesh.

Brad McGhee rolled away from the still-threatening rattler. His right leg felt the burn of venom beneath the skin, the pain fierce, as if his muscle and skin were on fire.

"Aghh!" he howled, scuttling across the desert floor on two hands and one knee. He lifted the right leg off the sand, dragging it behind him as the spill of agony spread across the back of his calf.

Would the snake strike again?

His injured leg collapsed onto the sand. The feel of it touching ground was savage. A rippling sheet of scalding water boiled his skin with every contact. He crawled, seven feet, eight feet, trailing pain.

Falling to the ground, far away from the snake —

far enough, he hoped—he stretched the leg out before him. The bite was at the outside of the calf. Tugging the right pant leg up and over his knee, he stared at the red and swelling flesh.

He had a knife; that was something he'd used often in the last few days. It was a tool he needed for many things, the knife: cutting mesquite branches for a fire, killing small game for food, spearing fish, and hacking prickly fruit from cactus. Opening the blade, he held it out before him. *Had to be quick. Had to be now.* He thought—Is the blade clean enough?—then knew it didn't matter, and stabbed the tip of the knife an inch deep into the meaty calf muscle of his leg.

"Aaahhh!" the scream tore from him, rolling through steaming blood and swollen flesh, rolling into the pitch-black meld of his mind.

The terror was . . . he had to do it again.

Brad used the knife first to cut and tear a strip of cloth from the raised pant leg and tie a tourniquet four inches above the wound. When he made the next cut, if he fainted. . . .

"Help me!" he pleaded, his fingers white rails on the knife, and stabbed the leg again.

Blood and venom oozed from the cuts onto his bare leg, sticky with sand. A weight pushed at him; the sky pressing against his head forced him back, forced him down. In the blazing heat of the afternoon, the sun faded, turning the broad sweep of cloudless sky into the blind tunnel of blackest night.

He awoke to the tear of flesh from his bone. An animal was ripping the skin from the muscle, its long teeth caught and sawing at the bloody wound.

303

A bear held the leg in its mouth, jaws clamped, shaking. Tearing the flesh from the—

"No!" Brad screamed, opened his eyes, and saw he was alone.

Nothing stood over him. Nothing tore at his leg. Only the sky was real, a blue-white blaze of heat and light, not the tenebrous dark of his dream. He'd passed out from the pain. The question was, How long had he been lying here?

The blood on his leg was still wet, but the area of the bite had swollen into a puffed and angry weal. The skin was tight, pulling at the edges of the cuts with the pressure. It hurt like hell.

With no way of knowing how long he'd been unconscious, the first thing he did was loosen the tourniquet. Loosen the constriction band for ninety seconds every ten minutes—that's what the survival guidebooks said. He'd read a few of them as a precaution when he first came to the desert, and many more since he'd learned he'd be living here alone.

The angle was awkward, but he managed to slide his leg in front of him, bend forward to reach the back of his calf, and suction the wound. The first mouthful made him gag, gritty sand, warm blood, and the slick, mucus slime of venom. He spat it from him and tried again.

In the resource building not far from the biosphere dome, there would be anti-venom injections. They would be in the emergency kits, along with penicillin tablets, bandages, a few minor pain and fever reducers, and a small vial of morphine. The way his leg was swelling, and with the strong possibility of infection from the deep cuts, getting to that medical kit was his only chance.

The biosphere dome and its adjacent offices down

the hill beyond it were over two miles away. It was over a hundred degrees in the direct sun. He'd fainted once already, and the worst thing anyone could do with a snake bite was to walk any distance — spreading the venom through their system that much faster.

If he didn't make it to the resource building, he would die.

There was no real choice.

He had no crutch or staff to lean on. Putting as little weight on the injured leg as possible, Brad started across the desert. Each step pumped the venom faster into his bloodstream. His leg bled profusely, and he worried that a hungry animal would smell the scent of blood and attack him.

"Oh, Mother!" he called out, holding onto the deeper cry of pain. It was not to his own mother that he called, but to she who had rescued him once, and who he hoped would save him again.

With each step, he thought of her. In his mind, he saw the image of her bending over him, lifting his body from the riverbed and carrying him to safety. The desert faded before his eyes, and he saw only her eyes, her face, and her arms held open to receive him . . . just a few steps ahead.

"Wait for me," he called to her fading image, pain and exhaustion narrowing him into a needy child.

She moved like an unreachable shadow — all the colors in a prism of light, her image — shining before him, leading the way.

"Wait!" he cried again, eyes watching only her eyes . . . and followed.

Chapter Thirty-five

Within the domed world of Biosphere Seven, the summer sun was muted by louvered ceiling and wall panels which could be adjusted as the heat of the day climbed and lowered, and by a cooling system which ran on solar energy. The temperature was kept at a comfortable seventy-two degrees, the air moist and moderate.

Grasses and crops grew year round in this controlled climate. A rich abundance of harvest swelled the granaries and storerooms. With the solar generator working as it should, there was no summer, fall, or winter. Every season was spring. Every day, perfect.

On a field of luxuriant grass, the three infants born to the world of Biosphere Seven slept on a nest of soft blankets, sheltered from the desert heat beneath the curved ceiling of the dome. They were another kind of yield, the continuance of human life.

On the twenty-first of July 2000, Trinity, son of Mike York and Maggie Adair, was fourteen months old and able to walk. Sidra, daughter of Cathe Innis and Josiah Gray Wolf, was ten-and-a-half months, crawling, and pulling up on everything in her eagerness to stand. Cameron, son of Jessica Nathan and Quinn Kelsey, was one month old that day.

For Cameron, and for the other two, the world of Biosphere Seven was their only home, their native land. It had allowed them life, when those outside the walls of glass had sickened and died. They were the children of their world, the only children. In them, lay all hope for the future of mankind.

For Trinity, his natural mother was dead, and his biological father ignored his presence. For Sidra, her genetic father was outside the dome—unaware of her existence—leading others to them. Only Cameron had both parents with him from the moment of birth. Of the three, he was the most secure. He cried very little, already slept through the night, and seemed to visibly grow stronger daily.

Which made Jessica's decision that much harder when she thought of risking his life by taking him Outside. Quinn said it was up to her. If she elected to stay, he would remain with her, but if she chose to go, he insisted they take the baby with them.

"Whatever the risk, I would rather our son die in our arms, than live with a wall forever separating us. No matter which way you decide, we go, or stay, together."

It wasn't only Cameron, but Trinity, too. She and Quinn had become foster parents to the boy. Jessica could no more leave him behind than she could leave her own son. Trinity was a cherub with blond curls, round face, and laughing eyes. He had just begun to say words, "Ma-ma" and "Da-da." He was theirs, as much as Cameron, but did they have the right to take him away?

Until now, Mike had paid little or no attention to his son. His promise to Maggie that he would love and care for their child had never held to be true. It wasn't that he meant to ignore the boy—at least, Jessica didn't think he did—but found that when the realities of a frequently crying, often demanding baby set in, he couldn't cope.

He watched Trinity from a distance, admiring him as a collector might admire a valuable piece of art. The fact that this *art* needed feeding and diapering, comforting and loving, was a complication. Mike didn't deal well with complications. He stood back and let Jessica and Quinn care for the boy. If they left the dome, would Mike let Trinity go?

If he didn't, would they take him anyway?

The children slept; a gentle stream flowed along the man-made channel beside them; from the center of the meadow, a raven spread its wings, and soared.

The sand was hot when Brad hit, stumbling full length onto the ground. His leg was hotter. The rattler's venom burned in him like a bubbling pocket of acid underneath the skin. He couldn't see for the rivulets of sweat pouring into his eyes. Where was the dome? Where was the access building?

It was all he could do to twist around and loosen the tourniquet. A fresh wave of pain surged with the return of circulation into the limb. The skin was purple, shiny and taut with blood, throbbing at each pulse beat. He felt the pounding of that pulse all along his leg, felt it in the muscle and the bone. Each thump shuddered as if his leg would burst open, and the steaming vent explode. A volcano.

He couldn't find the dome.

Jessica was there. His Jessica. *I'm not dead!* he

wanted to shout to her. *Not yet, Jessie.*

He couldn't get up; the leg wouldn't bend. Pain was solid, the venom moving through him, turning the inside of his calf to jelly. Moving up, past his knee, past the place where the tourniquet had been. . . .

He tied the tourniquet back on, cinching it tight.

Unable to give up, Brad rolled over, screaming when his kneecap connected with the ground. Crawling over the ocean of sand, he dragged the leg behind him, his toes leaving a trench. He couldn't stand, couldn't see where he was heading . . . but kept going.

To stop was to die. This wasn't where he wanted it to end.

If he died crawling on his belly in the middle of the desert, would anyone ever know? Would it matter? Where was she now? . . . the woman he had followed. He needed her to lead him out of this. Why had she abandoned him? He needed her.

The desert floor rose up to him, swirling like the stir of a teacup. His arms stretched out to brace himself, to catch his fall, fingers slipping into the moving sand. There was no more. His strength was gone. The hard light beat at his face until the cooling hand of unconsciousness shaded the heat from his mind. In that release of pain, he slumped forward, and was gone.

Brad felt strong arms lift him from the bed of sand. Pain rocketed through him with the touch. His leg was black, bursting with pressure from within, and enveloped in an agony at every movement.

309

"Brad? Is that you?" The voice batted at the swell surrounding him. "Brad! Open your eyes. Can you hear me?"

He felt a coolness dampen his face. Insistent words, calling him back from the dark, calling him to feel, to think. "Ahhh!" a groan of suffering rose from him, like the tormented cry of death, rose and lifted away the shield of unconsciousness. He became aware. And felt everything.

Arms were holding him down. The pain! His leg was on fire. *Put it out!* He needed to beat out the flames. *Had to stop it!*

"Don't sit up!" The strong arms pushed him back. "I know it hurts. We're here, Brad. We're helping you."

Opening his eyes, Brad couldn't believe what he saw. "How could you. . . ? Am I—"

"You're not dead, I promise you."

"Josiah?"

"It's me, Brad. We found you out here. We're taking you to the resource center in the van. You'll be all right, buddy. Here—" he held a canteen to Brad's lips—"take a little water."

He didn't understand any of it. How did Josiah get outside? Had everyone left the dome? Had Jessica?

More movement, someone carrying him to the van, and the constant rocking and jarring of the road as the wheels hit ruts and bumps. It was all he could think of, the excruciating line of torment, a straight line of hell he couldn't escape. The screams were awful. He wished someone would make them stop.

And then the van jolted to the left. His body slid, hitting his leg on the metal brace of a seat. Like a

310

drop of water in a pond, a corona of white pain
shot up from the deeper pool of his torment, crowning . . . crowning . . . until the coronet closed out
all awareness, and plunged him back into the depths
of that dark abyss where pain and awareness could
not enter.

In and out of consciousness: remembering the
wash of voices encasing him; remembering the hot
blade of the knife and the cries of, "Don't! Oh,
God, don't . . . don't!" Waves of pain rolled like a
shudder that would not ease . . . the sharp stab of a
needle . . . and the relief of morphine flowing
through him, damping the torment. Damping.
  It might have been a dream, Josiah's face above
his, what he thought he had seen in the desert. The
snake was real, he knew, and the pain, but the rest?
Now it was a bed of soft cushions beneath him and
a cool cloth on his forehead. It was a dream of Josiah, and Biosphere . . . and Jessie.
  He was in this place beside her—had he crawled
to the building by himself? If she knew, would she
come outside to him? Would she leave the dome
and risk her life for his? Was that what he wanted?
Jessie. Jessie. . . .
  Someone else was with him—a woman. She
waited while he slept, while the dream took him
into the unexplored caverns of his mind. In the
worst of it, when he feared to look, she was beside
him. Silent and enduring, she waited for the dream
to end.
  He was groggy, his thinking disoriented by pain
and exhaustion, even without the drug. Looking
around, he saw he was in the resource building,

311

near the communications room where he had given the press release on the opening day of Biosphere Seven. Nearly three years ago. So much had changed in that time, and so had he.

"How are you feeling?" a woman's voice asked.

He turned his head to see who spoke to him. Not Jessie. And not the woman from his dream. It was a young girl of not more than nineteen or twenty, with silky blond hair and soft green eyes.

"I'm Natalie," she said, looking solicitous of him, and attentive. "You shouldn't try to move until Josiah says it's okay. He said you'd be pretty weak when you woke up. Want something? A glass of water? Something to eat?"

She was pretty, healthy and young, but she wasn't the face he wanted to see. She wasn't Jessica.

"How long have I—"

"Not that long," she assured him. "We found you in the desert a few hours ago. You looked like a corpse. Josiah had to open the wound on your leg. It was pretty badly infected. He treated it with some antibiotics we found here. They kept a box of stuff for first aid. You were thrashing around a lot when we first brought you inside. He gave you a sedative, and another shot, too. Some kind of snake—"

"Anti-venom," Brad interrupted her amiable line of chatter. There was something more important, something he had to know. "Where's Josiah? Where did he go? I have to talk to him." His leg was throbbing heat, and now that he was fully conscious, he felt the pain return, emerging like a submarine from beneath an ocean depth.

"It's all right. He'll be back soon," she tried to calm him. She was a nice kid, and under other circumstances, he would have been touched by her concern. "He just went to let the people at the biosphere know we're here."

"What! He can't do that!" Brad tried to sit up, but pain like a steel blade slicing through his leg stopped him. "Please . . . Natalie—that's your name?"

She nodded, stepping back from the cot, out of grabbing range. Her eyes didn't look so full of sympathy and concern now; they looked a little scared.

"I'm sorry I shouted . . . please, Natalie . . . help me. You have to find him. Stop him from telling them that I'm here. Do you understand that? He can't let Jessica know I'm alive."

"Jessica?" She was staring at him with frightened eyes.

"My wife." The thought of Jessie forced him back down, flat onto the cot, all his strength gone in one instant. It had been too long. She believed him dead. She couldn't find out like this—not after all he'd done to keep her from knowing, to keep her from the truth.

"But, wouldn't she want to know?" asked Natalie. "I mean, if it were me, I'd want to know if my husband—"

"It's not you, and you don't understand!" he yelled, exhausted by the effort.

"I'm sorry," she said, backing out of the room.

"Wait. Don't go. Natalie!" he called after her; but the door to the room shut, and she was gone.

In the silence which remained, he heard the voice of his heart, a lamentation, mourning all that was . . . and all that could never be again.

He fought against it, but the sedative began to take effect. Closing his eyes, he saw once more the glow of light from the curving shape of Biosphere Seven, a warm circle of radiance he had sat and watched from the distance and secrecy of the hill. So hungry were those nights: for love; for the beauty of his wife's eyes; for the normalcy of other days; for the comfort of a band of friends.

He wondered, *Do I belong to that place anymore? To those people? Can any of us go back to what we once were? To what we once had?*

Sliding into a drugged and total exhaustion . . . sliding into the dream, the prophet followed the lure of the light.

Chapter Thirty-six

Josiah had led them back to the desert, to this place.

He went alone now, up the narrow macadam road, climbing the hill and walking the distance of two miles to the dome. All the others were left behind at the resource center. It would be dark soon. Brad's snakebite was proof enough that it would be safer for them to walk to the biosphere the next day, when they could see where they were going.

At the crest, Josiah set out across the plateau, crossing the white sand and scrub brush plain of the high desert, to the glass-walled face of the structure.

It was nearly sunset. The sky above and behind Biosphere Seven to the west was a mural wash of conch-shell pink, coral, and dusty rose. Thunder clouds were building in the higher reaches of the cauldron sky, their wispy haze softening the bronze and copper patina to a swirl of muted colors.

Walking toward the light, he was suddenly afraid. What was it he had brought to them? A promise of new life? Or further anguish in knowing they could not share in the bounty of the outside world? Would any of them leave the dome? Should they take that risk?

On this early evening, as he neared the end of

his pilgrimage and quest, he found himself thinking of Piper Robinson — the woman who had offered her life to save them all. In his mind's eye, he saw her again, standing at the water's edge before the Biosphere Sea, her dark eyes searching the horizon through the blocks of glass at the far side of the wall. Watching.

Was she watching still? He wondered. Did she see him now?

In a reckoning with death, he had left this place. His own fear of it had marked him, narrowing his breath with terror in those first silent days alone. When, he wondered, had the fear ended and a new perception begun? Would they welcome him back? Could they still accept him, as what they were, what they would always be to him? Family.

"Josiah!" The phantom voice came from the speaker system mounted onto the outside wall of Biosphere Seven. "By God, Gray Wolf, is that you?"

Had he changed so much? Inside, he was different. Between them was a lifetime of difference.

"I'm back, Quinn." His own voice sounded flat and unfamiliar, even to himself. Distant.

"Stay right there. Stay right there. I'll get the others. No, wait. Not yet. Go to the observation deck," Quinn told him, the hard bark of his voice excited and happy as a child's. "I want to look at you through something clearer than these rippled glass blocks. I can't believe it. You're back, man! Come on, meet me on the observation deck."

Josiah walked to the platform, climbed the outside ladder, and waited for Quinn to appear. A few seconds later, he saw a blurred rush propelling straight for him as the dark-haired Irishman took the inside ladder steps three rungs at a time.

316

Quinn's hands pushed at the thick pane of glass separating them, fingers spread out as if trying to grab and hug Josiah to him. "Jesus, Gray Wolf. Look at you! Better shape than when you left here. I wouldn't know you've even been sick."

"I haven't."

"What?"

"I never got the virus."

"Didn't get it? But everyone. . . ." Quinn's expression of amazement changed to one of avid interest. "How could you *not* get it?"

"Some people just didn't," Josiah told him honestly. "I wasn't the only one. I brought nine survivors back with me—nine healthy people. None of them had the virus."

A small silence followed. Josiah could almost see the questions sorting themselves in Quinn's mind, the evidence in the sudden frowns and the quick, sharp movements of his face.

"God! Tell me everything. What's it like out there? Where have you been? What have you seen? In here, we haven't heard anything . . ." he started to explain, then finished, "well, you know what it's like in here."

There was so much Josiah needed to tell him—needed to tell all of them—but there was one thing he had to let Quinn know first, while they were still alone. It was the best, and the hardest, thing he had to say.

"The people—is everything gone?" Quinn pressed for an answer. "Tell me. Is it as bad as we've imagined?"

Josiah didn't lie to him. "As far as I could see, other than the nine people I brought with me, it was total."

The happiness on Quinn's face pulled back, melting away into the hardness of taut muscles beneath the skin. "If no one who had the virus survived," he began, "how can any of us hope to ever live outside this dome?"

Josiah didn't answer.

"What you're telling me is that this is our only world and we'd better accept it," he said, lowering his hands from their place on the glass. "Going Outside . . . we'd all die out there—like Maggie, like Brad."

"Quinn. . . ."

"No, I need to get it straight. There's no hope of returning Outside. Good God, Josiah, I was the one who wanted to improve the earth, not go off and live on some satellite. And now . . . I'm here. Jesus," he said softly. "The only thing beyond this dome for us is death. We'd all—"

"Quinn, you need to listen to me. There's something I have to tell you, before Jessica knows I'm back. There was at least one person who had the virus and lived."

"What? But, I thought you said—"

"I said none of the nine people I found and brought here had been sick."

"Right . . . and that everyone else you saw while you were searching for survivors was dead." Quinn had pulled back, the look in his eyes wary.

"Yes." Josiah took it slowly; what he had to tell him would come as a shock. "Everyone else I saw on the journey, before I came here."

Quinn didn't ask the obvious question. He waited. The unspoken words hung between them, a thicker barrier than the pane of glass.

"We found someone when we got here, Quinn.

318

Someone who'd had the virus and survived." Josiah waited—letting the questions form and rise to the surface of Quinn's mind.

"Maggie?" There was something in Quinn's voice, a smallness, wanting the name to be that of anyone else's but the man he knew it must be.

"Quinn. It was Brad."

Josiah watched as the sound of that name hit Quinn like a hard blow to the face. His friend's eyes closed as he took the impact of it. "Oh, God," he said, the breath of his words trailing away into the terrible silence of his thoughts. "He had the virus. How could he—"

"I think he did have the virus," Josiah tried to explain. "He has pock marks on his face, but they're healed. Apparently, he survived it."

"Then—" Quinn couldn't understand.

"Brad was unconscious on the desert, almost dead from a snakebite when we found him," Josiah explained. "His leg was swollen twice its size, rattlesnake venom turning his muscles to jelly. He was still trying to crawl across the desert. I don't know if he'll live through this. He's desperately ill. We've done what we could for him—cleaned the wound, given him an anti-venom injection, tablets of antibiotics. It may not be enough."

Quinn opened his eyes again, and they were terrible to see. "Jessica will have to know."

"Yes," said Josiah.

"I kept her from going Outside to him once, Josiah. Remember?"

He nodded.

"We have a child between us now. Cameron. How in God's name can I keep her from going to Brad when she hears that he's still alive, but sick, maybe

319

dying? — that he needs her. She lived through his death once, Josiah. I was the bastard who kept her from him. Christ! Must we live through it again?"

"Would you like me to tell her?" The words felt like cracked ice in his throat, sticking, burning. He knew how this was tearing Quinn apart, and what it would do to Jessica.

What was he bringing them? The question that had troubled him earlier was answered now: He had brought them life, and pain, the twin certainties of human existence. "It might be better coming from me. If you'd rather I —"

"No," Quinn stopped him. "I'm the one. Give me until morning. Then bring the survivors here, Josiah. Let us see them; we need a vision of hope. I'll let everyone know. We'll be waiting for you."

"All right. I'll bring them at dawn." Josiah turned and started down the first step, anxious to be away from the hurt his words had caused.

"Gray Wolf," Quinn called after him. "If I forgot to say it, I'm sorry. Welcome home. And one other thing, when you come back tomorrow with the others, I'll introduce you to your daughter."

Josiah hurried away, his throat too tight to speak.

Jessica held her son's warm body close to her. Cameron's face was a roundness against her breast, his eyes closed in sleep. It was his last feeding for the night. She kissed his soft cheek, laid him in the cradle, and came back to sit beside her husband.

"Are you going to tell me now? What is it, Quinn? You haven't spoken more than a couple sentences all night."

He didn't answer.

320

"Look, if you've been waiting for the right moment, I think you've found it. We're alone. Cameron's asleep. Come on, I know something's wrong. What is it you have to tell me?"

He stood up, let out one hard breath, and said it. "Josiah's back. I saw him today."

"You saw him?" Red spots of anger bloomed on her cheeks. "And you didn't tell me?"

He made no excuse.

"I had a right to know." She was on her feet, moving toward him.

"Yes. You have a right to know everything, Jessica. I couldn't keep it from you even if I wanted to."

She stopped. "Keep what from me?"

She was his wife, the mother of his child. He loved her. What he was going to say next could change all that.

"Josiah came back with nine other survivors, people who have never had the virus."

"Never had the . . . Is that possible? My God, Quinn. That means. . . . Nine! That's wonderful news. Quinn, you scared me. The way you were acting, I thought—"

"Brad's alive." The words spilled from him in a break that couldn't be held back.

"Brad?" She moved away from him, the thought pushing her back.

"He survived."

She shook her head. "What do you mean? What are you saying? He had the virus. I saw the blisters on his face and hands. I saw them."

"He was sick, it's true. Josiah says the pock marks are on his face. I don't know how it happened, Jessie, but he lived. He's been here all along, only a few miles away, in a makeshift camp near us."

She couldn't accept it. He saw that from the expression in her eyes. "If Brad were alive . . . oh, God, if he were alive, he'd come to me. He'd tell me. Why would he — what would make him stay away?"

"I don't have the answer, Jessica. I wish I did. I'm telling you now because I wanted you to know the truth before you heard it from someone else."

"It isn't true. If he were alive, he'd come here. Why won't Josiah bring him here? Let me see him for myself." Her face was drained of color, and her eyes . . . her eyes were deep hollows, a hovering darkness on her soul.

"He can't bring him, Jess."

"Why not?" She was angry, pacing the room and angry. "You tell him. Make him come to me, then I'll believe it." She wasn't crying. He wished she were. She was strong, and that was the trouble. "I want to see him for myself. I want to —"

"They can't bring him!" Why had he shouted? Why was he hurting her? "He's been bitten by a rattlesnake and can't be moved. The truth is, he may be dying."

"No." The word was breath between them, an exhale, needle sharp. "Brad." The name. And then the cry. "Brad!"

In the torment of that cry, Quinn heard the tearing of his life . . . thin as paper chains, and the careful bonds ripping asunder.

And in the barren silence which followed, they waited for the dawn.

322

Chapter Thirty-seven

Morning came like dragonflies, ascending on the threaded lines of sky and wispy wings of clouds. Dawn. Even at this hour, summer veiled the land and held it wrapped in the unmoving stillness of a Texas August. The ground was dry-baked, white sand shimmering beneath unrelenting waves of radiating heat.

Josiah sat at the table before the picture window of the resource center, staring out across the sweep of desert, and further, at the distant hills. His back was turned to the room, so he didn't hear Elizabeth when she entered and crossed the floor to him. The night had brought no sleep; and the dawn, no answers.

"We're ready," she said, bending close and leaning her cheek against his. "Rosalina will stay with your friend this time. Yesterday, Natalie got a little spooked."

"She's too young," Josiah defended the girl. "I should have known better. As I remember, Brad could be a pretty tough guy."

"He must be, to have lived through what he has and stayed here by himself all this time. He's amazing."

"Yes." Josiah nodded. "He is."

"I only hope he's strong enough to live through this as well," she added. "Crystal had the watch last night. She said his leg was causing him a lot of pain, and that he was feverish. I wish there was something more we could do for him."

"There is. We could bring him his wife," said Josiah.

"Isn't that up to her? When she knows the truth, she's the one who'll have to make that decision. You can't take every burden on yourself. It won't be easy. From what you tell me, she's in love with the man she's with now, and they have a child. Whatever choice she makes will affect four people. It isn't simple, Josiah."

"I know." He stood up and started toward the door. His hand was on the knob when he turned back. "The strange thing is, he hasn't asked to see her. Not once. Brad may be dying, Beth. For the second time, he's chosen to face that alone, to protect her in every way he can and let her go."

"He loves her, Josiah."

"Love, yes. And what has that love cost him?"

"What does it cost each of us? Everything. A risk, but without it we might as well be dead. You ask your friend. Ask Brad. He hasn't stopped loving her, and he won't risk her, not to save his own life."

Josiah pulled Beth into his arms and held her close against him, never wanting to let go. "Stay near me today, Beth. I need you."

She nodded.

Joining the others, they left the resource center and set out across the desert, climbing the rose-white hill of dawn, to their future . . . to the biosphere.

At the summit of the hill, the land stretched away

324

to a flat palate of gray-green mesquite, scraped brown tableland, and scrawny cedar trees. The sun-dazzling brilliance of the Crystal Kingdom rose in the glittering dome, arched wings, and three-hundred-foot tower of Biosphere Seven.

"It's like a fuckin' palace," said Stephen Wyse.

"Doesn't seem real," agreed Skeet.

"Real enough," Elizabeth told them. "People live in there, a whole world inside those glass walls. Come on," she urged them, "they've been waiting a long time for us."

In a kind of awe, the company of ten survivors moved out across the scorched and arid land.

"It glitters like a jewel," Josiah heard Merry Logan whisper to Emily. "Just like a diamond in the light."

"Or a soap bubble," Emily answered, "shimmering with color. Beautiful."

"Well, I don't care," said Natalie. "I wouldn't live there for anything. I don't care how beautiful it is. It's a jail. They're all prisoners, and they can't get out. Not ever."

Hearing her words, and understanding all too well the meaning of them, Josiah stepped out in front and led the small party of survivors before the viewing window of the dome.

"They're here! It's them," called Mike York. "Josiah's back, and he's brought the others!"

The seven adults of Biosphere Seven crowded into the limited space before the observation window, three of them — Jessica, Cathe, and Quinn — holding their children in their arms.

"Five women and four men," said Griff. "Good

325

Christ, there's more of them than there are of us, and they've been on the Outside."

"There were a lot more of them to begin with," Cathe reminded him, smiling.

"Yeah, well . . . I guess so."

"Oh, yes. Come over here, sweet little mamas," said Mike in a low, hungry voice, staring at the three younger women.

His words were like ashes in Jessica's mouth, dry and bitter. She thought of Maggie, and wondered if he ever thought of her. Maggie, who had been so desperately in love. Maggie, who had given him a child, a son he completely ignored.

Quinn reached across to the far wall and switched on the outside speaker, nodding a go-ahead at her. The mike was in the wall-set to her right. She leaned in close.

"Welcome!" Jessica called to them. "All of you, welcome. Come up to the platform, please. Let us meet you face to face."

"Oh, God," breathed Cathe, standing beside her, Josiah's daughter in her arms.

"Easy," Jessica encouraged her. "It'll be all right."

Daniel stood at the back of the throng of seven with Quinn. His face was dark and sober. "The bastard made it back . . ." muttered Daniel, the words cold steel, only a breath above a sigh. "What am I supposed to do? Disappear?"

"Hang in there, buddy," said Quinn. "It's not over. Wait."

The ten Outsiders clomped up the metal staircase to the exterior platform, arranged themselves in a quick semblance of order, and stared back at those inhabitants within the enclosed world of Biosphere Seven.

326

Two were missing; Jessica counted. Quinn had said Josiah brought nine people. One wasn't here. And Brad. *And Brad.*

"Cathe," said Josiah, looking at the child in her arms, "Quinn said. . . . Is this my—"

"Your daughter, Josiah," Cathe broke in. "I named her Sidra. It means, inheritor of the stars. She looks like you: dark hair, Indian. She looks like her father."

"Sidra." He repeated and smiled at her. "She is my reward," he said at last. "I'm grateful, Cathe. I thought often of you, and the possibility of this child, on my journey, wondering if she existed, if she lived."

"And I thought of you," Cathe responded, "wondering the same—if you lived, and if you would ever return."

"Steady," said Quinn, giving Daniel a warning glance.

"The earth brings us home," said Josiah. "In her way, she found us all, and led us back to this place."

"He's gone wacko," murmured Griff derisively. "Right off his tom-tom."

"We're here," Josiah went on, "because we were called to this land, to these hills, to build our homes and settle near this biosphere. We are a single people," he told them, "even if we cannot live together—neither we among you, nor you among us. We are separated, and will remain so. Yet—" he looked at them all—"we are children of the same blood, of the same earth. For this reason, we have come home."

"Josiah," said Jessica, unable to wait any longer, "tell me about Brad."

"He's alive," he told her, "but I can't say for how much longer."

"Tell him for me—" She stopped, aware of all the others listening.

"What?" Josiah pressed.

Quinn was there. He would hear her words, and they would hurt him. Quinn.

"Tell him that I love him," she said. "Tell him that I've never forgotten—never for a single day—and that I will go on loving him all my life."

"Christ!" swore Daniel, turning to face Quinn.

But he was gone.

Quinn walked along the shore of the sea, holding Cameron in his arms. The day was "brewing," as his Irish mother used to say; plugged clouds of hashy gray percolated through the silver, bright sky. *Trouble weather.*

He sat near the water's edge and let the baby's feet splash and kick at the lip of the sea. He put his own feet into the cool water, and soon they were both wet to the knees.

"It's not a bad place to grow up, Cameron. It's the world you were born into, a world that saved your life, and mine. I wouldn't be in a hurry to leave it, son. You've got an ocean for fishing and swimming, a forest to dream in, and a rich land to grow your food and shelter you. No, it's not so bad, Cam."

Quinn lifted the boy to his shoulder. "See that over there? We built that tower, the men of this place and I. We built it with the work of our hands, and everything else that's here. It's a world we made, Cam. It's a world that let us survive, when the rest of mankind died. We're the caretakers

328

and the inheritors, keeping this place livable—for ourselves, and maybe for it."

He lowered the baby down into his arms and looked at him. "You've got your grandmother's eyes, and if you're lucky, her temperament, too. She was a nice woman, my mother. Siobhan Kelsey, that was her name—Roarke, before she was married. My brother was named after that side of the family, Roarke. He's dead now, I suppose, with the others."

"Don't you think he's a little young for family histories?" said Jessica, leading Trinity up the shady shelf of beach.

"Who knows what the mind keeps," said Quinn. "Besides, it may be the last time I'll have a chance to tell him."

"Why is that?"

"Well, you're going, aren't you?"

"Going?"

"Out to Brad. Outside. You're taking the boy and leaving."

She sat beside him. "Why did you think that, Quinn? Because of what I said back there?"

"Because you still love him," he told her, staring hard into her eyes. The hurt was more than he could stand, but he held it to him like a penance. *Mea culpa, mea culpa, mea maxima culpa.*

"Should I lie and tell you that I don't love him?" she asked, staring back just as hard. "Should I tell you that, when it isn't true?"

"Well, go to him then and be damned!" he shouted. "Go to him!" He rushed to his feet, making the baby cry.

"Give him to me," she said, holding her arms out for the child.

He handed her his son, knowing she would leave,

knowing she would take the boy and walk out of his life.

"I'll take the children back to the house. We'll have lunch waiting for you when you come home." She started away, carrying Cameron in one arm and leading Trinity by the hand.

"Dammit, Jessie, what are you saying?" He didn't understand, needed to have it clear between them.

"That I'll be there when you come home. That I'll always be there, Quinn. I'm not going anywhere. You're my husband; these are our children. And I love you. That's never going to change. When I love someone," she paused to let the meaning sink in, "I love them forever."

"And Brad?" He had to ask. Had to know.

She stood still, didn't turn back to face him, but balanced like a pendulum hanging on the breath of time. "He was of another time, another world ago. You're my world now, Quinn. This place is and will be our life, and all we hold within it. I won't ask more than that."

"Jessica?"

"Yes?"

"Do you remember, so long ago, when I called you Our Lady of the Sphere? You're still that to me—that, and so much more."

She walked away, this woman he loved. He watched her until only the footprints of her steps were visible in the damp sand. He watched, and filled his soul again with the vision of love she had shown to him. And then, when she was gone, when no one was near enough to see, he cried.

"Oh, God," he whispered into hands wet with the soothing release of tears, "thank you."

330

Chapter Thirty-eight

"I've decided," announced Mike York, "and I don't want anyone trying to tell me differently. I'm going out. I'm taking my chances on a real life outside this fishbowl."

Jessica wasn't surprised. She knew one or two of them would go. They'd be willing to risk everything for a chance at the kind of freedom they remembered.

"No one's going to stop you, Mike," she assured him. "We've known, since Maggie left, that we can send people out without contaminating the dome. It's all right if you want to leave, but we won't let you take Trinity. Not yet."

Anger flared in his face, suffusing the pale skin with wheels of spreading fire. "He's my son. I'm his father—not Quinn. I have the right to—"

"This isn't about rights," she stopped him. "You're risking your life, Mike. Think about that. Doesn't it make sense to wait until you're sure that the virus won't affect you, before risking the boy, too."

"There are ten people out there who never got it. Josiah's one of them. And Brad, he got it and lived."

"Ten out of how many?" she asked coldly.

He ignored the point. "The virus has changed, Jessica. Weakened. I'm sure it has. I wouldn't be taking this chance if I didn't believe that. I'm not stupid, or anxious to die."

"Good," she said. "Then, a little test of time won't matter, will it? Give yourself a month, Mike. If you show no signs of it by then, we'll send Trinity out to you. You're a parent, like you say. Act like one. You owe the child that much of a safeguard."

He wasn't satisfied, she could see, but caved in to her rationalization. Winning Trinity's custody was more a point of honor than something he really wanted. It was proof that he was independent of them.

Diana and Griff had decided on going out, too. "Nothing but the fear of death will keep me inside this crystal ball a minute longer than I have to be here," declared Diana at the meeting. "Griff and I are leaving with Mike."

"No. We can't allow all three of you out at once," said Jessica, knowing Diana would come back at her like a snarling cat.

"What do you mean . . . can't? Why not?"

Jessica tried to skirt around the issue. "It's safer to send out one at a time, to make sure you've settled in and everything's okay before we—"

"We're going together," Diana insisted. She wouldn't give in without a battle. "It's a waste to evacuate the air from the docking chamber three separate times. Makes much more sense to let us leave together. You only want to keep us here to try to change our minds. Don't lie."

"That isn't it, Diana."

"Okay, then, what is? Why don't you just sit back, quit playing queen, and let us do what we want?"

"Because, I need to see if whoever goes out first will die." She said it in the hard voice it deserved.

"There's no point in wasting three lives if you're wrong."

Diana pulled a wrap of silence over her, blocking out the words, the thought, everything. Jessica looked, but she couldn't see into Diana's eyes anymore; like steely doors to her soul, they had closed.

"You'll leave the dome one at a time, starting with Mike. In five days, if he's still okay, we'll send out Griff. Diana will be the last to leave the satellite—not because of any spite on my part, but because she's a woman, and therefore more valuable to us."

"Valuable in what way?" Daniel jumped into that one. Couldn't resist.

"She can bear children," explained Jessica. "If we're going to survive as a species, and as a community, we'll need all the women to bear children—as many as practicable."

"And," Quinn added, "we'll need to prevent inbreeding problems by allowing only one child per couple."

"One child?" asked Daniel. "I thought Jessica said—"

"One per couple," Quinn stressed the fine point, "and then we switch partners, at least for the purposes of conception."

"Kinky." Daniel looked too pleased.

"No," Quinn clarified the issue. "Genetics."

"And that's what you want, all of you?" Diana stormed at them. "To be some kind of breeding farm for the salvation of the human race? Well, no thanks. Count me out."

"It might not be any different Outside," Quinn told her. "Josiah might have to follow some kind of selective breeding system in order to keep the genetic pool bank sound."

"The genetic pool bank!" she repeated, furious. "Do you hear what he's saying? Cathe? Do you, Jessica? Is that what you want? Well, I don't."

"Fine." Jessica defused the bomb. "I think you've made it clear how you feel. Let's lay this over until four this afternoon. Quinn says he'll need that much time to get the override system ready. Everyone meet back here at four, to see Mike off."

She started back toward her room, hoping to avoid a confrontation with Diana, but wasn't quick enough. The woman caught up with her in the hall.

"Just a minute, Jessica."

"I'm really in a hurry." She tried to force the excuse.

"Make time," Diana insisted.

"All right, what is it?"

"You know, I can understand why Cathe would go along with this little plan of Quinn's; she's a plain woman, matronly, and desperate enough for a man to try anything."

"I don't see what—" Jessica tried to stop her, but Diana ignored the interruption.

"What I don't get is why you'd consider going along with it. Why you're planning to stay here in the first place. You've got a husband out there," she hurled the unspoken accusation at her. "What's the truth of it, Jessica? Is it that you'd rather stay here and play house with three men," she charged, "than to go Outside and be a wife to Brad?"

"Stupid bitch." Jessica wanted to hit her, wanted to force the vicious words back down her throat and seal them there forever. Instead, she walked away, pushing the door open to her room and shutting it firmly both on the hallway and Diana Hunt.

She was shaking. Anger roiled and seethed a rage within her. *Damn the woman. Let her go Outside if that's*

*what she wants so badly. What if she does die? Who cares?
God, let her.*

Diana's words had triggered more than anger.
They had triggered bright, stinging pain. For Jessica, one part of her *was* Outside, always would be.
With Brad. She crossed her arms over her waist
and held the ache of that hurt within her like an
unborn child.

"Brad, I'm sorry," she cried. "God forgive me, I'm
sorry."

The seven adults and three children of Biosphere
Seven assembled at four o'clock inside the savannah
wing. The double steel doors of the docking chamber were standing open, with the final, outside
doors remaining sealed.

"Remember," Quinn gave last minute instructions
to Mike, "when the inside doors close, you'll have a
ten-second delay until the exterior shields open.
Walk out immediately. The doors will reconnect
after thirty seconds, and all the air will be evacuated from the chamber. At that point, we've rigged
up jet nozzles around the room to spray the area
with a solution of bleach—to deactivate the virus. If
you're still inside, there'll be no way anyone can
save you."

Mike's face blanched a little at the thought.
"That's what I've always liked about you, Quinn—
your cheery insights."

"Just trying to save your life."

"Yeah, I know."

There was a feeling of loss, alive as another presence in the biome. They were an extended family—
had become one in spite of much bitterness—and so
few in number, it was like severing a limb to see

one of them leave.

"Are you ready?" Jessica asked him.

"Just a second."

Mike lifted his son into his arms. "I'm going to see you in a month," he said to the boy. "Until then, you keep this." He took the gold cross from around his neck and slipped it over his son's head. "I love you, Trin. When you come Outside, I'll try to be a real father to you, the way I should have been all along." He put the child down beside Jessica. "Wave bye-bye to Daddy, Trinity."

The boy turned to Quinn.

"Wave bye-bye to Mike," Jessica whispered to the child.

Four fingers uncurled from the chubby fist, thumb still holding the cross tightly to his palm. Like the sequential closing of a flower's petals, they spiraled down again, curving in one at a time.

"Okay," said Mike, moving to the center of the docking chamber. He turned to look at them as the interior doors hissed shut.

No one said goodbye. No one said anything. It was as if a curtain were being drawn, secreting a private life, a private world, away from them. It was not a time for goodbyes, any more than it would have been for a group of mourners at a deathbed. He was lost to them, but going on to begin another life. It was a moment of awe, and silence.

The interior panels sealed, dispersing a final hiss of pressure. Quinn counted aloud. "One, two, three . . ."

At ". . . ten," they heard the outer shields slide open, a loud, grinding sound celebrated by all within the biosphere.

"Good luck," said Quinn.

336

"And God protect him," added Jessica.

"What God?" asked Diana. "We're on our own, or hadn't you noticed?" She walked away, leaving them standing in the hard residue of her words.

"What now?" Daniel wanted to know.

"We wait," said Quinn.

"Quinn's right," Jessica told them all. "It may be quite a while before we know for sure whether Mike will survive Outside. Meantime, we go back to the business at hand—keeping this place running.

"I know all of you want to talk to Josiah and get to know the new people, but we can't forget that there's work to be done. Our lives depend on managing the livestock and the crops. We can't let that slide."

They moved away from the door, each heading a separate direction. Work was something that would keep their minds off what was happening Outside. *If Mike lived.* . . . Each of them was thinking of what Mike's survival could mean to him or her. More than one man's life was in the balance, more than one man's freedom tested.

Late that night, a message from Josiah to Quinn appeared on the main computer monitor. Still working on the final figures of the oxygen loss throughout the entire biosphere from the docking-chamber evacuation earlier that day, Quinn noticed the blinking green signal light on the terminal annex, and pressed receive. Line by line, the message appeared on the screen.

It read:

Mike York doing well. No sign of contagion. Spirits good. Outlook promising.

337

Brad gravely ill. Fever of a hundred and four. Lower half of leg appears markedly worse. May require amputation. No anesthesia. Surgery skills minimal. Advise.

Deciding against telling Jessica, Quinn typed out the reply.

Good news about Mike. Keep advised of status. Will inform Jessica as think necessary. Use whatever means needed. God help you.

Quinn sent the brief reply, erasing Josiah's earlier message from the monitor. At the moment, it was enough that only he knew of the difficult decision to be made. Unless there was no other choice, he would not notify Jessica of the situation.

He stayed by the monitor all night, waiting for a message he prayed would not come — word that Brad was dead.

For the next two days, Mike York lived with Josiah and the other survivors in the resource center near Biosphere Seven. He showed no signs of the virus: blisters, fever, or flu-like symptoms. He remained well through the morning of the third day, speaking to Jessica on the visual monitor.

"You should all leave the dome," he told her. "I feel absolutely fine. There's no reason for any of you to stay locked up any longer. I'm telling you, it's okay. And it's enormous out here, Jessica. I'd forgotten how wide the sky is, and how far you can see without walls."

"We'll wait awhile longer, Mike, just to be sure."

Jessica put him off. Didn't he remember Maggie, how it had been at first with her? Or was it fear that made him eager for them to join him? Her eyes searched his face for evidence of blisters, like the ones she'd seen on Brad.

"You don't need to wait; I swear it, Jessica. It's a risk, I know, but . . . I can't explain how I'm feeling, how wonderful it is to be in the real world again. It's where we all belong. Don't wait too long. Really, there's no need."

"I won't, Mike. I promise."

He appeared normal. Was this excitement only a natural part of his sense of freedom? Or was it the beginning of something else? She knew she was observing him with eyes that were overly watchful. Their future was held in the balance. She had to be sure, had to know for certain that he was well, and not that he just thought he was.

If Quinn knew anything about Brad's condition, he hadn't told her. That meant it was bad. She made herself not ask. Would anyone tell her, she wondered, if Brad died? Would they keep such news from her? With their silence, they said she was not strong enough for the truth. *And am I?* she thought. *Am I?*

In the early evening of the third day, Jessica stood in the computer room waiting for Mike's latest report. As the sentences appeared on screen, she knew the message was not from Mike. She read the words as they printed onto the monitor, knowing what it would be . . . knowing it meant Brad's death.

Situation grave. High fever, delirium, and convulsions. Not responding to any medications. Pulse weak. Advise treatment.

Jessica leaned against the table, adrenaline shuddering through her legs. He was dying. She had made her choice, and Brad was dying.

The words went on. Her eyes blurred, making it hard to read the rest of the message.

Brad showing marked recovery. Leg improving. Swelling reduced, fever down. For the first time, outlook hopeful.

Outlook hopeful. Jessica read the words again, realizing that it was Mike who was desperately ill — not Brad. Not Brad! One part of her knew a sense of shame at the absolute joy she fell at the news, while another part knew only relief and gratefulness that for whatever reason, Brad had been spared. She could feel no regret at the choice that had been made. Mike's life for Brad's? Was it a choice?

After the first moments of both grief and great joy, she realized that the message meant something more, too. It meant that none of the rest of them would be leaving the biosphere dome. Mike's illness was proof that the virus was still potentially deadly. They couldn't afford the risk to any more lives.

Brad would live, but she could never go Outside, never be with him. Her life was, and would continue to be, within these glass walls. It was a bargain she was willing to make for Brad's survival.

Quinn's words came back to her: "Our Lady of the Sphere." She held the thought, believing for a moment that it was true.

Late that night, Mike York died. With him went the hope of everyone remaining within Biosphere

Seven of returning to the Outside. His was a death for all of them, a final ending to the lives they had once known.

In contrast, in the days that followed, Brad McGhee fully recovered. He was known to those around him now as Prophet, and each day he grew stronger. For Josiah and the other Outsiders, he was still the spokesman, but now for the faith he carried within him, he was the spoke of the wheel, and a priest to his people.

Within the enclosed world of Biosphere Seven, the Insiders would continue, each of them the origin of a separate tribe of people. Each, a new beginning.

For Jessica Nathan, Quinn Kelsey, and all the others, it was not the end of their world. Mankind had not destroyed itself completely. If Josiah had found ten survivors on his journey, his pilgrimage, then surely there were others living in far-flung corners of the earth. Slowly, these survivors would repopulate the globe.

Now was a chance to live the myth of Genesis in reality, to renew the face of the planet with life of every kind, and this time, Jessica prayed, with a new understanding and respect for the living world they shared.

In April 1992, Pinnacle will publish J.M. Morgan's BEYOND EDEN, the next book in the thrilling *Desert Eden* trilogy. Here's a taste of the adventure yet to come . . .

BEYOND EDEN

by J.M. Morgan

The boy's back was broken. Wind savaged the
grassy Montana plains. The harsh, warning days
before winter had come like clawing wildcats, tearing great clumps of earth and gouges from the land.
It was a northern wind, holding cold, killing the
last of the season. Killing the boy.

The child was nearly ten. He was thrown from
his horse when the shearing wind spooked the animal. Falling, he heard the sound of his spine snap
when he hit the ground . . . then heard nothing
more until he awoke hours later, dark swelling up
around him, shivering in the fierce talons of howling death. Alone. His name was Cody, youngest son
of the Inuit man, John Katelo. And he was dying.

Through the long night, tunnels of freezing cold
swept over the boy, stealing the breath from his
lungs, the life from his body. His thin voice calling
to his father, to his mother, was hidden in the loud
and constant wailing of the wind. With the honey-
colored morning, the child's voice was silenced.

"What's that over there?" eighteen-year-old Seth
Katelo asked his one-year-younger brother, Jonathan. He pointed to small, snow-dusted mound less
than fifty feet from where their horses stood, the

345

animals blowing heavily in the icy air. They had been searching since before dawn.

Their father had gone out the night before, in the middle of the storm, looking for Cody. When Seth and Jonathan left home in the dark before morning, neither Cody nor their father had yet returned. In terror of losing not only her youngest boy, but her husband and two more of her sons, their mother, Salena, had pleaded with them not to go.

"I've given two children to this land." She spoke of the deaths of two babies between Cody and the birth of her youngest child, four-year-old Noelle. "As much as I love Cody—you know I do—we have to face the fact that he may be lost to us already." She hadn't cried. Her face had been hard-set as stone, her eyes, dry and terrible.

"The storm will hit us again before night. Don't make me live through losing you and Jonathan, too. I'd lose my mind then, Seth. I would. Then what would become of the rest of them?"

It was painful, watching his mother's tearless suffering. His own eyes had begun to fill with hurt for her. Still, Seth knew that if his little brother, Cody, had survived the freezing night, he would be in desperate need by now—perhaps near death—and could not make it home without help. Determined to find the boy, he had torn himself from the desperate clutch of his mother's fingers with the blunt words, "I won't leave Cody out there to die alone."

Jonathan made no speech, but had saddled his horse. They'd ridden out together. Now, hours later, the sky carried a ceiling of woven clouds, thickening with a weight of dark even as they watched.

Their horses snuffed the ground, furrowing trenches in the soft snow with their muzzles, and cropping grass. "I'll have a look," said Jonathan, urging the chestnut mare forward.

"No, we both will," Seth insisted, and gave a nudge with his knees to the dance-footed black. The horse gave up the sweet grass reluctantly, and trotted across the drifted plain, toward the mound.

Seth was hard pressed to believe it, even when he saw the familiar white rawhide fringes on Cody's jacket. The twisted angle wasn't right for the shape of a human—for the shape of a little boy. The body was bent back like a V, legs and arms pointing different directions.

"His back's broke," said Jonathan matter-of-factly, getting down from his mount. He walked the few steps to the body and brushed the powdering of snow clear from the child's face.

Seth needed air. A squeezing fist held his lungs so tight, he couldn't breathe. He was looking at Cody's face, but everything he knew of Cody was gone from it. The curled-lip mask staring back at him was a cruel mimicry of his brother. The boy's eyes were open, but they were glassy, like a doll's. No life to them.

Jonathan waited for a minute. When Seth didn't dismount, he began pulling the legs into a straight line with the torso. The sound was like the slow splintering of a tree from its trunk.

"Stop it! What do you think you're doing?" Seth shouted, swinging his booted foot over the side of the horse and jumping down. "You're hurting him!"

"It's all right." Jonathan straightened up from his task. There were tears standing unshed in his eyes. "He can't feel nothin', Seth. We've gotta take him on home to Mama . . . but not like he was. Not like that."

347

Seth bent down onto one knee, closer to Cody's body. His hand moved gently over his brother's hands and face, lingering with a scared, light touch. They were small hands, a small face. Just a little boy. Too young to die. Too young to die alone — like this.

"You did the right thing," he said to Jonathan. "You knew what was needed, when I didn't. Come on —" he slid his hands beneath Cody's shoulders — "help me lift him onto the saddle."

They rode slowly back to the house. There was no hurry now. Neither of them was anxious to break the news to their mother. Seth propped Cody's body against him, sitting up on the saddle. He wouldn't sling him over the horse's flanks like a camp blanket. Holding one arm around the boy's chest to keep him from falling, they made their way home.

John Katelo always spoke of the time when the sickness had come as the year of "bad spirits." He had seen their ghostly faces in the skies above his campfires that first winter — after he had broken out of the Siberian biosphere and fled across the frozen tundra — hunters, the old ones, young wives and children. He had heard the torment of their cries as they walked the earth, unable to find a way back into their world.

They had followed him, for he was alive, and life was what they wanted. If any man knew about bad spirits, it was John Katelo. He had been alone, except for a kind of brotherhood with the little pup, Kip, and he had seen them. He had asked their forgiveness for living when they were dead. He had hidden his fear, and spoken to them as "Brother" and as "Sister." The old ones, he called "Uncle," or "Aunt." Respectfully, he honored them with burial caches of their goods, with prayers to the Great Father, and with the songs of a Chukchi hunter. But he would not take shelter in their houses of death.

That first winter, he had worked hard to build shelters of his own, to teach the young dog to hunt, and to endure the winds of the tundra. For many days, he had heard nothing but the sound of those winds blowing against the cave of an ice igloo. In the sound were the voices of those spirits who had gone before him. He had heard them clearly, their cries beating against the outside of his shelter, the joined blocks of snow. From within, he had listened, and was afraid. Only the companionship of the dog had kept him sane.

Thoughts came to him now of the old dog. Kip had been gone five years this winter. He had been Katelo's only friend in that first turning of the seasons, after the death of the world, and had saved his life more than once since, earning a place of warmth and welcome in his old age at the Inuit's hearth.

Now, with the death of his youngest son John, Katelo knew that the boy, too, had heard the keening cries of the wind. Alone, the child had been surrounded by the hungry voices, and his spirit stolen.

More than any other thing he had endured, John Katelo felt this loss as a personal wound, lacerating him. He carried the injury of this child's death as an amulet of grief within himself. No one, not his wife, not the family he loved, could take it from him. No man should live among spirits of the dead; no child should die alone.

The hurt was still fresh, therefore, when after the new year's first thaw of spring, his eldest son, Seth, came to him and told him the longing of his heart.

"Jonathan and I must leave this valley," Seth said without apology. For his mother, the boy would have eased the words, but for his father, Seth said them openly. It was the way between men. Katelo understood this. He did not ask why.

"Where would you go?" he asked instead. He knew well enough that both Seth and Jonathan were men now, and could not be contained within their father's circle of family forever. The land in this valley had been good to them, plentiful with grass and planted seed. Here, Katelo and Salena had waited out the winter on their long trek down from the north. Here, six sons had been born to them, and three daughters.

It was a hollow between the mountains, this valley, protected from the worst of winter, and high enough to keep the cattle in grass all summer. They had stayed, finding a peace in this sheltered basin, beside a lake of blue water. Their house faced south, toward the beauty of that lake. Behind them, lay the spears of gray-black mountains, and the world of bitter cold.

"We'll go south," said Seth, "in the hope that we might find others."

Katelo knew they would be looking for wives. In his heart, he hated to send his children away from him, into the unknown, but to insist that they stay would only insure their loneliness. In the nearly twenty years that he and Salena had lived in this valley, they had seen no other living soul but that which they had made of their own flesh.

To see his first two sons leave home was a weight added to his heart, along with the grief he carried over the loss of the little one. It burdened Katelo, and he felt the power of this burden pull him down, but said nothing. He had lived through forty-three winters. By that spring, he felt every day of those years.

More terrible than his own sense of loss, he worried about what losing her two eldest children would do to Salena. Cody's death had brought a silence to her. She moved through her days without words, turned inward to a quietness his voice could not touch.

"We must keep this from your mother until you are ready to leave," he warned Seth.

But to his surprise, Salena knew, and had readied belongings for the boys to take with them on the journey. Katelo watched as her fingers moved over the clothes she had made for her sons to wear, smoothing the fabric and laying the shirts, pants, and warm coats into satchels for each boy. He watched, his heart locked in a tight pain at the sight.

"When you have found what you are looking for," she said to each of them, "you must come back to us. Bring your wives, your families, and return. This place is your home. Remember.

"Your father is no longer a young man. He will need your help in years to come. You must promise me — now, before you step one foot from this place which has been your home," she charged first Seth, then Jonathan. "Promise to come back," she demanded of her firstborn.

Seth was openly weeping, his will to leave visibly torn by his mother's words. "Keep me in your heart, Mother," he said, "and I will come home."

"Promise." She turned to Jonathan.

Katelo watched in breathless hurt.

Jonathan was like him, more Inuit than Seth or any of the others. His eyes were dry, and his voice steady. "If there *is* life beyond this place," he said gently, taking his mother's hands in his own, "I will find it — and I will come here, to tell you."

"Then, go from us with your mother's blessings," she said to them, kissing each, and holding these two sons one last time in her arms.

They rode out, Seth on the dance-footed black, and Jonathan on the chestnut mare, heading south, beyond the blue-gray oval of Mirror Lake. Behind them, the span of mountains pierced the sky. Before them, the land was open.

John Katelo stood in the field of grass and watched them go, knowing in his heart he would never see them again.